CW01642214

Secrecy

The Chaplain's Legacy Book 4

Mary Kingswood

Sutors Publishing

Published by Sutors Publishing

ISBN: 978-1-912167-59-3 (paperback)

V0

Cover design by: Shayne Rutherford of Darkmoon Graphics

Author's note:

this book is written using historic British terminology, so *saloon* instead of *salon*, *chaperon* instead of *chaperone* and so on. I follow Jane Austen's example and refer to a group of sisters as the Miss Wintertons.

About the book

One man with a secret. A family torn apart by the consequences.

Miss Teresa Nicholson, daughter of an earl's chaplain, has suffered two dreadful shocks. First, her father was brutally murdered, and then his will bequeathed her his entire fortune, but only if she marries a gentleman. Tess knows the reason for that - she loves a man who works with his hands, and that's unacceptable for the niece of an earl. But if she can marry a compliant man who won't interfere with her life, she'll be free to do as she pleases, won't she? If only she could find this mysterious fortune...

Edward, Lord Tarvin has his life exactly how he wants it - his mother confined to his northern estate while he enjoys a bachelor existence in London. But when he hears that Tess Nicholson has designs on his simple minded cousin, he knows he has to do whatever it takes to stop her. If only she weren't such an infuriating, conniving and downright beguiling woman...

This is a complete story with a happy ever after. A traditional Regency romance, drawing room rather than bedroom. Book 4 of a 6 book series.

Isn't that what's-his-name? Occasionally characters from an earlier series pop up, or are mentioned. Jeffrey Rycroft and his wife Jeanie were previously in *Stranger at the Hall*, when Jeanie's brother Cameron became Lord Saxby.

About the series:

Book 0: The Chaplain: a man adrift, dreaming of a home *(a novella, free to mailing list subscribers).*

Book 1: Disinheritance: a man freed, looking for a new purpose in life

Book 2: Determination: a man pursued, forced to outwit his adversary

Book 3: Anger: a woman alone, trying to choose a different path in life

Book 4: Secrecy: a woman neglected, scheming to secure her own happiness

Book 5: Loyalty: a man of dreams, torn between the past and the future

Book 6: Ambition: a woman thwarted, unswervingly set on making a brilliant debut in society

Want to be the first to hear about new releases? Sign up for my mailing list at https://marykingswood.co.uk.

Contents

Principal Characters

A partial list; for the full list, see my website at https://marykingswood.co.uk under Extras.

The Atherton family of Corland Castle, North Riding of Yorkshire:

Charles, 11th Earl of Rennington (55)

Caroline, Countess of Rennington (50)

Their children:

Walter, the former Viscount Birtwell (29)

Mr Eustace Atherton (27), living on his own estate nearby, Welwood-on-the-Hill

Josie (Josephine), Lady Woodridge (26), married to Viscount Woodridge; they have two sons

Izzy (Isabel), Lady Farramont (24); married to Ian, Viscount Farramont (35); they have two daughters

Mr Kent Atherton (22)

Lady Olivia Atherton (18)

The earl's blind sister: Lady Alice Nicholson (48)

Her husband, the earl's chaplain: Mr Arthur Nicholson (55, deceased)

Their daughter, Miss Tess (Teresa) Nicholson (20)

The Harfield Family of Harfield Priory, County Durham

Edward, 4th Lord Tarvin (27)

Mrs Edward Harfield (Alvira, 47), his mother

Lady Tarvin (Myrtle, 52), his aunt, widow of 3rd Lord Tarvin and sister to Lady Rennington

Mrs Jack Harfield (Joan, 42), his widowed aunt

Ulric Frith (22), her son from her first marriage

Her children from her second marriage: Aldith, Demelza, Isolda, Tostig, Elfleda, Oswin, Halbert

The Murder Investigators:

Captain Michael Edgerton (37), formerly of the East India Company Army

Mrs Edgerton (Luce, née Willerton-Forbes, 30)

Mr Pettigrew Willerton-Forbes (38), a lawyer

Mr James Neate, a lawyer masquerading as a footman

Mr Alexander Grant Saxby (Sandy, 25), now known as Mr Alexander

Miss Peach, a former governess

1: A Bereaved Daughter

CORLAND CASTLE: JUNE

It was worse than she could possibly have imagined... far, far worse. Tess had known something awful had happened, because of the screams. Mama never so much as raised her voice, yet she had screamed loudly enough to wake even the servants in their attic beds. Over and over again she had screamed, and when Tess had rushed to see what was happening, Walter had bundled her brusquely out of the room and sent her away. She and Olivia had dressed in silence, then huddled together in their bedroom, waiting to hear what had happened.

But this! It was incredible. Impossible to take in.

Grabbing her cloak, she tore down the back stairs, scattering maids with brushes and pails, then through the great hall and into the entrance hall where Wellum, used to her ways, raced to open the door for her. In her wake, her maid and footman scrambled to follow her, Harold loping along and Betty, puffing, half running.

On the path to Birchall, the trees loomed overhead, casting chilling shade as she tore along. She must get to Tom! He would comfort her, even if he could not make the nightmare disappear.

In the village, women out shopping curtsied to her, and men bustling past intently on some scheme of their own stopped and doffed their hats with a respectful bow.

"Good mornin' to 'e, Miss Nicholson," the brave ones called out, smiling at her. "Fine day for a walk."

They did not know yet. How would they react when they knew? Their faces would be filled with pity. Perhaps they would cry. She should cry herself, but she was still too shocked. It was too dreadful for tears.

Tom Shapman's workshop was wedged awkwardly into a narrow gap between two larger buildings, a bakery and a private house. Tom's door was closed, but Tess was not deterred by that. Lifting the latch, she opened it and walked straight in. At once, her nostrils were assailed by the scent of the different woods Tom used when he made furniture. Fully half of the workshop was taken up with racks of wood in a rainbow of colours waiting to be used, from large flat slabs to make the sides of wardrobes, to narrow strips to be turned for chair legs or ornamented as trimmings. On the workbench, a half-made travel box lay unattended, for Tom was not there.

Although the frontage was wide, the shop narrowed at the back to provide a small kitchen, and a storeroom for the latches and locks and bolts that Tom used when he fitted windows and doors. A narrow stair led up to a tiny bedroom. Perhaps she was so early that he was still abed?

"Tom?" Tess called. The only answer was silence.

"Fire's gone out," Betty said in disapproving tones, poking round the kitchen in a housewifely manner. Then, to Harold, "You can make yersel' useful and get this fire lit. I'll need hot water to clean they dishes."

Tess prowled restlessly about. Where was he? Why did he not come?

Not very many minutes later, the door opened and Tom Shapman came in, a bag over one shoulder. Tess drank in the sight of him, for there was no denying he was a fine figure of a man, tall, muscular and very, very handsome when he smiled. He was not smiling now.

"Miss Tess? What are you doing here, so early in the day?" His accent was not so harsh as some of the local working men, and his voice was pleasantly mellow. Or at least, it usually was. There was a hard edge to it this morning.

"Where have you been? You let the fire go out."

"Nowhere... just out."

"Before breakfast? Whatever for?"

"My time's my own, I believe," he said huffily. "I can come and go as I please, can't I? But what brings you here?"

"Something terrible has happened, Tom. My father is... dead."

"Oh, no!" At once, his face was wreathed in sympathy. Dropping his bag, he came and took her hands, his work-roughened fingers grating against her softer skin. "He was no age — what, fifty or so?"

"Fifty-five."

"But he always seemed to be in excellent health. What was it, an apoplexy? His heart?"

She shook her head, still reluctant to put words to so terrible a thing.

"An accident? A sudden fever?"

She shook her head again, and, perhaps recognising her distress, he fell silent.

"He was... oh, Tom, he was *murdered!*"

"Murdered!"

"Someone broke into the castle in the middle of the night and... and killed him while he lay sleeping in his bed. With an axe! And my mother discovered him!"

"Lord save us! Poor Lady Alice! But... how could she know?"

"You forget that her other senses are much sharpened. She may be blind, but she hears extraordinarily well, and her sense of smell... the blood... she knew something was amiss, and then she stumbled upon the axe, which had been dropped on the floor."

"Dear God! Poor lady! But *why*, Miss Tess? Why would anyone kill your father? The chaplain, after all... a man of God. How could a chaplain have any enemies?"

Tess did not have quite such a rosy view of her father, but still, it was hard to imagine that he had upset anyone sufficiently to cause himself to be murdered.

"I suppose there's one good thing to come out of this," Tom said with a quick grin. "At least when the will is read, you'll find out once and for all what your dowry will be."

Tess's spirits lifted fractionally. That was true! However dark the clouds may be, there was always a silver lining.

***

The will was read in the Earl of Rennington's study, in the presence of only the earl and countess, Tess and the two lawyers from York. Tess's mother, still too grieved at the tragic death of her husband, had not yet left her room. Tess and her aunt were in deep mourning, but although

Tess disliked herself in black, there was no escaping that. Anything up to six months in full black, and perhaps another six months or so in half mourning, with greys and lilacs and touches of white on darker gowns. Tess fretted a little at the necessity, but she had never been openly rebellious — that was not her way. So she sat meekly in her black gown, and waited patiently for the lawyers to shuffle their papers and clear their throats and begin the reading.

It was not so complicated as she had supposed. There were a few minor bequests first, for the servants — Papa's valet, several of the grooms, something for the butler and under butler. His pocket watch, which had come from an uncle, was to go back to his brother in Hampshire, to stay in the Nicholson family. Then there was Mama's jointure, fifteen thousand pounds in total, the income to be hers for her lifetime, and the whole to come to Tess after Mama's death, or on remarriage.

Remarriage! That was a strange idea indeed. Surely Mama would never take another husband?

But then the lawyer cleared his throat again and looked directly at Tess again. "*The remainder of my fortune to my daughter, Teresa Nicholson, on the sole condition that she marries a gentleman, and if she should not, or remains unmarried at the age of thirty, to be given to Pembroke College, Oxford, to found a Fellowship on whatever terms may be deemed appropriate. I appoint my wife, the Lady Alice Nicholson, as guardian to our daughter if she is not yet of age, and I appoint as trustees of her fortune until she marries the Right Honourable the Earl of Rennington and his heir, if of age, and if not, the most senior of the family lawyers. These same trustees to be also executors of this will.*"

The voices droned on with the final formalities, but Tess could barely wait for the last few words to trickle into silence before she burst out, "But what *is* my fortune? How much is it?"

The lawyer who had read the will removed his spectacles. "As to that, we cannot yet say, Miss Nicholson. It will comprise all your father's personal effects not otherwise disposed of, any money or valuables here or in the bank, any investments... we will have to investigate. There is also a house at Pickering which the late earl bequeathed him. That is now yours. We know of no other property."

The two lawyers exchanged glances, and the other one said gently, "I do not believe you should harbour unrealistic expectations, Miss Nicholson. Your father's stipend was very generous, but not such as would enable him to establish himself as a wealthy man. It may be that when he chose to use the word '*fortune*' in his will, your father meant only relative to his circumstances when he first arrived at Corland thirty years ago. When a man has nothing at all, then even savings of a few thousand will seem like a fortune."

"A few thousand!" she said, with something close to disgust. That would not do!

She went at once to Tom Shapman's workshop and unburdened herself of all her grievances into his sympathetic ears.

"A gentleman!" Tom said, the plane in his hand pausing its rhythmic movements. "Ah, that's my fault, Miss Tess. I did more harm than good by going to your father last year and asking for your hand. I thought it was wrong at the time, and now see what's happened — he's insisting you marry a gentleman, or you'll not get a penny piece."

"That is just like him!" she cried, perching on an unfinished travel box. "Even in death, he is controlling us... controlling *me.* I must dance to his tune, whether I will or not. He is determined that I shall never marry you, and I am just as determined that I shall."

"That's all very well, but he's right, isn't he?" Tom said, putting the plane down altogether and pulling over a chair. "You're the earl's niece. You shouldn't be looking at a man who earns his bread with his hands."

"I cannot think of a man more worth looking at," Tess said with a burst of laughter. "You are the best looking man in the North Riding, Tom."

He reddened slightly. "Now, now, none of your nonsense, Miss Tess. Even if that were true, it's nothing to the point. You should marry a gentleman, or a nobleman, like that lord that your lady mother wanted for you. Lord Tarvin. He'd be a fine husband for a lady like you."

"Pfft! Edward Harfield? The stuffiest man imaginable. I hate him!"

"You're just cross with him because he never danced with you that time he came for the ball."

"Never danced with me and never said more than *'How do you do?'* as we were introduced. He *ignored* me, Tom. Three days he was here, and he ignored me the whole time, as if I were too lowly a creature to be worthy of his condescension."

"You were barely fifteen," Tom said, smiling at her.

"And Olivia was *thirteen*, but he danced with her! And talked to her, several times. Not that he said anything worth hearing, Olivia said. Lord, but he is boring!"

"Hush now, Miss Tess. Don't be saying *'Lord this'* and *'Lord that'* like some of the rougher folk do. You've been brought up better than that."

A voice from the kitchen burst into mirthful laughter. "Aye, you tell her!" Betty said. "She takes no notice of anyone else."

"She takes no notice of me, neither," Tom said ruefully. "Does what she wants, and always has, and gets all of us jumping to her commands. It's your own family you should be talking to, Miss Tess, not the likes of me."

"Oh, pfft!" Tess said, but without heat. It was hard to be cross with Tom, so fine and handsome and *manly* as he was. Not like the namby-pamby gentlemen she met — her own cousins, and the oh-so-eligible Edward, Lord Tarvin. "Mama shuts herself away in her room, and nobody else cares about me. I have to look after myself and make my own friends. You are still my friend, are you not, Tom?"

"Of course, Miss Tess."

"You will never abandon me, will you?" She jumped down from her perch and knelt beside his chair, slipping a slender arm around his more muscular one. "You know how much I love you, and you are my only true friend — the only one I can depend upon absolutely. You will always help me when I am in need, will you not?"

"Now, now, Miss Tess, how can you doubt it, after all I did for you last year? You wanted me to go to him and ask for your hand, and didn't I do exactly that? And got thoroughly yelled at for my pains as a presumptuous upstart, which I have to say is nothing but the truth, but you wanted it, so I did it. You know how grateful I am to you for helping me establish my little business. I'd do anything to repay you for that."

"That's not very gallant, Tom. You should do it because you love me. You do love me, do you not?"

He shifted uneasily on the chair. "Between a lady and a woodworker, there's no call to talk about love, Miss Tess. Let's say I'm very fond of you and leave it at that."

"Fond of me?" she said softly, dropping a chaste kiss onto his delicious mouth. "*Fond* of me, Tom?" Another kiss. "How fond, precisely?"

A third kiss, a lot less chaste, did the trick, and for a while there was silence in the workshop, apart from the disapproving banging of pans in the kitchen as Betty tidied up.

"There, you see?" Tess murmured, when Tom finally pulled away with a rueful smile.

"You always could twist me around your little finger," Tom said. "But you'll have to look elsewhere for a husband, Miss Tess. Your father's will means you have to marry a gentleman, not a woodworker."

"Well, we shall see about that," she said. "At least now I shall soon know precisely what my dowry is, just as soon as the lawyers have tracked it down."

"But it may not be very much, they said," Tom said. "A few thousand. Were you expecting more?"

"A fortune — that is the word used in the will, so yes, I am expecting a lot more, and it is not at Corland. At least, if it is, it is very well hidden."

"It will be in the bank, won't it?"

"Perhaps. There is a house at Pickering, too. It must be somewhere, Tom, and it is not just a few thousand, either. It is a *lot* more than that, I know it."

"Wishful thinking, Miss Tess?"

"No, not at all. It is a vast fortune, and I know it exists because I have seen it."

***

Edward, Lord Tarvin, was in the best of good humours. Three years after the death of his uncle and his assumption of the honours of the barony, he at last had his life ordered precisely to his liking. The first year the family had been in deep mourning, and there had been so much to be done at Harfield Priory, his principal seat, that he had been able to make no more than a few swift dashes to town for recreational purposes. The following year, both his aunt and his mother had spent the entire season in town, and almost driven him mad with their attempts to pair him off with an eligible female. Last year, he had persuaded his aunt to retire from the fray, leaving only his mother to irritate him. But this year... ah, this year he had contrived to exile both the ladies to the Priory, and he had the Grosvenor Street house to himself. With all the principal rooms swathed in holland covers, there was no entertaining to be done, no feminine presence, nothing to interfere with his pleasant bachelor existence.

Today was Sunday, too, his favourite day of the week. His first agreeable duty was to write his weekly report to his mother. He had removed her from town by the simple expedient of telling her that her presence at his side inhibited all but the most dreary of marital prospects. No woman wanted to marry a man whose mother was forever at his shoulder, whispering in his ear, he had assured her. The price for her withdrawal to County Durham was a weekly letter from him, informing her of every dance partner, every meeting in Hyde Park, every chance encounter at Hookham's or the theatre with a suitable girl. The hour he spent on this creative endeavour was entirely worthwhile, he was sure.

'To Mrs Edward Harfield, Harfield Priory, County Durham. My dear Mother, I hope this finds you well and enjoying pleasant weather. Be assured that I am in the best of health, and although there has been much rain in the past weeks, we are now enjoying a spell of fine, settled weather, conducive to many outdoor activities. This week alone, I have received invitations to a Venetian breakfast, an expedition to Richmond and to Vauxhall Gardens. On Tuesday last, I attended a rout where I met again Lady E W, who

graciously conversed with me for some ten minutes or so. Also there was Miss Y, but I hear rumours that she is on the brink of an engagement, so I shall remove her from my list of young ladies of interest. Also on Tuesday, at a card party in Grosvenor Square, I saw Lady J M, but not to speak to. On Wednesday...'

He sighed. So many tedious and entirely predictable girls, smirking and fluttering their fans. As if he would marry any of them! Some were pretty and some danced well and some were accomplished musicians and one or two could even converse rationally, but there was not one of them who said or did anything to surprise him. He could not bear to spend the rest of his life entirely unsurprised. So he went through the motions of looking for a wife, without the least intention of finding one. But at least the weekly letters kept his mother safely tucked away at the Priory.

Three pages were required to encompass all the encounters with possible future Lady Tarvins, and some of them had even happened. He sanded, folded and sealed this missive, franked it and left it in the basket to be taken to the Post Office. Two less carefully crafted letters quickly joined it, after which it was time to walk down to St George's church for divine service, and another opportunity to rub shoulders with the higher ranks who inhabited the elegant streets of Mayfair.

And then, oh joy, his time of freedom. By the time he had returned to Grosvenor Street and changed into riding clothes, his horse had been brought round for him, his small overnight bag already strapped on.

"I shall be back on Tuesday morning, as usual," Edward said to his valet.

"Very good, my lord."

"If anyone asks for me—"

"You have gone out of town for a couple of days."

"Precisely so. If need be, you may mention that you believe I am visiting my former professor, and you have no idea where he lives."

"Of course." The valet bowed. "Enjoy your visit, my lord."

"Oh, I will. I certainly will." Edward chuckled as he mounted agilely into the saddle. "Until Tuesday morning, Deakin."

And then, at last, he was able to ride away to freedom.

2: Family Trouble

"Eleven thousand," Tess repeated, in disgusted tones.

The lawyers beamed happily at her. "It is a substantial sum, Miss Nicholson," one of them said. "A splendid dowry for any young lady. And in time you will also inherit your mother's portion of fifteen thousand pounds."

"A time far in the future, we must hope," the other said.

"Yes, indeed. All the Lady Alice's well-wishers must hope that it will be a great many years before such a large sum finds its way to you."

"Indeed, it is a very great sum," the other chortled. "You must beware of fortune hunters, Miss Nicholson."

The two men exchanged smug glances.

"What about the house?" Tess said.

"Ah, now, the house at Pickering is leased at a modest rental — ten pounds a year. The tenant is a respectable widow, a Mrs Mayberry."

"But what is the house worth?"

"Worth? If it were to be sold? A few hundred pounds, perhaps, but you would not wish to sell it, I am sure, Miss Nicholson."

"I might wish to live in it."

The earl had said nothing so far, but at this he frowned and leaned forward on his elbows. "Tess, my dear, you could hardly set up your own establishment, not a girl of twenty. If Alice were to go with you... but you know how impossible that is. She must stay here where all is familiar and she knows her way around, and that means that you must stay here as well."

Tess sighed. She had known she was asking for the impossible. Her mother had been blind since a childhood illness, and could not leave Corland Castle.

"But surely I can go and look at the house?" she said. "Since it is mine—?"

"And disrupt the tenant?" the earl said. "Tess, do not let this inheritance turn your head. The Pickering house is not yours, not until you marry, and then your husband will determine what is best to do with it."

Tess had nothing to say to that.

"When you are out of mourning," the earl said, "you may come to town with us, if you wish, and Lady Rennington will introduce you into society, and find you a suitable husband. You will have suitors buzzing all around you, my dear, so pretty as you are, and with a very handsome portion to offer. You will be able to choose just the man to suit you, you may be sure."

Tess could be sure of no such thing. A suitable husband! It was the last thing she wanted.

***

Tom Shapman was busy turning chair legs when she arrived, his coat off and sleeves rolled up above the elbow, revealing admirably strong arms.

"More chairs?"

"Aye, fourteen for the dining room at Langley Villa for Lord Birtwell and his bride."

"If they ever get to the altar," Tess said with a lift of one shoulder. "They have been betrothed forever, it seems."

"He's the heir, so it's not a simple matter of banns and a wedding," Tom said. "There'll be a lot to take into account. So long as they pay for their chairs, it's nothing to me when they marry, or if they marry at all. But what did the lawyers say? Are you a wealthy woman?"

She told him all that had been said, and he made sympathetic noises. "Well, there it is, then. No vast fortune after all."

"But there *is!*" she cried. "I tell you, I have seen it!"

"How can you see a fortune? It's all in the banks, isn't it? Or... investments of some sort."

"This was in Papa's safe," she said. "Gold bars, a great pile of them, and I know from the prices in the newspapers that they are worth far, far more than a measly eleven thousand. But then one time I looked they were gone, and now I have not the least idea where they are."

Tom looked up from his work, frowning. "Your father showed you what was in his safe?"

"Of course not! But I discovered where he kept the keys and I used to look. He kept Mama's jewels in there, and a bag of money — linen money, all rolled up, and coins — various documents, I know not what, and a pile of gold bars. But then the gold vanished."

"Perhaps he was holding it for someone else?" Tom suggested.

"No! It was all his, and now it is mine, if I can only find out where it is."

"And what would you do with it — buy a castle to live in?" Tom said vaguely.

She chuckled. "No! I should marry you, silly, and then you would not need to make chair legs over and over again. You could do nothing and be a gentleman."

He shifted uneasily. "I'd not like that, Miss Tess! I need to be working at something."

"Well, you could make the most beautiful furniture in the world, using the finest woods... or train up apprentices, so that they can earn a living themselves. That would be worthwhile, would it not? I should like to do some good with my money, but first I have to find out where Papa has hidden it."

"Why would he hide it?"

Tess made an impatient noise. "Why did Papa do anything? He was very secretive, but he had all manner of schemes going on. Even I cannot tell you all that he was doing, and I made it my business to find out, you may be sure."

Tom shifted uncomfortably, shaking his head. "You shouldn't meddle, Miss Tess."

"Aye, that's right enough," called out Betty from the kitchen. "Allus snoopin', she is."

"I like to know what is going on," Tess said with a careless lift of one shoulder. "Besides, Papa knew I was watching him. He caught me looking through the drawers of his desk one day, but he only laughed about it and told me I was a clever little puss, so he saw nothing wrong with it."

"I don't want to say nothing against your father," Tom said, "especially now he's dead, for he was a man of God, after all, but he shouldn't have encouraged you in that."

"Why does everyone become so mealy-mouthed about the dead?" Tess cried impatiently. "A wicked man does not become a saint as soon as he dies."

"Miss Tess!" Betty protested. "Don't you go suggestin' that your father was anythin' but a good man at heart. Human, like everyone, and likely to make the odd mistake, but a good man."

"He was an evil and selfish man, who never cared for anyone but himself… and Mama, I suppose. He certainly never cared for *me* or he would never have left my inheritance so horridly tied up. That money is *mine*, but can I get my hands on it? No, only my trustees and then my husband. And where is the rest of it, that is what I really want to know? Where are all those gold bars?"

"Perhaps these people investigating the murder will find them," Tom said, tossing a finished chair leg onto the pile and starting another. "They seem to be very thorough."

Tess sighed. "That is a possibility. They are turning the castle upside down and shaking it thoroughly. If the gold bars are here, they will find them… surely."

"And even if they don't, they'll find out who killed your father," Tom said.

"Do you think so?"

Tom looked up in surprise. "Of course! A wild killing like that — someone breaking into the basement, finding an axe on the stairs and then going to your father's room — whoever it was must have left some traces behind, and must be quite mad."

"A wild killing? Nothing of the sort," Tess said. "This was no madman."

"What makes you say that?"

"This was planned. How could a passing madman break into a house and find his way unerringly to one specific bedroom?"

"But that's just the point, Miss Tess. He broke in, and that wasn't hard, given that the scullery window had a broken latch, then he wandered about here and there — he could have stumbled into any number of rooms. He could even have looked into *your* room. But when he came to your father's room... perhaps something disturbed him, or your father woke and saw him and he panicked, he slashed at him with the axe he'd picked up, then, realising the terrible thing he'd done, he ran away. Surely that's how it happened?"

"But where did the axe come from? It belonged to Eustace, part of his collection, and he had arranged it as part of the display on the main stairs, but *nobody saw it.* It was there for more than a week, but even the maid who dusted the display never saw it there."

"Maids never see nothin'," Betty called out.

"Maybe it was there and no one noticed," Tess said. "Or maybe it was not there at all."

"What are you suggesting, Miss Tess?" Tom said.

"Just this — that the murderer was not a passing madman, but a very clever man who planned his wickedness carefully. I doubt he came in by a window, not when there are four doors into the basement. The garden door with the broken bolt, perhaps, and then straight up the service stairs to the great hall. Then he collected the axe from where he had hidden it, and—"

"Wait! He had hidden the axe somewhere? Why? And where?"

"Why? So that it would be waiting for him when he came to fulfil his wickedness. As to where, I imagine he took it from Eustace's display and then slipped it into one of the urns."

"Urns?"

"Giant Chinese vases. There are two of them on the stairs, one on either side of the display. A good place to hide a weapon, do you not think? Then up the stairs to Papa's room, do the deed while he sleeps, drop the axe and back out the way he came in."

"It could've happened that way, I suppose," Tom said thoughtfully. "But I still think a madman is—"

"No!" she cried. "It was planned, I tell you. I know it, Tom. And that is better than an unpredictable madman... who might come back at any moment."

"That broken latch has been fixed," Tom said, "and the bolt on the garden door, and all the locks changed. No one can break in now."

"Not at Corland, but a madman might go anywhere. No, the murderer was a man with a specific grudge against Papa. He wanted my father dead and he *is* dead, and it is better by far to leave it at that."

***

Edward lay contentedly in bed, watching Nellie dress. She never liked to wander about in her nightgown, so as soon as she rose, she began methodically to don her clothes. He enjoyed watching her deft fingers tying and buttoning and straightening. Especially the stockings — there was something mesmerising about a woman's stockings. Nellie's concentration was intense as she carefully slid them up her legs and tied the bows, and he loved that brief glimpse of leg as the shift was pulled up. He had seen

Nellie without a stitch on, but that quick view of leg as she dressed was still appealing.

"I suppose you'll be off straight after breakfast, as usual," she said, looking up from her work momentarily.

"It is Tuesday morning," he said, although not without regret. "Sunday night and Monday night, that is all I can spare."

"You don't really get your money's worth from me, do you?" she said with a throaty chuckle. "This house, the servants, the food and drink, pin money, the occasional present — which I appreciate very much, you may be sure — it must cost a fortune, yet I only see you two nights out of seven."

For about three seconds he was tempted, for he was only human and a man, after all. But one could not spend every minute in bed, and the prospect of more hours of Nellie's inane chatter was unappealing. One did not engage a mistress for her wit or ability to discourse on the state of the world, but a little conversation above the banal would be welcome.

"I am occupied for the other five nights. As a baron, I have a position in society to maintain."

"You could come here afterwards. Or maybe an afternoon now and then. I don't know what I'm supposed to do with myself the rest of the time, and it's not as if you have a wife to object to you keeping a mistress."

"Thank heavens!" he said with a quick laugh. "You could spend my money. Go shopping and let me have the bills next time I visit. Go out with your friends. You do have friends, I take it?"

"Oh yes. I have friends," she said, with a wry laugh. "Lots of friends since you set me up here. Some of them are even respectable."

"There you are, then," he said. "Keep yourself busy for five days a week, but be here for me from Sunday to Tuesday. Is it not the ideal arrangement? And the best of it is that my mother knows nothing about it."

He laughed again. Oh yes, life was just perfect!

***

The earl's summons was definitely ominous. The whole family was to attend, not just Tess, and Uncle Charles was not one for dramatic meetings, so there was clearly something intriguing afoot.

Tess found the darkest corner of the library to hide in, sheltered by one of Eustace's precious suits of armour. With her black gown, she was confident of passing unnoticed as the rest of the family arrived. Walter was the first, but that must have been by the earl's wish, too, for he was waiting for him by the study door.

"Am I late?" Walter said.

"No, no, not at all," Uncle Charles said, his voice unsteady. "You are early, but that is all to the good. The more time we have before the others get here, the better."

"Whatever has happened?" Walter said. "It must be something dreadful, I am sure. I have never seen you so agitated."

Then he was inside the study, the door closing behind him, and Tess heard no more, but those few words were alarming enough.

Gradually, the rest of the family arrived in the library. Tess's mother was amongst the first, on Aunt Caroline's arm, the two sitting silently side by side as they waited. Then cousins Kent and Olivia, Kent joking as always, his ill-timed wit rousing Olivia's ire.

Olivia had chosen to be tearful today in anticipation of bad news. Once Tess and Olivia had been the best of friends, and they still shared a bedroom and sometimes clothes, too, but gradually they had grown apart. Olivia was destined for London, the season and a splendid marriage into her own rank, whereas Tess has no such expectations. Not that she wanted a splendid marriage, or any marriage at all, but as the two girls had realised their very different destinies, they had drifted apart.

The Westwick Heights family appeared then, making the room seem crowded and noisy, as greetings were exchanged. Uncle George had the same patrician air as Uncle Charles and Tess's mother, but then they could not help being the children of an earl. Aunt Jane made straight for Mama, seeing her as the greatest object of compassion in the room. Tess did not dislike Aunt Jane, for there was nothing objectionable about her at all, but she had never attracted her aunt's attention. She was far too healthy to be an object to a lady whose only interest in life was ailments — her own and everyone else's.

At noon, the appointed time for the meeting, the study door opened and they were allowed inside. As they drifted across the library and squeezed into the little round room, one of the corner towers of the castle, Tess's cousin Bertram asked how she was. He was the only person to address her.

Then, because Eustace was late, as usual, they all had to wait for him to arrive, giving everyone plenty of time to detect the shocked expression on Walter's face and the grey, tear-stained cheeks of Aunt Caroline. Bad news, then, without a doubt.

Tess could not have imagined just how bad it was. Her father — her wretched, *wicked* father — who had been chaplain at Corland Castle for thirty years, who had married Uncle Charles and Aunt Caroline, had, it appeared, never been ordained at all. He was not a clergyman, and not qualified to conduct marriages. The earl's marriage was invalid and all his children rendered illegitimate.

No wonder Walter was shocked. As the heir to the earldom and all the entailed estates, he had held the courtesy title of Viscount Birtwell. Now, thanks to Tess's father, all that had been taken from him. He had *nothing.* No inheritance, no title, not even the modest comfort of being a legitimate son. Uncle George, the earl's younger brother, was now the heir presumptive, and Bertram after him, and the two of them looked as shocked as anyone else.

There were many questions asked, of course, but nothing could make things right and set everything back the way it was. The women wept, the men were grim-faced and Walter left almost at once to inform his betrothed, Bea Franklyn, that she would never be the Countess of Rennington, merely Mrs Walter Atherton.

Tess crept away to her favourite hiding place, a small balcony high above the main staircase, and pondered her situation. She was one of the few unaffected by the change in the family's fortunes. Her own father's marriage had been conducted by the parish parson, so she herself was still legitimate, still bound by the terms of that stupid will. Her uncles, aunts and cousins were in disarray, but her life had not changed at all, except that her father's perfidy was now revealed for all to see. She had always known him for a rogue, but she had never suspected that his wickedness stretched so far.

She saw the others emerge below her, dispersing to their own favourite places to ponder their broken lives. They were silent, by long habit saying nothing in front of the servants, but that was mere foolishness. This could not be hidden from anyone, not the servants, not acquaintances, not the malicious section of society in London that would gloat over such a downfall. It would be in the newspapers, very likely, and the entire world would know the worst of her father.

What a wicked man he had been! No wonder someone had murdered him. Tess had always known that he was lining his own pockets at the earl's expense, always suspected that there was more she did not know, but this was beyond anything. To pretend to be a clergyman for all these years... to put himself forward as a pious, God-fearing man, and yet to be living such an enormous lie — it was incredible!

The castle fell into its afternoon slumber. A carriage arrived at the front door, but was turned away. No one was receiving callers today. After a while, the Westwick Heights family appeared, their carriage was summoned and they departed. Then silence again. Below her, only the occasional footman striding past importantly on some unknown errand disturbed the afternoon's tranquillity.

All at once, Tess could not bear to be still. There was nothing more to be learnt at the castle, so she would unburden herself to Tom, her faithful friend. Betty and Harold, her mother's watchdogs, were nowhere to be seen, for once, so Tess slipped down the service stairs and out through the garden door, collecting an ancient bonnet from a peg as she passed by. Then she was free, striding down the path to Birchall.

Tom was out, only the village woman who cleaned for him busy at the workshop, and she was soon finished. Tess made herself a pot of tea and waited for Tom to return. But he did not come, only Betty and Harold, indignant at being left behind.

"You shouldn't go off on your own, Miss Tess," Betty scolded. "Anything could happen if we're not by to protect you."

"What could happen to me in Birchall village, where everyone knows me?" Tess said.

"If you come callin' on Tom Shapman all by yourself, you know what folk'll say 'bout *that,*" Betty said. "We're here to look after you."

"And tell my mother everything I do," Tess said with a spurt of anger. "Do not imagine me ignorant of your true purpose."

"She *does* ask, it's true," Betty said, lifting her chin. "After all, she can't see herself, so she has to have other eyes watchin' over you. But we don't tell her all you get up to. No point in worryin' the poor lady, now is there? You'd be amazed if you knew how often you pray in church or deliver potted meat to the poor." She chuckled. "Leastways, that's what we tell her ladyship. But we're loyal to *you*, Miss Tess, first and last. We'll keep you safe, but we won't betray your secrets."

Tess did not for one moment believe them, but it was beneath her dignity to argue with servants, even such familiar ones as Betty and Harold. Betty had been a junior nursemaid when Tess was still in the nursery, a well-built girl willing to wade into fights between the older boys and haul the combatants apart, or carry a younger child bodily, but for ten years now she had belonged to Tess alone, acting as lady's maid as well as chaperon. Harold had been added when Tess was twelve, and already showing a propensity for wandering far and wide. Her mother had never attempted to stop the wandering, merely providing an escort to rescue her if she got into too much trouble.

Eventually, Tess gave up waiting for Tom, and set off back to the castle, Betty puffing in her wake and Harold loping along behind. Almost the first person she met as she crossed the great hall and set foot on the stairs was Captain Edgerton coming down them, light-footedly skipping from step to step. He was an unlikely person to be investigating her father's murder, having been a soldier in India, and still displaying a military air, a sword always hanging at his waist. He was amusing, however, and polite, too.

Now he stopped on the half-landing beside Eustace's display of armoury and made her a flourishing bow.

"Miss Nicholson. I trust I see you well?"

"As well as ever, Captain. Have you discovered who killed my father yet?"

"Not as yet, ma'am, but progress is being made, I feel."

"Is it?" she said disbelievingly. "And have you found any trace of my fortune?"

Instantly, he was wary. "There was nothing in your father's safe beyond the items already disclosed to you, Miss Nicholson — around a thousand pounds in cash, a few documents of no great moment and your mother's jewels."

"And nothing elsewhere? Under the floorboards? Up the chimney? A secret drawer?"

He grinned, showing a fine set of gleaming teeth. "Nothing like that, and believe me, we have looked. We have looked *everywhere.*"

"What about this house at Pickering?"

"Let on a long-term lease, and the tenant says that Mr Nicholson never went there. All her dealings have been through the attorney. Miss Nicholson..." He looked sorrowful suddenly. "I would love there to be a great fortune awaiting you, but your father was a sensible man. Whatever wealth he possessed would be held in the bank, not stuffed up a chimney."

"I am sure you are right, sir," she said demurely.

But she was entirely certain he was wrong. The house at Pickering... that had possibilities. She would talk to Tom about it.

3: An Under Housemaid

The talk at dinner that night was all about the disaster that had engulfed the Atherton family, and what Walter was to do, since Bea Franklyn had jilted him, now that he was not to be an earl. No one spoke to Tess, beyond the minimum that politeness decreed. What was there to say? She was not responsible for her father's misdemeanours, but her presence was a constant reminder of him. As soon as Aunt Caroline led the ladies away from the dining room, Tess slipped away to see her mother.

Lady Alice still spent virtually all her time secluded in her private sitting room, one of the round tower rooms at a corner of the castle. She had emerged for the family meeting only because her brother had ordered her to attend, and as soon as she was released, she returned to her sanctuary, having sworn she would not emerge until her husband's murderer was caught. She was deeply offended by Captain Edgerton, too, who had as good as accused her of murdering her own husband.

Malling, Mama's personal maid, admitted Tess with a low-voiced admonishment. "Don't distress her ladyship, Miss Tess. I'm sure you wouldn't, and she'll be pleased to see you, I know, but don't mention the murder."

Mama sat straight-backed on a small sofa, the only light in the room being a candelabrum set behind the chair where Malling was mending a shift or nightgown. From the window, the sun's dying rays gave the room a ghostly glow.

"Miss Tess, my lady," Malling said.

Mama turned her sightless eyes towards the door, looking at a point somewhere beyond Tess's left shoulder. "Tess! Come in, my dear. Were you at this dreadful meeting today? You understand what has happened? But you must not think badly of your father over this. I am sure he did not know... he could not have realised... he never intended such unfortunate consequences. It was a misunderstanding, I am sure. He must have believed he was ordained, or he would never— He was not a bad man, Tess, and you must never think ill of him."

Tess hardly knew how to answer her. How was it possible to *believe* oneself ordained if it were not true? She had heard the story many times of how her father had encountered the late Lord Rennington by chance as they both travelled north. Snowed up at an inn, they had fallen into friendship and the earl had brought his new friend north to be chaplain at Corland, and how could he have done so unless the man had told him he was ordained? And his first act was to marry Aunt Caroline and Uncle Charles, knowing full well that he was not an ordained clergyman, and everyone knew a marriage was invalid without a proper parson. And then to say nothing before Walter was born. Six children altogether, all illegitimate, the entire inheritance in disarray, and all because of her father. Yet somehow, her mother clung to the fiction that he was a good man.

And yet to her, perhaps he was. They had always been a loving couple, so wrapped up in each other that there had never seemed to be room for Tess. She had felt superfluous to their perfect intimacy, beyond their notice, somehow. Mama's condition made her dependent on Papa for so much. He helped her with food at dinner, he read to her for hours at a time, wrote letters for her, walked or rode with her, or simply talked to her. They never tired of each other's company, and there was no room for a child in such an arrangement.

Tess had never resented their closeness. There was a freedom in being so often overlooked. Aunt Caroline had kept an eye on her when Tess was a girl, but the prospects for a chaplain's daughter were so different from the futures laid out for her own daughters that gradually even Aunt Caroline had forgotten her. There was no season in town to arrange for Tess, no eligible match to look out for, no useful connections to invite her to stay in a house with marriageable sons. So Tess had felt free to make her own friends and arrange her own future with Tom Shapman, whose manly body and warm kisses set her shivering all over.

"Mama, it is a little awkward for me here just now, under the circumstances."

"Dear Tess! It is not as if anyone blames you for this… situation."

"No, indeed, but it is difficult for the family to speak freely before me. I thought I might go down to Helmsley for a couple of days, to see about more mourning clothes. I could stay with Susan Bullock."

"Bullock? Oh, the grocer's daughter."

"Mr Bullock retired from his trade more than twenty years ago, Mama. He died last winter, if you recall, so Susan is still in mourning."

"Then she will not encourage you to attend any unsuitable engagements?"

"No, indeed. She lives very quietly with her aunt now. She would be company for me, however, and perhaps a little shopping would cheer me up. If you can spare me, of course. I should not wish to leave you if you have need of me."

"No, no, I am no company for a girl of your age, not at present, and Helmsley... you cannot get into trouble at Helmsley. It will do you good to get away from home for a while. Do not rush back — stay over the Sabbath, at least. I confess, I do not like you going down to Birchall on Sundays, now that we cannot use our own chapel. You are bound to meet *that man* there, and there is a danger that you will be drawn back into his sphere. You have not seen Shapman lately, have you? Other than at church, that is?"

Tess pretended to think about it. "I believe I passed him outside the parsonage one day. He bowed, I made the smallest inclination of my head, he moved on."

"Well done! You must do nothing to encourage him. How presumptuous to think that we should ever allow you to marry a man like that, a man of trade, earning a living with his hands. You are not a great heiress, but you are the niece of an earl, and that should mean something, after all. But I dare say he mistook your natural friendliness for something more, and is now mortified by his mistake. Let us hope that is all in the past, and your father, in his wisdom, has taken steps to ensure that you are never again importuned by anyone so unworthy."

Tess could not quite see the matter in that light, but there was never any point in arguing with her mother, so she merely said, "May I have the carriage tomorrow, to take me to Helmsley?"

"Of course. And you will have Betty and Harold with you, so you will be quite safe. Remember to take one or other of them with you whenever you go out of doors."

"Of course, Mama."

Her trip thus approved, Tess left to tell Betty and Harold of the delight in store for them, and to order the carriage.

***

Susan Bullock was a well-rounded girl of twenty-three, who had admired Tess ever since their accidental meeting over the same ribbon at the haberdashery. For some years now, Susan had been Tess's friend and confidante, offering a place to stay when she needed to escape from home, and a place to pretend to stay when she wanted to go adventuring. Mostly, her adventures had involved Scarborough and the slightly rakish air of a seaside town. This adventure was more serious.

"I am going to try to find my fortune," Tess told her friend, as they sat in the best bedroom, the one always assigned to Tess. "It is not at Corland Castle, so it must be at the house at Pickering. *My* house, in fact, although my trustees will not allow me even to go there. But I am going to go, despite them, to see what I can find."

"Ooh, Tess, you're so brave!" Susan said, wide-eyed. "I should never dare! But what will you do? You can't just walk up to the front door... can you?"

"I am not sure yet," Tess said with a frown. "However, if it is left to the lawyers nothing at all will be done, so I must find a way to get inside. The widow who lives there must have callers. Friends, perhaps. I shall befriend her."

"How clever you are!" Susan said.

Tess was not so sure. Susan might be impressed with the idea, but Tess knew perfectly well that she would need to be a great deal cleverer to find any secret hiding places in the house. One could not drink tea in the drawing room with the lady of the house, and immediately institute a search for hidden treasure. There had to be a better way than simply befriending the widow. What was her name? Mayberry. Mrs Mayberry of Apstead House.

"Your aunt will play the game?" Tess said anxiously. Miss Bullock was a lax chaperon, but there was no saying when she might choose to exert her authority.

"Oh, yes. She is used to you, and she is too much in awe of you ever to try to stop you."

"Good. I have told Mama that I will be gone for a few days, but she knows my ways and will not worry about me if it is longer. If anyone should come looking for me, you need only say that I stayed a while and then went on elsewhere, but you do not know where. I had better send Harold to buy seats for us on the coach. With luck, we may be away this afternoon."

"I wish you could stay longer," Susan said wistfully. "It's not that I mind helping but we have such fun when you stay here properly, not just pretending."

"With luck, I shall be back in a week or so, and we can have fun then," Tess said. "But I must find my fortune, you do see that?"

"Oh, yes, of course! It is quite shocking that your lawyers cannot find it themselves, but I am sure you will manage it, and then you will be rich, won't you?"

"Rich and independent," Tess said with satisfaction.

With coach tickets obtained, Tess changed into the drab old clothes she kept for her adventures. She had only a small portmanteau, filled with more drab clothes, and a few coins in her reticule, but three purses of money were hidden away on her person. She may have been pretending to be poor, but she had no intention of actually being so, and there was no knowing when she might need to lay out her blunt in a hurry.

The common stage coach was always an adventure to Tess. Harold sat on top, as usual, but Tess and Betty shared the inside with an attorney, a severe looking widow with a snappy dog, a girl travelling to Scarborough to take up a position as a maid and a cage full of ducklings. The widow unbent sufficiently to offer the new maid some advice about working hard and avoiding single gentlemen. The maid said nothing beyond *'Yes, ma'am'* and *'No, ma'am'*, but the exchange gave Tess an idea.

"Housemaids!" she hissed in Betty's ear as they descended from the coach at Pickering.

"What?" Betty said. "What do we want housemaids for?"

"No, we do not want them. We shall *be* housemaids. Mrs — the widow in question — must need servants, surely."

"You, a housemaid?" Betty said. "That I'd pay good money to see."

"Well, how hard can it be?" Tess said. "Nothing but flicking a duster about."

Betty only laughed.

It being quite late in the day now, Tess sent Harold to procure rooms for them at the inn where they had arrived, not having much interest in finding anywhere better. They took dinner in the common room, and then set out to find Apstead House. It was not a very prepossessing place, just a modest house in a line of similar houses, except for a certain air of neglect. The gardens were in good order, but the rest of the house had not seen fresh paint for some years, windows were cracked and the one smoking chimney, no doubt from the kitchen, billowed forth dark clouds.

Tess walked past once, turned at the end of the road and then walked past again. "Mrs Widow definitely needs a housemaid or two."

"And a footman?" Harold said hopefully.

"Unlikely," Tess said. "A widow is likely to keep an all-female household. But we can find out. Harold, go and ring the front door and ask if Mr Smith is at home."

"There is no Mr Smith there," he said, puzzled.

"Of course not," she said impatiently. "You will be told that and then you apologise and say that you must have mistaken the house. But we wish to see who answers the door — a butler or footman, or a housekeeper or maid. Do you see?"

Belatedly, he did. Tess and Betty stayed out of sight behind a neighbour's high hedge until he returned. "Housekeeper," he said. "Very starchy one, too. Looked down her nose at me. I don't look like a footman, do I? I'm not in livery."

"No, but you do not look like a gentleman, either. But there you are, Harold. The widow will not want a footman. What did the hall look like?"

"Um... like any hall."

"Shining furniture? Smell of beeswax polish? Fresh flowers on display?"

"Oh — no, dust everywhere. Smelt fusty, like damp clothes."

"Aha!" Tess said. "Then she definitely needs maids."

"We need to find out how folk get their servants here," Betty said. "It might be all word of mouth, or it might be done at the market, but there could be a registry."

"We can ask at the inn," Tess said happily.

There was no registry, they soon discovered. Most positions for servants were filled by word of mouth, or on market days there was a room at the inn where they might wait and those wanting servants would come and look them over.

"That is no good," Tess said, as she and Betty readied themselves for bed in their tiny room. "We are not looking for just any position. We want to work in that particular house. We are just going to have to take a risk and go to the door."

"I don't know anyone who'd take on servants who just came and asked like that," Betty said dubiously.

"We can only try," Tess said. "If the widow is desperate enough, she might do it. If not, I shall have to think of something else."

The following morning saw the two of them outside Apstead House at an early hour. This time it was Harold who lurked out of sight behind the neighbour's hedge, as Tess and Betty walked boldly up to the front door.

"You know what to say?" Tess hissed. Betty, being older, had been given the task of talking to the housekeeper.

"Aye. Sisters. Just arrived from Thirsk. Had to leave the last place because the son was a pest."

"Our undimmed virtue should ensure the widow's sympathy, at least."

Tess knocked briskly at the door. After several minutes, the starchy housekeeper appeared, a large bunch of keys dangling from the waistband of her gown.

"Yes?"

"Good day, mum," Betty said. "We heard you might be in need of two honest, hard workin' maids. Just arrived from Thirsk."

"References?"

Betty handed over the glowing letters of recommendation that Tess had written that morning.

"Hmm. There is nothing here within the last three years."

"We had to leave the last place in a hurry," Betty said. "The son of the house had wanderin' hands, and when we objected, the mistress turned us off. We're looking for a place with no young men."

The housekeeper laughed suddenly. "Oh, there are no young men living here, or old men, either. Only me and my nieces. I can certainly use you, if you truly are honest and hard-working. For some reason, I have had trouble getting maids locally, and I cannot tell why, for we are a quiet household, and the work is not arduous. Twenty pounds a year for the two of you, since you come as a pair. Come in. I'm Mrs Mayberry, by the way."

Nieces? That was a surprise. And this was no starchy housekeeper, but the widow herself. They followed her meekly into the house.

"You will rise at five," she said, to a squeak of alarm from Tess, "and clean these four rooms around the hall, and the hall itself. Then upstairs, to my dressing room and the young ladies' dressing rooms. Ah, here is Margaret. She is head housemaid here. She will supervise you just at first. New under housemaids, Margaret, starting today. I have told them the first duties. What comes after the dressing rooms?"

"Staircase and then servants' breakfast, madam. Then the bedrooms, corridors and passages, and whatever special tasks there are — rugs to be beaten, or curtains shaken out, windows cleaned and so on. Dinner at one, then the linen to be repaired. During dinner, you help the kitchen maid with the dishes and see that everything's put away properly. You'll get into the way of it soon enough."

"Show them their room, Margaret."

"Can we go to the inn to collect our things, ma'am?" Betty said.

"If you're quick about it. Back here and at work within half an hour."

So began Tess's career as an under housemaid. For several days, she hardly knew where she was or what she was about. Betty hauled her from her bed at five o'clock every morning — five o'clock! An hour Tess had scarcely known existed except as a time to fall into bed exhausted at the end of a ball. From then on, there was nothing but scrubbing, or so it seemed. No wonder Betty had laughed when Tess had talked about flicking a duster here and there! Margaret wielded the duster, Betty had a jar of furniture polish while Tess, the most junior of them, was delegated to clean the fireplaces.

She had never guessed there was so much work involved. Even though there were no ashes to empty at this time of year, she had to rub the bars and fire irons with oil, then with emery paper and finally with scouring paper. Then the backs of the fireplaces had to be black-leaded twice weekly. And finally, the marble surrounds were washed in soapy water, dried and rubbed over with a linen cloth. And that was just the fireplaces. In addition, the rugs were to be lifted, the floors dusted, or mopped on Tuesdays and Saturdays, and mirrors and windows cleaned. All this for five downstairs rooms and the stairs before breakfast.

And so the day went on relentlessly, until Tess fell exhausted into her bed at close to midnight, only to be shaken awake immediately, or so it seemed. She counted the minutes until the next meal, for at least the food was good and there was plenty of it. The ladies upstairs did even better, for Tess saw every dish of expensive delicacies that went up to the dining room. It seemed this was a recent innovation, for the cook sighed often as she worked and remarked on how pleasant it was to have the best cuts of meat for a change.

"It's almost like it was in Miss Carlisle's day," she said with a beatific smile, but when pressed about Miss Carlisle, her face closed up and she said primly, "My lips are sealed."

Gradually Tess learned to get through the work speedily, so that there were moments of respite, when she could gaze out of the window at the neat gardens at the back of the house, or the road at the front. Never for long, for Margaret was always around, watching her with what Tess was sure were suspicious eyes. Did she suspect? She must be aware that Tess had never been in service before, her white, unblemished hands giving her away more surely even than her obvious lack of expertise. Still, she could not possibly know who Tess was or what her true purpose was.

Tess had earned some respect from Margaret early in her employment, by voluntarily taking down mirrors and paintings, and opening cupboard doors. "I like to dust the backs properly," she had said blandly. Margaret had nodded approvingly, but the effort only proved that there was no safe tucked away anywhere in the main rooms. Nor could she see any loose floorboards when she moved rugs here and there. When she occasionally helped Betty with the furniture, she could detect no sign of secret drawers. It was all very dispiriting.

Ten days passed without any discoveries at all. At church, they managed a few words with Harold, who was conducting his own enquiries about the town. By telling people he had worked at Corland Castle, he had found the subject of Mr Nicholson, the murdered chaplain, aroused great curiosity, but he could not find anyone who knew him, or remembered him being in Pickering.

Shortly after this, a curious incident occurred. Tess and Betty had seen nothing of Mrs Mayberry's nieces, for the junior servants were kept out of sight when the young ladies were about. One afternoon, however, as Betty was pressing undergarments, and Tess was diligently mending sheets, Margaret came through and whispered, "Come to the scullery window."

The scullery was at the front of the house, with a narrow window overlooking the area. Phyllis, the kitchen maid, was already there, pointing excitedly to the road, where a fine carriage stood, with four horses, two coachmen and two footmen in livery.

"Callers?" Betty said, but Margaret laughed.

"Miss Rochester is going out for the evening. Wait, and you'll see her in all her finery."

Within a very few minutes, Mrs Mayberry appeared carrying a portmanteau, and then a girl of perhaps twenty or so, in a rather over-decorated evening gown and cloak, her abundant black curls elaborately dressed.

"Ooh, so pretty!" Phyllis said in hushed tones, as a footman held open the carriage door for Miss Rochester. "Such pretty hair."

"That's a wig," Margaret said. "Her own hair is brown and straight as a stair-rod, but the gentleman likes black curls better."

Miss Rochester stepped inside the carriage, the footman closed the door and tossed the portmanteau up to the coachman on the box, then hopped onto the back of the carriage. Almost at once, it creaked into motion, the horses stepping smartly away from the house and disappearing down the road.

"Where's she off to, then?" Betty said.

"It's not for the likes of us to know where madam's nieces go to," Margaret said repressively.

"She ought to have a chaperon," Betty said.

Margaret looked about to speak, but then closed her mouth firmly.

They all drifted back to the servants' hall and their afternoon chores, Betty still wondering aloud who owned the smart carriage, and where the girl might be going with an overnight bag. Scarborough, she decided. No doubt there was a ball or some such going on there.

Tess did not have to wonder quite so much. She had recognised the carriage, the coachmen and the footmen's livery.

The only question in her mind was what Cousin Eustace's interest was in Miss Rochester.

4: A New Plan

For the rest of the day, Tess could think of little but the unexpected sight of Eustace's carriage taking Miss Rochester away. She had never thought Eustace had anything to do with Pickering, but she supposed he might have friends in the town. He had friends all over the place, and rarely seemed to be at home. As a single man, he could not entertain ladies at his own house, and there would be no evening parties at Corland, not with the family in such disarray, so presumably Miss Rochester was being taken elsewhere as Eustace's guest.

Betty was still wondering over it, too, as they climbed into bed that night. "Wherever she was goin', she should have had a chaperon," she said sourly.

"There was no one else in the carriage that I could see," Tess said.

"Don't matter," Betty said. "Her aunt should have gone with her... if she is her aunt, that is."

"Why should Mrs Mayberry say she is the girls' aunt if she is not?"

"Aye, that's the question, ain't it? This is a strange house and no mistake, Miss Tess. Mrs Mayberry is the mistress here, supposedly, but she acts more like a housekeeper than a respectable widow. And four young ladies in the house, but they never go out callin', nor no one calls here. Ten days we've been here and that's the first time any of those so-called nieces has left the house."

"We never even see them," Tess said. "We do the bedrooms while they are at breakfast, and we are stuck in the kitchen all afternoon and evening."

"Aye, well, I nipped out to the privy in the garden the other evenin', when Margaret were upstairs," Betty said. "I saw a *man* goin' up the garden path and round to the side door, the one by the stairs. So they do have callers, gentleman callers, but only to the back door and only in the evenin'."

"Well, there is nothing in that," Tess said. "A man might be hesitant to make a formal morning call to an all-female household, but he might be invited to join the ladies for tea after dinner."

"But not goin' anywhere at all, and then that girl sets off all alone with an overnight bag in a fancy carriage like that. Someone rich sent that rig, you may be sure."

"Did you not recognise it?" Tess said. "That was Eustace's carriage."

"Master Eustace?" Betty cried. "No! Was it? But—?"

"Precisely," Tess said with a smile.

"Hmpf," Betty grunted, pulling the thin blanket up to her chin. "This place is too strange by half, Miss Tess, and we're no further forward findin' any trace of your father here. We've been into every room in the house, even the attics, and found nothin'. The sooner we get out of here the better."

"A few more days," Tess said. "I should like to know how long Miss Rochester spends with Eustace first. That is an odd pairing. Very odd indeed."

***

Miss Rochester returned the next day, late in the afternoon, again in Eustace's carriage. Betty had discovered there had been a public assembly in Scarborough that evening, so she was satisfied that the lady had been dancing the night away. Tess said nothing, disbelieving, for the girl had worn an ordinary evening gown not the more elaborate ball gown. She determined that she would watch Eustace more closely when she returned home.

She was almost ready to abandon Apstead House and accept that her father had never been there when she made a discovery. Like many houses of a size suitable for a gentleman's family, there was a small coach house at the bottom of the garden backing onto a quiet lane. It was from the lane, she presumed, that the gentleman caller had come, walking through the garden to the house. The garden itself was neat and tidy, for Mrs Mayberry was indefatigable with a trowel in her hand, and no weed dared to show its face. The coach house was less well cared for. It contained an ancient gig, but there was no horse and no groom, nothing but a few wisps of rotting hay and a great many cobwebs. Outside stairs at one side led to an upper floor, perhaps intended as accommodation for a groom. On the other side was the privy.

Tess had explored a little, while supposedly visiting the privy, and discovered that the door to the upper floor was firmly locked. She thought nothing of it until the day that, hidden behind the privy door, she had seen

Mrs Mayberry go up the stairs. Creeping quickly around to a better vantage point, she watched Mrs Mayberry unlock the door, go inside and emerge a few minutes later with a heavy purse in her hand. She hastily tucked it away into a pocket of her old-fashioned skirts, but Tess had seen enough.

"There is *money* in there!" she hissed to Betty. "We have to get inside."

"Lord, Miss Tess, you're like a dog with a bone!" Betty said. "There's nothing amiss with a lady keepin' a little cash locked away safe like that. If your fortune were in there, d'you think she'd be livin' in a little house like this, with not enough servants? And why don't she have more servants, anyway? She's got to be desperate, taking *us* on."

"True, but if she has money of her own hidden away, why is the better food such a recent innovation? The furnishings are good — Turkish carpets, I would swear, porcelain everywhere and some fine paintings on the walls. And Miss Rochester's clothes were not cheap. Have you looked through the young ladies' wardrobes? Not in the first stare of fashion, but good quality fabrics."

"Cut too low, and too flimsy, if you ask me," Betty said darkly.

Tess only laughed. "You should see what Izzy wears sometimes. Very low cut, very flimsy."

"She's a married lady," Betty said. "I don't care what you say, Miss Tess, I don't like this house. I don't like it at all. There's something not right about it."

"I dislike it, too," Tess said, "and as soon as I have seen inside that room above the coach house, we can leave."

Betty sighed and rolled her eyes. "You'll need the keys, and the mistress hangs them from her waist."

"Only during the day. When she dresses for dinner, she leaves them in the housekeeper's room. This evening, when Margaret is upstairs serving the tea, Mrs Harris is asleep in her chair and Phyllis is in the scullery — that will be my opportunity."

The first part of this plan went remarkably well. Mrs Harris, the cook, did indeed nod off, Phyllis was occupied washing dishes in the scullery and Margaret was serving tea upstairs when Tess crept along the passage to the housekeeper's room, slipped inside and took the large bunch of keys. Then she scuttled to the kitchen door and out into the garden, as if going to the privy. Instead, she ran light-footed up the stairs to the groom's apartment and began to work her way through the keys on the ring, trying to find the one that opened the door.

Male voices from below caused her to freeze. Two men walked past the end of the coach house, passing directly below the stairs on which she crouched, trying to make herself as small as possible and fade into the shadows. The sun was not yet set, and if they had looked up they could not have failed to see Tess. They did not look up, passing on up the garden, absorbed in their own conversation — it sounded as if they were discussing a horse race. A burst of laughter, and then they were gone.

Tess turned quickly back to the locked door, and finally, with almost the last key she tried, the lock turned and the door opened.

The room was disappointing. It was, at first sight, just what one would have expected, sleeping quarters for a groom. There was a low bed, devoid of mattress or blankets, a washstand, a chest of drawers and wardrobe, and a battered wooden table set in front of a window, set with paper, ink and pens. There were some pegs in the wall for hanging coats, and a few nails where pictures might once have hung. Curiously for a disused room, it was clean and tidy, with none of the cobwebs so prevalent in the coach house below. Someone, then, cleaned regularly.

But where had the money come from? With light from the lowering sun pouring through the window, she began pulling open drawers. They were full. Some contained bills, mostly from Pickering businesses, some were letters or business documents that she would need to read carefully to understand. And finally — success! One drawer contained account books neatly annotated in her father's hand. A metal cash box contained four hundred and twenty pounds in notes and guineas, and a quantity of smaller coins.

Triumphantly, she let the coins slide through her fingers. Her father *had* been to this house, had kept an office here, had kept records of his expenses. But there was no sign of her fortune, or a safe where it might be hidden, and no other cupboard, apart from the wardrobe. With a rush of excitement, she pulled open the wardrobe door, and there it was — a neat safe, undoubtedly containing a multitude of gold bars. *Her* gold bars.

She could see at a glance that none of the keys on the ring would fit the safe. Now, where would her father keep the key? On his person? No, the key to the safe at Corland had been hidden on the underside of the desk, and undoubtedly the same was true here. All she had to do was search carefully.

Just as she was about to crawl on the floor looking under the writing table, the door creaked open and a dark figure loomed in the doorway. Mrs Mayberry, resplendent in purple, with Margaret hovering behind.

"I told you I saw someone moving about," Margaret said.

"Well?" Mrs Mayberry said. "What have you to say for yourself, you little thief?"

Tess jumped to her feet and rubbed her dusty hands on her skirt, and laughed in their faces. "Oh no, you have that wrong. *You* are the thief, not I. Did I not see you come in here and take money away?"

"That is my money," Mrs Mayberry said. "All of this is mine."

"On the contrary, all of this is *mine*," Tess hissed at her. "This house and everything in it was left to me by my father who owned it before me. Everyone said he never came here, but he did, this room proves that he did. That money you have been stealing was his and is now mine, and the contents of that safe were his and are now mine."

The two women gazed at her, open-mouthed in astonishment. "You? You are Miss Nicholson?" Margaret whispered.

"I am."

"Nonsense," Mrs Mayberry said robustly. "We'll see what the constables have to say about *that.* But whoever you are, you can pack your things and leave within the hour, you and that so-called sister of yours."

"You cannot throw me out of my own house," Tess said.

"I am the tenant here and I have the right to peaceful occupation, and no disruption by the owner until the tenancy expires. So you leave and you don't come back, understood?"

Tess was quite prepared to argue the point, but she recalled something of the sort that the lawyers had mentioned. When she married, her husband could reclaim the house, but until then her trustees insisted on leaving the tenant in place.

"Very well, but there is four hundred and twenty pounds in the cash box, and I shall expect there still to be four hundred and twenty pounds when you leave, and the contents of the safe untouched, for I know what is inside it." At least, she sincerely hoped she did. "If anything is missing, I shall see you hanged or transported. Understood?"

Mrs Mayberry did not deign to reply.

"Where is the key to the safe, do you know?"

Still no reply. There was nothing for it but to leave with as much dignity as she could manage. Within an hour, she and Betty were back at the inn, settling down in the common room to a second dinner, this time with wine.

"Now what, Miss Tess?" Betty said. "Back to Corland?"

"Heavens, no. That would be far too tame. I shall not give in so easily, you may be sure. At least now I know where my fortune is. All I have to do is get hold of it."

"That's just what you can't do, Miss Tess. You'll not get near it again, not with those women watching."

"No, and they will change the lock on that room and hide the new key, so there will be no sneaking in."

"If you tell the lawyers, maybe they—?"

"No," Tess said quickly. "Not the lawyers. What I need, I think, is a husband." She giggled suddenly. "And I have the very man in mind."

"Now, Miss Tess, what are you up to?"

"You will see." She giggled again. "I think it is time I paid a visit to my aunt's sister."

***

The first priority was to return to Helmsley to collect her boxes from Susan. Tess had no desire to subject herself to the common stage again, so she hired a post chaise and four.

Susan grabbed her arm anxiously when she saw her. "Oh, Tess, there have been so many people looking for you! First, a groom from Corland, and then your cousin, Mr Kent, and finally a Scotsman who was sent by a Captain Somebody—"

"Edgerton," Tess said with distaste. "Nasty, snooping man."

"That's the one, although the Scotsman was very pleasant, but Tess, I couldn't pretend you were here. Well, I've never been any good at lying. Still, I wouldn't tell them where you were. I swear, I never told them anything!"

"Not to worry," Tess said easily. "It is of no consequence. My mother need not know everything I do."

"She wrote to you just a few days after you left," Susan said. "Here... but nothing after that. I suppose when you didn't write back, she realised you weren't here and sent people to find out where you were."

"Well, this is excellent news," Tess said, swiftly scanning it. "Aunt Caroline has gone to Harfield, which gives me even more of an excuse to go there myself."

"Harfield Priory?" Betty said. "How are you goin' to get a husband there? I thought you disliked the new Lord Tarvin."

"Everyone dislikes Edward," Tess said disdainfully. "A starchier, more disagreeable man would be hard to find, but he will still be in London, we must hope. But he is not the only man at Durham."

"Well, I'm sure I don't know of any others," Betty muttered, but Tess only smiled at her. The more she considered her new plan, the more perfect she thought it.

Bidding Susan a fond farewell with a pretty little necklace and some expensive tea for her aunt, to thank them for their help, Tess made her way north. Their route passed by Corland Castle, but she chose not to stop there, even for one night. Even though her mother would perhaps not try to dissuade her from going to Harfield, it would be an unnecessary delay. She had written from Helmsley to tell Lady Alice her plans, and that, she felt, satisfied the proprieties.

She stopped at Birchall village, however, for she had not seen Tom for three weeks and who knew when she might be back at Corland? She had no great desire to see any of her family, but not seeing Tom would be insupportable.

He was busy at work, but he laid down his tools, turning to her with a wide smile.

"Miss Tess! Haven't seen you for an age — gone off to Helmsley, so I heard. Or maybe not. There were some odd stories of you disappearing altogether."

"I have been looking for my fortune. Oh, kiss me, Tom, or I shall run mad. I have missed you so much."

"Well now, Miss Tess, we really shouldn't. Not now you have to marry a gentleman."

"Nonsense!" She pushed him onto the nearest chair and settled herself firmly on his lap. "I shall marry where I please, once I have my fortune in my hand."

His arms crept round her waist, but he said, "It'll be in your husband's hand, not yours."

"Not if I get to it before the lawyers do. Can you not see? All those gold bars are like coins — very expensive coins. Once a coin is in your pocket, no one knows where it came from or who owned it before. It belongs to whoever has it. Once I have those gold bars, which are *mine*, may I remind you, no one can take them away from me, and I shall be free to do whatever I like."

She pressed her lips against his, and for a moment he allowed it, but then he drew back. "Do you know where they are, these gold bars of yours?"

She giggled. "I do! They are at my Pickering house. That widow, Mrs Mayberry, she told everyone my father had never been there, but she lied.

He had an office there, well hidden, but I found it, with bills and account books — and a safe! I could not find the key to the safe, but the gold is inside it, I am certain."

Again she leant towards him, but he held her away from him. "You've been there? Inside?"

"Yes! Betty and I worked there as housemaids."

"Housemaids! You, a proper lady, working as a housemaid? That's not right, not right at all."

"No, and it was hard work, I can tell you. You cannot imagine how much needs to be done just to keep one small house clean. I am quite worn to the bone. But I found the office and the safe, although I was caught before I could get the safe open. So now I have to find a different plan to get my money."

He picked her up and set her bodily on her feet, rising himself. "You and your schemes! You're such a clever little thing, Miss Tess. But I might be able to help. I know how to get into a safe — some safes, that is. If there's just the one key to it, I *might* be able to pick the lock."

"How good you are, Tom, but there will be no need for lock-picking. I shall find the key, never fear, just as soon as I can take possession of the house. But until then, my fortune is quite safe. My trustees will not go there, and the lying Mrs Mayberry will keep thieves away from it. She is as good as a watchdog! But I must find a way to get her and her nieces out of the house, and get into it myself, without the trustees elbowing their way in."

"Because they would take control of your fortune?"

"Exactly so! The only way for me to be free is to have those gold bars in my possession, and no one else knowing anything about them. If the trustees find them first, that is the end of that. They will be taken to the bank to await the pleasure of my gentleman husband, and I shall never see them again. But if I get to them first…"

"You'll be free," Tom parroted with a smile. "I'm sure you're clever enough to do it, too, and I'll help if I can, you know that. I want you to have whatever makes you happy."

"And then we can be married, and no one can stop us," she said with a beaming smile.

5: A Visit To Harfield Priory

After leaving Tom to his work, Tess's post chaise wound its way further into the hills, passing Corland Castle and the small village surrounding it without stopping. Some while later, they passed Eustace's house at Welwood-on-the-Hill, making Tess wonder all over again about his connection to Miss Rochester. Another thought occurred to her, as they rattled past the gates of the estate. Given the time she had left Pickering, it was perfectly possible for the girl to have reached Welwood in time for dinner. Had she, then, come here for her evening engagement? But Eustace was a single man who had never been known to host parties for ladies as well as gentlemen. He would have needed his mother or one of his sisters to act as hostess, and that seemed unlikely. He had never done so before, and with the family in its present disarray, it was surely impossible. It was a mystery.

It was late the following day when they arrived at Harfield Priory. Tess had often stayed there, for her mother had liked to send her to visit relations — *'It will broaden your horizons, dear,'* she had always said, but Tess suspected it removed her from her mother's presence. She had not expected to have children at all, and had never quite known what to do with Tess. It was easier, therefore, to dispatch her here and there, and leave her to be raised by others.

The Priory was one of Tess's favourite places. Unlike Corland, which looked medieval but was actually modern, Harfield was truly ancient, with a great hall dating back to the original manor house, a chapel that had been part of the abbey, and a multitude of odd, mismatched wings with long, dark passages and unexpected stairs. Best of all, it was tucked into a narrow valley, so even the garden was all changing levels and tightly winding paths. It was a place where a secretive girl could hide away indefinitely.

The butler, who seemed as ancient as the house, emerged wreathed in smiles. "Miss Tess! What a delightful surprise! We were not expecting you, I think?"

"No time to write, Jeffries. Is all well here?"

"Very lively, at the moment. Lady Rennington is here, and also Lady Woodridge, and we've had both Lord and Lady Farramont visiting, but they've both left now. I expect the ladies will tell you all about it. Good day, Betty, Harold. You know your way, of course. I'll have your usual room made up, Miss Tess. Come inside, do."

The great hall was pleasantly cool. The Priory was a nightmare of draughts and perpetually chilled rooms in winter, but in summer it was a relief to be inside after the heat and dust of the road.

"The ladies are in the Blue Parlour, Miss Tess," Jeffries said. "Will you see them first, or go to your room?"

"I had better see them at once," Tess said. "Just in case they decide to throw me out."

Jeffries laughed at this little jest, but Tess was not entirely joking. Lady Tarvin was Aunt Caroline's sister, and a kindly soul, who treated Tess as if she were her own niece, but Mrs Edward Harfield, the mother of the present Lord Tarvin, was not quite so tolerant. It was not clear to Tess which of the two was in fact the mistress of Harfield, the widow of the former Lord Tarvin or the mother of the present one, but it would never do to be backward in any attention, or to take her welcome for granted.

She followed Jeffries along a multitude of passageways to the Blue Parlour. Three ladies sat there, looking up with surprise as the door opened.

"Miss Nicholson, my lady," Jeffries said, leaving Tess in no doubt as to who he regarded as the mistress of Harfield.

Aunt Caroline rushed across the room to wrap her in a perfumed embrace. "Tess! Dear girl, what a delightful surprise! I thought you were staying with a friend somewhere."

"So I was, but after three weeks I felt like a change of scene and Corland is..." She hesitated. What could she say of Corland that would not distress Lady Rennington?

But Aunt Caroline took up the idea at once. "Oh, indeed, Corland is a very dismal place just now. You are very sensible to stay away from there. Your poor mama is inconsolable, so even your presence could not bring her any comfort, those investigators are turning the place upside down, and then there is the Dowager Countess, still lingering. It is not a healthy atmosphere for a young girl. I just wish I could bring Olivia out of there, but she will not leave her father, the dear girl. Myrtle, is not this a delightful surprise?"

Her sister Myrtle, Lady Tarvin, agreed that Tess's unexpected arrival was indeed a delightful surprise. The two ladies fussed over her until she almost felt guilty for her devious plan. Almost, but not quite.

The third lady present, Mrs Edward Harfield, merely nodded to Tess and made some commonplace remarks, without enthusiasm, but it was enough. Tess would not be thrown out on her ear. Satisfied, she retired to her room where a bath was already being filled for her. She had bathed and swaddled herself in a robe when there was a brisk knock on the door. Before Betty could reach it, the door opened and a head peeped round.

"Tess! How lovely!"

Tess's cousin Josie was the eldest of the three daughters of Lord and Lady Rennington. She had taken her time to marry, settling eventually on Viscount Woodridge, the heir to an earldom, but hers was a love match and she exuded contentment. Tess wondered sometimes what it must be like to marry for love, when the loved one was also highly eligible. There would be no compromises needed in such an arrangement, no need to convince a reluctant father to agree to the match, no quibbling over a dowry. How pleasant that would be!

Josie came fully into the room, and pulled over a chair to sit beside Tess. "You look tired, cousin," she said. "But then it is only six weeks since your father's death, and you must feel it dreadfully, especially with that shocking will. Marry a gentleman, indeed! And to leave you a fortune, but only on such conditions! It is the outside of enough. I feel for you, Tess, truly I do."

That was as neat a way of accounting for her tiredness as any other, and no need to mention five o'clock starts and scrubbing floors.

"Thank you, Josie. How are you? And the baby?"

Her face softened. "Gerard is a darling, and I love having him all to myself. However, my mother-in-law is to leave Throxfield in a day or two, and it will be safe for me to go home again." She gurgled with laughter. "But until then, it will be delightful to have you here. We are all still catching our breath after Izzy blew through — you know what Izzy is like. It will be charmingly peaceful with you here."

The evening brought another opportunity to try to determine who was the real mistress of the Priory.

"Dinner is served, my lady," the butler said.

"Thank you, Jeffries," Mrs Harfield said, immediately assuming the position of hostess. "Shall we go through, ladies?"

Lady Tarvin merely smiled, while Lady Rennington and Josie exchanged amused glances.

Josie's prediction that Harfield Priory would be peaceful was rather too true for Tess's taste. Dull was another word for it. The five ladies struggled to manage a simple conversation at dinner. After asking in a desultory fashion after Tess's stay at Helmsley, for clearly the information that she had not been there at all had not filtered through from Corland, there seemed no other safe topic of conversation. Everything at Corland was too dreadful for discussion in a civilised dining room, it seemed.

Happily for Mrs Harfield, there was the latest letter from her son in London to be shown off, for she carried it even at dinner. Edward, the 4th Lord Tarvin, was twenty-seven years old, and according to his mother, the most eligible bachelor in town. Apart from the Priory, he owned his father's estate of Hunsworth Hall, as well as a highly desirable London house in Grosvenor Street, and had an income of twelve thousand pounds a year. Tess would even grudgingly admit that his mother's description of him as *'the handsomest man one ever saw'* was not entirely erroneous. But the perpetual scowl of disparagement that usually graced his features did nothing to improve his looks, and his manners were cold and unfriendly, as if he disapproved of the world and everything in it.

She was amused to discover, however, that he had successfully exiled both his mother and his aunt from town this year, by telling them that he would never attach a suitable young lady with the two of them constantly at his side. So here they sat, trying to pretend that they were not bitterly missing the whirl of society in town, while he wrote a weekly letter to report on his progress in the delicate business of finding the next Lady Tarvin.

"I do like the sound of Lady Henrietta," Mrs Harfield said. "The daughter of a marquess! That would be a splendid match, indeed, and she sounds most attractive. *'Modest and well-mannered... most accomplished on the harp and pianoforte, and sings, too.'* Does not she sound most agreeable?"

"What is her dowry?" Lady Tarvin said.

"He does not mention... oh, no, here it is. Ten thousand. Well, that is not very much, is it? He could do much better than that."

"Miss Amsworth is the most well dowered, is she not? Was it fifty... no, sixty thousand."

"Oh yes, but only a plain Miss, not even an Honourable. Edward is a baron, after all, and must marry into the nobility."

"Has he seen Lady Anne this week?" Lady Tarvin said. "I liked the sound of her. A spirited rider, which would suit Edward better than all these modest, well-mannered girls."

"Oh, *no*, dear!" Mrs Harfield said. "We must have a quiet girl, who will not disrupt our lives too badly. Let me see... the Honourable Miss Brock, Lady Susan, Miss Smith— What is he doing looking at a Miss Smith? She cannot be— Ah, here it is. He called upon Lady Anne and invited her for a drive in his curricle, but she had a prior engagement and was unable to accept. How disappointing for her! But perhaps next time, although she sounds a little too lively for Edward. He is not, in general, a lively boy himself."

That was a sentiment with which Tess could entirely agree. Tiring of all this talk of eligible young ladies, she said, "Why does he need to marry just now — or at all? He is only twenty-seven, after all, and could easily wait a few more years. Many men do, after all. It is not as if the barony would become extinct, is it?"

Both Lady Tarvin and Mrs Harfield shuddered. The previous baron had been one of three brothers, and having no issue himself, the middle brother's son, an only child, had inherited. But until he married and produced a son of his own, his heir was the son of the youngest brother, a thoroughly disreputable man, by all accounts.

"Allow Jack's boy to inherit? Never!" Mrs Harfield said robustly. "He was ramshackle his whole life and even though he had the good grace to die young, he married a wife as bad as himself, and he has left behind an entirely ramshackle family."

"It is just as well he died young," Lady Tarvin said, smiling. "With seven children in nine years of marriage, who knows how many they would have ended up with, and Joanie not even forty yet. Still, given that Matthew and I had none at all, and you and Ted only the one, Alvira, perhaps it is just as well. As Tess says, at least Edward has an heir — three heirs, in point of fact."

Mrs Harfield moaned slightly. "But *Tostig*, my dear sister! Whatever sort of name is that for a baron? And the younger ones no better — Oswin and Halbert. It is all very well for Joan to call that strange son of hers Ulric, for that was her first marriage and nothing to do with us. But when she married into a baron's family, she should have taken thought for the future and given the boys, at least, sensible names. John, like their father, or other good, solid English names. Charles, Henry, William, Richard. Or from the Bible — Matthew, Mark, Luke and John."

"Nebuchadnezzar," Tess said. "Ichabod. Hezekiah. Mephibosheth."

Josie laughed. "Yes, there are some very odd names in the Bible. Is anyone going to eat that last chantilly cake? I still have a little corner that it might conveniently fill."

"Dear me, Josie, have you not eaten sufficient yet?" Lady Rennington said faintly.

"Those of us with a baby to feed are perpetually hungry," Josie said cheerfully, as Tess pushed the plate nearer to her.

"That is what wet nurses were invented for," Mrs Harfield said disdainfully. "At least then you would be able to sleep at night."

"Oh, but I adore babies when they are so tiny," Josie said, with a sigh, as she took the last cake. "Gerard is so warm and sweet and lovely, and he will become a grubby little boy with scraped knees all too quickly. I could not bear to hand him over to anyone else just yet." She devoured the cake in two swift bites. "I believe I could manage another mouthful of the orange jelly."

Tess laughed and reached for the dish, but the older ladies all sighed and shook their heads.

***

Tess was too shrewd to reveal any part of her plan prematurely. For three days, therefore, she explored the gardens of the Priory in the mornings and sat demurely in the Blue Parlour with her needlework in the afternoons. If there was an outing to call on neighbours, or shopping in Durham, she obediently went along too. When Josie received word that her mother-in-law had left and it was safe to go home, Tess helped her pack and waved her away in a little train of coaches for her house high on the cliffs to the east.

But there came a day when nothing else was planned, and Tess ventured to take a step towards her objective.

"If there is a carriage unwanted today, might I go and call upon Mrs Jack?" she said casually at breakfast. "I should not like her to think I am ignoring her."

"That is a kind thought. One would not wish to be backward in any attention," Lady Rennington said. "I should call, too, since I have not been since shortly after I arrived here. Josie came, and what with one thing and another, poor Joan went quite out of my head. It will serve as a farewell. We shall both go, Tess, dear."

"Farewell? You are leaving?" Tess said, surprised. "Returning to Corland?"

Lady Rennington looked somewhat conscious. "Not that, no. I thought I might visit the cousins at Lochmaben."

"*Scotland?* But why?"

"Oh... the duchess invited me," she said, waving an arm vaguely in the air. "And I do not like to outstay my welcome here."

"I thought you would have gone to Josie, if you do not wish to go home," Tess said. "Or Izzy, perhaps."

"Izzy is travelling," Lady Rennington said. "There is no knowing where she is, but she is not at home. She left her carriage here, as well as her maid, her footman and half her luggage, and just... vanished. You know what Izzy is like. But I have a feeling that she might end up at Lochmaben, and if she does, there I shall be. As for Josie, she does not need me. But I should like to see Mrs Jack before I leave, so I shall come with you, Tess, dear."

Tess did not mind that. There was plenty of time and she had no wish to *'rush her fences'*, to use an expression of her father's. She rarely bothered to ride, and certainly not to hunt, so jumping fences was not a thing she ever did, but she understood perfectly about not rushing at things. She had rushed rather over Tom, pushing him into going to her father to ask for her hand, and look what had come of that. Not only had Tom been thoroughly chastised for his presumption, but he had not even managed to winkle the vital information out of her father of how much her dowry might be. And her father had gone straight out and changed his will, to hobble her entire future.

Or so he believed. She smiled as she thought about it, for if her plan came to fruition... Slowly and carefully, that was the way to do it. Step by cautious step.

Mrs Jack Harfield, the widow of the third Harfield brother, suffered the usual difficulties of those married to younger brothers. Jack had had no estate of his own, no career or income beyond the charity of his brothers. The eldest brother had inherited the title, the Priory and a fine income. The middle brother had married a woman of wealth with an estate of her own. Jack had never taken thought for the future at all, and thus had left his widow in relative poverty.

Holly Cottage was not quite so small as its name implied, but containing, as it did, Mrs Jack and her seven children, her son from her first marriage, a couple of spinster relations to help with the children, and an ever-varying array of servants, it always felt to Tess like an over-full asylum.

There was not a room in the house free from chaos, or a chair unmarred by discarded sewing or a broken toy.

Mrs Jack and the spinsters rushed around collecting up this and that to make room for the two visitors to sit down, then the spinsters disappeared to the kitchen to arrange for tea, and, Tess suspected, to whip up a batch of biscuits or a cake, for there would be none in the house.

For a while, the usual pleasantries were exchanged. Mrs Jack said nothing about the shocking events at Corland Castle. One would imagine that a murder, followed by the disinheritance of the earl's entire family, might be worthy of some comment, but she was entirely absorbed by the doings of her own family. As one child or another, or more often three or four at once, barrelled into the room, inevitably knocking over some ornament-strewn small table, or tripping on a badly laid rug, their mother would smile fondly.

"Ah, Oswin! Such a fine boy, although he will run into things. He lost a couple of teeth only last week. Dear Isolda! She is learning the pianoforte, you know. Do play something for us, darling. Elfleda! Have you torn your gown again?" Laughing, she added, "Such an energetic girl! Aldith, do bear me company, child. She is not quite out yet, but she is becoming quite the young lady."

Aldith, a well-grown girl of fifteen, did indeed sit still for perhaps two minutes, long enough to display her tousled hair and a gown sporting a multitude of stains. Mrs Jack's gown was none too fresh, either, and the younger children all looked as if they had spent a week living out of doors. The spinsters came in eventually with a tray of tea, and as Mrs Jack poured, Tess thought it time to move closer to her objective.

"And how is Ulric, Mrs Harfield? I have not seen him for an age."

Her perpetually anxious face softened. "Ulric is well, as always. Nothing ever ails him, thank God. He is at Myercroft today, but on market days he helps out at the Queen's Head and of course Dan Smith could not do without him. Any difficult beast, and Ulric is sure to be sent for."

Tess nodded and said all that was proper. Ulric's affinity for horses was legendary — in fact, it was the only interesting facet to his character, for he had suffered an unfortunate incident as a baby when an inebriated nurse had dropped him on his head. The poor boy had never been right since. Still, he had inherited Myercroft from his father, which was let to tenants but with the proviso that he might stable his extensive collection of horses there. A good proportion of the income from the house went to funding his hacks and hunters. In his spare time, he acted as ostler at the coaching inn, and helped the smith.

Ulric was not likely to put in an appearance, so Tess set her sights on the three eldest daughters. Before the half-hour visit was over, she had arranged to bring journals showing the latest fashions to the eldest, a novel for the middle sister and some music for the third. She left well satisfied with her progress.

6: A Lady Friend

Tess moved forward slowly. From her tentative approaches to the three eldest girls, she progressed to the younger ones. Within a week, she had instituted regular lessons for all seven children. There was no money to spare for a governess, and Mrs Harfield herself took little notice of her offspring, spending her days mostly below stairs, for she was constantly caught up in one domestic drama or another. It was therefore left to the two spinsters, Miss Frith and Miss Emily Frith, to teach the children, and their timid natures meant that the designated schoolroom was usually empty. Tess was not timid, however, and ruthless when she had an objective in mind, so she speedily found ways to keep the little ones occupied.

It was not very long before all the ladies declared that they could not imagine how they had ever managed without Tess, and would she be willing perhaps to come and stay for a while? Tess graciously agreed that she would indeed be willing, and thus found herself ensconced in a tiny attic room next door to a very disgruntled Betty.

"It's not fittin', Miss Tess," she grumbled. "And you the niece of his lordship, sleepin' under the roof like a scullery maid. At the very least, one of they great lummoxes should have moved for you."

"The Miss Friths have been here for years, Betty, and they will still be here long after I have moved on," Tess said, amused. "This is no worse than the room at Pickering, is it? Better, since here your snoring is next door, instead of sharing my bed."

And so it came about that, ten minutes before dinner was due to be served, Tess's quarry finally came into view.

Ulric Frith was twenty-two years old, and had he not had his unfortunate accident as an infant, would have had every marriageable female in the northern counties at his door, for he was as handsome as a Greek god, tall, fair and perfectly featured. Even so, there were plenty willing to set their cap at him, to be mistress of his pretty little estate. A wife would have to compete with his precious horses for his attention, of course, and there was no sign whatsoever that he took the least interest in females.

"Evening, cousin," he said in his curiously flat voice with a nod to Tess, when her presence was pointed out to him.

"Good evening, Ulric. You are looking well. Life agrees with you, I can see."

He blinked at her. Polite chit-chat was not his strongest suit. "Did you ride over?" he said. "Got a good mount, have you?"

"No, I came in Lady Tarvin's carriage."

"The blacks?"

Tess correctly interpreted this as an enquiry about the horses. "No, they were a brown colour with black tails."

"The bays." He pulled a face. "No good. Should have taken the blacks. Sweet steppers, the blacks."

"I shall remember that next time, cousin," she said calmly. They were not cousins, of course, being only distantly related by marriage, but Ulric could never remember names.

They went in to dinner just then, and Tess contrived to sit beside Ulric, plying him with questions about his work at the inn and the smithy, and his stable at Myercroft, questions to which he replied with enthusiasm. He was easy to engage, so long as one were prepared to talk endlessly about horses.

After dinner, at which Ulric was the only male present, he promptly disappeared, presumably to the stables, while Tess, Mrs Harfield, the two spinsters and the three eldest girls, who were deemed old enough to join the adults, played a noisy game of Speculation. Tess had played the game often, but never with such a cavalier disregard for the rules, or even fairness. Mrs Harfield liked to win and so at every point where she might be at a disadvantage, a new rule was invented or an existing one set aside. They only played for coppers, but nevertheless her winnings mounted.

After an hour or so, Ulric returned and the game was switched to vingt-et-un. Even Ulric, it seemed, could count to twenty-one. The game was too dependent on chance and the rules too simple for Mrs Harfield to manipulate them in her favour, but since Ulric never knew when to stop adding cards to his hand, he almost invariably went bust so all the other players did very well out of the game. The Miss Friths looked especially pleased.

Over the tea cups and cakes later, Tess again contrived to sit beside Ulric. Since she would make no progress with him by sitting around the drawing room, she made a bold move.

"Have you anything in the stables here or at Myercroft suitable for me to ride, cousin? If I am to stay here for a while to help your mama, I should like to take some exercise every day, and riding is such a pleasure in the summer, is it not?"

That was a mistake. Ulric could only handle one question at a time, so he answered the second one. "Riding's good any season."

"True, although it can be somewhat bracing in the coldest months."

"Not if you ride fast and hard," Ulric said, stuffing a small cake into his mouth whole.

"Perhaps," she said doubtfully. "So do you have anything suitable for a lady?"

"Brandysnap," he said. "She takes a side-saddle."

"Is Brandysnap a gentle beast... or spirited?"

He pondered that while he chewed. "Lady's horse," he said eventually, as if that was all the answer the question needed. "Takes a side-saddle."

"Is she here or at Myercroft?"

"Myercroft. Nothing here but a hack for the gig."

"May I come to Myercroft tomorrow to see Brandysnap?"

He had just reached for another cake, but now his attention was turned fully on Tess. "You want to ride her?"

"Yes, please. If she is suitable for me."

"Lady's horse. Bound to be suitable. Come at ten. I'll take you out."

That was promising! "Thank you, cousin. I shall be there."

Myercroft was a fine Tudor house in excellent condition. Ulric had been born there, and had his mother not remarried, they would both have lived there still. But along had come Jack Harfield with his handsome face and roguish twinkle in his eye, and swept the widow into matrimony. She had been incensed to discover after the event that she had lost not only her generous jointure, but also any right to live at Myercroft. Ulric had been only six at the time, and his trustees had closed ranks and remained firm.

She could take Ulric to live with her at her new marital home, for she was his guardian and they would not separate a child from his mother, but his estate was to be preserved for Ulric's use only, when he was old enough. Nor had they ever wavered from that position. Myercroft and its two thousand pounds a year were for Ulric's benefit alone, and she now existed on the very modest jointure from her second marriage, and a small stipend from Myercroft to cover Ulric's board at Holly Cottage.

Tess set the children their lessons for the day, told them sternly that she would test them on all they had learnt when she returned, and went to don her riding habit, before setting out on the half-mile walk to Myercroft. She was not an enthusiastic rider, far preferring the comfort of a carriage, but if she was to have any success with Ulric, it would be necessary to ride. If, however, Brandysnap turned out to be as highly strung as Ulric's hunters, then she would just have to hang around the stables as often as possible.

Ulric was not a man to shilly-shally around. When Tess arrived, Brandysnap was already saddled. Within moments, Tess was tossed up as if she weighed nothing and Ulric had mounted his own horse and was leading the way out of the yard. There was no time to assess her mount or grow accustomed to her gait, for almost as soon as they left the stables behind, Ulric set off at a smart canter.

Fortunately, Brandysnap was exactly as Tess had hoped, a steady lady's mount with no sign of incipient temperament. She was willing, however, and although she could not match the long legs of Ulric's mount, she gamely followed behind at a steady pace. Although she would have liked a slower start, Tess soon realised she was not about to be terrified by an excessive burst of speed, or tipped unceremoniously into a bush. For an hour, therefore, she followed behind Ulric, who occasionally remembered she was there and waited for her, before she declared herself ready to turn for home.

"Already?" Ulric said. "We've barely got going."

"I am not as used to riding as you, cousin. Perhaps with a little practice I shall be able to go further afield."

"Good inn just over the next hill," he said. "Strong ale. Take you there tomorrow."

The ale was not much of an inducement, but an hour at an inn to rest the horses would be a good opportunity to talk to Ulric. She was not sure that talking to him was going to advance her cause very much, but if she could persuade him to call her Tess instead of cousin, she would be satisfied with that. So they turned back towards Myercroft, made an arrangement for the following day and she trudged wearily back to Holly Cottage, her legs aching.

When they reached it the next day, the inn was obviously often frequented by Ulric, for he was greeted as an old friend, a large tankard of ale and an enormous meat pie brought to him at once.

"Well, now, yer've got yerself a lady friend, Mr Frith," the innkeeper said with a knowing smile at Tess.

"Cousin," Ulric said.

"I am Miss Nicholson," Tess said. "From Corland Castle. Lady Tarvin's sister, Lady Rennington, is my aunt."

The man's eyes widened. "Nicholson? Not... not *that* Nicholson? That poor man what was done in wi' an axe?"

"He was my father," she said calmly, unsurprised to find that such a juicy piece of news had penetrated even to County Durham. It must be all over the country by now, and even the lowest classes would have heard about it.

"Well!" he said, and then, "Well!" again, clearly unsure quite what to say. What could one say to the daughter of a murdered man? "Will you take a glass of something, milady? Something to eat?"

"A glass of wine. Nothing to eat, thank you."

"Aye. At once."

He came back quickly with the wine, followed by a little round dumpling of a woman, probably his wife, bearing a plate of sweet cakes with a spicy aroma.

"You poor dear," she said, patting Tess's hand. "Try one o' my teacakes, still hot, they are."

Dutifully, Tess sipped the wine and nibbled a teacake, as Ulric downed two tankards of ale and chomped his way through the pie. There were several other men in the inn's common room, mostly farmers refreshing themselves between bouts of... whatever farmers did. Tess was vague on the details. The farmers, too, greeted Ulric as an old friend, said how pleased they were to see him again and wished him good fortune with the birds when the shooting season should begin.

The shooting season! Tess froze for a moment. Only another week, and Ulric would be off with his guns and she would not see him. No time to be lost, then.

But as the farmers headed for the door, their ale finished, one or two looked at Tess and winked at Ulric.

"Yer a dark 'orse, Mr Frith, and no mistake," one said.

"Be an announcement soon, will there?" said another, with an even broader wink.

"Pretty lady," said a third, bolder than the rest.

Ulric was not clever enough to understand the other allusions, but he knew when Tess was referred to.

"Cousin," he said, in his flat voice.

"Ah, keepin' it in't family," one said, and they left in a noisy gaggle, laughing at what passed for wit amongst them.

It was too good an opportunity to miss.

"Have you ever thought of getting married, Ulric? A wife to take care of you — would you not like that?"

"Wife?" he said blankly.

"Every man wants to get married, surely," she said. "You must have thought about it. You could live at Myercroft then, with your horses, instead of at Holly Cottage."

No need to mention that he could live at Myercroft any time he wanted, with or without a wife. It was his house, after all.

"Like to live at Myercroft," he said.

She said no more, perfectly satisfied. Another day or two, and she would proceed to the next step.

***

It was almost a week before Tess had an opportunity to speak to Mrs Harfield alone, for that lady was always dealing with some domestic crisis or other, and Tess was generally trailed by two or three of the children. But eventually, they were both out in the kitchen garden picking beans, and for once unattended by servants or offspring.

Tess lost no time in raising the subject. "Ulric seems very settled now — very easy to manage."

"Oh, he has never been a *difficult* boy, not really. Not so long as he has his horses."

"I wonder if you have taken thought for his marriage?"

"Marriage! Ulric can never marry, that much is certain. If he had any interest in women… but he never has."

"But he is very eligible, with Myercroft, and such a handsome man. There must be those who—"

"Of course. Plenty of women look at him and wonder, but he has never shown any sign of forming an attachment."

"As to an attachment, I dare say not, but that need not preclude his marriage, need it?"

Mrs Harfield stopped picking and turned to stare at Tess. "My dear, Ulric is hardly fit husband material for any woman."

"Not in the usual way, no… not a marriage of equals, certainly. But with the right woman, one who would not fuss over him, but would allow him to go on just as comfortably as he does now… well, with the *right* wife, he could have the trust wound up and reclaim Myercroft. And the right wife could ensure that he would have his family about him, just as he likes it."

Mrs Harfield was quick to see the possibilities. "The right wife? You? But you hardly need Myercroft. Your father left you well provided for."

"Indeed. But you know my situation, ma'am. To claim my inheritance, I must have a husband. For Ulric to reclaim Myercroft and its full income, he needs a wife. It seems to me that we could do each other a good turn."

"A marriage of convenience?"

"Of course. Once you and Ulric have Myercroft and I have my own money, well… there will be no need for us to spend much time together. Ulric will go on just as before, except that you will all be at Myercroft instead of Holly Cottage, and think how agreeable that will be."

She could see that Mrs Harfield was indeed thinking of it, her eyes alight with excitement. But then she frowned. "The trustees will forbid it."

"They have no power to forbid it. Ulric is of age, after all, and I shall be so in just a few months. A short betrothal, then we marry. Or it may even be that there will be no need to marry at all, for the betrothal might be enough to do the trick. Who are Ulric's trustees, by the way?"

"A couple of the Frith uncles, very elderly gentlemen now. *They* will be no trouble. But the third is Lord Tarvin, who took on the duty after his uncle died, and he is not an amenable man, not at all. If anyone is to give us trouble, it will be him."

"Nonsense!" Tess said robustly. "He cannot refuse to wind up the trust once Ulric is married — can he?"

"True, for Ulric was only a babe when his father drew up his will, and we did not know then how he would be when he grew up. Henry thought he would grow out of his... well, his *oddness.* So the terms of the trust are the usual ones. It may be wound up once he is of age, if Ulric himself requests it, or at any age if he marries. Of course, once we understood his affliction better, we never thought the trust would need to be wound up at all. He will never ask for it himself, so it is all set up in the most advantageous way — an allowance for Ulric's keep, his horses paid for and Myercroft leased to a very dependable family. And no one ever expected him to marry, but with a *wife*... yes, that would change everything. But Edward will fight it tooth and nail. He is fiercely protective of Ulric."

"And so are we," Tess said cheerfully. "Who should know better than his mother what is best for Ulric? Yes, we can deal with Lord Tarvin, I fancy."

***

Lord Tarvin breakfasted late, as usual, after an evening spent at a musical soirée and a rout. There were not so many evening engagements now as during the season — in fact, there were very few — but he needed material to send to his mother in his weekly report so that she would be satisfied that he was diligently searching for a wife, and not feel any urge either to descend upon town herself or to summon him back to County Durham. He was not a sporting man, so the opening of the game season held little appeal for him. He had friends — male friends, thankfully, devoid of unmarried sisters or cousins — who could be depended upon to invite him to visit over the autumn, and then the weather would be too bad to travel north. Perhaps in the early spring he might spend a week or two at the Priory, just to ensure that his mother would stay at home for another season. Lord, but it was pleasant to be single and alone in town! A man might do as he pleased, and no one could gainsay him.

Deakin, who acted as both valet and butler in the reduced household prevailing at Grosvenor Street, entered bearing a fresh pot of coffee and a silver salver.

"The morning mail, my lord."

"Thank you, Deakin."

There were several invitations on the salver, together with a bill or two, a letter from his banker and another from his mother. He opened the invitations first. No balls, thankfully, but three invitations to dine, one to be a guest at someone's estate in Surrey — someone with a marriageable daughter, he recalled with a shudder — and a sprinkling of card parties and the like. He would accept everything except Surrey — another shudder — but these quiet evenings were very much to his taste.

At a ball, one was obliged to dance with a succession of hopeful young ladies, and very often take one into supper, too, and very tedious it all was. If only he could just dance once or twice and then head for the card room and male company, but that would only encourage speculation surrounding the chosen ones. Almack's was positively the worst, for his very presence excited the rapacious mamas beyond all reason. As an unmarried baron with an income of twelve thousand a year, he could not possibly escape their notice. But his mother would never believe he was seriously looking to marry without regular visits to Almack's. Thank heavens that was all finished until next year.

He glanced without interest at the bills, read the letter from his banker with quiet satisfaction, for his finances were in very good order, and then turned with a sigh to his mother's letter.

'My dearest son, You must come at once for the most dreadful thing has happened."

Edward sighed. "Deakin! *Deakin!* Ah, there you are. Brandy, if you will. I have a feeling I am going to need it."

'Or at least, it has not happened yet, but I feel certain that it will happen soon for that woman is conspiring to make it happen and she has not an iota of sense, or care for the dignity of this family.'

Deakin came in at a trot bearing a decanter and glass on a tray.

"Ah, good man. Pour me a large one, will you?"

'Mind you, she would never have thought of it if it had not been for that girl, who looks as meek as milk, but is all the time a wicked serpent plotting her nefarious mischief.'

Edward took a large gulp of brandy, and then a second one. Letters from his mother fell into one of two categories. Either they were filled with trivia, such as the uninteresting doings of the neighbours or wild speculation on the young ladies mentioned in his own letters, which could be safely ignored, or burnt if he were feeling in a particularly rebellious mood. Or else there was some dreadful doom about to fall on their heads which only Edward's presence could resolve. These required brandy, and a degree of ingenuity to find a suitable excuse for not rushing north to the rescue.

'I speak, of course, of Tess Nicholson, who seemed to be so friendly and helpful to that woman and worked a positive miracle with the children — Joan said that even Tostig minds her, as I wrote in my last. But instead she was scheming and plotting, as cool as you please, and you will not guess what she plans to do!'

Edward sighed. No, he could not guess, nor was he very interested. He vaguely recalled that she had turned up at the Priory a week or two ago, and had then decamped to Holly Cottage to be useful to Aunt Joan, none of which sounded very threatening. No doubt she planned to reorganise the still room, or throw out the worn linen, or some such tragedy. Or perhaps she proposed to beat some sense into the obnoxious Tostig, which was what he needed. Edward's heir, as his mother never ceased to remind him.

'She set out right from the start to wheedle her way into Ulric's good graces by riding with him every day, but now — you will never believe it — indeed, I can scarce say the words — "

"Oh, do try," Edward muttered, reaching for the brandy glass again.

'She plans to marry him!'

"What!"

A little brandy slopped over the side of the glass as he slammed it down on the table.

"Deakin! *Deakin!* Have the carriage brought round in... one hour, shall we say. And go and pack. We are going north."

"Very good, my lord. How long a stay, my lord? Shall you require evening dress?"

"Yes, everything. I shall stay as long as it takes, Deakin. As long as it takes to detach a leech. She will not get away with this, I swear it! I shall put an immediate stop to it."

"Yes, my lord," Deakin said, without knowing a thing about it.

"What are you waiting for?" Edward yelled. "Carriage, pack, at once!"

"Yes, my lord." Deakin bowed himself imperturbably out of the room.

7: Lord Tarvin Arrives

Tess received a steady stream of letters from Corland, sent to Harfield Priory, where she was presumed to be staying, and brought to Holly Cottage by a long-suffering groom. Her mother wrote regularly, but without saying anything of interest. Olivia spoke only of her own complaints, and the blighting of her prospects now that she was illegitimate. Josie wrote reams of motherly advice, offering the comfort she supposed Tess to need. And occasionally Tom Shapman wrote.

'Miss Nicholson, I hope you are well. Captain Edgerton has been here. He knows about our friendship. Wants to talk to you. If you don't come back, he says he'll have you arrested. Your friend, T. Shapman'

Tess laughed long and hard at that one. Tom was a man of few words, but she had no doubt he was reporting Captain Edgerton's words faithfully.

'My dear Tom, You must not worry about Captain Edgerton. He cannot have me arrested. If he wants to talk to me, he may come here, if he pleases,

but I am too much occupied to return home just now, but do keep me informed of what they are up to. Tess'

The next letter threw her into a spin.

'Miss Nicholson, I hope you are well. You asked for news of Captain Edgerton. Rumour says he's looking to Pickering now. Your father had businesses there as well as the house. Your friend, T. Shapman'

At once she dashed off a reply.

'Tom, This is dreadful news! Businesses? What businesses could Papa have had? I cannot understand it, but it hardly matters for if it gives Captain Edgerton an excuse to start snooping round Pickering, then I am sunk! He will go into the house and be bound to find the safe. Or perhaps my fortune is secreted in one of these businesses, but whatever the truth, the captain will find it all out and I shall never get my hands on my fortune. This is a disaster! If only there were some way to call off the captain once and for all, but I fear that he is one of those people who never, ever gives up. Oh, Tom, whatever am I to do? Your distraught Tess'

With this worry at the back of her mind, Tess became more than ever determined to secure Ulric, at least in a betrothal until she came of age, for she was under no illusion that her mother would approve of the marriage. With this in mind, she began to talk very frequently to Ulric about Myercroft and how pleasant it would be for him to live there, just as he had as a small boy, with his mother and younger brothers and sisters. He had some memory of living there, surprisingly, and he had dined with the tenants, Sir Ernest and Lady Peterson many times, and he agreed that it would be pleasant to live there.

"Like to live with Sir Ernest and Lady Peterson," he said. "Always have a good dinner."

"If you were to live there, then Sir Ernest and Lady Peterson would leave," Tess said. They had ridden out to a different inn — Ulric knew every inn within riding distance of Myercroft — and were sitting on a bench in the sunshine outside, their backs resting against the inn's rough stone wall.

"Why do they want to leave?"

"I dare say they do not, but it is your house, Ulric. If you want to live in it, the Petersons would have to move out."

He frowned. "Why?"

"Because that is how it works. They only live there because you do not, and the house would be empty otherwise. You would like to live at Myercroft with your horses, would you not?"

"Like that," he agreed. "Like to live at Myercroft with the horses."

"Your mama would like to live there, too, I am sure."

"Yes. Mama would like that."

"She would. Indeed she would," Tess said happily. He was getting the point.

But then Ulric frowned again. "Cousin Edward won't allow it. Mama tried, last year. Wouldn't allow it."

"Your mama does not have the right to ask, but if you were married, Ulric, your wife would certainly have the right to ask for Myercroft to be given back to you." He had the right himself, but there was no point confusing him.

"Don't have a wife."

"No, but you are a grown man, now. You can marry whenever you please. All you have to do is find a friendly female who would like to marry you." And in case he did not see the obvious, she added, "Someone who enjoys the same things that you do — like riding, for instance."

He made no answer to that, but she was content to have sown the seeds of the idea in his mind.

In fact, progress was so promising that she felt emboldened to write to her uncle, the earl, and hint that she might very soon be engaged to be married, and would be able to take possession of her house, pointing out that she would take it very much amiss if anyone else, such as Captain Edgerton and his friends, had been poking around there before her. That, she hoped, would be enough to preserve the safe above the coach house until she could get to it.

***

Tess had been out for an even longer ride with Ulric, one that involved no fewer than three different inns, and was trudging wearily back to Holly Cottage. Rain had caught them out on the final stretch, and although it was not heavy, she was thoroughly damp and mud-bespattered, the jaunty feather in her hat drooping sadly, when she emerged from the shrubbery onto the drive.

There, drawn up in front of the entrance, was a fine carriage, a little travel-stained but with the coat of arms on the door clearly visible. A man was just stepping down from it, and Tess did not need the insignia to identify the owner of such a vehicle. Lord Tarvin's stern face was all the evidence she needed.

The whole family had gathered on the steps to receive him, the children in varying degrees of excitement, and the ladies looking terrified.

"Oh! Tess!" Mrs Harfield cried, hand to mouth, as if warning her of some impending disaster. Too late for that.

He turned, saw her and his expression darkened even more. "You!" he cried, in a rousing voice worthy of Drury Lane. "You are the cause of all this trouble."

It was far from the meeting she would have wished. She felt all the disadvantage of situation — he as immaculate as if he had just that moment left his dressing room, and she looking as if she had been crawling through ditches. A little warning would not have gone amiss, so that she could have slipped in through the kitchen door and up the back stairs. But perhaps his coming was a surprise to all of them. Still, there was no avoiding it now, and Tess was not about to be cowed by a supercilious baron.

"Good day, Lord Tarvin. I trust your journey was satisfactory." She made him an ironic little curtsy although it was doubtful if he had the capacity to recognise irony.

"No, it was not satisfactory," he thundered. "It was, as all journeys are, uncomfortable and tedious. Nor should it have been necessary. It is most inconvenient for me to leave town just now, but something must be done to put a stop to your nonsense. You cannot marry Ulric."

"Why not?" she said sweetly.

"It should be obvious, even to you, why not. I shall not permit it."

"What are you going to do, forbid the banns?" she said, with a spurt of laughter. "Try not to make a cake of yourself, sir. Ulric is of age, and may marry whenever and whomsoever he pleases."

He crossed the drive in three paces, and stood not a foot away from her. "Not if I have anything to do with it," he hissed. "You will pack your bags and return to the Priory with me."

"I am here as Mrs Harfield's guest, to help with the children."

"She will have to manage without you."

Tess looked at Mrs Harfield, and saw at once that there was no help to be had there. "Do you wish me to leave, ma'am?" she said, but she already knew the answer.

"Best to do as Edward says, my dear."

There was no point in fighting it. "Very well. I shall have to change, as well. I am not sure how long—"

"You have an hour," he said uncompromisingly. "Is Ulric at Myercroft? Very well, I shall walk over there to see him. When I return, I shall expect you to be ready to leave. You have a maid to accompany you?"

"I do, and a footman."

"The maid will sit inside the carriage with you, and the footman will sit on the box with Timothy Coachman. Timothy, bait the horses and be ready to leave again in an hour."

And he strode off without another word.

Tess hurried inside, a little dismayed by this setback, but not yet ready to surrender the point.

"I am so sorry, my dear," Mrs Harfield said, rushing after her, "but there is never any point in arguing with Edward, you know. He has very fixed ideas, and besides... he is... kind when there is a problem. Oh, he grumbles, naturally, and rings a peal over me, but he always bails me out when things get difficult."

"He pays your debts, you mean? Yes, I can see why you would not take up arms against him. Nevertheless, I do not mean to let him hinder my plans. I shall find a way to get back here, and then I must tie Ulric up in a betrothal, a proper one that he understands, so you must explain to him what he must do."

"What must he do?" she said, wide-eyed.

"Why, propose to me, of course. Make it clear to him that if he marries me, he will get Myercroft and as many horses as he wants. New, bigger stables, if he chooses, because all his income will be in his control. Well... yours and mine, but he will think he is in control, and that is what matters."

"Oh, my dear, you are so brave!"

"Nonsense! Bullies like Lord Tarvin do not frighten me. But I must get out of this habit and into dry clothes, and Betty must pack. Send her up to me, will you? It seems we are going back to the Priory."

***

Edward's talk to Ulric was frustrating in the extreme. No matter how much Edward pointed out the advantages of living at Holly Cottage, Ulric would reply that he would like to live at Myercroft with his horses and his mama, always listed in that order. Then he would frown and say it was a pity that Sir Ernest and Lady Peterson would leave because they always had good dinners.

"Ulric, we talked about this last year, if you remember, and it was agreed that you and your mama would stay at Holly Cottage."

"Mama wanted to live at Myercroft," Ulric said.

"And it was agreed in the end that it would be best to keep things as they are."

"Mama had no right. A wife would have the right."

"You cannot marry, Ulric."

"Yes, I can. Grown men can marry, and I'm a grown man. Cousin Tess said so. I like Cousin Tess."

Edward gave it up, for it was obvious that Tess Nicholson — or the witch, as he had begun to think of her — had already cast her spell over the gullible Ulric, and her dangerous ideas had wormed their way into his mind and lodged there. It was going to take more than a flying visit to restore the situation to equanimity.

He walked back to Holly Lodge to find the girl herself awaiting him in the hall, already outfitted for travel in neat black. She looked remarkably presentable, in fact, all trace vanished of her dishevelled appearance of a hour ago. She was a slender creature, small and dainty, with elegant hands, he noticed. She had not yet put on her gloves, and her fingers were long and rather beautiful. He liked such hands in a female. So often a woman removed her gloves at the dinner table to reveal ugly, pudgy fingers that quite disgusted him. He was, he supposed, fastidious in such matters and was quite proud of his own well-manicured hands. Now he was surprised to find such an appealing feature in a woman he was determined to dislike.

The carriage appeared, the boxes were loaded on, farewells were made. Mrs Jack stood on the steps wringing her hands, no doubt torn between her desire to repossess Myercroft and be the lady of the manor again, and her need to keep on the right side of the man who controlled her entire income. Not that he would ever interfere with her basic allowance, but she could never keep out of debt, and it suited him for her to live in fear that he would not rescue her from such difficulties. A woman who depended on his generosity was a woman who could be constrained to act as he wished.

Tess Nicholson, on the other hand, was not dependent on him at all. Different methods were necessary for her.

As the carriage bounced down the rutted drive, Edward gazed wordlessly at the cause of all this difficulty, placidly sitting beside her maid with an innocent expression on her face, and pondered his next move. Ulric and his mother he could manage, but this girl was not so easy. He would have to be ruthless.

Not a word was spoken in the carriage until they reached the Priory. Just as the horses slowed to a stop, Edward said, "Do not get settled here, Miss Nicholson, for tomorrow you will be returning to Corland Castle."

The impudent chit had the temerity to laugh at him. "Lord Tarvin, you may be able to browbeat your own relations, but may I remind you that you have no authority over me. If you throw me out of the Priory, there are plenty of inns and hotels in Durham which would be happy to accommodate me. Frankly, it is all one to me where I stay."

The girl's footman had jumped down to open the door, but Edward could not be silent. "You will do as you are bid, my girl!"

"Or what? Are you going to carry me bodily all the way to Corland? I wonder what my uncle would say to that."

"Pft!" he said, and only years of training kept the curses that rose to his mouth from emerging. He jumped down from the carriage and strode into the house, the annoying girl's laughter following him all the way.

Dinner that evening was tense. His mother and aunt were largely silent, only talking in whispers when absolutely necessary. Edward himself felt as if he would explode. Never in his life had he been so abominably treated! To say he had no authority over her! She was his aunt's sister's niece, which made her a relation of sorts... a connection, at least, and this was his house, so his wishes must prevail. How dared she defy him!

And yet she sat there calmly, quite unperturbed by the distress she was causing everyone. In some ways, he could only admire such coolness, and in evening dress she was rather appealing, he grudgingly conceded. Black suited her, and with her shining black locks piled on top of her head, only a few stray curls left to frame her face, she was almost pretty. Or she would be if she were not so damnably irritating.

By the next morning, he had calmed a little. Being angry did no good, in fact she seemed to derive strength from it, or at least amusement. It was annoying that she knew the terms of the trust, such that it must be wound up if Ulric married, there was no getting around that. But without trustees to make sensible decisions about the management of Myercroft, who would be able to do it? Not Ulric, that much was certain, and not his feckless and spendthrift mother. But Tess Nicholson was no better fitted to run an estate. How could a slip of a girl know how best to deal with tenant farmers and attorneys and neighbouring landowners? How could any woman? Females were no more suited to business than butterflies flitting from bush to bush, beautiful but with no thought for the morrow.

It was clear that Miss Nicholson could not be ordered about as his female relations were, so a different strategy was needed. He was not sure that she had any better nature to be appealed to, but it was worth a try.

When he found her alone in the breakfast parlour, therefore, he lost no time in saying, “Miss Nicholson, we got off on slightly the wrong foot yesterday, I think you will agree. I am sure that, when we discuss the matter rationally, we will find that we both have Ulric’s interests very much at heart, and can perhaps find common ground there. You would not wish to distress him, I am certain.”

“Not for the world,” she said at once. “But I do not believe that living at Myercroft would cause him distress.”

“Any disruption to his routine is potentially upsetting for him, and having a wife always about him — a relative stranger ordering his life — is bound to disturb his equanimity.”

“I have no intention of always hanging about him, Lord Tarvin. He may live his life much as he does now, except that his surroundings will be more gracious and his horses will be closer to hand.”

"So he is to be kept occupied in the stables while you and his mother bleed the estate dry, is that it?"

"Heavens, what do you take me for, sir?"

"I take you for an avaricious and devious woman, madam."

She laughed in his face. Lord, how irritating she was! "You really would be best advised not to judge my character without knowing more about me. We met twice as children, if I recall, and once at Izzy's wedding five years ago. How, after so little acquaintance, do you dare to label me as avaricious? I say nothing about devious, in fact, I take it as a badge of honour that I should be thought so, but avaricious? No."

"How else would you describe the behaviour of a woman who seeks to seduce a wealthy man into marriage? I hold to my opinion, Miss Nicholson."

"Only a willing man can be seduced," she said with deceptive sweetness. "And now, if you will forgive me, I must change into my riding habit. I have an appointment with Ulric, and I have further to go than usual."

"You will not take my carriage... or any of the carriages."

"I assumed that would be the case, so I took the precaution of sending my manservant to the nearest inn to hire a horse for me."

Edward was left speechless as she swept from the room. However, when she reached the stables, neatly attired in a different riding habit from yesterday's muddy affair, he was waiting for her, his own horse ready saddled.

"I feel like a ride myself, this morning," he said blandly.

"Oh, that is better!" she said, smiling up at him. "You look almost human when you stop scowling at me and pretend to be good-humoured. Will you help me mount, or shall I ask Harold to do it?"

Gritting his teeth, he tossed her up into the saddle. She weighed nothing at all — such a dainty creature! And a pretty heart-shaped face... with enticing lips...

No. She was a witch, and the embodiment of evil.

They rode in complete silence all the way to Myercroft, where Ulric greeted them with a broad smile.

"Cousin Tess!" he yelled, as soon as they clattered into the yard. Then, at the top of his voice, he went on, "Will you marry me?"

Edward swore under his breath. The girl gave an *'Oh'* of pretended surprise, and slid from her horse in ungainly fashion.

"Ulric! I should be honoured... much obliged... yes, I should be delighted to marry you."

And she turned to Edward with an expression of pure triumph on her face.

8: Letters From Corland

Tess was astonished to have achieved her goal so easily. Her words to the suggestible Ulric had planted the idea of Myercroft and a wife in his head, and Mrs Jack had done the rest, simply telling him what to say to Tess when he next saw her. And he had done it!

Even if nothing came of this and she failed to recover her fortune, it was entirely worth the effort just to see the blind fury on Lord Tarvin's face. He had wheeled his horse about, and taken off at speed, not to be seen again. Tess spent the rest of the morning riding with Ulric, visiting every inn within a ten mile radius, so it seemed, while Ulric shouted to everyone he saw that he was getting married.

When they returned to the Myercroft stables, there was a girl waiting there, a plump person of perhaps twenty-five, who greeted them unsmilingly.

"Is it true, Ulric? You are to be married?"

"Yes. A wife. Cousin Tess. Live at Myercroft."

"Then... we shall have to leave?" She spoke too quietly for Ulric to hear, for he was already leading his horse into the stable building.

Tess slid from her horse. "You are one of the Petersons?"

"Fanny Peterson, yes. We've lived here for sixteen years, and will be very sad to leave Myercroft."

"Then I am very sorry to turn you out, but Ulric is of age now. It is time he took back his own home."

"Oh, yes, but we never thought he would! Lord Tarvin always assured us— But that cannot hold, naturally, if he is to marry. You will... take good care of Ulric?"

"Of course," Tess said. "You may be easy on that head. I mean no harm to him."

"No, but that's not quite the same thing," she said, looking Tess straight in the eye. "I don't know what your reason is to wish to marry Ulric, but I don't think his well-being is foremost in your thoughts. Forgive my bluntness, but I don't know you, and have no reason to suspect that you have any great affection for Ulric."

"I mean him no harm," Tess said again, but Miss Peterson's clear-eyed gaze was unnerving all the same. It was true that she was using Ulric for her own purposes, and even if he benefited in the end, that was not her principal concern, and she could not but be uncomfortable about that. She would not surrender her purpose, but her conscience prodded her rather.

That evening was difficult. Even the servants were jumpy, for the butler knocked over a glass of wine and a footman dropped a dish of vegetables. Amongst the diners, there was no conversation, and the older ladies retired early to bed. Tess would have gone, too, but Lord Tarvin peremptorily asked her to stay.

"We should talk about Ulric, Miss Nicholson."

"What is there to say?"

"You should be aware that the Petersons have Myercroft on a repeating lease, renewable every Lady Day. They cannot be removed before next Lady Day, therefore."

"That is no difficulty. I do not imagine that Ulric and I could be married before I come of age in the spring. My mother is very likely to take your side in the matter and refuse her permission."

"You do not feel that your mother's opinion should carry some weight in your mind? Your uncle, too, will no doubt disapprove of such a—" He stopped, slightly flushed.

"No, do speak your mind. You have already abused me soundly, so nothing you say could give me a worse opinion of you."

"I beg your pardon. I should not have spoken so intemperately."

He was breathing heavily, as he attempted to rein in his temper, then he rose and crossed the drawing room in quick steps. Pouring himself a brandy, he returned to the sofa where Tess sat, and pulled up a chair to sit a little closer to her.

"Miss Nicholson, I must speak openly with you, although I hope without insult. I can see that Ulric is a tempting prize, but you do not know him as I do. He may seem meekly biddable now, but as a boy he was not so calm. He was prone to outbursts of rage which could be violent at times. He was for a while somewhat difficult to control, until we realised his affinity for horses, and kept him occupied that way. For some years now he has been quite content, and such behaviour is a thing of the past. However, if he marries, the change in his circumstances... there is no predicting quite how it will take him, and if you, as a relative stranger, have inserted yourself into his life, living in close proximity to him... you can see how things might take a nasty turn. I should not wish you to be exposed to any danger of that sort."

"I shall not be in danger, Lord Tarvin."

The frown reappeared instantly. "You are over-confident, madam! You cannot know how Ulric will react, and he is a big man, a powerful man, and you are a such a dainty creature. I should not wish you to be hurt by him."

"And I shall not be, sir. I am confident that this is so, for I shall not be living at Myercroft with Ulric."

The frown changed to bewilderment. "Then what on earth is the point of this charade? If not Myercroft, what *do* you want? His money, is that it? A large settlement so that you can go off and live as you please? You will catch cold at that, for the lawyers and I will take the greatest care over the settlement, you may depend upon *that.*"

Tess could hardly believe he knew nothing of her situation. "I care nothing for Myercroft, or Ulric's fortune!"

"Nonsense! You are not doing this out of the goodness of your heart. If it is not Myercroft you want, it must be money. How much?"

"What?"

"Let us get to the point, Miss Nicholson. How much will it take for you to relinquish your hold on Ulric? Ten thousand? I can do that if it will get rid of you."

"How dare you! I do not want your money!"

"Twenty thousand, then."

"Did you not say you would avoid further insult, sir? And yet you see fit to try to bribe me! Your money is nothing to me, nothing. I do not want so much as a penny piece from you or from Ulric. How should I, when I have a fortune of my own, if I can get my hands on it? Did your Mama not tell you about me — about the terms of my father's will? No? My father left me his entire fortune, since I am an only child, but only on condition that I marry a gentleman. Ulric is a gentleman, is he not? He will serve my purposes admirably. In fact, I may not even need to marry him. A betrothal may be enough. *Now* do you understand?"

His eyes glittered for a moment, and she held her breath. Would he erupt again, or would he see the logic behind it? "I did not know that," he said stiffly. "That does not improve my opinion of you. It was low when I believed you were merely in pursuit of Ulric's wealth, but it is even lower now that I know you mean to use him for your own purposes and then discard him when he is no longer of use."

"What do I care for your opinion of me?" she said impatiently. "And how is Ulric harmed by this? If we marry and take control of his estate, then he and his family will have a more pleasant home to live in and a more agreeable life, without you needing to dip into your pockets to rescue them from debt. So long as Ulric has his horses, he will be happy."

"Do you know what will happen if his mother moves back to Myercroft?" he said tersely. "She will run through his fortune in two years or less, and then I shall be called upon to dip into my pockets, as you describe it, far more than at present. I do not begrudge the allowance that is paid them, nor the few pounds here and there when the children need new boots or the butcher's bill becomes pressing, but I will not fund that woman to live like a great lady at Myercroft."

Now it was Tess's turn to frown. That was a problem! She had assumed that Mrs Jack lived in seeming poverty because her funds were too limited for her numerous family, and that with a larger income she would be comfortable. She had not taken her for a spendthrift. Yet now she thought about it, she had seen the trunks in the attic filled with bolts of cloth that had been determined after all to be unsuitable, the furniture still with years of use in it replaced, and the vast amount of waste in the kitchen. Mrs Jack looked eagerly forward to invitations to card parties, yet bemoaned her poor luck.

"I shall consider that," she said. "There must be a way to ensure she has no way to overspend. If I were there... but I shall not be. Even if I could persuade Ulric to let you have the management of his finances, you are not always here, either, and his mother would be there every day, dropping hints in his ear."

"Exactly so," he said, with an unexpected smile. Oh, but he should smile more often! How handsome he was when he was not scowling.

"We will both consider the problem," Tess said. "Of course, if I can get hold of my fortune without marrying Ulric, that would make the question moot, and everything could go on as before. That is what you want, is it not?"

"It would be for the best."

"I shall write again to my uncle, and see if I can persuade him to— Well, never mind. My betrothal must carry some weight with him, so I will write and see what may be done."

"Would it help if I write, too?" Lord Tarvin said. "He may listen to the urging of another peer."

Tess sat up straighter. "Now that is better! We should not be enemies, should we? We both want the same thing, after all — for me to go away and leave Ulric in peace, which I shall be very happy to do once I have my fortune. If you write, be sure to mention the house in Pickering. I need access to that — will you tell him so?" She made no mention of safes or gold bars — he had no need to know about that.

"I shall be sure to do so," he said. "Anything to be rid of you."

They both laughed, and since Lord Tarvin wanted to know more about the terms of the will, they talked for some time in perfect amity, only retiring to bed when the clock struck midnight.

***

Tess was not trusting enough to leave Lord Tarvin to write his own letter to Lord Rennington, for who knew what he might say and what mischief might be caused as a result? So she rose early and loitered in the hall until he descended the stairs, and then supervised as he wrote the letter in the library.

It was rather cleverly done, she had to admit. Lord Tarvin appealed to the earl as one lord to another, and one trustee to another. Since he would be winding up his cousin's trust fund and drawing up settlements for his marriage to Miss Nicholson, he wrote, it would be convenient for him to know the full extent of her fortune. In particular, there was a house in Pickering which had not yet been examined and valued, and might he send a trusted man of his to view the interior and assess the value? Then he franked his letter and Tess's too, and dispatched a footman to get them at once to the post.

While they awaited replies from Corland, they went over to Myercroft every day, and rode with Ulric. Tess found these rides far more agreeable with Lord Tarvin's presence. Unlike Ulric, he rode at an easy pace, stopping often to admire a particularly picturesque view, or to comment on the signs of burgeoning prosperity or incipient neglect in Ulric's land, or simply to pass the time of day with a farmer or cottage wife or some boys painstakingly digging out a ditch beside the road. And in between, he chatted easily about this and that. If he was especially interested in Tess herself and her Corland life, that was not to be wondered at since she was betrothed to Ulric.

In the evenings, they made up a four for whist with Lady Tarvin and Mrs Edward Harfield, where Mrs Harfield apologised to Edward for every infelicitous play the other ladies made, and glared defiantly at him for her own mistakes. He uttered no reproof but wore his most disapproving expression.

If the ladies declined to play, or retired early to bed, Tess and Lord Tarvin played chess, and his frowns disappeared. Especially when his mother was not present, he was an agreeable and even amusing companion, as if he had forgotten that Tess was supposed to be his enemy. Only when Ulric was mentioned did his sour face return until he became absorbed in the game again. She discovered that they were evenly matched in the game, but she felt it expedient to allow him to win most of the time, since it kept him in humour.

"Did your father teach you to play?" he asked her one evening as they set up the board.

"No, he was a cards man. Piquet, principally, but he would play any card game, especially if there was money to be won. My cousin Kent taught me to play chess when his brothers showed no aptitude for the game."

"It is a slow game that does not suit everyone. Most people prefer cards, I suppose."

"Too slow for Walter, perhaps. He learnt all the moves, but he never bothered to apply himself to improving. But Eustace — he would have played well, for he has a clever mind, and the patience to let a strategy play out to its end, but board games are not his strength. He confuses left and right, and so he frequently goes wrong. He could never play backgammon at all, for he would keep moving his pieces the wrong way. He can only play cribbage if someone else moves the pegs."

Lord Tarvin laughed. "Poor fellow! How does he manage? Does he lose himself when he rides, or perhaps he takes a groom with him every time he ventures out?"

"At the end of his drive, he has *'Corland'* painted on one gatepost and *'Stokesley'* on the other, so he knows which way to turn. After that, his horse knows the way."

"Truly? That I should like to see."

"Oh, it is very subtly done, with ivy all round so no one notices, but the signs are there, all the same. Are you going to move, or shall we just sit here indefinitely?"

He laughed again, and moved a pawn briskly. "So tell me, why did your father leave your inheritance in so odd a way? That whole business of marrying a gentleman is rather insulting, as if he did not trust you to marry suitably."

"And he did not," she said, moving her own pawn.

"Why should he think so? Have you given him reason to mistrust you?"

She hesitated. That was a perceptive question! But there was no secret about Tom, after all. "There was a man… a woodworker from the village near Corland. Tom Shapman. I have been friendly with him and last year he went to my father and asked for my hand. Papa refused, naturally, but it must have been after seeing Tom that he wrote this *stupid* will."

Lord Tarvin reached for a knight, then lowered his hand. "One can see his point. A woodworker is hardly a suitable husband for the niece of an earl. But why did he do it? The woodworker, I mean. You must have given him some encouragement."

"Of course I encouraged him," she burst out indignantly. "He would never have done anything about it if I had not."

"But you would never marry him — would you?"

"I would far rather marry Tom than anyone else. At least he is a real man doing real work, not an idle, selfish, overdressed clodpole, like most gentlemen. He is so clever with his hands! He makes some wonderful things, but he spends so much of his life turning chair legs and making coffins and doors. More than anything, I want him to be able to let his artistic nature have full rein, which he will be able to do if he marries me. But unless I can somehow get my hands on my fortune without marrying anyone else, Tom is out of the question."

She could not quite keep the regret out of her voice, and perhaps he noticed it, for he said sharply, "Then your father has succeeded in his aim of protecting you from fortune hunters."

"Tom is no fortune hunter!"

"But he is by no means your equal, in rank, education or wealth," he said dismissively. "Are you going to defend your bishop?"

"Pah!" she said, in annoyance, and was so cross with him that for once she played to win, and trounced him handily. They parted in an atmosphere of mutual dislike.

***

The replies from Lord Rennington, when they arrived, were not encouraging. To Tess he said only that the matter would be considered when she was suitably married, which thoroughly enraged her.

"Suitably married? Who is to be the arbiter of that if not myself? A gentleman, that is all that is required, and Ulric is a gentleman, is he not? And we are betrothed, and therefore as good as married, so why should I not have access to my own house? All I want is to see inside it. Is that so much to ask?"

Lord Tarvin wisely made no response to this diatribe. His own letter from the earl was longer, but no more helpful.

'Lord Tarvin, While I appreciate your concerns, be aware that my niece will not be of age until May of next year, and therefore there is no urgency in the matter. My sister, while pleased that her daughter is inclined to comply with the terms of her father's will, is by no means agreeable to granting permission for the match before then. In fact, given the volatile nature of my niece's affections over the past year, it may well be that they will shift again before too long. For these reasons, I will not agree to any precipitate action. The house my niece has inherited is well tenanted by a respectable widow, and it has been agreed that she need not be disturbed unnecessarily. You will understand, therefore, that I must respectfully decline your proposal at this time. If my niece's intentions remain fixed over the next six months, then I shall reconsider my decision. Yours in friendship, Rennington.'

That set Tess off again. "Volatile! He thinks my affections may shift again, indeed! Well! So that is what he thinks of me. I am glad to know of it, but I shall not sully your ears with my opinion of *him.*"

Lord Tarvin laughed. "No, better leave it to the imagination. I confess, I am disappointed. You are officially betrothed, after all, so some discussion of settlements ought to be undertaken. Apart from the house, how much is this fortune of yours?"

"Eleven thousand."

"That is not insignificant, yet it is what one might expect a chaplain to leave. I suppose this house comprises the bulk of his fortune. Is it a large estate?"

"It is not an estate at all, just an ordinary house in a small town."

"Oh. Then surely—?"

"You think there is nothing valuable there? It may be so, but it was bought years ago by the 10th Earl who was very free with his money. There is no knowing what treasures may be found within." Especially in the safe, she must hope. But there was no need to mention that. Only Tom knew her innermost thoughts on that subject.

Another letter arrived, this time from her mother, congratulating her in stiff terms on her engagement, and inviting her to bring Ulric to Corland so that she could meet him.

"That would not be a good idea," Lord Tarvin said sharply, when the letter was shown to him. "Ulric does best on familiar ground."

"Although I could probably tempt him there," Tess said, mischievously. "The Corland stables are magnificent, and stuffed to the rafters with excellent horseflesh. Ulric would love it. He could ride a different horse every day for a month."

"Please!" Lord Tarvin said, wincing. "Do not even think it. Your plans will be quite sunk if your family actually meet Ulric."

"Do you think so? And yet he is indisputably a gentleman, no one can argue otherwise. No, no, do not look so agonised. I shall not do it. But he *would* like it there."

"You are a wicked girl to tease me so, Tess," Lord Tarvin said. "But what are we to do about this house of yours? Shall I send someone to Pickering to have a look at it? As Ulric's trustee, I do have a right to know what his future wife brings to the marriage."

But while they were considering ways to accomplish this, news arrived from Corland that drove all thought of houses and fortunes out of Tess's head altogether. She was in the drawing room with the ladies one afternoon, pretending to work on some tapestry, while Lord Tarvin read out snippets from last week's London papers, when Jeffries came in bearing a silver salver.

"Your letters, my lady. Quite a few today, after the rain further south flooded so many roads, but the mail is finally getting through at last."

"Oh, good," Lady Tarvin said. "I wondered why everything has been local for the last few days. Alvira, several for you. And Tess, one for you, from Corland. Your uncle's hand, I fancy."

Tess could not have imagined as she broke the seal and unfolded the letter the dire news contained within.

'My dearest niece, You must prepare for a very great shock, for the most unexpected event has occurred. Your friend Tom Shapman walked into the castle yesterday and confessed to killing your father. You may imagine how...'

Tess could read no more. She screamed, and then she screamed again.

Lord Tarvin crossed the room in a few swift strides, and caught her as she fell insensible from her chair.

9: Journey To Corland

Tess came abruptly to her senses, a vinaigrette wafted under her nose. She was lying on a *chaise longue*, Lord Tarvin's arm still around her back, his concerned face just inches from her own.

"Enough, aunt. She is coming round," he murmured, and the horrid vinaigrette was whisked away.

Mrs Harfield's voice murmured in the background. "Someone has confessed to the murder of Mr Nicholson, but that should make her happy, surely?"

"Who is it, Mother? Who has confessed?" Lord Tarvin said.

"Someone called Tom Shapman," she said. "Do we know a Tom Shapman? I have never heard of him."

Tess pushed herself upright. "I must go to Corland — at once! There is no time to be lost! He could hang for this!"

"And quite right, too," Mrs Harfield said robustly. "If this fellow killed your father—"

"Of course he did not! Oh, I must go at once, *at once!* There is not a moment to be lost. Lady Tarvin, may I use your carriage? I must go into Durham to pick up a post chaise."

"No, we will go in my carriage," Lord Tarvin said. "It will be quicker. Mother, ring the bell for Jeffries."

"*We* will go?" Tess said, staring at him.

"Of course, *we.* You do not imagine I would let you go alone, do you? Ah, Jeffries, my carriage in one hour, if you please. Four horses. Tell Deakin to pack at once, and also Miss Nicholson's maid and manservant. We leave in one hour for Corland Castle."

"Very good, my lord. Is this to be a long visit, or short? Evening dress?"

"Yes, everything. I have no idea how long this will take. Never fear, Tess, we shall rescue your friend."

"But he could be hanged in days."

"Only the Assizes deal with murder, and the judges will not be on the circuit again until next year."

"Oh! Thank God!" Relief flooded through her, leaving her weak and barely able to stand. She would be in time to save him, her poor, deluded Tom.

***

Edward watched Tess as the miles rolled past, her eyes seeming huge in her white face. She had said very little, and that only pertaining to the journey — how long would it take? And where would they rest overnight? He had answered her just as briefly.

Now she gazed out of the window, but he knew she was not even seeing the fields with their stone walls, the villages they passed through or the hills on the horizon. Her mind was fixed on Tom Shapman. She did not cry, but occasionally her eyes would fill with tears as some unhappy thought intruded, and then she would blink rapidly and look down at her hands, smoothing her kid gloves, or the skirts of her travelling pelisse.

Such a determined little creature, seemingly so selfish and absorbed in her own affairs, yet her feelings ran deep. So complicated, so puzzling, so contrary, but so intriguing. And not boring! To a man jaded by the stultifying lifelessness of London society, Tess was a howling gale of vitality, energising Edward as nothing else had done in all his twenty-seven years. He felt alive for the first time, wanting nothing more in that moment but to do whatever would please her. He had begun by disliking her intensely, yet now that he saw her suffering, all his protective instincts were aroused. However strong she appeared to be, inside she was still fragile.

At the first post house, as their own horses were detached and hired teams with postilions were hitched to the carriage, he said gently, “There is food in the hamper, if you are hungry.”

“Thank you, but no.”

“Coffee? Tea? A glass of wine? Or just a rest. They have parlours here.”

“No rest,” she said. “I know he will not be hauled off to be hanged for months yet, but I do not want to delay.”

“I understand.”

Once they were under way again, he ventured to say, “Tess, are you quite sure he could not have done it? It would be very odd to hang for a crime one did not commit.”

“He imagines he is protecting me, I suppose. What an idiotic thing to do!”

“Protecting you? How? Does he imagine *you* killed your father?”

She looked at him fully, then, a little frown marring her smooth forehead. "He must know I did not, just as I know he did not. We have been friends for two years now — more than friends — and we know each other well enough for that. But I cannot imagine why else he would confess."

"We will find out when we see him," he said easily.

"Yes." She gave him a tremulous smile. "You will come with me to talk to him, then?"

"Of course."

"Thank you! You are very good. I know we have not always got along as well as we should, but I could not be more grateful for your help and support now."

"Say nothing of it, I beg you. Do you suppose I could sit tamely at home and leave you to rescue your self-confessed murderer single-handed? This is an adventure, Tess, and I want my share of it."

The smile was wider, then. "Thank you," she said, a little shyly. "I cannot tell you how comforting it is to have a man to arrange everything... or what it costs me to admit that."

He laughed out loud at that. "A man's loud voice and imperious presence can be very useful, it is true. The coat of arms on the carriage door does not hurt, either. But since we are being honest, let me acknowledge that I find it surprisingly pleasant to have a lady to take care of. I must have danced with every unmarried female in town over the last three years since I came into my title, and not met a single one who is not boring and dull and downright insipid. But you are not in the least insipid, my dear. In fact, I am never sure from one moment to the next what you will get up to, and I am quite certain that I have barely scraped the surface of your many mysteries. And perhaps that is part of my wish to accompany you back to Corland — it gives me an opportunity to uncover some of your secrets."

Tess only smiled enigmatically, and turned her head to look out of the window again. Beside her, her maid Betty raised her eyebrows at this conversation, and chuckled a little.

***

Had they left earlier in the day, and the roads been tolerable, and no mishaps occurred, the journey to Corland could have been accomplished in a single day. As it was, they stopped at Northallerton for the night, where Tess ate nothing and arose so pale of face that Edward presumed she had not slept, either. They set off at an early hour the following morning, but they had reached the area recently gouged by summer storms and their progress slowed abominably. It was therefore almost the dinner hour before their carriage, its wheels and horses liberally plastered with mud, drew up outside Corland Castle.

Tess was out of the carriage and tearing across the bridge into the house as soon as the steps were let down. Edward followed more slowly, with a glance of distaste at the austere frontage of the castle. It was imposing, of course, but unlike many castles, it was not an original Norman edifice. It was newly built, designed to look as if it had been there for hundreds of years, but inside fitted out with every modern convenience. Not for Corland the oppressive gloom of echoing stone, and narrow spiral stairs. Instead, there were soft carpets, fashionable wallpaper and a wide, elegantly branched staircase.

In the entrance hall, he caught a glimpse of Tess, already whisking away into the interior. The butler greeted him with a slightly puzzled, "My lord?"

"Lord Tarvin," Edward said helpfully. "Last here for Lady Isabel's wedding."

"Of course, my lord," the butler said, bowing. "A room will be prepared for you at once."

"Where did Miss Nicholson go?"

"She asked for his lordship, my lord, who is in the drawing room. Shall I show you the way?"

"If you would."

The butler led him down a wide corridor to the great hall, two storeys tall and filled with light from a glass roof far above. The walls were covered from floor to ceiling with a fearsome array of ancient weaponry. Edward was ushered past the stairs, with its suits of armour guarded by a pair of Chinese urns on the half landing, to the prettily appointed drawing room, where Tess was already kneeling at her uncle's feet.

"Miss Nicholson and Lord Tarvin, my lord," the butler intoned, his voice signalling clear disapproval of those persons who rushed into a room without even waiting to be announced.

A dozen or more pairs of eyes, currently fixed on Tess, now swivelled to Edward. Into the silence, Tess's voice was clear and high.

"He did not do it, Uncle Charles, he did not! He is innocent."

"But he confessed to it," the earl said querulously. "I do not see what I am to do about it if a man stands up and says he killed a man. Am I supposed to say, *'No, I do not believe you'*? He confessed, the investigation into the murder is over, we have got rid of that Edgerton fellow and his prying, thank the Lord, and that is the end of the matter. "

Tess sat back on her heels. "May I see him?"

"Edgerton?"

"No! Tom Shapman."

"The murderer? Certainly not!"

"Is he here? Or... where is he?"

"Why would he be here? He is in York Gaol, awaiting the Assizes."

"York Gaol!"

Edward crossed the room, and laid a hand on her shoulder. "You may go to York tomorrow, Tess, but just now I suspect everyone is awaiting dinner."

"Oh. Of course," she said in a small voice, rising smoothly to her feet. "I beg your pardon, uncle."

"Dinner will be put back, naturally," the earl said, rising also. "Tarvin, you are welcome here. You are both welcome, but do you go and change, Tess. We will talk more about this later."

"What is there to talk about?" she said in angry tones, before striding out of the room with a swish of her black skirts.

Edward bowed to the earl and followed her from the room. A footman led him up the stairs to an elegant room aswirl with activity. Two maids were hastily throwing sheets onto the bed, another carried a wobbling tower of linens, while a fourth rushed in with a steaming ewer of water. Meanwhile, several footmen were manoeuvring boxes under Deakin's supervision. There was a dressing room, fortunately, so Edward was able to escape the chaos and dress as swiftly as it took Deakin to remove the appropriate garments from one of the trunks.

He returned downstairs to find the drawing room deep in a multitude of intense conversations. With no one to announce him this time, no one looked up as he entered, so for a while he loitered near the door, unwilling to put himself forward in such a family crisis.

Eventually, one of the men came forward, quite young, no more than one or two and twenty.

"I am Kent Atherton, Lord Tarvin," he said with a grin. "One of Tess's many cousins. Shall I introduce you to everyone, or do you plan to pretend to remember us all? Or is a drink the most urgent requirement?"

Edward laughed. "A drink first, definitely, and then introductions. It is five years since I was here, and I never got everyone straight at the time. I cannot remember you at all."

"Ah, the forgettable one of the family! Such is the fate of youngest sons everywhere," Kent said cheerfully, deftly steering Edward to the sideboard where decanters of wine and sherry sat.

Thus fortified, Edward allowed himself to be taken across the room and introduced to Lady Alice Nicholson, Tess's mother. Her widow's attire would have identified her instantly, and her still-luminous beauty was very memorable, but he had forgotten, until she turned towards him and fixed her gaze on his ear, that she was blind.

"Lady Alice," he murmured, bowing. "May I offer you my sincere condolences on the recent death of your husband."

"Thank you, Lord Tarvin," she said with a gracious bow of her head. "Pray sit beside me and tell me all that my daughter is about these days, for she is not the world's best correspondent. She is betrothed to your cousin, I understand?"

"Indeed. He is my aunt's son from her first marriage. His father is long dead, and I am a trustee for his fortune, a duty I inherited from my uncle, the late 3rd Baron."

Unexpectedly, she blushed slightly. "I knew your uncle very well," she said, with a soft smile. "In fact, a marriage was proposed between us, but he preferred Myrtle Horncastle and I preferred Arthur Nicholson, so it all worked out very well in the end. Although it was a pity she had no children. Not for you, of course, but a marriage without children is a strange, half-formed beast, like a meal without meat. We were very happy when Tess came along. But do tell me about this young man with the strange name — Ulric Frith. Lady Tarvin writes to her sister, the countess, of course, but Mr Frith has been but little mentioned. What sort of man is he?"

How on earth to answer that question? Should he tell the truth? But really, there was no need to trouble them with the details. With a possible marriage at least nine months away, anything could happen. "He loves horses," he said finally. "Tess has been riding with him every day."

"Has she, indeed? That will be good for her, at least. But I must tell you, Lord Tarvin, that I am not at all inclined to favour such a hasty match, and to a man who is not at all known to us. He is a man of some wealth, she assures me, and presumably he is of good standing in his own neighbourhood, but we know nothing of him and he does not accompany her on this journey, which does not speak well of his care for her. If you have any influence with her, and you must have or you would not be here, I hope you will advise her to consider carefully before taking such a step. Marriage is not something to be undertaken impulsively, on a whim."

"I regret that my influence over her is negligible."

"Mine also, sadly," she said with a wry shrug of one elegantly clad shoulder. "I do not think she takes the least notice of any of us."

"It may be that this Tom Shapman has more of a hold on her mind than we had supposed," Edward said carefully. "She seems very upset by his confession."

"Tom Shapman!" she said, her expression hardening. "That man killed my husband, Lord Tarvin. If she cares anything for him, then she has poorer judgement than I had ever suspected."

Tess arrived at that moment and dinner was announced almost at once. Edward was scooped up by Lord Rennington, and Tess by Kent and a pretty young woman. He searched in his mind for a name, and since pretty young women were more memorable than youngest sons, he quickly identified her as the earl's youngest daughter, Olivia. At dinner, Tess was far from him, too far to hear what she said, although what glimpses he caught of her showed her drooping and eating very little. By the time Edward was able to escape from the dining room, she had already retired to bed.

He went up himself as soon as he decently could, but he had not been in his room long, and had done no more than loosen his neck cloth with a sigh of relief and pour himself a bedtime brandy, when there was a scratching at the door. Deakin went to answer it.

"Tell whoever it is I have gone to bed," Edward said, throwing himself into a chair beside the fireplace, where a low fire burned.

As soon as the door opened, Tess rushed in, wearing only a nightgown and robe, her hair in a long plait reaching to her waist. "I must talk to you!"

"No, no, no, no, no!" Edward cried, jumping up and grabbing her by the shoulders to propel her back to the door. "Talk, yes, but not in my bedchamber at this time of night... or any time, come to that."

"We cannot talk out in the corridor."

"If it is urgent, you can get dressed, I can restore my neck cloth and we can go downstairs to the drawing room, with a proper chaperon — your mother, ideally, but any member of your family would do, and Simpson would be about, too. Good heavens, Tess, have you no sense of propriety at all?"

"Oh." She deflated at once, her face desolate. "I... yes, of course. How stupid of me."

"If it is not quite so urgent, we will have all day to talk in the carriage tomorrow."

Her expression brightened. "You will come with me, then?"

"Of course I will. I would not miss it for the world."

"You make it sound like an amusement — a balloon ascension, or a juggler, or some such," she said sullenly.

"Tess, you infuriate and intrigue me in equal measure, but you and your problems are far more interesting than a balloon ascension, I assure you."

She grinned impishly. "I infuriate you, do I?"

"You do, especially when you turn up in my room at this time of night. What time is it? Gone eleven, and we have an early start tomorrow, so go and get some sleep. If we can be on the road by eight, we will be at York by the middle of the afternoon, all being well. Go now. Go on. Shoo."

Laughing, she skipped away, and Edward closed the door firmly behind her.

"That girl will be the death of me, Deakin. What am I to do with her, eh?"

"Whip her until she submits to authority," Deakin said, as he eased Edward out of his coat.

"Would that work? I have a feeling it would not. She might very well *pretend* to submit, but go her own sweet way in secret. Yes, I am sure she would, for I suspect she has been doing it for years. Any other ideas, Deakin?"

"Lock her up in an asylum."

"And yet, I do not think she is insane. She may appear irrational, but I suspect she has a good reason for everything she does. All I have to do, if I can, is to find out what those reasons are. I should like to know, for instance, why she betroths herself to Ulric when she is clearly very attached to this woodworker fellow, and even encouraged him to offer for her. And why, I wonder, is she so obsessed with this house of hers in Pickering, which sounds like a very ordinary little house to me, not likely to hold any great treasure. It is a puzzle."

Deakin carefully unbuttoned Edward's waistcoat and gently removed it. "If you ask me, my lord, I should say you were getting in very deep with that young lady. She'll have you wrapped round her thumb as quick as winking, if you let her."

"You think I should be careful, do you?"

"No, my lord. I think you should cut and run back to London as soon as you can. She's trouble, that Miss Nicholson, big, big trouble, and you're one who's always been so clever about avoiding troublesome young ladies. You need to escape from her as fast as you can, before you find she's caught you so tight in her web there's no getting away at all."

"Thank you, Deakin," Edward said evenly. "You may go now. I can manage the rest."

"Very good, my lord," Deakin said, gathering up discarded clothes and bowing himself out of the room with his usual imperturbable dignity.

Edward donned his nightgown and robe, then returned to his chair by the fire, brandy in hand. He was thoughtful, but a little smile lingered on his lips. Coming to his room! And a balloon ascension, indeed! There was just no knowing what she might say or do next, the tantalising little minx.

10: York Gaol

The carriage had lumbered down the hill to Helmsley, the horses changed for a hired team of four and they were well under way again before Edward ventured to break the prevailing silence.

"Tess, you wanted to talk to me last night. Do you wish to talk now? If you prefer to speak privately, we can stop the carriage and we may walk into these woods on our left, so that Betty and Deakin will not overhear us."

She looked at him thoughtfully, chewing her lip. "It is not private," she said eventually. "I only wanted to know how we can get Tom out of York Gaol."

"Not by springing him," he said with a little smile. "I will do much to accommodate your wishes, Tess Nicholson, but I will not break the law quite so outrageously."

That brought a hint of a smile to her lips. "Oh, not that. Besides, I do not know how it might be done, for gaols are always fearsomely well-guarded, are they not? So it would have to be some clever stratagem, and without seeing the place, I cannot think how it might be done."

"You have clearly given the matter careful thought," he said.

"Well, I have, yes. One must consider every option, however unlikely. But if he simply retracts his confession, would anyone believe him? That is the problem. And no matter how much his friends protest that he could not possibly have killed anyone, the judges will say, as my uncle did, that he has confessed and that is an end to it."

"These questions are imponderable," Edward said. "Of course, we are bound to ponder them anyway, that is only human nature, but we cannot yet answer them. Our first course is to talk to Shapman and find out why he confessed to a crime he did not commit. After that, we must find Captain Edgerton and see what he thinks about it."

"Captain Edgerton! Why?"

"Because he was in charge of the investigation into your father's death. He must have had suspicions as to who might have done it. If we can convince him that Shapman is innocent, then he can start looking for the real murderer again. That is the very best way to clear Shapman's name, you see — to find out who really did it."

"Ah," was all she said, but he could see that she understood.

Their progress was slower than he would have liked, but Tess seemed more at ease, and when there was a delay in replacing the horses at the final post house, he took a parlour, ordered some food and was pleased to see her eat a little bread and ham. They arrived in York at an hour when working men were beginning to think of going home for the evening, and the gentry were watching the clock for the hour to change for dinner. There was the business of finding accommodation to be accomplished first, but as soon as rooms had been secured, Edward left Deakin and Betty to unpack, while he, Tess and Harold headed for the gaol at the castle.

The gaolers were disinclined to produce Shapman at such an inconvenient hour, but Edward's title and the coins he pushed into their hands did the trick. They were shown into a small room furnished only with a table and a few rickety chairs, and a few minutes later, a man in manacles was led in.

Tess hurled herself at him, throwing her arms around his neck and sobbing, "Tom! Oh, Tom!"

With his hands confined, he could offer her no physical comfort, simply murmuring, "There now, Miss Tess, it's all right. I'm fine."

Edward saw at once why Tess was so enamoured of him. It would be hard to imagine a handsomer man, and built as so many working men were, with broad shoulders and muscular arms. In the rudest of rude health, he was a striking contrast to the slenderness of Kent Atherton, or the earl's middle-aged portliness. He looked tired and very dishevelled, with straw clinging to his coat and breeches, and he wore no neck cloth, but that perhaps only made him more attractive to Tess. All her protective instincts would be roused by it.

He persuaded Tess to sit down, which she would only do if Tom's seat was right beside hers so that she could cling to his arm with one hand, and wrap her fingers around his manacled hands with the other.

"Oh, Tom, why have you done this? Such a foolish thing to do! You had nothing to do with my father's death, and everyone must know that."

"They were quick enough to believe me, though," Shapman said. "Not Captain Edgerton — he made me go through it step by step, but everyone else just sighed with relief."

"Go through it step by step? What do you mean?"

"I had to tell him exactly how the murder was done."

"But how could you do that? How did you know?"

"Well, it was you that told me how it might've been done, Miss Tess, don't you remember? I said I thought it was a madman, and you said, no, he was clever not mad. And you thought up that whole business of hiding the axe in the big vase thing. It was your story... oh, the captain asked if I got covered in blood, and I knew the murderer must have been, so I said yes, but I wore an old smock and burnt it later. That was my own invention, but he seemed satisfied with that. Heavens, Miss Tess, I did this for you. I thought you'd be pleased with me. I didn't mean you to come galloping down here. You wanted the captain called off the investigation and now he is."

"But Tom, I do not want you to hang!"

"I'm not going to hang!" He laughed, quite at his ease.

"Will you retract your confession, then?"

"No, I've got a better way than that. You're not to worry about me, Miss Tess. It's not very comfortable in here, but as soon as you've found your fortune, you let me know and I'll do what I need to do to get out of here."

"Is that what this was about?" she said in a small voice. "My fortune?"

"Of course. Once you get your hands on that, you'll be free to do what you want and I can go back to my workshop. I've left my brother to keep an eye on it, but I'd not like to leave it for too long, for all that. So you get on with finding what's yours, you hear?"

They returned to the hotel in silence, Tess striding ahead, Edward in her wake and Harold marching some little way behind. Edward had ordered dinner to be served in a private parlour with their own servants attending them, but even so, nothing at all was said beyond the practical.

Eventually, the meal was cleared away and the servants disappeared to their own quarters. Edward poured himself a brandy and waited.

Yet still she said nothing, sitting sunk in thought at the table, nursing the half glass of wine he had poured for her an hour before.

Someone had to say *something* about Tom Shapman. "He will go on more comfortably now, I trust. I paid those men to ensure he has a cell to himself, with a mattress and blankets, no rats and decent food. Or as decent as it can be, in a place like that."

A sigh, and then she pushed the glass away. "I have to go to Pickering," she said, as if he had said nothing.

"This house of yours?" She nodded. "But you cannot get in. No one can enter without the permission of the trustees, or the tenant."

She fell silent again.

"Tess, what *is* this fortune that you expect to find at the Pickering house? Whatever it is, it is part of your dowry and therefore is not truly yours. Your trustees will control it until you marry and then it will be your husband's."

Again she said nothing.

He sipped his brandy and waited again, but she seemed to have nothing further to say. Well then, he would say his piece and give her something to think about.

"It seems to me," he said slowly, "that you have to make a major decision, one that will affect your whole life, and perhaps you are torn. Perhaps the options seem limited. Certainly your family is no help, but then I cannot imagine you would accept any advice they offered." That brought a wan smile. "I shall not offer you advice, either, since I believe you are perfectly capable of making a rational decision by yourself. You have to decide who to marry... well, I suppose, if we are to be entirely logical about this, there is always the option not to marry at all, but then you have nothing — no fortune, nothing. So let us suppose you must marry. At the moment, you have but three choices. One, you could marry Tom Shapman, who is a fine figure of a man, I grant you that, but not your class, not educated, not the cleverest of men, since he presently resides in York Gaol on a hanging charge. But let us suppose he can be extricated from his predicament and you marry him, you would find yourself with no fortune, no chess in the evening, no conversation over dinner. Where would you live? Have you thought about that? In his workshop?"

"In a cottage in the village," she said, her eyes flashing. "He could still have his workshop, if he wants it, and do the work he loves."

"A cottage," Edward said thoughtfully. "So... a parlour and a kitchen downstairs, and two bedrooms upstairs, one for Mr and Mrs Tom Shapman, and one for all the little Shapmans. The maid of all work will sleep on the kitchen floor, I suppose."

"Not *that* sort of cottage," she said smiling.

"Oh, a cottage with a drawing room and a dining room large enough to seat twenty-four, I suppose. How many footmen will a woodworker's wage pay for? Grooms? Horses? A lady's maid, perhaps? How many gowns a year do you think he can buy you?"

"I hope I shall have enough money to pay for such an establishment myself."

"Ah, so you will be the great lady, and he will still be the village woodworker, except living on his wife's money. That will gratify him, I am sure. He will be the envy of all his friends."

She frowned at him. "What are the other two choices?"

"Number two is to marry Ulric. You would have your fortune, and although it will be technically Ulric's, if you can keep him docile, and keep his mother from persuading him to make it all over to her, you will have full control of it. You can leave Ulric at Myercroft with his beloved horses while you do… well, whatever you want. But you would still have no one to play chess with and no conversation over dinner." He hesitated only a moment. "Or…"

"Yes?"

"Or you could marry me." There! He had said it, and now let the dice fall however they will.

"You? Why would I marry you?"

That was not the reaction he had expected. "For the obvious reasons — fortune, chess, conversation," he said sharply. "I am assuming that such trivia as my title, income and standing in society hold no attractions for you."

"Certainly not! Nothing about you holds any attraction for me."

The sudden pain took him entirely by surprise. Did he care so much for her good opinion? Apparently he did. "Hmm. That is certainly comprehensive, but bear in mind that you could marry me tomorrow, or at least as soon as the banns could be read. Your mother would be delighted with the match. Did you know she almost became Lady Tarvin herself at one time? So she could have no possible objections, and you would have your fortune immediately, including this house of yours."

"No, *you* would have my fortune," she spat. "Do you think I am stupid? That I would take one look at you, and roll over instantly? Oh, look, a baron with a fancy house — naturally I must marry him immediately! Pah! You are just trying to get my fortune for yourself. I love Tom Shapman, Edward, and I intend to marry him, whether you like it or not. All I have to do is get my hands on my fortune."

"Then I wish you joy of your cottage," he said angrily. Fool of a woman! What did he have to do to make her see sense? And why exactly did he care, anyway?

***

Edward waited until Tess had retired to bed, then took a bottle of wine and two glasses, and made his way back to the gaol. It took considerably more coins this time, but before too long he was sitting opposite Tom Shapman again in the drab little room.

"Wine, Shapman?"

"I'll try some, but I don't often have it. Is this a good one?"

Edward took a sip. "A middling sort, I should say. I have much better stuff in my own cellar."

Gingerly, Shapman tasted the wine, his face assuming a surprised expression when he found it palatable. "You want to talk to me without Miss Tess weeping all over me, I dare say."

"Something like that. I want someone who will be honest with me... straightforward, because frankly Tess is as unpredictable as a squirrel. There is no knowing which way she will jump, and I have to know what is going on if I am to help her."

"*Are* you going to help her?"

"That depends," Edward said. "Answer me this, Shapman — why do you want to marry her?"

"Oh, I don't," he said, sounding surprised. "Heavens, no! She's way above me. I'd never presume. I know she has this funny idea that we'll wed, but it's never going to happen, is it?"

That was unexpected! "So why did you go to her father last year and ask permission to address her?"

He shifted in his chair and pulled a face. "It wasn't quite like that. She wanted to know how much her dowry was, that was the purpose of it. She said if I went to her father and said I was thinking of marrying her, but if she had a large dowry it would be impossible... well, she imagined he'd say something like, *'You'll not get your hands on my daughter's twenty thousand'* or whatever it was. Then she would know what was hers. But he just said I'd never see a penny piece of her money, he'd make sure of it, and he has, hasn't he? This will of his has stitched her up good and proper."

"But she still thinks she will marry you. There is something about getting hold of her fortune."

"She thinks that if she gets her money in her own hands, she'll marry me. But I keep telling her it will never do. Her uncle is an earl, for heaven's sake. She's grown up in Corland Castle. How could she lower herself to marry a man like me?"

"But if she finds this mythical fortune, what then? She would be rich enough to keep both of you in comfort. You need never work again, or you could do only the jobs that interested you. Would you marry her then?"

He sighed. "Look, she's a lovely lady and she's been very good to me and helped me get the business started, and I confess that when she comes to me with kisses and sweet words... well, I don't fight her off as perhaps I should. It's never gone beyond that, but I defy any man to refuse a kiss from a girl like Miss Tess. She's as sweet as pie, and if she were a farmer's daughter... but she ain't, and that's the long and the short of it. I have my life all planned out, and she's no part of it."

"So... is there, in fact, a farmer's daughter?"

He went bright red. "She's a farrier's daughter, actually, and she works as a poultry maid on Gowland's farm. That's about ten or so miles west of Birchall. Will Gowland's her uncle. I've been courting her for about three years and we should have been wed by now, but when Miss Tess came along and seemed inclined to be friendly, we agreed not to do anything to discourage her. Make use of her, like, and she helped me get business when I was struggling a bit, so I'm grateful for that. But we never supposed she'd start talking about marriage. I keep thinking she'll forget about me, but she's not going to, is she?"

"Not unless you tell her about the poultry maid."

"There never seemed to be a good moment for that. Besides, Miss Tess has a way of beguiling a man so he just wants to do whatever she wants. It's how I ended up going to her father, and how I came to be in here, and if she gets her money and starts on at me to wed her… well, I'm not sure I'll be able to fight her off, and that's a fact. She just never takes no for an answer. I want her to find her fortune, if that's what it'll take to make her happy, and I don't want to fall out with her, but I'd like my life back the way it was. So if you can persuade her to leave me alone, that would be a kindness, my lord."

"I'm not sure I can persuade her to do anything, but I shall do what I can. But what about you? You said you have a plan to get out of here. I trust it does not involve tunnelling out or bribing the gaolers, because I am not sure either of those ideas will fly."

Shapman laughed. "Nothing like that. I was over at Gowland's farm visiting Ruby the night of the murder. I go there about once a month, walking over the night before, have supper, sleep in a room with Gowland's four sons, leave again at six to walk home. There are about a dozen people who'll swear I was there. All I have to do is get word to them, and they'll go to the magistrate."

"But not until Tess has found her fortune."

"Exactly!"

Edward laughed, for finally his way forward was clear. "Then we must make sure that her fortune is found as soon as possible."

When Edward returned to the hotel, leaving the wine bottle with Shapman as prisoner currency, he found Tess pacing backwards and forwards in the parlour. At least she was fully dressed this time.

"You went out!" she said accusingly. "You took wine — I saw you from my window. Where have you been?"

"Back to the gaol to talk to Shapman again. There was much left unsaid earlier."

"Was there? What else is there to say?"

"I wanted to know more about your fortune," he said, having no intention of telling her the real reason for his visit. "I *still* want to know more about this mysterious fortune of yours that you think is lurking in some nondescript house in Pickering, for I will tell you openly, Tess, I do not believe any fortune exists that is not already known about."

"Well, that is where you are wrong, Mr Oh-So-Clever. It *does* exist, I have seen it and I know precisely where in the house it is."

"How can you possibly know that? No one has been into the house."

"I have been in, as a housemaid until I was caught. I found my father's office over the coach house, and there is a safe in there. That is where my fortune is."

"Oh, there are bags of coins in there, are there? Diamond necklaces?"

"Gold bars," she said. "Lots of gold bars."

"Excellent!" he said with a grin. "Then let us go to Pickering forthwith. What an adventure this is turning out to be!"

11: Pickering

Tess was exultant. Finally, someone took her seriously and would do something sensible. Lord Tarvin accepted that there was a great heap of gold bars in her house, and he was determined to find a way to get them out, and without her trustees being any the wiser. He would not say much about how he intended to do it, for he said he would need to see the house first, but he would surely find a way.

The whole journey to Pickering had been filled with his questions about the house. He wanted to know the exact layout of all the rooms, and even made her draw a map. Then he wanted to know all about the people who lived there, both the widow and her nieces, and also the servants. He was particularly interested in their habits — when they went out, when they went to bed, what visitors they had and much more besides. And finally, he wanted to know about the office over the coach house and the safe.

"It just had one lock? Not two? Trying to find two keys might be difficult."

"No, only one key. Papa's safe at Corland only had one key, and he used to keep it on a hook under his desk. Another minute and I might have had the Pickering safe open."

"We will have it open soon enough," he said soothingly.

And then, finally, the fortune her father had wilfully tried to withhold would belong to her, as it should by right. And then... and then... she could marry Tom at last.

Here her heart quailed momentarily. Edward's sarcastic words rang in her head. *'He will still be the village woodworker, except living on his wife's money. That will gratify him, I am sure.'* He would not like that! A man like Tom, so proud of his little business and making his way by his own skills would not be at all content to be funded by his wife. Perhaps he would not even like to live in her cottage, being used to far more modest accommodation. But he could hardly expect her to live in a hovel, with a maid of all work! The practical aspects had never even crossed her mind, except that she knew she could never live in that tiny room above the workshop.

It was a conundrum, and she was only surprised she had never thought of it before. Still, there would be time enough to work out the details later. The first priority was to find her fortune. Then Tom could be released from prison and they could begin to plan their future together, whatever it was to be.

***

Captain Michael Edgerton was cross. He was cross a great deal of the time just now, ever since Tom Shapman had walked into Corland Castle and confessed to the murder of Mr Arthur Nicholson, the earl's chaplain. Nine weeks Michael had spent at Corland, nine long weeks of painstakingly interviewing everyone from the earl himself down to the scullery maid, and then the neighbouring families, and not even come close to identifying the murderer. The miscreant rested in York Gaol now only because his conscience had troubled him and he had confessed.

Although even now doubts remained in Michael's mind. The means of it, the way the fellow had entered the castle, retrieved the axe, gone up the stairs to Nicholson's room, and then escaped afterwards — all of that was plausible. He had even explained how it was that no one had noticed the axe in the display on the stairs, since he had hidden it in one of the Chinese urns so that it was handy for his enterprise. But as to *why* he had killed the chaplain, his explanation was deficient. He had wanted to marry the chaplain's daughter, and been refused, not surprisingly. A woodworker was not a suitable husband for the niece of an earl. So, a year later, he had killed the chaplain, and now he would hang. That made no sense to Michael, when all he needed to do was to wait a few months until the lady was of age and they could marry anyway. Even if he hoped that Tess would inherit a great fortune, was it worth risking the hangman's noose for?

Now he had another problem. His investigation had finished two weeks ago, ever since Shapman's confession, but Michael had still to recover the last of his team. Miss Peach was an elderly spinster, once Mrs Edgerton's governess, but brought out of retirement to play the part of companion while they resided at Corland Castle. The intention was to give her a pleasant holiday, sitting in the drawing room with all the latest journals to amuse her, while she was supplied with endless cups of tea and currant buns. Instead, she had hurled herself into the investigation with glee, initially elbowing her way into the rector's wife's circle to hear all the gossip, and latterly in Pickering, pursuing Mr Nicholson's ventures there.

And now she had disappeared. Michael had been looking for her for two weeks, without any success. It was enough to make him leave off his investigator's hat once and for all, and go back to army life. At least there everything was regular and orderly, and he had only to do what he was told and not think too deeply about any of it, or chase round after elderly ladies who vanished off the face of the earth.

So he returned to the inn at Pickering, accompanied by Sandy, his Scottish colleague, in a thoroughly despondent frame of mind. His wife, Luce, was alone in the parlour.

"Anything?" she said eagerly.

He shook his head, removing his sword and laying it on the battered deal table that filled the centre of the small parlour. "No one has seen her, not for weeks."

"Ah, well, there is a letter for you from Pettigrew, so perhaps he will bring good tidings from Corland."

While Sandy poured wine for them all, Michael broke the seal on his letter and read the contents aloud.

'To Captain Michael Edgerton, Black Swan, Pickering. My good friend, we have had an interesting visitation. Miss Tess Nicholson arrived from Harfield Priory late yesterday, just as we were gathering for dinner, in a great state of agitation, having heard that Tom Shapman had confessed to the murder of her father. She protested loudly that he is innocent, but the earl would have none of it. She did not know that Shapman was held at York Gaol, and left this morning to go there. Curiously, she was accompanied by Lord Tarvin. If you recall, he came storming up from town to protect his simple-minded cousin, Mr Frith, although it seems he was unsuccessful, since Miss Nicholson is now officially betrothed to Mr Frith. He is chosen to be the gentleman who will unlock the terms of the late Mr Nicholson's will, and

release her fortune. However, the Lady Alice will not give her permission, so they must wait until the spring before they can marry. I should very much like to know why Lord Tarvin so concerns himself in Miss Nicholson's affairs that he undertakes to drive her here and there in his carriage. He has gone with her to York, but I do not think it likely that they will be able to have Shapman released. Do you suppose she has any reason for believing in Shapman's innocence, or it is merely her affectionate female heart that makes her say so? You have never been entirely convinced of Shapman's guilt, so perhaps this is the key to unlocking that particular mystery. Is there any news regarding Miss Peach? I am becoming quite alarmed by her continued disappearance. I remain your good friend, Pettigrew Willerton-Forbes'

There was silence for a long time, as the three occupants of the room pondered this interesting news. Michael sipped his wine, Sandy absent-mindedly chewed a slice of cherry cake that had been abandoned on a plate, and Luce placidly mended one of Michael's shirts.

"She is a very odd sort of girl," Luce said eventually. "Last year she wanted to marry the woodworker. Now she is betrothed to a man she barely knows, of whom strange things are said, and yet when she hears that the woodworker is in prison, she comes haring south in... what did Pettigrew say? *'A great state of agitation'*. She is fond of the woodworker, yet she is to marry this other man."

"Is that not the fate of many women of her class?" Michael said. "Herded into London and married off to the first eligible man to offer for them, or worse, a match made by her parents when she was in the cradle. Few aristocratic women marry for love."

"Oh indeed, and many of them live to regret it," Luce said at once. "An earl's niece and a woodworker? It would never do, and they would both be miserable."

"And you are a baron's daughter and an earl's cousin, and yet you married a common soldier," Michael said softly. "You hide your misery very well, my dear."

Luce laid down her sewing and smiled at him. "Michael, you cannot compare our situation with theirs. You are a gentleman's son, after all, a great many rungs on the social ladder above a woodworker. I had only a modest dowry, so you brought more money to the marriage than I did. A common soldier indeed!"

"I notice ye dinnae deny being miserable," Sandy said, and ducked as Luce threw her thimble at him.

"Foolish Scotsman!" she murmured.

"Aye, but are we off tae York or not?" Sandy said.

"Of course we are!" Michael said. "I suppose it is too late to go now?"

"It is," Luce said crisply. "Dinner in an hour, followed by a leisurely evening and a good night's sleep. Tomorrow you may go tearing off to York, if you wish."

But this plan was soon forgotten, for the dinner hour saw the return of another of Michael's colleagues, James Neate, an unobtrusive man whose great skill was to sit unnoticed in tap rooms and hear all the gossip.

"Any news of Peachy?" were his first words, but when Michael shook his head, James went on at once, "I bring interesting news. Guess who is staying at the White Swan? No, you will never guess. Miss Nicholson and a lord... Lord Tarvin. Do we know a Lord Tarvin? I thought she was betrothed to a commoner?"

"Miss Nicholson? Lord Tarvin?" Michael said, stunned. "But Pettigrew has just written to say they are gone to York. Wait... what date is on the letter? Well, I suppose if they only stayed one night in York... How long have they been at the White Swan, James?"

"Two or three days. They have been very furtive, using false names. He is Lord Frimley, and she is his sister, Miss Frimley, but the carriage has the coat of arms on it, and the servants are... a bit careless in their talk, especially when plied with ale. I am very good at plying servants with ale."

"Two or three days!" Michael cried. "Who knows what they may have been up to in that time. And what are they even doing here?"

"I overheard the servants talking about a house," James said. "I would wager that is Miss Nicholson's house."

"But what can they do about it?" Michael mused. "They cannot enter it... but perhaps they can. Lord Tarvin is Mr Frith's trustee, I believe, so now that Miss Nicholson is engaged to marry him, he might be able to persuade the attorneys that he has a right to go in. But then, why the false names? They are up to something, that much is certain. We must keep an eye on them."

"False names... masquerading as his sister... and ye think they're up to something?" Sandy said. "Well done, Michael! Ye should take up a career as an investigator."

It was as well Michael had no heavy object in his hand, for he would surely have thrown it at Sandy's head, but the rest of them laughed long at his discomfiture, and he was not brought back to good humour until cajoled with a dish of sweetbreads and several glasses of very good claret at dinner.

***

Edward fizzed with excitement. He had spent three whole days looking at Apstead House from every possible angle, and loitering nearby to observe the comings and goings. He quickly discovered that few people went into the house and even fewer left it, just as Tess had said. But the gentlemen arriving in the evenings by way of the garden were interesting, so he sent Deakin to patronise every inn in town and make certain discreet enquiries. That brought surprising intelligence. Apstead House, it appeared, was in business as a rather exclusive and very expensive brothel.

That would make it easier for a gentleman to be at the back of the house, near the coach house, in the evening. There were bushes in abundance to hide behind, and an ancient apple tree meandering its way up the side of the coach house, easily climbable, and half hiding a window large enough for a man to scramble through into the office. Tess had told him that she had been spotted moving about, so he had only to keep below the level of any windows on the house side of the office. It should be easy.

Tess was very cross to be excluded, naturally, but he insisted that she and Betty should keep well out of sight. They had been confined to the inn since they arrived, or at least, he had told them to stay there. With Tess, there was no knowing what she might get up to when his back was turned. That was what made her so fascinating.

"It would never do for you to be recognised, especially as we are not using our own names," he said. "It would look deeply suspicious."

"We are not doing anything illegal," she said. "That house is mine, after all. I am entitled to enter it."

"Well... perhaps. I am not sure that a magistrate would be convinced by that argument."

"I have more right to get into it than you have."

"Tess, I am going to climb a tree, and then force a way in through a closed window. That is no venture for a female, especially as we have no idea what might be waiting inside. For all we know, Mrs Mayberry may have hired armed guards to protect that room. You must stay here, do you understand?"

She smiled and nodded and assured him that she had no thought of climbing trees, but he mistrusted her all the same.

"Do you want me to watch her while you're gone, my lord?" Deakin said when she was out of the room.

Edward sighed. "Really she needs tying to the bedpost, and the servants with her, for they are totally loyal to her and cannot be trusted to protect her. No, let her do as she pleases, but if she should leave the inn, please do your level best to keep her out of trouble."

He left early enough that there would still be light enough to see by, for lighting a candle would be fatal to his hope of secrecy. He had planned to wear his normal evening dress, to attract less suspicion, but Tess had pointed out scornfully that his usual pale silk breeches and stockings would be easy to see, so he had settled on black pantaloons. And then he was out of the inn, making his way towards the small house where he, a peer of the realm, was going to break in and steal whatever was in the safe.

The thought amused him, and he had the comfortable notion that even if he were caught, he had the justification of acting for Tess, whose house it was, and neither she nor her trustees would pursue him for his crime. The only point in the plan that gave rise to a degree of apprehension was the prospect of meeting a man with a pistol in his hand, but it was six weeks since Tess had been there, so he was optimistic that the affair had been forgotten.

Edward took his time walking through the streets. Pickering was not a large town, so he had to meander a bit, but eventually he found himself at the back of the house, and hastily dodged out of sight in the shrubbery behind the privy. Here he paused to catch his breath, calm his thumping heart and prepare for the next stage of his adventure.

Climbing the tree was easy, and he was mostly hidden from the ground by the still expansive foliage, although the ripening apples kept bumping him as he climbed, or else fell with soft thuds to the ground below. The highest part of the tree was above the roof of the privy, but thickly growing ivy provided shelter from anyone watching from the house.

Then he was at the window, and here he paused, wondering if this was the point where he acknowledged defeat, for the glass was filthy and he could not see where the latch was. He had brought a flat metal bar with him, purchased by Harold from a tiny shop near the church, so he started to worry away at the window in a couple of places where he thought the latch might be. To his surprise, the window abruptly swung open, knocking him from his precarious perch, so that he slithered a few painful feet down the tree before grabbing a branch firmly enough to stop his descent.

For a few minutes, he could think of nothing but the pain in a particularly troubling place, but as soon as that subsided enough for his brain to function again, he climbed up to the windowsill and gingerly clambered over it.

He was in! For an instant, exhilaration rose unstoppably and he laughed out loud. But he could not linger, for the sun would soon be gone and he would have to make the descent down the tree before it was too dark to see.

The room was long and thin, with windows on all sides. That meant plenty of light to see by, but he must be very careful not to show himself at any of the windows. Dropping to the floor, he crawled across the room to the writing desk and felt underneath for the key. There it was! Exactly as Tess had predicted, it was in the same place as at Corland. Then across to the wardrobe, manoeuvre the door open without standing up, and there was the safe. Excitedly, he fumbled with the key, dropped it with a metallic clang, tried again, the door swung open.

So much gold! He sat back on his heels, astonished. Everything Tess had said was true, was his first thought. He had never quite believed in the existence of her great fortune, assuming it to be a few pieces of gold — worth a few hundred pounds at most. But this! He could not even begin to guess at its value.

He picked up the topmost bar… and then froze.

Behind him came the distinct sound of a gun being cocked.

"I should not move, if I were you, my lord," came a voice.

12: The Black Swan

The man had a cultured accent, that was Edward's first thought. The second was that the fellow knew who he was. He was not, then, a hired guard who might panic or shoot accidentally.

"You will not shoot me," Edward said with more confidence than he felt, but he did not move all the same.

The man chuckled. "What makes you so sure of that?"

"I am a peer of the realm, I am unarmed and I am fully entitled to be in this house."

"The first I concede, the second is at present unconfirmed and as to the third, opinions may differ on the point."

Now it was Edward's turn to chuckle. "I concede your last point. May I turn round? My back is not my best feature."

"Slowly, and stay on the ground, Lord Tarvin."

Edward did as he was bid and saw that the man was standing just to one side of the window facing the house. He was a small man, a pistol in one hand and the other resting on a businesslike sword.

"You have the advantage of me, sir."

"Captain Michael Edgerton at your service, my lord. Forgive me if I do not bow. A cocked gun is a delicate creature, not liking too much movement."

"You could always uncock it," he said.

The captain laughed. "Not yet, my lord. Let us complete the introductions. My colleague just entering through the window you helpfully left open is Mr James Neate. He will bow to you, since his pistols are still in his pocket."

"You seem to have everything in hand, Michael," Neate said, making a flourishing bow.

Edward could not help laughing at the two of them. "So what are you going to do, Captain? Arrest me? Send for the constables? Ring a peal over me?"

"None of those," Edgerton said. "My lord, you look uncomfortable crouched like that. Perhaps you would care to sit over there with your back to the wall. Yes, keep hold of that gold bar. If you have that in your hand I need not worry about you reaching for a knife or pistol. James, check what is in the safe, will you?"

Edgerton sat on the floor, too, the pistol still steady in his hand, while Neate crawled over to the safe. "Some documents... purchase documents for properties... certificates relating to investments. Miss Nicholson's trustees will want to know about these. The rest is the gold bars. Shall I count them?"

Edgerton agreed and for some time there was silence as Neate shuffled the bars about. "Seventy five," he said eventually. "Seventy-six with his lordship's. Some variation in size. They will need to be properly valued."

"True," Edgerton said. "Now put them back in the safe and lock it. I will keep the key."

"Now wait a minute," Edward said in alarm, as Neate instantly complied. "That gold belongs to Miss Nicholson, and it should be given to her, not left here."

"Ah, yes, the question of who owns this is an interesting one," Edgerton said, his grin revealing rows of gleaming teeth. "It is not for us to determine, that much is certain. You may keep that one bar to show Miss Nicholson, if you wish, Lord Tarvin, and you may want to have it valued. That will give you a rough idea of the fortune in the safe. But we do not want to linger here, and risk discovery. Shall we all repair to the Black Swan to discuss this further, preferably over a glass of something decent?"

"Is there anything decent at the Black Swan?" Edward said with sudden interest. "For there is nothing drinkable at the White Swan."

Neate laughed. "Oh, there is, but you have to know how to ask for it. There is all manner of excellent wine that makes its way here from the coast, but the innkeepers prefer to keep it under wraps until they are sure of you. We have had some splendid brandy, have we not, Michael? Oh, for heaven's sake, man, put away that gun. Here, take the key, and let us get out of here before someone spots us."

They made their way back down the tree, Edward first, then Neate, and finally Edgerton, who made an effort to secure the window. They crept through the shrubbery, listening carefully for anyone arriving at or leaving the house, but all seemed quiet.

As they neared the end of the garden, however, Edgerton said in an urgent whisper, "There are people in the lane. Wait here."

Neate pulled Edward down behind a small bush while Edgerton crept forward to see what was happening. He returned in a moment, not bothering to hide or lower his voice.

"Come and see," he said grinning.

As soon as Edward showed himself, a figure shot forward, the skirts of her pelisse flying open. "Edward! Did you find it? Who are all these people?"

"Tess, do you think I told you to stay at the inn for my own amusement? Betty, Harold, take her back to the inn at once. Knock her over her stupid head and carry her if she protests. Ah, Deakin, there you are. You can help, too."

"Edward, I—"

"Back to the inn! This instant!"

"But I want to know what happened!"

"And I shall tell you everything, but later. I must talk to Captain Edgerton first."

"Captain Edgerton! I thought I recognised him. What is he doing here?"

"That, too, I shall explain, but later. Will you please go?"

With a rumble of laughter, Edgerton said, "Lord Tarvin, pray bring Miss Nicholson to the Black Swan. I believe she is entitled to hear our deliberations on this evening's activities."

"Thank you, sir," she said, making him an ironic little curtsy. "At least *someone* treats me as a rational person."

With a sigh, Edward accepted the inevitable, and offered Tess his arm as they made their way the short distance to the Black Swan.

The Black Swan was not very different from any other modest inn, and Captain Edgerton's parlour was no better than their own, for Pickering inns were unused to customers from the highest ranks. They found the captain's wife awaiting them there, together with a blond Scotsman rejoicing in the name of Sandy.

The servants were dispatched to the common room to wait for them, for they absolutely refused to leave Tess unattended and go back to their own inn. Even Deakin stayed, for if Betty and Harold watched over Tess, he seemed to think it his duty to watch over them.

Food and drink were sent for and the table was soon spread with an array of edibles. Edward had eaten little over the last few days, his nerves stretched by anticipation, so now he found he was ravenous and tucked in as though he had not seen food for a month. Tess, meanwhile, was content to sample the rather good wine that was offered and nibble a cake. The rest of the group, having presumably dined well, merely sipped the wine.

As soon as the inn servants had withdrawn, Edward, still chewing, reached into a pocket of his greatcoat and pulled out a large golden bar.

Tess gasped, running her fingers over the smooth surface. "You found it, then! But where is the rest of it?"

"Still in the safe, and Captain Edgerton has the key," Edward said shortly, between mouthfuls. "Seventy-six bars altogether."

"Then I am rich!" she said, with a giggle of excitement. "When will you go and get the rest?" Then, with a frown, she added, "Why does Captain Edgerton have the key?"

"Ask him," Edward said, cutting himself another thick slice of ham.

"I am holding the key to ensure that nothing vanishes unexpectedly from the safe."

"Very well, but when can I have my fortune?"

The captain's face was impassive. "That is an interesting question, Miss Nicholson. Is it indeed *your* fortune? That is the first point to be established."

"Of course it is mine!" she cried. "It was my father's, it is in the house he left me, therefore it is mine."

"Unfortunately, we cannot be sure of that. There is a tenant in the house, so the gold bars may be hers. They may belong to some other person entirely, who is simply using the safe. We cannot say at present. It will be necessary to examine the records left in the office for some indication of ownership — receipts for purchase, for instance. It will be necessary to talk to the widow who rents the property. And it will be necessary to obtain permission from your trustees to do all that, since at present there is a very clear instruction that no one is to enter for any reason."

"But if you tell my trustees, then they will take it all away from me!" she cried fretfully. "It is mine! They must not get hold of it!"

Captain Edgerton frowned. "If it transpires that it is indeed yours, Miss Nicholson, then you will have it."

"No, *they* will have it, and then my husband will have it, not me."

He still looked puzzled, and Tess gave a huff of annoyance. How could she possibly explain?

It was Edward who reached for the gold bar and picked it up, weighing it in his hands.

"This is solid gold," he said. "Just like a gold coin, it has intrinsic value. One could take this to a bank or perhaps to a reputable goldsmith, and exchange it for coins or notes to the value of the gold. Anyone who owns such a thing has no need to ask for money or give reasons or wait for next quarter day. Anyone who owns many such things will be able to live life as he pleases... or as she pleases. A lady with such a fortune in her own hands may marry wherever she wishes, or not at all."

"She might marry a man who is not a gentleman," said Captain Edgerton, getting the point.

"Exactly so."

"I am going to marry Tom Shapman," Tess said.

"You want to marry a murderer?" the captain said.

"Tom did not murder anybody. He is entirely innocent, and once I have my fortune safe in my keeping, I shall get him out of prison and we shall be married. That was the whole purpose of Edward climbing trees and breaking into safes, to get my fortune for me so that I can marry Tom."

"And that would be a disaster for both of you," Edward said sharply. "On the other hand, if these gold bars simply become part of your dowry in the trustees' care, then you will marry Ulric Frith and that would be another kind of disaster."

"What is the objection to Mr Frith?" Mrs Edgerton said.

"He is simple in the head, and only interested in his horses," Edward said. "I have been doing my best to prevent both these disasters, but the good captain and his pistols have sunk my plan."

"Your plan?" Tess said in a small voice. "You were never intending to give me my fortune, then?"

"And have you run straight off and marry Tom Shapman? No, certainly not."

"Then what were you going to do with it? Not hand it over to my trustees, in case I marry Ulric. So what *did* you intend to do with it?"

"Keep hold of it myself, and use that as a way to persuade you to marry me instead."

For a long moment she was silent, then she burst out laughing. "You meant it, then, when you suggested that the other day? You really think I would marry *you?*"

"Better than Shapman or Ulric, anyway."

"Not for me!" she burst out. "I could never marry you!"

"As you please," he said, although again the pain of her words cut him deeply. "Then I had better write to Lord Rennington to tell him what we have found."

"No! You cannot... oh, you are a hateful man!"

"Yes, probably, but I have your best interests at heart, Tess."

She gave a squeak of pure frustration, jumping up from her chair to prowl about the room. "After all this effort, to be denied at the last moment! It was I who told you about the gold bars I saw in my father's safe years ago. It was I who worked out that they were here. It was I who found the safe. I thought you were my friend, Edward. I thought you were on my side."

"I am on your side, if you will only see it."

"No, you are not. You are only on your own side. You want my fortune for yourself, that is all you have ever wanted, and you think to marry me to get your hands on it. Well, I shall never marry you, *never!* If you keep my money from me, then I shall marry Ulric and that will serve you right!"

"Tess, I—"

"Oh, leave me alone. I am going back to the White Swan, and tomorrow I shall go back to Durham to see Ulric. My betrothed, in case you had forgotten. It will suit me very well if I never see you again." Her gaze swept the room. "Any of you."

She stormed from the room, slamming it behind her.

Edward waited until he heard her footsteps disappear into the distance, then rang the bell for a servant. When he appeared, he said, "My valet, Deakin, is in the common room downstairs. Kindly ask him to step up here."

When Deakin arrived, Edward said, "I want you to go to every inn in this place, which should not take long, and tell the head ostler in each that Lord Tarvin will be extremely grateful to him if he does not hire out a post chaise or horses to Miss Nicholson. I will see that he is not the loser by it."

"Yes, my lord," Deakin said, with the glimmer of a smile on his dour countenance. "Shall I obtain some manacles, also, my lord? Or strong rope to tie her up?"

Edward could not help laughing at the image this conjured. "I would not dare! It will be enough if she cannot escape from Pickering."

"I wouldn't put it past her to cadge a lift out of town on a farmer's wagon," the valet said.

"Nor would I, but she will not get far that way. If she truly wants to go, she will doubtless find a way, for she is an enterprising lady, but we will not make it easy for her."

When Deakin had gone, Captain Edgerton placed another bottle on the table and a clean glass. "It seems as if brandy might be in order at this point."

"Ah, good man," Edward said, pouring himself a large measure, and then, on reflection, doubling it.

"Do ye truly want to marry that termagant?" Sandy said.

"For my sins, I do."

The Scotsman spread his hands. "But *why?*"

There was a ripple of laughter around the room.

Captain Edgerton said, "I confess, I wonder the same thing. She would be a troublesome wife indeed, I should think."

"Oh, yes," Edward said easily, for he had long since come to terms with his own feelings on the matter. "She is the most prickly, irritating, contrary, infuriating, unpredictable and downright abominable girl I have ever met. She is also the most fascinating. I must have met her at Corland when she was still a child and forgotten her entirely, but now... now she is very much unforgettable. The instant I met her grown self, I realised she was unlike any woman I had ever known before, and within a week that I wanted to marry her. It is a forlorn hope, I regret to say."

"Yer better off without the lassie, if you ask me," Sandy said.

"But she is indeed fascinating, do you not think?" Neate said. "Have you ever before met a gently born woman who would prefer to marry a woodworker than a baron? And when denied the woodworker, she says she will marry the simple-minded fellow who only loves his horses?"

"I think she does not want to marry at all," Mrs Edgerton said. "The woodworker and the simple man are both people over whom she has great control. The woodworker will have the natural respect of his class for the aristocracy, so she will be able to dominate him easily — at least at first. And the simple fellow who is only interested in horses — she would have the mastery of him, too. But you, Lord Tarvin — that is another matter. A marriage of equals, a marriage of affection, a *real* marriage — that she cannot stomach."

"You say *'at first',*" Edward said. "You think, then, that would change?"

"All men expect to be master in their own house," she said. "So long as there is mutual respect, and husband and wife keep to their own spheres and do not try to interfere with each other too much, all is well, but I do not think Miss Nicholson would be very good at keeping to her own sphere, do you? She would be constantly telling her husband what to do, and a woodworker, however much he loves her, will eventually push back against such interference. And then she would discover all the disadvantages of her situation."

"It would be the same with Ulric Frith," Edward said. "He appears biddable now since he has his horses and no disruptions in his life, but if Tess marries him... I do not know how he would react. This is precisely why I feel Tess would be better off marrying me — or anyone else of her own class, if she prefers."

Captain Edgerton refilled his wine glass, and sipped thoughtfully. "Miss Nicholson's marriage notwithstanding," he said slowly, " it seems to me that we are in an awkward position. Lord Tarvin can claim that he broke into the house on Miss Nicholson's authority, and... well, he is a peer of the realm, no one is going to transport him for it. As for us, we observed a man climbing a tree and entering a house, so we were merely acting as concerned citizens in preventing a theft. I do not like to admit to breaking into a house, but we could argue our way out of that. But what do we do now? Let us assume for simplicity that these gold bars are, in fact, Miss Nicholson's property. We have been cut loose by Lord Rennington, so we have no right to pursue any enquiries regarding the late Mr Nicholson. But equally, we have been given no authority to act for Miss Nicholson's trustees, either, and her marriage is absolutely none of our concern. Yet those gold bars sit in the safe still, and I hold the key. The question is, what should I do with it? I cannot simply put it back, nor can I give it to the widow who lives in the house. Whether I give the key to Miss Nicholson's trustees or to Lord Tarvin or to Miss Nicholson herself, then I am in effect making a decision on how Miss Nicholson may marry, which I have no wish to do. How do I solve this conundrum?"

For a while they argued back and forth, reaching no consensus. Edward worked his way steadily through his glass of brandy, and then refilled it, saying nothing.

After a while, he said, "There is a way to remove Tom Shapman from the board."

"Hang him?" Sandy said.

Edward chuckled, but shook his head. "He is not going to hang. He has an alibi."

His words caused outrage. Captain Edgerton seemed like a mild-mannered man, but now he grew so apoplectic with rage that Edward truly believed that if Shapman were in the room at that moment, he would be in serious danger of being throttled.

It was Neate who calmed down enough to ask the obvious question. "How do you know that, my lord?"

"He told me so when I talked to him in York Gaol. On the night of the murder, he was ten miles away at a place called Gowland's Farm. He walked there the day before, stayed overnight, walked back the next morning. Any number of people will vouch for him."

Edgerton's eyes narrowed. "How convenient! Relations, perhaps?"

"Not yet. He is courting the poultry maid so—"

There was another outbreak of outrage.

"Do you mean to tell me," Edgerton hissed, "do you *seriously* tell me that the fellow is not even planning to marry Miss Nicholson? Even though he asked her father's permission? And confessed to murder to protect her? Sandy, do stop laughing. Does the lady know of this?"

"He said it never seemed quite the right time."

"So he would never have married her, anyway?"

"As to that, she has him so bedazzled that he might well do it if she pestered him enough. She can be remarkably persistent, and look what she has already persuaded him to do. I would not wager sixpence on the chance of him resisting her, if she sets her mind to it."

Sandy was still laughing unstoppably. "I'm goin' hame tae Edinburgh," he said, wiping streaming eyes. "Ye English — yer all mad. Completely mad."

Edward chuckled, too. "I know. It is ridiculous, is it not? But if we can get Shapman out of prison and married to his poultry maid, that will put a stop to that. Better for him, better for his poultry maid and better for Tess, too."

"And better for you, too, my lord," said Neate. "It shortens the odds considerably."

"I think my odds are impossibly long, sadly, and I am not sure I see a way of protecting Ulric from her, which is what I set out to do."

"I cannot see a way either," Edgerton said. "But there is one very bright spot in all this swirl of subterfuge. If Shapman has an alibi for the murder, then we can go back to Lord Rennington and get permission to resume our investigations. If we can persuade him to allow us access to Miss Nicholson's house, and with these businesses of Nicholson's in the town we definitely have enough evidence to look at it, we shall be able to discover the safe and the gold bars legitimately, and there need be no mention of tree climbing or breaking in."

"You will still have the problem of what to do with them," Edward said.

"True, but it gives us a little time. Or rather, it gives you time to get Shapman married off, and to convince Miss Nicholson to marry you instead."

"Good luck with that," Sandy said, grinning at him, and raising his wine glass in salute.

Edward smiled, but he rather thought he would need more than luck. He would need a miracle.

13: Truth And Lies

Tess was pacing round the parlour when Edward returned from the Black Swan. Naturally she was. He would expect nothing less of her.

He smiled to see her, wondering for an instant if her antics would always seem so amusing to him. Would there ever come a time when he sighed, and wished for once for a quiet life? He could not imagine it. He had enjoyed a quiet life for twenty-seven years, and it had been so tedious that sometimes he had wondered if he should provoke a duel with someone just to make life exciting. But then he remembered that being dead or horribly injured or forced to flee the country would be even more tedious, and gave up the idea. He had his own little secret excitement in London, although even that was becoming a trifle dull. But then Tess had come along and all thought of boredom had flown out of the window, never to return.

"Well?" she said, hands on hips.

"Well what?"

"Am I to have my fortune or not?"

"That is not yet decided. It is out of my hands, now. Tess..." He hesitated. Was this the moment to push? Not ideal, perhaps, but he had to try. "Tess, I know you despise me, but if you cannot get hold of your fortune any other way, you would do well to consider my offer. I could ensure that your settlement is generous, and that you have as much freedom as you want. I promise I would not constrain you."

"Promises, promises. Why should I trust you?" But he could see that she was thinking about it, and she had stopped pacing.

"Because I give you my word."

"You promised you would give me my fortune, but you never intended to."

"I made no promise, other than to try to find it, which I did. I am attempting to find the best future for you, Tess, I wish you would believe me."

"Marrying you? What sort of future would that be?"

"One that does not set you at odds with your family or society at large."

She paced again, chewing her lip. "Why do you want to marry me anyway? Why not find yourself a demure little earl's daughter, someone who knows her place and will make you a proper wife?"

"London is full of demure young women, and there is not one of them has half your strength of mind. I want a wife who will challenge me, Tess, not a doormat."

She gave a little grunt of laughter. "Oh, I would challenge you, all right. You may depend upon it. Would it be... a marriage of convenience?"

"No!" he said sharply. Then, more gently, "I am a peer, so I have to have an heir, to displace my wild cousin Tostig. You have met him, so you know how unsuitable he is."

"He only needs something to occupy his mind. Leaving a lively child to the care of a couple of elderly spinsters is bound to lead to trouble. I liked him."

"Oh." That was interesting.

"Why not give him tutors? Send him to school? Eton would knock him into shape," she said.

"Because I never imagined he would ever inherit. I always planned to marry and have sons of my own," he said tersely.

"And now that is to be my duty. How lovely for me."

"A child or two is not too great an imposition for a wife, surely? I would make no other demands on you."

She nodded pensively, and he could see that she was, for perhaps the first time, seriously considering it. Time, perhaps, to press home his advantage.

"At least with me you would have something you would never get from Ulric," he said softly, moving a little closer.

"What is that?" Her voice was low, too, picking up his mood. That was encouraging!

"Gentleness," he said, reaching one hand to her. "Tenderness. Affection." As soft as a butterfly wing, he ran one finger down her smooth cheek. Then, brushing aside the heavy curls that fell onto her forehead, he stroked her eyebrows and then all the way down to her chin.

He took another step nearer, but she made no move to back away from him, standing stock still as he reached now with both hands to cup her face. Her lips parted, and astonishingly she closed her eyes, lifting her face a little in invitation.

Slowly, so slowly, he lowered his face until he was only an inch away from her, his lips hovering close to hers. He could feel her warmth, smell the perfume she used, hear her rapid breath. He was breathing heavily himself. So close! He could almost hear his own heart pounding, the blood rushing in his ears. How was it that no other women had ever stirred him in this way? The cream of London society left him unmoved, but this strange chit of a girl had him all of a quiver. He must have her, he must!

Yet she trembled in his hands like a baby bird. Was this the moment where he scared her away altogether?

But he could not have drawn back at that point, not even if Captain Edgerton had held a pistol to his head. He wanted this so badly he could not help himself.

His lips touched hers, and it was as if a fire shot through him. He wanted nothing so much as to pull her tight into his arms and kiss her until she swooned at his feet, but he dared not. He must not scare her away! It was the lightest, most delicate of kisses, and she returned it in the same gentle way, making no resistance. It was glorious.

When, at last, they separated, she tipped her head to one side. "Why did you do that?"

"Because I wanted to," he said with a spurt of laughter. "And to show you what you will never get from Ulric."

"But I can get kisses from Tom," she said, flashing a smile at him.

Tom Shapman again! When would she forget about him? How could she even think about him, after the moment they had just shared? In sudden anger, he shot back, "You will never marry Tom Shapman!"

"If I get my fortune—"

"No. He is engaged to a poultry maid on Gowland's Farm."

He regretted it as soon as the words were out of his mouth. It was not for him to tell her, after all. Still, he supposed it was not so bad. She had to know some time, after all.

Her eyes were huge in her face. "I do not believe you."

"It is the truth. He has been courting her for three years. That is where he was on the night your father was murdered, so he knows he will never hang. Gowland and his family will vouch for him. You dazzled him, certainly, but he has never loved you, Tess."

The grief on her face tore at his heart. "I do not believe you," she said again, but the words were barely above a whisper, and her eyes filled with tears. "No. It is not true. It *cannot* be true."

Then she turned and fled, tears spilling unchecked down her cheeks.

Nothing was left for Edward to do but to kick the fire irons savagely and curse his stupidity.

***

Tess sent Harold out first thing to secure a post chaise and four, but he returned, dispirited, an hour later.

"No one has anything for hire, Miss Tess," he said glumly.

"Nothing? But there are several vehicles in the coach house here and any number of horses, I have seen them!"

"All reserved, they say. Same at the other inns. Mebbe tomorrow, they say."

"That is ridiculous!"

"I dare say, Miss Tess, but there's nowt we can do about it."

"Let me talk to them. All it needs is a few sweet words and coins in their hands."

But she returned, baffled, in a very few minutes.

Captain Edgerton was waiting for her in the parlour. He rose and bowed with a flourish. "Miss Nicholson! A pleasure to see you again so soon."

"Lord Tarvin is not out of his bed yet."

"It was you I hoped to see. I am going down to York to have a word with your friend Shapman. If he is as innocent as you say, I should like to know why he confessed to a crime he did not commit and see if we can find a way to release him from prison. I wondered if you might like to come with me."

She would see Tom again! He could hear the good news that her fortune was found, even if she had not yet got hold of it, and he could retract his confession or whatever was needed to get him out of prison.

"I should like it very much, but there is no post chaise to be had in the whole town."

"I have my own carriage."

"There are no horses either."

He smiled. "I have already bespoken horses. Mrs Edgerton would accompany us, for propriety."

"Is Lord Tarvin to be invited?"

"Oh, I do not think we need his lordship, do we?" He grinned, and then winked, making her laugh.

"I should have to bring my maid and manservant. My mother insists I take them everywhere."

"Perfect, for we shall have to stay at least one night in York, or perhaps two. After that, I can see that you get to wherever you want to go. May I collect you in... an hour, say?"

She agreed to it happily. She would see Tom again! Then he would be able to tell her that Edward's talk about a poultry maid was nothing but moonshine. Captain Edgerton would get him out of prison and they could go back to Corland together and plan their future. Assuming she could get hold of her own money, that is, but now she would have an opportunity to wheedle that safe key out of Captain Edgerton's care. This unpromising day had just become incomparably better.

She set Betty to packing, and sent Harold to convey a message to Edward's man that she was going to York with Captain Edgerton, and he need not wait in Pickering for her. She would make her own way from now on, and Lord Arrogant Tarvin could do as he pleased.

Captain Edgerton arrived with two carriages, his own neat travelling carriage for himself, his wife and Tess, and a post chaise for Betty and Harold.

Any journey with Captain Edgerton could not be dull, for he made it his business to create lively conversation. If nothing else offered, he would retell some improbable tale of his days in the East India Company Army. Tess assumed these were so embellished that any resemblance to the truth was pure accident, but nevertheless she was well entertained. There seemed to be no object passed by that could not inspire him to begin, "That reminds me of the time when..." and away he would go again. Mrs Edgerton listened with a smile on her face, saying nothing, for doubtless she had heard every tale many times before. It was left to Tess to protest at the implausibility of the stories, but she enjoyed them, nevertheless, and it seemed no time at all before their carriage was clattering over the cobbled streets of York.

With accommodation secured, they left Betty to unpack, while Captain and Mrs Edgerton and Tess, trailed by the ever-faithful Harold, went to York Gaol.

There was less trouble in obtaining a meeting with Tom this time. Whether that was Lord Tarvin's influence and the fistfuls of coins he had pressed on the gaolers, or whether it was Captain Edgerton's military air, just as authoritative in its way as any lord, they were admitted promptly to the bare little room, and Tom was brought there within a few minutes.

He looked better, Tess thought, less tired and dishevelled, and although his wrists still bore the marks, he wore no manacles. He bowed and smiled as if he were happy to see her, but he eyed Captain Edgerton warily. He made another bow as Mrs Edgerton was introduced. Tess was not tempted this time to fly to his arms, or weep all over him. Edward's words still rang in her ears. *'He is engaged to a poultry maid on Gowland's Farm.'* Could it be true? He had never once mentioned Gowland or a poultry maid, and yet she could not imagine that Edward would invent such a tale.

"Tom?" she said hesitantly, as they settled themselves around the table. "How are you?"

"Oh, well enough, Miss Tess. Lord Tarvin must've greased the guards' palms with plenty of silver, for I've a cell to meself now, and decent food, too."

"Tom, I have been to Pickering and found my fortune, just where I thought it was, but..." She threw the captain a fulminating glance. "Captain Edgerton was there, and *he* has charge of it now, so it may go to my trustees after all, and that is no use to me."

"Ah, I'm sorry for that," he said. "I know you'd set your heart on having it in your own hands. Was it as much as you'd thought? The gold bars?"

"Lots of them. Seventy-something — that must be worth quite a lot, I should think."

The captain reached into a pocket and laid the gold bar on the table. "I shall have this valued tomorrow, which will give us a rough idea."

Tom's eyes widened. "By all the saints, that is... well! And you have over seventy of them?"

"Seventy-six," the captain said crisply. "Some larger than this and some smaller, and without weighing them all, we will not know the exact value, but I think it may safely be said that Miss Nicholson is a very wealthy woman. If the gold should turn out to be hers, of course. That has yet to be determined."

"So nothing is settled yet," Tom said, in disappointed tones.

"But at least you can stop this foolish confession business," Tess said. "Tell the captain the truth, Tom — that you made it all up."

"Aye, tis true, sir," he said sheepishly. "I'm right sorry for misleading you but it had to be done."

"Had to be done, did it?" the captain said tersely. "Would you explain to me, Mr Shapman, why you *had to* confess to a murder you did not commit? Why you *had to* shut down my enquiries, thereby leaving the real murderer free? Why you *had to* mislead everyone, including the murdered man's widow, into believing that the terrible time was at an end, and all was resolved? Because I can tell you that I am very tempted to leave you to hang for it anyway. It is no more than you deserve."

"I'm not going to hang," Tom said, with a little laugh. "I have people who'll swear I didn't do it."

"And *I* have a written confession, signed by you and witnessed by the magistrate, that swears you did. What do you think the Assize judge will believe, eh?"

"I'll just tell him that—"

"Tell him? *Tell him?* Do you know what will happen at your trial, Shapman? Your confession will be read out and you will be sentenced to hang, that is what will happen. You will not be allowed to say anything, and even if you were, no one will listen to a self-confessed murderer claiming to be innocent, no matter how many people swear to it."

Tom blanched and Tess cried out in horror. "But he did not kill anyone! English justice will not hang an innocent man, surely?"

Captain Edgerton laughed. "English justice is not always as wise as one would hope, Miss Nicholson. However, even if the courts would condemn an innocent man, I would not, so I will get you out of here if I can. Who are these people who will swear to your innocence?"

"Will Gowland, of Gowland's Farm. About ten miles to the west of Birchall. His four sons will speak for me, too."

Tess exhaled sharply. So it was true! Gowland's Farm... and the poultry maid.

Captain Edgerton produced a notebook. "Names?"

Tom listed them as the captain wrote.

"And you were there at the time of the murder — around four in the morning?"

"I were there all night."

"Relations, are they?"

"No, just friends."

"Do you often stay overnight?"

"Maybe once a month or so. Walk out the afternoon before, spend the evening there, sleep until about six or thereabouts, then walk home."

"Why?"

"I... what?" Tom said, frowning.

"Why do you go there?"

"I just enjoy their company."

"No, the real reason," the captain said.

There was a long silence. Tom looked at the ceiling, he looked at Tess, he looked at his hands — his calloused, work-worn hands, so unused to idleness. He sighed, he twitched at his sleeves, then he looked at the ceiling again.

Tess could not bear it. "I expect he went there to see his poultry maid," she said, her voice quavering.

Tom's head shot round, eyes wide. "You know about Ruby?"

"Oh, is that her name? I know of her existence, yes. I know that you have been *lying* to me all this time, Tom Shapman."

"Nay, I never lied! I may not have mentioned Ruby, that's true, but I told you no lies, Miss Tess."

That was so disingenuous that Tess could not even respond to it. For two years — two whole years — he had led her to believe that he loved her as she loved him. Oh, he had never said as much, and he had always argued that she was too good for him and anything between them was unsuitable, but he had never once suggested by even the smallest hint that he did not feel the same way about her. And that was as good as a lie... or as bad, perhaps.

Grief poured through her like a rainstorm. Her pleasant dream of a fine, handsome husband was gone. She had wanted a real man who worked for a living, unlike the soft and selfish aristocratic men she met, men who cared more about their clothes and their horses than their women. And then she remembered Ulric, who also cared more for his horses than anything else on earth. Did she really want to marry a man like that? Or would she be better off with Edward, who had promised her both her money and her freedom? What a strange, desperate thought.

Captain Edgerton's harsh voice cut through her introspection. "You have still not explained to me *why* you felt it necessary to risk your neck to the noose."

"Why, so Miss Tess could find her fortune, of course. You'd started looking at Pickering and she panicked a bit, thinking you'd find her fortune before she did. She wanted you called off, so… I confessed. Of course, it was all for naught, seemingly, for you found it anyway."

The captain buried his head in his hands. "Sometimes I despair," he muttered. "I thought at the very least you were protecting the real murderer." His head shot up. "And perhaps you are! As a proven liar, Shapman, why should I believe a word you say? I always doubted the reason you gave for killing Mr Nicholson, that he thwarted your marriage to his daughter, but this is also implausible. You must have known… at least, Miss Nicholson must have known that her trustees had forbidden anyone from entering her house in Pickering, so you could not have had any fear for whatever was inside it. No, you are protecting the murderer, that much is plain."

"No!" Tom cried. "I've no idea who killed Mr Nicholson, truly."

"So you say, but again, why should I believe you? And there is only one person who might inspire you to confess to protect her from suspicion."

"No!" he yelled. "Miss Tess never hurt anyone! She'd never kill her own father."

"So says the man who invented a story about murdering someone. No, that will not do, Shapman. If you did not kill the chaplain, then the most likely murderer is Miss Nicholson herself."

Tess stared at him in horror. Everything was going wrong! Her fortune was in Captain Edgerton's hands, Tom would be free but would marry his poultry maid, and now she herself was suspected of murder.

It was so shocking she could not even cry.

14: Leaving Pickering

Michael concentrated on the delicate task of unfastening the many buttons on the back of his wife's gown. He always took his time over it, savouring her nearness, the sweet perfume that hung about her, the soft sound of her breathing. There was the anticipation of the night to come, too, which was by no means the least of his pleasure.

He kissed her neck gently. "I am so glad you got rid of that lady's maid," he murmured.

She chuckled softly. "So am I. She was only there to impress the Corland people. Now that we have been ejected from the castle, I no longer need the air of respectability she gives me. It is far more fun with just the two of us."

"I entirely agree, wife." He slipped his arms around her waist, kissing her shoulder this time.

"Do you truly believe that Tess Nicholson could have murdered her father?"

He returned to the long line of buttons. "Not for a moment. She shared a bed with Lady Olivia, after all, and it seems impossible that she could have crept out of that bed, run downstairs for the axe, back upstairs to kill her father, then got back to her own room unnoticed. She would have been covered in blood, after all. Did she divest herself of a blood-stained nightgown, wash any remaining blood from her hands, put on a clean nightgown and just climb back into bed? Lady Olivia must be a remarkably heavy sleeper not to notice any of that."

"She could have gone somewhere else to change and wash."

"But then there would have been a bowl of blood-stained water to dispose of, as well as the nightgown. No, I cannot see her as a vicious murderer, but this will be a good excuse to get her back to Corland and ply her with questions, as I have long wanted to do."

"You always say that anyone is capable of murder."

"And I believe it, but murder by means of an axe in the middle of the night? That is a certain kind of murderer. Miss Nicholson, I feel, would use a more subtle method."

"Rat poison in his bed-time brandy," she said.

"Something like that, yes. Do you not agree?"

"I do. You have stopped unbuttoning, husband. We shall never get to bed at this rate."

For a while he worked in silence, removing first the gown and then the stays. But when Luce sat down to unroll her stockings, he said fretfully, "What am I to do with these gold bars, Luce? Every option is fraught, it seems to me."

"You must do the right thing, Michael."

"That is all very well, but I have no wish to push Miss Nicholson into marriage just so that she can have control of her own fortune. There is much to be said for a woman controlling her own destiny. If she has her fortune in her own hands, then she can decide her own future. She is a spirited little thing, and I think her family neglected her somewhat. It is hardly surprising that she wants to be free of them, and it seems a pity that she should be thwarted in the end." Luce said nothing, so he went on, "On the other hand, perhaps Lord Tarvin is the right person to deal with all this. He seems to want her, after all, unfathomable as that is, and she would be safe with him. What do you think? Advise me, Luce. Tell me what I should do, for I have not the least idea."

"You should do what is right."

"But what is that? What is the right thing to do?"

"Michael, you know the answer to that, in your heart. Are you ever going to get undressed? Or do you want me to help you?"

"You are just trying to distract me from the problem."

"Is it working?"

"It might be. It just might be."

***

Captain Edgerton was as good as his word, and went off straight after breakfast to find a goldsmith to value the gold bar. Tess was thrilled to discover that it was worth over five hundred pounds.

"Five hundred! So seventy-six of them... that would be..."

"Around forty thousand," the captain said. He seemed subdued this morning, not his usual ebullient self.

"But some of the bars were bigger, so it could be more," she said happily.

"And some were smaller," he said sharply. "Miss Nicholson, what would you do with such a sum if it were yours absolutely?"

She deflated at once. "I had planned to marry Tom. The money would have paid for a decent house for me — servants, a carriage, clothes, that sort of thing. All the necessities of life that Tom's earnings could not provide. He would not need to work, except for special projects. I thought we might start a little school for orphans or... or neglected children. He could teach the boys woodwork and I could teach the girls a bit of sewing. But now... I cannot say. I could buy a small estate somewhere, I suppose."

"As a single woman?" he said.

"Oh, I could find a companion."

"It would still be scandalous," he said. "And have you thought what would happen if it were seen that you have money of your own? Your trustees might well wonder how you came by it."

"You are as bad as Lord Tarvin, trying to dissuade my from pursuing my dreams."

"No," he said evenly. "I am only trying to point out the possible pitfalls."

"You think I should marry Lord Tarvin, I suppose."

He shook his head. "I have no opinion on who you should marry, except that I hope you are as fortunate in your choice as I have been. Shall we walk around the town, ladies? Do a little shopping?"

Tess was never averse to shopping, although she bought little except a book, some new stockings and a small box of bonbons.

As it was the Sabbath the next day, Captain Edgerton and the servants went to the Minster to attend divine service. Tess was too restless for a sermon, so she stayed at the hotel, and Mrs Edgerton kindly kept her company.

Tess quickly abandoned her book, a rather melodramatic novel, while Mrs Edgerton placidly wrote letters and then took up her needlework.

After a while, Mrs Edgerton said, "What is it that upsets you the most, Miss Nicholson — Tom Shapman's treachery or Michael withholding your money?"

"Both!" Tess said with a sudden laugh. "And Lord Tarvin's perfidy, too, and then there is the small matter of Papa's will, not to mention Lord Rennington, who smiles and pats me on the head and tells me that he knows best. Every man thinks he knows best. Ha! Men are slippery, untrustworthy creatures, and I wish I need have nothing to do with them."

Mrs Edgerton laid down her needle. "Yet you are betrothed to this man at Durham."

"Poor Ulric! He deserves better than me. Yet who else can give me what I want?"

"Lord Tarvin?" Mrs Edgerton said archly. "I will not enumerate the advantages that would befall you as the wife of a peer, since you must be aware of them, but as a man, he is not so dire a prospect, is he?"

"He is autocratic, as all men are. When I first became friendly with Ulric, Lord Tarvin came tearing up from London as if his hair was on fire, telling me what I must and must not do. He was thoroughly obnoxious."

"That does sound very bad, but perhaps he has softened since then? He seems very fond of you."

"If he were fond of me, he would do what I want!" she said pettishly, fully aware that she sounded childish. "Or at least, he would be honest about his plans. He wants my fortune for himself, that is the truth of the matter. Besides, like all gentlemen, he is stuffy and dull and boring."

Even as she spoke the words, she recalled his enthusiasm for climbing trees and breaking into houses at night, calling it an adventure. And that kiss! That was not stuffy at all! But she was not minded to be generous towards him.

"You prefer men like Tom Shapman."

"I love Tom," she said in a small voice. "He is part of the ordinary world, where people work for their living instead of idling the days away in mindless amusements, just to pass the time between breakfast and dinner. I love to watch Tom at work, his hands so deft, so certain, his expression so intent. It is hard to explain."

"No, I completely understand. It is physical work that he does, too, and there is an attraction in that, especially if his coat is off. There is something compelling about a man in his shirtsleeves engaged in some physical activity. One would not take pleasure in watching a clerk at work, I think."

"Yes, that is exactly it," Tess said, pleased. "You *do* understand."

"Oh, certainly. That was how I fell in love with my husband, after all. There was a great gathering at my uncle's house to celebrate a betrothal, and Michael was there as a very minor guest, invited mainly to fill the card tables in the evening. He was very amusing, very chivalrous, a little flirtatious and so, so charming. I *liked* him at once. But one day, I found him in the long gallery with a sword he had taken from the wall. This sword was long, almost as long as Michael, but he wielded it with such confidence, and as intently as if he were in battle."

"He loves his sword," Tess said. "I rarely see him without it."

"He loves all such weapons and he has great skill with them, too. There was a little taunting amongst the men, and Michael became embroiled in a fencing match with one of them, with duelling rapiers. He was mesmerising to watch. My goodness, but he looked so... so *distractingly* attractive as he fought."

Tess laughed, and said, "Did he win the fight?"

"Oh, yes. Michael usually wins, although he was slightly injured, so I had the very great pleasure of bandaging his arm. He was obliged to remove it from his shirt sleeve, and oh heavens, the sight of it had me almost overset. Bare skin... and muscles! Michael is very well endowed with muscles. And we talked and talked, and by the end of it I was nine parts in love with him. So I entirely understand the attraction of a man like Tom Shapman, Miss Nicholson. But he is very far from your equal."

"It hardly matters now, does it?" she snapped. "He is going to marry his poultry maid."

"Who is certainly his equal," Mrs Edgerton said crisply. She bent her head to her stitchery again, saying softly, "I do not presume to advise you, Miss Nicholson, for you must be the best judge of the man who would suit you, but you should be aware that if a gentleman, even a stuffy, dull gentleman, is peeled out of his confining garments — the starched cravat, the perfectly fitted coat, the tight waistcoat — he might display to just as much advantage as a working man."

"As Captain Edgerton did?"

"And still does," she said blushing slightly. "I can see that your cousins are not promising specimens in that way, except for Mr Walter Atherton, perhaps. He is a fine figure of a man. But Mr Eustace? Mr Kent? Mr Bertram? I do not think many muscles lurk beneath their shirts. Lord Tarvin, on the other hand—"

"Ah, I knew we should get back to Lord Tarvin sooner or later," Tess said. "You think I should marry him, do you not?"

"I think you should marry someone of your own class, certainly. It does not need to be Lord Tarvin. However, I would disagree with you on one point — I do not think he is interested in your fortune. He has an income of twelve thousand pounds a year, and unless he has an unsuspected liking for the gaming tables or an expensive mistress, he cannot spend even half of it."

"I would like him better if he were a gambler or had a mistress," Tess said. "At least that would make him a degree less dull. But of course he is interested in my fortune! Anyone would be interested in such an amount — fifty thousand pounds in total, including what was in the bank. I suspect he thought I was making it all up about the gold bars. He imagined he would break in and find the safe empty, or full of nothing but dusty old documents, but when he saw all that gold, he decided he would have it for himself."

"Yet he offered to marry you before he knew what was in the safe," Mrs Edgerton said.

"Oh, I see you are determined to paint him as a hero," Tess said crossly.

"And you are determined to keep him as a villain," Mrs Edgerton said, smiling.

She was so good-humoured that Tess could not help smiling too. "If you had seen him at Harfield Priory, all aristocratic hauteur, you would understand that he is a natural villain. I will not admit to a single virtue in him. Hateful man!"

Mrs Edgerton laughed and shook her head. "Have it your own way, my dear."

***

From the window of his bedchamber at the Pickering inn, Edward watched Tess leave for York in the company of Captain Edgerton and his wife. At least he knew she could get up to no mischief under the captain's watchful eye. Then he made the rounds of the ostlers and grooms who had refused to provide transport for Tess, and gave them suitable recompense. After that, there was nothing else for him to do but to pay his shot at the inn and climb once more into his own carriage, with only Deakin's plain features to distract him.

He closed his eyes and allowed Tess's pretty face to fill his mind. He had not thought her at all well-looking the first time he had seen her, her riding habit muddied from hem to neck, her hat drooping and her wet, windswept hair making her look like a vagabond. But clean, dry and in her neat black gown, she was pretty indeed, and especially when she was berating him for some perceived misdeed or other. How her eyes flashed fire at him! He almost laughed out loud at the thought of it.

There was no cause for laughter in the decisive way she had spurned him, however. *'Nothing about you holds any attraction for me.'* So she had said, but later, when she had begun to think about it more seriously, she had seemed to soften towards him. Certainly she had allowed him to kiss her without protest. But then he had spoilt the moment by telling her of Shapman's poultry maid, and now she had gone off with Edgerton to see her woodworker again.

Another man might have been downhearted by these difficulties, but Edward was a patient man. He had arranged the visit to Shapman with Edgerton, after all, as a way of keeping Tess out of the way of his own plans. His first objective was to get Shapman out of prison and safely married to his poultry maid. Then he could begin to devise a way to separate her from Ulric. And then... perhaps then, when her alternatives were gone, she might turn to him.

His journey was pleasantly uneventful. He went first to Corland Castle to deposit Deakin and his luggage, before borrowing a horse and a groom to show him the way to Gowland's Farm. His business there satisfactorily concluded, he had time to call on Sir Hubert Strong, the magistrate. Sir Hubert was a sensible man of middle age, who accepted the news of Shapman's retracted confession with aplomb.

"You have talked to Gowland himself?" Sir Hubert said, handing Edward a glass of Canary.

"And two of his four sons, and the parson, who called that night. His sister is married to one of the sons, so he often spends the evening there."

"They are quite certain of the date?"

"They are. Mrs Gowland keeps a diary."

"Hmm." Sir Hubert frowned. "I do not quite see why the fellow would confess to a crime he did not commit. It seems... irrational. Unless—?"

Edward had no wish to raise the subject of Tess's fortune, so he said only, "Captain Edgerton suspects he is protecting Miss Nicholson from close enquiry."

"I can see that he might think that, but surely *Tess* would not—? I mean, such a quiet little thing, and surely too delicate to wield an axe with such... with such..."

"Quite," Edward said hastily. "One expects the murderer to be a man, naturally, but the captain likes to address all possibilities."

"Well, I suppose I must go out to Gowland's Farm myself and take written statements from them all. Then perhaps we can get Shapman out of York Gaol. It is all most inconvenient. Now Edgerton has to start all over again, I suppose, and his wife's companion is still missing, too, or she was the last I heard. The poor fellow is not having much luck, is he? After all this time, and still no satisfactory conclusion."

"I suspect the real murderer is long gone now," Edward said. "As for York Gaol, I have some business in York, so it would be easy enough for me to collect Shapman for you, and bring him back here, if that would be agreeable to you?"

"That would be most obliging of you, Tarvin, if it would not be too great an imposition."

"Not the least in the world. I should be delighted to spare you the journey. If, when you have talked to the Gowlands, you are satisfied with the veracity of their assertions, then you need only write the appropriate letters of authority, and it would be my pleasure to see it done."

He returned to Corland Castle well satisfied with his progress. The butler greeted him with relief.

"We were beginning to wonder if we should send out a search party, my lord," he said. "You have just time to change before dinner. Allow me to show you to your room." As they proceeded up the stairs, he went on, "There were some letters for you, which your man is looking after. Also a person called, asking to see you."

"A person, Simpson? What sort of person?"

"A Mr Ramsbottom, my lord."

"I am sure I know of no one by that name."

"He wouldn't write a note or send a letter. He wished to speak to you in person, but he wouldn't say whether it was a business or personal matter, only that it must be conveyed to you in person. He was informed that you had gone on to York."

"How very mysterious!" Edward said, amused. "I did not come across him in York, so I dare say he has given up and gone home. Wherever home might be."

Dinner was a fraught affair, as everyone plied Edward with questions about Tess and her sudden betrothal, and then, when they discovered it, the news about Shapman. On both subjects there was much that he could not say. Nothing, for instance, about climbing trees or forcing open windows or opening safes. Nothing at all about the contents of such safes. Nothing about Shapman confessing to give Tess time to find her fortune. Not too much about Ulric, either, except his status as a gentleman, although something of his nature was already known.

"Lady Tarvin says he is not right in the head," Olivia said pertly, as they sat in the drawing room with their tea after dinner. "I hope that is not true, for Tess's sake."

"Ulric is perhaps not the cleverest of men, it is true," Edward said cautiously. "It is my opinion that he would be happiest not marrying at all, but I cannot prevent him from doing so if he wishes."

"Is he a suitable husband for my daughter, Lord Tarvin?" Lady Alice said. "She can be a trifle wayward at times, and I would prefer her to marry a man of strong character who can rein in her little quirks."

"I cannot claim to know your daughter well, Lady Alice, but I have known Ulric for a great many years, and I believe they would be very ill-suited. Ulric devotes all his time to his horses. People are of less interest to him, and if he were married, his wife would be of small consequence to him. I am doing what I can to prevent the match, for both their sakes, but it may be that I cannot prevent it, in the end."

"We must all hope you are successful," Lady Alice said. "She cannot marry him until she is of age, for I shall not give my permission. She has chosen this man purely to comply with the terms of her father's will, I doubt not. Mr Frith is a gentleman, and therefore Tess's trustees must release her inheritance to him if he becomes her husband, but it sounds as if she will be at liberty to do as she pleases thereafter, and that is not healthy for any woman. I always hoped she would make a marriage of affection, Lord Tarvin. I have been so fortunate as to experience that felicity, and I very much wished that for Tess, too. For that reason I never encouraged her to go to town for the season. I am told she is very pretty, so undoubtedly she could make a good society match, but I do not think that would satisfy her. A good, kind man who loves her — that is the ideal."

"And perhaps she may yet make such a match," he said evenly. "I hope so, certainly."

"Ah." She turned more fully to face him, her sightless eyes fixed on his nose. "I share your hope, then, Lord Tarvin."

She turned the subject after that, but he felt that however blind her eyes might be, Lady Alice saw into his heart with unnerving accuracy.

Later, in his room, he found a neat pile of letters awaiting him. Some had been forwarded from London to Harfield Priory and then on to Corland. He recognised the strong hand of Sir Ernest Peterson.

'Tarvin, You have been so good in the past as to send one of your experienced grooms to Myercroft and take on our new recruits to be trained up at Harfield. May I ask you in your kindness to do so again? We have a lad of twelve just started in the stables, very keen but with no experience of horses at all. You know what Ulric is like! He is a dear boy, but he has no patience with any degree of incompetence, and I should like to remove the young groom from Myercroft until he knows what he is doing. Six months under your head groom would teach him the basics and give Ulric no cause to shout at him. However, if it should be inconvenient, I shall quite understand and shall find some other use for the boy. Yours respectfully, Ernest Peterson, Bart.'

Edward sat down at once to pen his reply.

'Peterson, It would be my pleasure to oblige you in the matter of the groom. It shall be done as soon as I can manage it. I am currently staying at Corland Castle, home of the Earl of Rennington, and also the home of Miss Nicholson, Ulric's betrothed.'

At this point, he was struck with a sudden thought. This might be just the opportunity he needed. He finished his reply with a smile on his face.

'I feel it would be salutary for the betrothed couple to get to know each other a little better, and for the lady to see her future home. Might I suggest that you issue an invitation to her to visit you at Myercroft before too long? Ulric may make one of his periodic stays with you, and if you extend the invitation to me also, then we may begin to make plans for the future. It would, I feel, be an interesting visit and much good may come of it. Yours, Tarvin.'

The final letter was from his mother, and it was, for once, brief.

'Edward, We have had a man called Ramsbottom here wishing to speak to you. Kindly tell your acquaintance to make an appointment before descending upon us, or better still, get rid of him. We are a respectable household. Your affectionate Mother.'

Edward laughed out loud. Who was this Ramsbottom fellow?

15: A Journey With The Edgertons

Tess had hoped that Captain Edgerton would help her to return to Durham and Ulric, but he had other plans.

"Since you are currently at the top of my list of potential suspects," he said, "I should like you to return to Corland with me. I need to talk to the magistrate about releasing Mr Shapman, and I shall hope to persuade Lord Rennington to allow me to continue my enquiries, in which case I shall want to talk to both you and Shapman at some length."

"What about Peachy?" Mrs Edgerton said softly.

The captain shook his head sorrowfully. "I cannot myself undertake to continue the search for Miss Peach. My duty is to Lord Rennington and the murder of Mr Nicholson. However, I shall leave Sandy and James in Pickering — and you, if you wish it."

"I had sooner be with you," she said quietly, and the two exchanged a look that Tess could interpret all too well.

Oh, to be so well loved that it was imperative to stay together! For a brief moment she envied them that, and grief for the loss of Tom gnawed inside her like a physical pain. But that would never be her fate now, so there was no point in repining. Her fortune — that was the door to her future freedom, and another journey with Captain Edgerton would be an opportunity to wheedle the safe key out of his pocket and into her reticule.

She found that the captain was too wily to be wheedled out of anything. Whenever she raised the issue of the gold bars and whether perhaps her property ought to be in her own hands, he would merely say, "We shall see," and deftly change the subject. Only one small piece of information did she coax out of him. When she asked how he had just happened to follow Edward up the tree and into the office where the safe was held, he laughed and said, "We were watching him. We discovered who you were very quickly — you really should teach your servants to watch their mouths. Since you were using false names, we knew you were up to something, so we watched you both. There is no mystery about it."

On the other hand, he was adept at drawing information from Tess.

"Have you no brothers or sisters, Miss Nicholson?" he said, with his ready smile.

"No, none. Plenty of cousins, however."

"Mrs Edgerton is in the same case," he said. "No brothers or sisters but vast numbers of cousins. And you have grown up with yours. They have been there all your life. You shared the schoolroom with the three girls, I expect."

"That is true. Josie and Izzy were a little older and Olivia is two years younger than I am. We did everything together, just as sisters do, but... it gradually dawned on me that I was different from them."

"In character... or circumstance?" the captain said.

"Both, I suppose, but mostly it was that our destinies were very different. They were to be given grand come-outs in London, with no expense spared, and would marry into the peerage, and I... well, I was the chaplain's daughter. No grand come-out for me."

"Did you want one?" he said gently.

"Heavens, no! All that fuss, and eyeing up every man as a potential husband, and knowing that he would be looking at me in the same light. How horrid *that* would be! That and having to be chaperoned every moment."

"You do not like being chaperoned, Miss Nicholson? Yet you have your maid and a manservant always with you."

She chuckled. "Oh, yes! My faithful Betty and Harold! Mama thinks they give me consequence and protect me from pickpockets, and perhaps they do. They are also supposed to tell her what schemes I dream up, and perhaps they do that, too. But their great advantage to me is that they allow me to go wherever I want, and do what I want. At first, I was very cross about Harold in particular. Why should I need a manservant dogging my footsteps everywhere? But I soon saw how useful he is, organising the hire of post chaises or buying tickets for the stage coach."

"Do you often travel by stage coach?"

"Not often. Only when I want to be an ordinary person and not the niece of an earl."

He laughed, and said, "What fun! Being an ordinary person myself, I have travelled on stage coaches more times than I care to remember, and mail coaches, too, and as a consequence I am always deeply grateful for the comfort of a private carriage."

"That is true, but one meets with such interesting people on a public vehicle. All my best ideas come from passengers on public coaches."

"Such as?"

"The idea of being a housemaid. That was how Betty and I insinuated ourselves into Apstead House."

The captain sat forward so suddenly that he almost fell off the seat. "You were *inside* the house? As a housemaid?"

"Well, yes. How else do you think Lord Tarvin knew where the gold bars were hidden?"

"I just assumed you knew... or your father had told you. Tell me about the house. Tell me *everything*, Miss Nicholson."

Tess could see no reason not to comply. She told him all about her stay there, and if she skated over any details, he asked questions until he knew everything. He was interested in the recent improvement in finances, and the gentlemen callers in the evenings, but when she reached the episode of Miss Rochester, the captain was astonished.

"It was Eustace Atherton's carriage? Are you quite sure?"

"Positive. I recognised the coachman, and the footmen's livery."

"Footmen on the back? How many?"

"Two, and two coachmen, and four horses. Eustace was doing her proud — no expense spared. He is not noted as being free with the readies, so it must be quite a romance."

The captain rubbed his nose thoughtfully. "As to that... I do not think he is courting Miss Rochester."

"Then why else send his carriage for her?"

He exchanged a glance with his wife. "We have heard, Miss Nicholson, that the ladies of Apstead House are... Luce, how would you describe them?"

"They are not of the first respectability," she said crisply. "Not the sort of female that any gentleman would marry."

"Oh, like opera dancers," Tess said.

They both burst out laughing. "What does an innocent young lady like you know about opera dancers?" the captain said.

"Only that they are not at all respectable. Are they like mistresses? Grandfather had an opera dancer in London, once, and a mistress in Yorkshire, and Walter had a mistress, too, but the earl and countess put a stop to it."

The captain laughed even more, but his wife frowned. "I cannot approve of anyone telling you about such things. It is most improper."

"No one told me," Tess said, with a wry smile, "but when one is small and insignificant and likes to hide away behind the curtains or sofas with a book... well, one hears things."

The captain chuckled. "You are a lady after my own heart, Miss Nicholson."

"So Miss Rochester is... a mistress? Or an opera dancer?"

"Well... something of the sort," the captain said, waving an arm vaguely. "Most likely all the young ladies in that house are of that type, and Mrs Mayberry manages them, but on no account should you mention that to anyone, and especially the connection to Mr Eustace. What tricks he plays are entirely his own affair."

"Not a word shall pass my lips," she said, but she chuckled all the same. What a delicious titbit of information to discover about Eustace! She had never particularly liked him, for he had teased her unmercifully when she was a child, but she could respect a man who had his own little secrets.

***

Nothing had changed at Corland Castle, Tess speedily discovered. The Dowager Countess lingered on, asleep for most of the day, and not fully aware even when she was awake. Olivia was still weepily miserable. The earl was still oddly distracted. Kent was still annoyingly cheerful. And her mother was as cool and composed as ever. Apart from the occasion when she had found her husband hacked to death in the marital bed, Tess could not remember her ever showing the least emotion. Sometimes she wondered if she was devoid of the capacity for it, but then she remembered the way her voice had softened when she spoke to her husband, just as his had. But neither of them had ever spoken to Tess that way.

"So you are back, are you?" Lady Alice said, when Tess first arrived. She was sitting in the library while Mr Alfred Strong read extracts from the newspaper to her.

"I am back, Mama, for a while. Captain Edgerton wished me to return. There have been developments in the matter of the murder."

"We heard all about the *developments*," she said, her mouth making a moue of distaste.

"We thought that business was all settled," Mr Strong said. He was a neighbour, a genial man of about Lady Alice's age. He held a government position at the Treasury, but with Parliament not currently sitting, he lingered in the north. "Now the fellow has retracted his confession, and we still have not the least idea who might have killed poor Nicholson."

"So you know of it already?" Tess said, surprised.

"Lord Tarvin told us," Lady Alice said.

"Oh, him! He is here, then."

"He was at Corland, but I believe he left this morning. He has been very helpful," Mr Strong said. "He went straight to my brother to inform him, as magistrate, of the new information, and he has also talked to these people who say Shapman was with them on the night of the murder."

"Gowland's Farm," she said in disgust.

"That is the place. A good ten miles from here, and Shapman did not leave there until about six and then walked home. He could not have reached Birchall before eight at the earliest."

"It was a little after that," Tess said. "I remember now, I had gone to see him very early, well before breakfast, to tell him that Papa was dead, but Tom was not in his workshop. He came in with a bag a little while later and would not say where he had been. It must have been half past eight, at least."

"There you are, then," Mr Strong said, triumphantly. "You have verified the truth of it yourself."

"Tess, whatever were you about, going to see this man in his home?" Lady Alice said sharply. "I thought you had given up all thought of that foolish business. An earl's niece cannot marry a common labourer."

"He is a woodworker, Mama," Tess said indignantly, "not a common labourer — a cabinet maker with his own business. You need not worry about me marrying him, for he is betrothed to a poultry maid at Gowland's Farm, but he is still my friend. He is the only *true* friend I have in the world, for he was prepared to hang to protect me, and there is not one gentleman who would even have thought of it. Tom is a hero."

"I would not call making a false confession of murder especially heroic," Lady Alice said. "Time has been lost that could have been employed in pursuing the real murderer."

"His family must have been distressed by it, too," Mr Strong said. "Imagine the feelings of his mother and father! How grievously they must have suffered."

"That is hardly likely," Tess said. "They must have known, as I did, that he could not have done such a thing."

"Yet he was still in York Gaol awaiting a judge to condemn him to be hanged," Mr Strong said sharply. "Indeed, there remains a possibility that my brother may not be able to get him off. A confession is a powerful matter, Miss Nicholson, not lightly to be set aside. A man says one thing and then he says another, and who is to say which is the true version of events?"

"But he was not even there! Mr Gowland and his family will vouch for him."

"If he is betrothed to the poultry maid at the farm, they are hardly impartial witnesses."

"But I saw him return that morning."

"From somewhere, and carrying a bag, but you cannot know where he had been and you are by no means impartial yourself," Mr Strong said.

Tess felt as if she stood on a sandbar in the midst of a fast-rushing stream, with the water rising all around her. She had been so happy that Tom was to be freed! Angry and hurt that he preferred a poultry maid to her, but still, he would be released and his life would return to normal.

Yet now there was no certainty at all! His retraction might not be believed, the testimony of the Gowlands might be set aside, and everyone might say, *'He confessed, so let him hang.'* And it would save the bother of trying to find the elusive real murderer.

But Mr Strong, seeing her distress, reached forward and patted her hand. "Not to worry, Miss Nicholson. Happily for Shapman, the parson was also at Gowland's Farm that evening until close to midnight, and his word must carry weight. Since no one imagines that anyone could walk over those hills at night, your friend must be released from suspicion."

He smiled at her and she thanked him for the thought, but she had a vague memory that the moon was close to full that night. Surely by moonlight the track would be clear to see? And if Tom could walk the distance in two and a half hours, he had time to walk to Corland, kill her father and then walk back to Gowland's Farm afterwards.

"Tell me a little about this Ulric Frith that you propose to marry," Lady Alice said.

For once, Tess was happy to talk about Ulric. Anything to turn the conversation away from Tom and the murder and the nagging fear that he might have murdered her father after all.

***

Captain Edgerton did not look forward to explaining Shapman's retraction of his confession to the earl. At least, he had to attempt an explanation. Lord Rennington had been cross that Michael had failed to identify Shapman as the murderer and it had only been known when he confessed. He was even more cross that the confession might not even be true.

"How can this happen? How could you not know?" he spluttered. "You accepted his word without a second thought?"

"Not at all, my lord," Michael said. "I made him explain every detail of it at great length, but his story was perfectly consistent with the facts."

"Yet he just made it all up? Every word?"

"So he says, my lord. He claims to have an alibi, which needs to be verified."

"Yes, yes, so Tarvin said, and Strong has been looking into it, but why were *you* not doing so?"

"You dispensed with my services, if you recall, my lord," Michael said mildly. "If you would like to re-engage me, then—"

"Of course, of course, but so much time has been lost. Do you really believe you can find the murderer after so long? Three months, Edgerton! Three months since my poor brother-in-law was slaughtered in his bed, and do you have any more idea of the perpetrator's identity now than you did when you arrived?"

That was not a question Michael wished to address, for the answer could not possibly reflect well on him. However, he gamely said, "I have a few matters on which to make further enquiries, my lord. The illegitimate son, for instance. I did not pursue that path after Shapman's confession. Then there are Mr Nicholson's Pickering businesses, and his house there — I should very much like to have a look round inside. I also hope to talk at greater length to Shapman, and to Miss Nicholson, for I feel certain they can shed more light on matters."

"Talk to Shapman and my niece? Well, I cannot see why. Shapman had nothing to do with it, seemingly, and my niece is an innocent girl, not to be dragged into this affair."

"I only wish to talk to her, my lord. It may be that she has some information about her father — quite unwittingly, of course, not realising it might be significant — that would help shed light on events."

"You have already talked to her, I recall."

"Indeed, but that was before I knew of her friendship with Tom Shapman and she has been away from home since then. His confession put her in a curious position, and it would relieve my mind to determine that she knows nothing about the murder, and is completely innocent of any involvement."

This was the right note to strike, for the earl nodded sagely. "Ah yes, determine her complete innocence. That would be acceptable, but the house... I cannot see the need to enter the house. The respectable widow who lives there is entitled not to be importuned and Nicholson was never there, you know. Everything was done through the attorneys."

Michael made no attempt to explain that the respectable widow ran a not at all respectable brothel, so instead he said, "It is a question of leaving no stone unturned, of settling once and for all that the house is not connected in any way with the murder. Then, you see, we may restrict our investigations to more promising lines of enquiry."

"Yes, yes. Very well then, but you must ensure that the widow is not unduly inconvenienced by it all. The minimum of disruption, mark you, Edgerton, the very minimum. You have turned Corland upside down, and one understands that and makes allowances, but a respectable widow... one would not wish to unsettle the poor lady. Hmm, so I suppose we shall have all your associates here again, shall we? That Scotsman who flirted so outrageously with Olivia, for instance."

"My wife is with me, my lord, and Mr Willerton-Forbes is still here, I believe, looking into some legal and financial affairs on your behalf. Mr Alexander has remained behind at Pickering to continue the search for Miss Peach."

"Miss Peach?"

"My wife's companion, my lord. An inoffensive lady of middle years. She vanished about four weeks ago."

"Ah, I remember now. A quiet creature, as I recall. Well, I hope you find her soon, Edgerton. I shall see you at dinner, no doubt."

Thus dismissed, Michael made his way upstairs to the old school room, where his friend was hard at work.

"Hail, Pettigrew, and well met!"

"Michael! Where have you been? Mrs Edgerton looked in an hour ago, at least."

"I have been with the earl, who offered me not a drop to drink and made me stand for the entire time," Michael said, pulling a wry face. "But he did not throw me out, and he has agreed to let us go into the Pickering house."

"At last!" Pettigrew said, pouring glasses of Madeira for them both. "Although I am not sure what good it will do. Even if it is a bawdy-house, I cannot see how that might be connected to the murder."

"Oh, it is definitely a bawdy-house, although with only four light-skirts it must be rather exclusive. One of them was collected in Mr Eustace Atherton's carriage, replete with four horses, two coachmen and two footmen on the back."

"No!" Pettigrew's face lit up with amusement. "How diverting! But we know he is that way inclined, since he had a woman with him on the night of the murder. But is it certain?"

"Quite certain. I did not see it myself, but I have it on very good authority. Also, there is more money about the place than there used to be, so I suspect the charming Mr Nicholson was taking all the profits."

"Oh, very likely," Pettigrew said. "That would be the purpose of the chandlery and the ironmongery Nicholson owned, to take in the immoral earnings and turn them respectable."

"Of course. How ingenious. But what of your own investigations?" Michael said. "Are the earl's affairs coming into sharper focus?"

Pettigrew sighed. "Yes and no. Yes, in that I now have a much clearer idea of how deep Mr Nicholson dipped into the late earl's pockets, thanks to Lord Farramont. He suggested that the tenant farmers would know to the penny how much rent they paid, and he was quite correct in his advice. Nicholson recorded lower amounts and pocketed the difference. But no, in that it is such a large amount of money that it should have turned up by now."

"How much?"

"Altogether? Taking into account his spurious charitable activities, and his wife's jewellery, replaced with paste and the gems sold, it would be above forty thousand pounds, and perhaps as much as fifty. Yet his bank account held only ten thousand with another thousand in the safe here. That leaves perhaps forty thousand pounds unaccounted for, and where can such a sum be hidden?"

Michael laughed and said smugly, "I might have an idea about that."

By the time he had told Pettigrew the whole story of the safe with the gold bars, and how Tess Nicholson had masqueraded as a housemaid to discover them, the Madeira decanter was seriously depleted.

"What on earth am I to do about these gold bars, my friend?" Michael said. "Hand them over to Miss Nicholson and pretend I never saw them? Give them to Lord Tarvin to deal with? Or tell the earl about them, whereupon they are whisked into Nicholson's estate, giving the trustees full control over them, and Miss Nicholson must marry to have any access to her own money?"

"It is worse than that, Michael," Pettigrew said sadly. "The sainted chaplain stole that money systematically over many years. By rights, it belongs to those from whom it was stolen — the earl, principally, Lady Alice, for the jewels, and the generous benefactors to Nicholson's non-existent charities. If that were to be done, then there might very well be nothing left for Miss Nicholson at all."

"She would be penniless!" Michael said, appalled. "That is dreadful! Yet... it must be so, must it not? Luce told me I must do what is right, and now I understand what she meant. Poor Tess! She has lost the man she loved and now she has lost her fortune, too. But at least she need not be told just yet. When I go back to Pickering and get into that house, I will discover the safe and the gold bars, as if for the first time, and that will be the time to tell the earl of their existence. Until then, let the poor girl keep her dreams."

16: An Axe And An Urn

Tess was surprised to find herself disappointed that Edward had left already. Why had he come all the way to Corland, which was not on the way to or from anywhere, only to leave again almost at once? He seemed to have told everyone about Tom already, so perhaps that was his sole purpose, and now he had gone home again. She felt oddly bereft.

She was one of the last to enter the drawing room before dinner, sidling into an unexpectedly full and noisy room.

"Tess! Dear girl, where have you been all this time?" The familiar face of the earl's brother loomed out of the crowd.

"Oh, here and there, Uncle George."

"And betrothed, I hear," he said, with an arch look. "I wish you joy, my dear."

"Thank you, uncle, but it will be a lengthy engagement, I fear, since Mama will not give her permission."

"You must bring your young man to meet us all. I am sure once your mama is assured that you have chosen wisely, she will not withhold her consent. But my goodness, what a summer it has been for betrothals. Walter is to marry Winnie Strong — did you know that? And Bertram is engaged to Bea Franklyn."

"Bertram? Bea Franklyn? And Walter and Winnie? No, I did not know that! I am all astonishment, uncle."

"So were we, to be frank," he said in a lowered voice. "You young people, you seem to make up your minds to it all in a rush."

"I thought you and Aunt Jane had a very quick courtship," Tess said. "Five weeks, was it not?"

He looked a trifle abashed. "Oh well... yes, that is true. Sometimes, one knows one's own mind. So tell me about this young man of yours — Mr Frith, is it not? He has an estate near Durham, I understand?"

Tess said what she could about Ulric, but when Uncle George asked her what in particular attracted her to him, she was hard pressed to answer. The truth — that he was a gentleman, but one who was so uninterested in her that she could do as she pleased — was not an idea she wished to put into words. Uncle George was sweet to pretend that this was a normal betrothal based on mutual affection, but he must know perfectly well how things stood.

Happily, Aunt Jane soon interrupted them to introduce a friend of hers who was staying for a while, a Miss Hannah Snellgrove, so Uncle George drifted away, leaving the three ladies to make laboured conversation. Tess was not much minded for the usual inane chatter of the drawing room when her head was so full of her own problems, and Miss Snellgrove seemed not to have much conversation, either. Fortunately, Aunt Jane was perfectly capable of talking for three, and moreover soon took her friend away to meet the Edgertons, who could at least be relied upon to dredge up suitable drawing room chatter.

Tess retreated to a poorly-lit corner where she could skulk and not be called upon to talk. If she had had Edward there... but he was gone, and there was no one else who knew all her secrets and to whom she could unburden herself. She watched the milling crowd in the drawing room in a detached way, almost as if she were the audience watching a play on the stage. She had nothing in common with these people. Tom, with his shy smile and his clever hands turning plain wood into beautiful objects, that was where her heart lay. And Edward, too, understood her. At least he could give her a tolerable game of chess. But her own kin? No. Almost she felt she must be a changeling, she was so different from them.

At last they went through to the dining room, Miss Snellgrove on Uncle Charles' arm, as the guest of honour. The earl looked at the lady rather strangely, Tess thought, almost as if... no, surely not. Lord Rennington was long married, and would not be so crass as to display open admiration for another woman, would he? It was true that Miss Snellgrove was rather pretty, and many men would be delighted to strike up a flirtation with her, but not the earl, she would have said.

But when they were all seated, Tess found herself next to her cousin Kent, who grinned and said, "Father seems to like this one better than the others."

"You refer to Miss Snellgrove? What others?"

"Aunt Jane has been inviting likely candidates for weeks now, but this is the first really pretty one. Oh, did you not know? Candidates to be the next Countess of Rennington."

"But what about Aunt Caroline?" Tess squeaked.

"It was her idea," Kent said. "Now that we know that your perfidious father was never ordained and Father's marriage was never legal, he needs to get more sons. Legal ones, that is. Mother is too old for that, so she has stepped aside to allow him to choose a second wife. This one might just catch his fancy, do you not think?"

Tess was too shocked to answer. Poor Aunt Caroline! Cast aside after thirty years of marriage, to be replaced by someone younger, able to bear sons. She had said nothing about it when Tess had seen her at Harfield.

For a while, everyone concentrated on the food, but once the soup was removed with a shoulder of lamb and ribs of beef, and all the dishes had been passed around, conversation began again. Tess noticed Miss Snellgrove talking animatedly to the earl, while he said very little, shaking his head occasionally.

"What do you suppose they are talking about?" she whispered to Kent. "Whatever it is, she seems more enthusiastic about the subject than Uncle Charles."

Kent grinned, and called the butler over. "What topic is it that has so animated Miss Snellgrove, Simpson?"

"Essays on morality, sir," Simpson said in an undertone.

Tess felt her eyebrows rise. "Can it be that the very pretty Miss Snellgrove is a bluestocking?"

Kent laughed. "How amusing! Do keep an eye on Father. Another five minutes of philosophising on morality and his eyes will glaze over. So what should we talk about, cousin? You will not have much to say about your betrothed, I dare say, and although I should like to know where you were when you were supposed to be in Helmsley, I doubt you will tell me."

"Are you quite sure I was *not* at Helmsley? When you called at my friend's house, I might have been indisposed or out at the modiste's."

He lowered his voice conspiratorially. "Any half-trained servant knows how to deal with an enquiry for a young lady who is indisposed or out shopping. I should have been told very calmly that Miss Nicholson was not at home. But instead, the whole house was thrown into a spin, so I knew at once that you had gone scampering off on one of your mad starts. Miss Bullock is stout of heart, and would not tell me where you truly were, although she went the colour of beetroot when I mentioned Pickering. Where your house is, is it not so, cousin? But you need not worry, I have told no one your little secret. Whatever mischief you were up to, you need not fear that I would betray you."

On her other side, Eustace leaned towards her. "But I might, now that I too know your little secret, cousin." He grinned wolfishly.

"I had rather you did not mention Pickering. After all, most of us have secrets we would rather not have revealed, is it not so, cousin?" She smiled at Eustace benignly, and was pleased to see the tiniest frown mar his forehead. That would give him something to think about! She could reveal a thing or two about a certain young lady from a certain house in Pickering, if she chose.

Eustace recovered quickly. "I am only teasing you, cousin. Family secrets stay within the family, is it not so, Kent? I value loyalty above all things."

Kent looked uncomfortable, and turned away to attend to Emily Atherton on his other side, but Eustace laughed and reached for a dish. "Some more fritters, cousin? They are quite delicious, are they not? Or may I pass something else to you?"

"The fish, if you please," she said.

As he attended to her request, she glanced at the earl at the foot of the table. Miss Snellgrove was still talking with great enthusiasm, one hand waving a piece of bread for emphasis. The earl's eyes had glazed over.

It was not until the ladies withdrew, leaving the gentlemen to their port, that the true horror of Miss Snellgrove became apparent. Several of the ladies brought out embroidery to work on, but when Penelope Atherton admired her sister's work and said, "Is it not exquisite, Miss Snellgrove? Emily has such a talent for delicate stitchery, do you not agree?" she sniffed disdainfully.

"It is well done, I suppose, although I have no time for such a pointless occupation. Practical needlework — that I concede is necessary, but ornamental work serves no purpose, and ruins a female's eyesight for no good reason."

"You think, then, that a woman should confine her needlework to the mending of shifts and the darning of stockings?" Penelope said.

"If she can find no better occupation, yes."

Mrs Edgerton looked up with a gentle smile. "What would you regard as a better occupation, Miss Snellgrove?"

"Why reading, of course."

"There are journals on the table over there," Olivia put in helpfully. "May I fetch one for you?"

"Journals! Repositories of frivolity and trivia, to corrupt the mind," she said scornfully.

"Perhaps we might have a little music," Lady Alice said quickly. "Miss Snellgrove, would you care to—?"

"I do not play! Music can uplift the spirits, if played by a true proficient, but schoolgirl performances are a dull affair, to be endured rather than enjoyed. I have never wanted to add myself to the number of those who play but a little, and that little not well."

"I am not so nice in my requirements," Lady Alice said with asperity. "We have a number of ladies here whose performances give me great pleasure. Mrs Edgerton, would you oblige the company? We have so missed your spirited playing. And Miss Snellgrove, perhaps you may care to find a book to read in the library. We have a number of volumes suitable for persons of a serious disposition, not at all frivolous. Olivia will show you the way."

As soon as they had left, Aunt Jane burst out, "I am so sorry, everyone! What a crashing bore she is. I should never have inflicted her on you if I had known. It is no wonder she is still a spinster at her age. She would drive any rational man to distraction."

"She would certainly drive Charles to distraction," Lady Alice said. "He is no intellectual, that much is certain. He is an outdoors sort of man, happy to ride to hounds, to shoot and fish, to play cricket on the lawn with the children. He never picks up a book beyond the Bible or the Book of Common Prayer."

"Riding..." Aunt Jane said. "Yes, that gives me an idea."

Just then, Mrs Edgerton began to play a lively tune, and conversation lapsed. Tess took the opportunity to creep out of the room and scurry away. She would find her favourite hiding place where she could be peaceful, free of foolish chatter, and wonder how soon Tom would be released from prison.

***

For two whole days, Tess sat in the former schoolroom with Captain Edgerton, while Mrs Edgerton placidly sewed or read a book as chaperon. The lawyer, Mr Willerton-Forbes was there occasionally, too, and Harold stood guard outside the door, ready to rush in the instant she summoned him. On a shelf sat the axe, a disheartening reminder of their purpose.

The captain wanted to know every little detail that Tess could remember about her father — who his friends were, where he went, even trivia like where he got his clothes and his food preferences.

"So long as there was a decent claret on the table, he never minded what he ate," she said.

"I know someone like that," Mrs Edgerton said archly, with a glance at her husband.

"There is nothing wrong with an appreciation of good wine," said Mr Willerton-Forbes, and they all laughed, even Tess.

By the second day, she found herself drawn almost against her will into a kind of camaraderie with the captain and his friends. He said nothing to distress her, made no accusations against her and was even generous towards Tom, and it was clear that his only objective was to find her father's murderer.

Since he already knew a great deal about the Pickering house, she found herself telling him everything she knew about the gold bars, explaining how she used to sneak into her father's study when he was away from home and root around in his papers. It was thus that she discovered the safe, and without much difficulty the key, and saw the pile of gold bars inside.

"How many, would you say?" the captain said, lifting his pencil from the notebook where he was recording interesting details.

"Not so many as at Pickering, I should say, although I did not count them."

"So he continued to add to his collection after that point. How did you think he acquired such a treasure trove?"

"Not from saving his pennies, that much is certain!" she said, laughing.

"How do you know that?"

"Because I know to a nicety what he was paid as chaplain, and what Mama's portion was." When the captain looked at her quizzically, she shrugged and said, "I used to look around Uncle Charles's study, too. I never got into his safe, but he had a drawer labelled *'Important papers'*, so I looked in there."

The captain laughed. "If only everyone were so helpful as to label drawers in that manner. It would make snooping so much easier. So how do you think your father made all that money that became gold bars?"

She frowned a little, for it was a question that bothered her, if she were honest. But she gave the explanation she had settled on years ago. "He used to win at cards a great deal, especially when he played piquet against Grandfather late at night — five or ten or even twenty pounds, so that would add up, would it not?"

"Even small amounts would add up, over time," the captain said. "If he made five pounds in a night, and repeated the feat every week, say, then... let me see, the late earl died ten years ago, so over twenty years... hmm, that would be five thousand pounds. Assuming he did not spend his winnings."

"He never spent a penny of his own money if he could help it, and if it were ten pounds, three times a week...?"

"Hmm. Thirty thousand. Even so, it seems a great deal just from cards. Is there any other way you can think of that he might have accumulated so much money?"

"His businesses in Pickering?"

"A chandlery and an ironmongery. We will look into them, of course, but it seems unlikely that they would be quite so profitable, and if he had any other businesses, we have yet to hear of them."

"A haberdashery," Mr Willerton-Forbes said. "There was talk of a haberdashery."

"So there was. But that could not have been so profitable, either. Let us be generous and suppose he made twenty thousand from cards, over the years. That still leaves twenty thousand to account for."

"Perhaps he was involved with the smugglers," Tess said, laughing.

"Is there smuggling here, so far from the coast?" Captain Edgerton said, blandly, but Tess had a feeling he knew more than he was saying.

"There is smuggling everywhere," she said. "The goods may come in at the coast, but they get distributed far beyond that."

Captain Edgerton nodded, and scribbled away in his notebook, and Tess hoped she had deflected him from further enquiry. She did not know precisely how her father had acquired so much money, but he could not have come by it honestly, on that point she was certain.

When he looked up from his writing, he said, "Tell me about Shapman's confession."

"I know nothing about it."

"He never talked about it to you? It was not, perhaps, your suggestion?"

"*No!* I would never have—! And I know he did not do it, so why would I—? No! But I think it was my letter that set him off. When I heard you were at Pickering, looking into my father's affairs there, I panicked a bit, in case you found my fortune." She lifted one shoulder with a sigh. "Well, you found it anyway, but I wrote to Tom and said I wished there were some way to stop your investigations, and Tom took me at my word. But I had no idea of any confession beforehand. I was shocked when I heard."

"But you must have talked to him about the murder. You walked into Birchall regularly, I understand, so—?"

"What does that have to say to anything?" she said sharply.

Captain Edgerton smiled. "I mean no censure, I assure you. What you do or who you see is not my concern. I am only interested in Shapman's confession, for I have to tell you, it was very convincing, and it puzzles me how he got all that information. I wondered if perhaps he had discussed with you how the murder might have been done."

"Oh... I am not sure... there was only one time..." She frowned, trying to recall the occasion. "He said it must have been a madman, someone who just broke in through the window in the scullery with the broken latch, then wandered about here and there, picking up the axe on the stairs and entering my father's room by sheer chance. But I said it could not be so."

"Yes?" the captain said encouragingly, when she paused.

"I thought it was all planned."

"What makes you think so?"

She paused, wondering just how wise it was to answer that question truthfully. Reticence was as natural to her as breathing, but she could not see the harm in it and perhaps it might be the vital clue that allowed the captain to solve the murder. She glanced at the axe on its shelf, a silent nudge to her conscience. "Because of the axe," she said slowly. "The axe was hidden."

"Was it?"

"Nobody saw it," she said. "Eustace said he put it in the display, but nobody saw it because it was hidden, ready for the murderer to use."

"Where was it hidden?" the captain said.

"In one of the urns, of course," she said scornfully. "Where else?"

"I could think of scores of places where it might be hidden," the captain said.

"No, it was in one of the urns."

"What makes you think so?"

"I do not *think* so, I *know* so. I saw it there."

The captain uttered an exclamation of surprise, and dropped his pencil. Even Mr Willerton-Forbes raised his eyebrows in astonishment.

"Miss Nicholson, you could not possibly have seen the axe in the urn. It must be taller than you are."

She smiled at him. "Not from alongside it. From above. There is an alcove that overlooks the stairs, and when the sun is at just the right height, the light from the glass ceiling shines directly into the urn. I could see the axe inside it."

"Show me! Show me at once!" Captain Edgerton cried, jumping up and grabbing the axe. "Pettigrew, will you be so good as to take the axe down to the stairs and put it in the urn? Now, Miss Nicholson, show me your alcove."

The alcove was a small rounded balcony overlooking the great hall, made with a carved stone balustrade. It was set to one side of one of the bedroom corridors, its great attraction being a curtain that hid anyone lurking there from those passing by in the corridor.

"When we were little, we were allowed to sit here to watch guests arriving for a ball," she said. "Everyone used to gather in the great hall before going in to dinner or through to the gallery to dance. We could peer through the balusters and admire the gowns and jewels. Nowadays, I believe I am the only one who remembers its existence. It is an excellent place to hide if one does not wish to be found."

"And it has a splendid view of the stairs," the captain said.

Down below, Mr Willerton-Forbes waited with the axe, with Mrs Edgerton.

The captain leaned over the balustrade and called down, "Put it in the urn, Pettigrew."

As he moved to do so, Tess cried out, "No! Not that one! The other one, Mr Willerton-Forbes."

"But that is the one that Shapman said he used."

"Well, he made it up, did he not?" Tess said, laughing. "It is only possible to see into the nearest urn, Captain, not the one at the other side of the half-landing."

"Of course," the captain said slowly. "And there is no balcony on that side. Very well, this urn, Pettigrew if you will."

When he did so, the captain leaned over the balustrade. "No, I still see nothing."

"The handle is too dark. It is the metal blade that shows up," she said. "Mr Willerton-Forbes, can you place the axe so that the blade is on the side furthest from us?"

"Ah! Now I see it," the captain said. "Excellent."

"It shows up much better when the sun is directly on it," Tess said. "Oh! I have just thought of another reason why Tom could not have done what he claimed. Those urns are fitted with a platform about halfway up so that a vase of flowers may be placed inside without damaging the urn itself with water. Without that, the axe would slip right to the bottom and be out of reach. Tom would not have known that."

"Who would have known it?"

"The family, and the older servants. I cannot recall that flowers have been put in there for years — not since my grandfather's day."

"How very interesting," the captain said, with a flash of gleaming teeth. "I shall make enquiries, but this does account for why Shapman knew about the axe being in the urn and yet chose the wrong urn. I suppose you did not happen to see who put the axe in there, Miss Nicholson?"

"If I had, I should have told you all this a very long time ago, Captain Edgerton, because whoever it was, he must have murdered my father."

17: A Wedding

Captain Edgerton retreated to the old schoolroom with mixed feelings. Luce lifted the Madeira decanter, but Michael shook his head.

"Brandy, I think."

Pettigrew chuckled. "So is she telling the truth?"

"About the axe in the urn? Possibly. The fact that she and Shapman chose different urns speaks to her honesty, for if they had arranged their story together, they would surely have named the same one. No, it is what she knows about her father that worries me."

Pettigrew passed him a brandy, and settled down with his own glass. "You think she is aware of what he was involved with?"

"He was involved with a great deal, and none of it recorded officially, so I am not sure she could have known anything about it. Taking a share of the rentals, the paste jewellery, the brothel — none of that was written down. The chaplain had no drawer labelled *'My illegal activities'*, sadly. The charitable contributions were public knowledge, but no one knew that no such charities existed. She knew about the existence of the gold bars because she saw them in his safe, and she knew about his winnings at cards because there was no secret about that. The late earl no doubt grumbled about it. *'Another bad night at the card table. Nicholson took twenty pounds off me this time.'* That sort of thing. And that is all legal, a debt of honour, paid without the least protest or hint of cheating. So it seems to me that she would naturally assume all that gold came from the card tables. But I wonder... she wanted that gold so badly that she went into the house as a maid, which cannot have been easy for her. And when that scheme failed, she recruited Lord Tarvin to break in. Why the urgency? If she knew that her father had been systematically stealing from the late earl, she might have wanted to get the gold safely spirited away before it was reclaimed by her uncle."

Luce had picked up her needlework again, but now she laid it down. "It seems to me that Miss Nicholson's desire for independence is sufficient to account for all she has done. Having control of her own money would give her the freedom to live as she pleases, without the need for a husband."

"I agree," Pettigrew said. "I also think Miss Nicholson's money is a distraction from our principal objective."

"But I have to decide what to do about it!" Michael said. "I could still give her the key and let her take what is hers."

"It is not hers," Pettigrew said quietly. "My investigations are not yet complete, but I have done enough to show that most, if not all, of that gold was stolen from the Earl of Rennington."

Michael deflated at once. "You are correct, of course. Luce told me to do what is right, and so I must. The earl must be told of this."

Pettigrew beamed. "That is more like yourself, Michael. You are too soft-hearted sometimes, especially when a pretty young lady is concerned. In another week or two, I shall have an accurate calculation of the amount stolen from the earl, and you will be able to send someone to the Pickering house to value the entire collection of gold bars. Then we shall know how large a fortune Miss Nicholson has inherited."

"If any," Michael said sadly.

"Yes, if any. But the earl will not necessarily decide to recover all that was taken from the estate. He might choose to leave some of it as a dowry for his niece."

"So he might," Michael said, brightening. "He is a generous man, after all, and fond of her, I am sure. As soon as I have accurate estimates of the amount stolen and the amount of gold, I shall see the earl and put that point to him."

"And then we can all get back to looking for Mr Nicholson's murderer."

Michael sighed. "That man! He has caused us so much trouble. It is fortunate that he is already dead, or I should be tempted to murder him myself."

***

Tess emerged from her talk to Captain Edgerton with a feeling that she had done her duty, and given him some useful information for his pursuit of the murderer, without revealing too much of her father's thievery. Not that she knew precisely what he had been up to, but he had not amassed such a fortune by legitimate means. If she had only been able to rescue her gold bars before anyone knew about them! But that ship had now sailed, and her fortune was in Captain Edgerton's hands.

Tom's future, too, was in other hands now. Despite the poultry maid, Tess still loved him, but unless she had her fortune, he was beyond her reach. Still, there was one way she could help him, and that was by helping the captain to find the real murderer. She had been too shocked at first to consider possible murderers, assuming like everyone else that a stranger must have broken in. Only later, when she remembered the axe in its hiding place, had she realised that the murder was planned.

And now that she had remembered the platform inside the urn, it was obvious that the murderer was someone who knew all about it. An empty urn of that size would not normally be a suitable place to hide a short weapon like an axe. A sword, perhaps, or a spear, but an axe would slide to the bottom and be out of reach without tipping the urn onto its side. But with the platform filling the full width of the urn, it rested with the handle conveniently just below the rim.

So the murderer must be someone who knew about the platform, and must be tall enough to reach inside to retrieve it. A man, most probably, or a very tall lady, and she could not think of any female who would be tall enough. But who knew about the platform?

Here she shivered, for surely only the family would remember a time when flowers were placed inside the urns? The footmen, possibly — they were always tall. Male servants of shorter stature were sent to be grooms or gardeners. Only the two butlers, she thought, Simpson and Wellum, had been at the castle long enough.

She retreated to her room and drew a sheet of paper towards her, and began a list of possibilities.

'Uncle Charles...'

Immediately she stopped. Her uncle? The earl himself? But she must include all possibilities.

'Uncle Charles,

Walter,

Eustace,

Kent,

Simpson,

Wellum.'

It was a remarkably short list, and she could cross three names off immediately. Uncle Charles had no need whatsoever to murder her father, since he employed him. If he had ever had a serious disagreement with him, he could simply have asked him to leave Corland. Eustace was at his own house on the night in question, twelve miles away. Simpson was married, and lived with his wife in the village. Besides, it was hard to see a man of his age and with his arthritic knees creeping about in the middle of the night. That left just three names.

'Walter,

Kent,

Wellum.'

Walter? He had been very quick to arrive on the scene that night, and very quick to push her and Olivia away, so that they would not see the dreadful sight of her father's body. Such quick thinking might be because he had not just been woken that minute by Mama's screaming. Could he have crept about the darkened castle, retrieving the axe, slaughtering her father in his bed, then quietly creeping away, only to emerge at the first scream?

Yet the planning involved in hiding the axe seemed unlike Walter. He was an idiot who had drifted into his engagement to Bea Franklyn because he had not the wit to avoid her, so the jump to calculating murderer was too great to be believable.

As for Wellum, his father and grandfather before him had both been butler at the castle, and he was hugely proud to be the third generation to achieve such a distinction. His parents and his grandfather still lived in the village, and he had a sweetheart at Birchall that he hoped to marry in a year or two, so would he jeopardise all of that? Could he truly hate a man so much that he would risk throwing away everything just to be rid of him? It seemed unlikely.

That only left Kent, the perpetually cheerful man who never disliked anyone enough even to utter a harsh word about him, let alone kill him. What reason would compel him to do so?

That was, of course, the ultimate question — why? Why would anyone want to kill her father, who was not a good man by any measure, but his transgressions were not such as to call for murder, one would have thought.

Disgusted, she crumpled the paper and threw it forcibly into the fire.

***

Tess was curled up in an armchair in the library one afternoon pretending to read, but in reality wondering where Lord Tarvin had gone and how she might find out, when Betty sidled in looking big with news.

"I've just been downstairs pressing that green gown of yours, Miss Tess," she hissed excitedly, so as not to disturb Lady Alice and Mr Alfred Strong, who were chatting on the other side of the room.

"And?"

"That lad of Mr Parker's came by with a turkey for Sunday, and you'll never guess what he said."

"Yes?"

"He's seen Mr Shapman!"

"What!" Tess sat up abruptly. "Tom? Where? When?"

"Yesterday, in the village. He's home, seemingly. Micky said he only glimpsed him in a big crowd outside Tom's Ma's house, but it were definitely him."

"So he is out of prison," Tess said with satisfaction.

"Aye. I just have to hang up that gown and put away a few things, then I'll find Harold and fetch my cloak."

But Tess could not wait even those few minutes. As soon as Betty had gone, she raced down to the garden door in the basement, retrieved her old cloak and bonnet, and she was gone, scurrying away to Birchall village in the greatest excitement. Tom home at last! Sir Hubert had accepted that he was innocent, then, and let him go. She would see him again and surely she would be able to distract his thoughts away from his poultry maid? What was so attractive about a poultry maid anyway?

She raced down the path to the village, and surely her feet had never flown there so fast. In no time, it seemed, she was in the little lane where Tom's workshop was and lifting the latch to go inside.

He was not there. Her disappointment was so acute that for a moment she could not breathe. Yet clearly he was expected, for the fire in the kitchen was burning merrily, the kettle was on its hook ready to swing over the flames, and there were teacups set out on the table, together with an uncut cake and a small vase of field flowers. There were new curtains at the window, she noticed, a cheerful yellow colour which made the tiny kitchen seem sunny and warm despite the grey skies outside.

She waited for a few minutes, but Tom did not appear. It occurred to her then that if he was but newly out of prison, he would have wanted to spend time with his parents. Perhaps she could look for him there, although Mrs Shapman disliked her, she knew that. She had muttered disapprovingly of '*you grand ladies and your games with humble folk*', as if Tess were just amusing herself with Tom! So she had avoided the rest of Tom's family as much as possible. But this was different. Surely she could presume on her long friendship with Tom to ask for him there?

She made her way back to the main road through the village, where she saw a great crowd of people filling the street, laughing and cheering and making their way slowly towards her. She saw Tom at once, for even though he was at the centre of the group, he was tall enough to tower over most of the others.

Eagerly she set off towards him, as the crowd flowed down the street towards her. Gradually, one by one, they noticed her and the excited chatter slowly died away as the crowd parted. And there she was, face to face with Tom, various members of his family at his back, and on his arm a girl with flowers in her hair.

"Miss Tess!" Tom said, his face a picture of guilt. He licked his lips, and shuffled his feet, but the girl rested her other hand on his arm and looked up at him with a troubled expression. As if she had spoken, he nodded, then patted her hand. "Miss Tess, this is... this is Ruby... Mrs Shapman... my wife. We were wed this morning. I hope you'll wish us joy."

There were occasions when it was a great inconvenience to be brought up as a lady, and be coolly polite at all times, no matter the provocation. Tess's mother was an expert in such manners, but Tess had never before been put to such an extreme test. How much more satisfying it would be to scream and rant and hit out and slap faces and pull hair. It took all her twenty years of training to plaster a smile on her face.

"I will... I do... I felicitate you, Mrs Shapman. Both of you. May you enjoy a long and happy marriage."

"Thank you, milady," the girl said, with a beaming smile, bobbing a little curtsy.

"Where will you live?"

"We'll live over the workshop just at first," Tom said. "Then when my little sister Sally goes into service after Christmas, we'll have a room with Ma and Pa, just until I can afford a place of my own."

"May I send you a wedding gift?" Tess said, the smile stiffening her face.

"That'd be right kind, Miss Tess," Tom said. "Will you... I mean, we're going to show Ruby her new home. You're welcome to—"

"No," she said quickly. "No, I must get back to Corland." Then, with genuine feeling, she added, "I wish you every happiness, Tom."

"Thank you," he whispered, flushing a little.

And then the procession flowed on down the street and away, leaving Tess stranded like a starfish on the beach after the tide has gone out.

She fled, reaching the blessed privacy of the path back to Corland where, hidden by the sheltering trees, she allowed the tears to flow unchecked. Striding along, her eyes too full to see where she was going, she crashed headlong into a figure pelting down the track towards her. She would have been bowled clean over by the impact had not the person grabbed her forcibly and kept her upright by holding her tightly against his chest.

"Tess! Oh, Tess, I am so sorry!"

Edward's voice! Not a stranger, not a neighbour who must be fobbed off, and best of all, not Betty or Harold, who might relate the whole to her mother. It was Edward, her friend, who understood.

"He is married!" she sobbed, burying her face in the shoulder of his greatcoat.

"I know," he murmured. "I have been looking everywhere for you to tell you myself, so that you would not find out in this horrid way. Did you see him?"

She nodded. "And her."

"Oh, Tess darling, I am so, so sorry."

For a long time he held her tight while she wept and wept, making a soggy mark on his coat. When the storm had abated somewhat, she lifted her head to look at him, and saw his face filled with compassion for her.

"My poor darling," he murmured, and somehow, she could not tell how, they were kissing and it felt so right, so infinitely reassuring that she had no mind to push him away. With his arms around her and his lips warm and gentle on hers, the world did not seem such a hostile and painful place as it had just a short while before. There was strength in those arms, one around her waist and the other wrapped firmly around her back, pulling her close to him. Nothing could hurt her when Edward was there to take care of her!

That was a strange thought. She had never needed or wanted anyone to take care of her before. She had been fiercely proud of her independence, gleefully following her own path. Yet in Pickering, it had been good to have Edward's enthusiastic support for her plans, to plot and plan and do things together.

With a sigh, she rested her head on his shoulder.

"Better now?" he said, still holding her tightly.

"A little," she said. "But where were you? You were here and then you disappeared. Now here you are again."

"I went to York to get Tom Shapman out of gaol."

Her head shot up excitedly. "*You* did that? How good you are!"

"Sir Hubert wrote the letters of authority to have him released, but I undertook to make the journey. I got back with him yesterday."

"But then... how is it that he is married today? When were the banns read?"

"No banns. He was married by licence."

"By *licence?* But how? That must be expensive..."

For the first time his expression slipped into a tiny frown. "Well... I paid for it, of course. We got it from the archbishop's office in York. Shapman would not have known how to obtain such a thing."

She pushed him away angrily. "So *you* did this! You arranged for him to be married to that... that *female*. A poultry maid! When he could have married me!"

"He would never have married you, Tess," he said in a low voice. "Believe me, he did not want it. All I did was to make it possible for him to marry the woman to whom he was already devoted."

"He was devoted to me!" she cried. "He loved *me*, not some stupid poultry maid."

"No. He never loved you, although you dazzled him so much that he would do anything you asked. He even jeopardised his own life to please you. Believe me, everything I have done is for the best, for Shapman and his wife, and also for you, Tess, and one day you will understand that."

"You are an arrogant, overbearing, interfering man. I wish you would just stop meddling in my life!"

"If you give up this foolish idea of marrying Ulric, then perhaps I will."

"How else am I to get my hands on my own fortune?"

He gave a quick laugh. "You could always marry me."

"Never! Never, never, never! I hate you so much, I would sooner die a penniless spinster than marry you."

Pushing past him, she ran on up the track towards Corland. Oddly, she was crying again, and this time, it was not for Tom.

18: Money Considerations

Edward stood frozen, watching Tess's retreating back. Well, he had made a mull of that! There she had been, in his arms, allowing him to kiss her and everything comfortable between them, and he had gone and ruined the whole thing — again. Every time he thought he was making a little progress with her, he found himself on the wrong side of her temper.

For once, his eternal optimism entirely deserted him. He would have to watch her marry Ulric, thereby ruining who knows how many lives, and it seemed there was nothing at all he could do about it. Such an amazing girl, to be thrown away on a man who could never appreciate her, and would never even see her except as someone to ride with occasionally. If she never went near the stables, Ulric would undoubtedly forget her very existence.

Yet Edward would have loved her forever and cherished her as she deserved to be. No one in her life had truly cared about Tess, or protected her as a girl should be protected. She had been left to find her own way in life, her mother restricted by her blindness, and her aunt, who might have taken an interest in the girl, occupied with her own brood. Tess had grown secretive and devious because of that neglect, and Edward was perhaps the only man of her class who did not mind that. Did not mind? He adored that aspect of her nature, for he was secretive and devious himself, if truth be told.

Eventually, voices approaching on the track from Birchall drove him to turn and walk back to the castle. He wondered forlornly where Tess had gone and whether, if he looked for her and apologised abjectly, she might be less hostile. Perhaps she might even let him kiss her again.

As he strode over the bridge to the castle's main entrance, the butler rushed out to greet him.

"Oh, my lord, there you are! We wondered... when you dashed away so precipitately after Miss Nicholson... but she is here now. She returned a few moments ago."

"I have seen Miss Nicholson."

"Ah. Excellent. Captain Edgerton was enquiring for you, my lord."

"Tell him to go and boil his head," Edward said savagely.

"My lord?" the butler said, startled.

Edward sighed. It was hard to set aside the roiling emotions inside him and bring his mind back to more mundane matters. "Oh... tell him I will see him in a few minutes. Where is he?"

"The old schoolroom, my lord. Bedroom floor, south-eastern corner."

"And remind me where my room is?"

"The south-western corner, my lord." He flicked a finger and a footman jumped forward. "William will show you the way, my lord."

Edward was grateful. Most great houses were modelled on a central block with wings to each side, and it was easy enough to navigate to one side or the other, but Corland was a solidly square house. He remembered, as he followed the silent footman up the stairs, that he needed only to turn to the left on the half landing and his door was directly opposite the top of the stair, but in his disordered state of mind, he was certain to have taken a wrong turn somewhere.

"Shall I send your man up?" the footman asked.

"No need."

In the sanctuary of his room, he tore off his greatcoat, hat and gloves and sat on the bed in despair. It was a moment of unrelieved gloom. Just a few weeks ago, he had pridefully congratulated himself on having ordered his life perfectly to his own wishes. He had removed his mother and aunt from his orbit and established a delightful bachelor existence in town, and although he had to show himself at the occasional ball or musical evening or the wretched Almack's to appease his mother, he could otherwise do as he pleased. It had amused him greatly to have a secret life that she knew nothing about and therefore could not scold him for. And how she would scold, if she knew what he did when she was not there to keep him in check!

But a mere few days in Tess Nicholson's company had torn all his pride from him, and filled him with a conviction of his own worthlessness. He was rich, he was a baron, he was accounted handsome and pleasing to females, and yet none of that made him an acceptable husband to that shameless chit. She preferred her uneducated woodworker or poor horse-obsessed Ulric to Edward, Lord Tarvin of Harfield Priory and Grosvenor Street, London.

What was he to do now? Nothing. There was nothing he could do to win her.

***

Tess hid away in her favourite secret place, the balcony overlooking the great hall. The great advantage of wearing black, and possibly the only advantage, was that hiding was much easier. A flash of white muslin glimpsed between the balusters would perhaps attract attention, but in her mourning gown she was invisible, with no need to swathe herself in a dark cloak as she used to do.

For a few minutes she seethed with rage at Edward, who had taken it upon himself to interfere in her life. If she had been able to talk to Tom, to kiss him, perhaps, she could have turned his mind away from that stupid poultry maid, she was sure. Tom was as soft as butter in her hands, easy to mould to her own wishes. Easy to distract. All men were foolish where women were concerned. But men had power, too, the power to obtain a licence so that Tom could marry the poultry maid instantly, and put himself forever out of Tess's reach.

Not that he had been within her reach, without her fortune. If she could only have got her hands on those gold bars! But there again, the interfering Edward had taken that option away from her. Such an arrogant, high-handed man! Now there was only Ulric left to her.

A shiver of uncertainty hit her, as she remembered Edward's words. *'I can give you something you can never get from Ulric,'* he had said, and then he had kissed her. She trembled as she remembered his kisses, soft and warm and gentle, infinitely tender. Tom's kisses were enthusiastic, certainly, but had nothing of Edward's comforting affection. And from Ulric, there would be no kisses at all, and could she live with that?

Below her in the great hall there was a bustle of activity, as one of the footmen who waited there was summoned to the entrance hall, returning moments later to lead a man of nondescript appearance up the stairs.

"I didn't catch your name, sir. How shall I announce you?" the footman said, as he passed below Tess's vantage point.

"Just say, *'A person to see you'*," the man said.

"Is the captain expecting you, Sir?"

"Oh, yes."

Neither his face nor his voice were familiar to Tess, but nevertheless, she thought she recognised something about him. He looked like a bailiff or perhaps a farmer, in the sort of hard-wearing, somewhat outmoded clothes that would be practical for outdoor work. She would not know anyone of that nature, but perhaps in a different context...

She had it! He had been a footman in the not too distant past, although a rather unusual one. Not one of theirs, a visiting one, although she could not remember whose. That was intriguing.

Impulsively she jumped up and slipped through the door to the service stairs, and up to the attic floor. There were a few tiny bedrooms for the servants there, but around the perimeter was a low space, just the right height for a smaller-than-average child to walk in. As an adult, she had to stoop but she could still creep about up there. Over the years, she had gradually loosened and shifted boards or even drilled small holes so that she could hear what was going on below her. It was only the bedrooms, so although she heard much snoring and other odd noises, there was little conversation to be overheard. A man discussing the arrangement of his neck cloth with his valet, perhaps. The women were more interesting. Aunt Caroline gossiped dreadfully with her lady's maid, and Tess had learnt much of interest from her. Walter and Eustace had quarrelled sometimes, before Eustace had inherited his own house and moved out. And of course Izzy had always been entertaining with her melodramatic tantrums.

The old school room had not been used for a number of years, but now, with the arrival of Captain Edgerton and his associates to investigate her father's murder, there was much that was worth listening to. Now she crept along the low space until she was above the room and could hear voices below. Then she stretched out on her stomach and laid her ear to the gap between the boards.

"...this letter, James."

That was Captain Edgerton's voice with its clipped military tones. For a while, there was silence, apart from the faint scratching of a pen.

"There! That should do it. Give that to the attorney, and this one from his lordship, and that should get you inside. You are to give them due notice — two days at least."

"They will have hidden everything of interest," a second voice said. The quiet tones of the man on the stairs.

"Yes, but those are the earl's explicit orders. We cannot do otherwise. But then straight in. Take Sandy with you, and those two from the inn — the big fellow and his brother, and the attorney, of course. You have a bailiff arranged to value everything, I assume."

"Of course. A Scarborough man. I wish you could be there, Michael."

"So do I! But I must talk to Whyte."

"Nicholson's natural son?"

"That is the fellow. Shapman's confession took him off my list for a while, but now I must talk to him. He is one of the few people who has a genuine grievance against Nicholson, and a quarrelsome family who just might turn to violence against the man who fathered a child on a girl and then refused even to acknowledge him. Not so much as a mention in the will, either. So I must see Whyte without further delay. I talked to the smith and a couple of the sons, and they hardly seem the type to break into the castle at dead of night and murder a man with an axe. A brawl in the street, certainly, and possibly a hostile delegation to talk to Nicholson and persuade him to do the right thing by the boy, but they are not secretive types, I should have thought."

"And the boy is only sixteen."

"Precisely!" Captain Edgerton said. "It seems most implausible, yet who else do we have? Only Miss Nicholson, who is even more implausible, and Shapman, who has a rock solid alibi. James, I depend on you to find me something useful at the Pickering house."

"Apart from Miss Nicholson's gold bars, you mean?"

"Yes, apart from that. Nicholson's papers there may have something of interest."

Tess heard a door open and close again.

"Ah, Lord Tarvin! Do come in, my lord. Thank you for attending so promptly. Rumour has it that you succeeded in setting Shapman free from prison."

"And he was imprisoned again this morning, in the Holy state of matrimony," Edward said.

"My goodness, that was quick work!" That was Mrs Edgerton again. "How did you pull that off?"

"With a bishop's licence from the Archbishop of York, a fraught evening arranging everything and then running my carriage between Birchall and the bride's church all morning. I had to spend last night at the parsonage to make everything work. I thought it best to get it done before Tess has a chance to insinuate herself into the situation again."

"Does she know yet?"

"Unfortunately, she heard Shapman was free, rushed down to the village to see him and ran straight into the wedding party. She was... a bit upset."

"Poor girl!" Mrs Edgerton's voice was full of sympathy. "She has not had an easy life, and it is not getting any easier."

"Not an easy life?" the captain said. "Born into an earl's household? Never wanting for anything in her life?"

"Anything material," Mrs Edgerton said. "Love... I think she has been starved of love."

"Which she would not have got from Tom Shapman," Edward said, a harsh tone in his voice. "Nor will she get it from Ulric Frith."

"It seems to me that she wants money, rather than love." Now who was that? The lawyer fellow, Tess thought. Mr Willerton-Forbes.

"And she shall have it, just as soon as we can extract those gold bars from Apstead House," Edward said.

"That is precisely what Neate is about," the captain said. "Do you remember my associate, James Neate, my lord? He has just arrived from Pickering to collect the letters of authority enabling him to gain admittance to the house. And the key to the safe, of course. In the course of investigating the house, he will discover afresh the safe and its contents, and be able to obtain a proper estimate of the value of those gold bars. There is a goldsmith coming up from London for the purpose."

"Excellent. This news may cheer her a little," Edward said.

"Unfortunately, there is a small problem," the lawyer said in his ponderous way. "The late Mr Nicholson was helping himself to a sizeable proportion of the late earl's rental income. The present earl engaged a land steward to deal with such matters, and so Nicholson devised other schemes to line his own pockets, but there was a substantial loss to the estate from the earlier depredations. The earl quite naturally wishes to recoup some of the losses."

"But not to the extent of Miss Nicholson's entire fortune, surely?" Edward said.

"My investigations are not yet complete," the lawyer said slowly, "but my current estimate is that Mr Nicholson's embezzlement may amount to forty thousand pounds or even more." A long pause. "Do you still wish to tell Miss Nicholson?"

"No. Good God, no! This is dreadful! She could end up with nothing... not a penny!"

There was a profound silence from the room below.

Tess was too experienced at listening in to reveal herself by an injudicious sound or movement, but she was hard put to it not to squeak with shock. This was a severe blow! She had suspected her father's perfidy for a long time, ever since she had realised that he bought a new coat or a fob for his waistcoat or a trinket for Mama after he had collected the Lady Day rents. Why should he have extra money to spend after gathering in the earl's income? He was not usually free with his money, but once a year, he was a little more generous.

Once, she had tested her theory by asking him if she could have a new gown.

"Your Mama is the person to ask," he had said absently, busy with his accounts. "She handles your allowance."

"But you have plenty of money just now, so I thought you might share some of it with me."

His head had come up sharply at that. "It is true that I have been fortunate at the card table lately."

"The card table? Is that where it comes from?" she had said in innocent tones.

He had looked at her penetratingly. She could not have been more than nine or ten at the time, and he must have wondered whether this was truly childlike innocence or something more subtle.

Eventually, he chuckled, and set his pen down. "You are a clever little thing, Tess. Tell me, why do you think Lord Rennington is such a powerful man?"

"He's an earl, Papa."

"True, and everyone bows down to him for that reason. But the real power in the world is money. If you have money, you are a person of consequence even if you are lowly in other ways. Money is security and freedom and the ability to live your life however you choose. Money permits a recovery from any disaster, large or small. Money is independence, Tess, and not being beholden to anyone. Not being *owned* by anyone. How much would you like for your new gown?"

Tess had no idea what a gown would cost, but she knew that her father regularly won twenty pounds from the earl at piquet and the earl laughed it off. That was a trivial amount, then.

"Fifty pounds," she said brightly.

He was so shocked she almost laughed. "Fifty pounds! Great heavens, Tess!" But then he began to laugh. "Still, such brazen impudence should be rewarded." He opened a drawer and counted out five gold coins. "There. Five guineas. That should buy you a new gown and a pair of stockings, too. But never ask me for money again, do you hear? Everything I possess will be yours after I die, so you will get your hands on it then and not a moment sooner. Now leave me in peace, you little monkey."

She had never again asked for money, but knowing where he kept his coins, it was not difficult to help herself to a few shillings now and then. After all, it would be hers one day anyway, so she was merely taking a small advance on her inheritance. She was very careful only to take small amounts, and only silver or copper, never gold. Even a careless man might know precisely how many guineas he had, and her father was anything but careless about money. Did he ever notice? If he did, he never gave any sign.

Now she wished she had taken more, and hidden it away instead of spending it. At least it would be hers, and no one could take it away from her. Now she would be penniless…

But not if she acted swiftly. There was yet a possibility of getting hold of some, at least, of her fortune.

The group below began to talk about Mr Neate's journey to Pickering, and under cover of their conversation, Tess crept away, brushed off the accumulated dust and cobwebs her gown had acquired, and descended the service stairs to the ground floor. In the great hall, Simpson and Wellum were conferring, breaking off their discussion as she approached.

"Miss Nicholson? How may I be of service?" Simpson said.

"Is my uncle free at the moment, Simpson?"

"I believe he is not engaged at present," the butler said, in his ponderous way.

"Would you ask him if he could spare me a few minutes?"

He could and did, returning very soon to say, "His lordship will see you now, Miss Tess."

And there was that little niggle of discontent that always bubbled up. Josie and Izzy and Olivia were always *'my lady'*. Even now, the servants still called Olivia *'my lady'*, and not *'Miss Olivia'*, as she should be, but Tess would always be *'Miss Tess'*. Or Mrs Shapman, as she should have been, she thought resentfully. Mrs Frith, perhaps. Or Lady Tarvin. That made her scowl even more. As if she cared tuppence for him or his title! It was a question of respect, that was all.

Simpson led her through the ante-room to the library, and into the earl's study.

"Miss Nicholson, my lord."

"Tess! My dear girl! Come in, come in, do. How delightful to have this little chat. I do not see you often enough, not to talk to, for one cannot talk properly over dinner, can one? May I send for some tea for you?"

"I will have a glass of Madeira, thank you, uncle."

His eyebrows rose a fraction, but he willingly dismissed the butler and poured a small glass for her and a larger one for himself.

"And how are you, my dear? You are well, I can see that, and happy, I am sure, with your future so well settled." If only that were true! "We cannot wait to meet your young man, my dear. Such a whirlwind romance! I cannot tell you how happy it makes me, and your aunt..." A shadow crossed his face as he mentioned Lady Rennington. "I am sure she will be pleased about it, too, when she hears. Have you written to her?"

"Not yet, uncle. Everything is very much up in the air at the moment, so I hardly know what I am about. Have you not written to her?"

"Oh... not recently, no. She... she prefers me not to. Just until... things are settled. If I find someone to marry. But as to your happy news, I dare say your mama has told her all about it, although she would be glad to hear from you, I am sure. Was there anything in particular that you wished to talk to me about?"

"I am thinking ahead to my wedding in the spring. It cannot be sooner since Mama has not given her permission, but I should like to be prepared — wedding clothes and so forth. Under normal circumstances, my father would have paid for such things, but perhaps I could have the money he left me to begin with. Ten thousand in the bank, and a thousand in cash. That would enable me to make my preparations... put some renovations in hand at Mr Frith's principal seat, that sort of thing."

The earl frowned, and she knew at once that he was not going to fall for her stratagem.

"Ten, eleven thousand for wedding clothes, my dear?"

"And a carriage and horses, uncle. Perhaps two. I want to begin some work in the grounds, too. A summer house... a lake... a fountain..."

"Most of these plans, worthy though they are, are for your husband to undertake, Tess. Your wedding clothes... perhaps something might be done there, but a carriage? Building works? Wait until you are married, my dear. Your husband will have all your money then, and he will be the best person to decide what to do with it. There will be settlements, and so forth... your pin money, widow's jointure, all that sort of thing. More important than a lake, I should think."

"I am sure you are right, uncle, but perhaps something for wedding clothes now?"

"When you are still in deep mourning? My dear girl, it seems a little disrespectful to be thinking of such things now. When you have set a date for the wedding, talk to your mama about what you will need, and then come to me for the money. We shall not send you into matrimony in rags, you know! There now, you are excited about entering the married state and cannot wait to make a start, and that is perfectly natural, but you will have the rest of your life with Mr Frith, after all. A few more weeks to wait for wedding clothes is neither here nor there. Do not forget to write to Lady Rennington, will you? I am sure she would love to hear from you. And if she writes back to you, as I am sure she will, do not forget to let me know what she says and how she is, will you?"

Tess drank the rest of her Madeira in one mouthful, and left with as much politeness as she could muster.

Everything was going wrong! What a horrible day this was turning out to be.

19: Tears And Kisses

Edward was in sombre mood that evening, dressing for dinner in silence, and steeling himself for the inevitable questions in the drawing room. No one in the earl's household would be so crass as to say, *'What are you up to, Lord Tarvin?'* or to ask when he might be leaving again — that question would come later, perhaps. But they would wonder, all the same, and he would be obliged to offer some explanation. Releasing Tom Shapman from prison was one thing, a mere charitable gesture, but arranging his marriage? Obtaining a licence, fixing a time with the parson and the families, ferrying people back and forth? The marriage of a woodworker and a poultry maid was not something with which a baron would normally concern himself.

Perhaps the time for secrecy was past. He had already hinted to Lady Alice that he had an interest in marrying Tess, but it could be useful to him now to be more open, and declare his intentions publicly. It was unorthodox, for Tess was officially engaged, but he would be a far more acceptable suitor than Ulric. If he could win Lady Alice's approval, they could be married at once, and able to secure Tess's fortune for her. If there were any fortune left to secure, that is to say.

The drawing room was already full when he entered it, and for a moment he panicked, recognising no one. Who were all these people? But then the earl loomed out of the crowd.

"Tarvin! There you are! Come and meet a few people. Let me see, you will not remember the Cathcarts, I expect."

Edward let himself be herded around the room, smiling and making the polite noises expected of him, but all the time he was looking for a diminutive figure in black. Dinner was announced and there was a general movement towards the dining room before it dawned on him that Tess was not there at all. Shapman's marriage had hit her hard, then. He had another burst of panic — had she run away? She was good at that.

He allowed himself to be seated beside Lady Alice once more, on her left hand this time, with one of the multitude of Cathcarts in the place of honour on her right. As the rest of the guests chose seats and settled themselves, he murmured in a low voice, "Is Miss Nicholson not joining us tonight, Lady Alice?"

"Is she not here?" she said. "One never knows what is going on with Tess, but if she had other plans for the evening, she has not intimated them to me."

Mr Cathcart helped Lady Alice to several of the dishes laid out on the table, and then the two were engaged in conversation for several minutes. Edward attempted to talk to the young lady seated beside him, but she was monosyllabic and in the unquietness of his mind, conversation was too much effort and he fell silent, waiting for Lady Alice to turn her attention to him.

As soon as the opportunity arose, he said quickly, "Lady Alice, have you talked to Miss Nicholson at all today?"

"I have not," she said, "but that is by no means unusual. Are you concerned about her, Lord Tarvin? She has her maid and footman to watch over her, you know."

Edward knew perfectly well that Tess was easily able to evade her watchdogs whenever she wished, but that was not something her mother would wish to hear. Instead, he said, "I am a little concerned, it is true. Her friend Tom Shapman was married this morning to a poultry maid from Gowland's Farm, and she was a little upset to discover it."

"Married, is he? And to a poultry maid? I am very glad to hear it, since he will pester Tess no more, but I do not know why she should be upset about it. That business was scotched by my husband last year, and now she is betrothed to a much more suitable man."

It was the opening Edward had hoped for. "I would not entirely agree that my cousin Ulric is more suitable. More fitting than a woodworker, certainly, for he is a gentleman and has an income sufficient to support a wife, but..."

"*But*, Lord Tarvin? You know of some flaw in his character, perhaps? You must know him well, and I would much sooner know the truth than to be left guessing. One hears... rumours, and I notice you have not expressed the flattering remarks usual in such circumstances — that he is the best of good fellows, a man of respectability who will make any woman an excellent husband. That is what I expected to hear from you, Lord Tarvin, and yet I did not. I conclude, therefore, that you dislike him."

"No, indeed, I like him very well, but he is not a man who should ever marry. That is my considered opinion, Lady Alice."

She raised her eyebrows a delicate fraction at this robust statement. "Oh. Then I must presume that he is a man of vicious habits."

"Not that, no. Let me be very blunt — my cousin is simple-minded. He is happy enough if he has horses to ride and to care for, but he has not the intellect for family life. He has been cozened into this betrothal by his mother and Miss Nicholson."

"Why?" she said sharply. "If he is all that you describe him, why would they wish him to marry?"

"When Ulric marries, he regains control of his estate, which his mother desires greatly. Miss Nicholson, of course, obtains control of her fortune, for although it would in law belong to her husband, he would easily be persuaded to cede control to her. As one of Ulric's trustees, you will appreciate that I am doing all in my power to prevent this marriage from ever taking place. I have already taken the woodworker out of contention by arranging his marriage, and—"

"You did that?"

"I did, and I hope to intervene with Ulric, too, but that is... more difficult to predict."

"Is your cousin's welfare your sole objective, Lord Tarvin?" she said, with such a sweet smile that he could not take offence. "Or do you have some other plan in mind for my daughter?"

That, too, was an opening. There was no point dancing around the question, not any more. "I hope to marry her myself, Lady Alice."

"Ah," was all she said, and began enquiring about Edward's estates, very much a mother with an eye on her daughter's marriage prospects.

Edward was quietly pleased. Lady Alice's approval would not weigh with Tess, naturally, who would always go her own way, but it could do no harm.

When the ladies withdrew, Edward made a point of asking if any of the gentlemen had seen Tess that day.

"She came to see me this afternoon," Lord Rennington said. "We had a pleasant little chat. She is to write to Lady Rennington to tell her about her betrothal."

"Is that what she wanted to talk to you about?" Edward said, puzzled.

"Oh, no. She wanted money for her wedding clothes, but it is a little premature for that. Frankly, I am not sure she will stick with your cousin, Tarvin. Is he much smitten with her? She can be a taking little thing when she sets her mind to it, but lately I cannot tell what is in her head, not at all. First, this Shapman fellow, who is not at all suitable, and now this man at Durham, which is a very sudden start and I have a feeling her heart is not engaged as it should be. Will he be much upset if she bolts, do you think?"

"I imagine he would bear up nobly under the loss," Edward said carefully.

"Of course, of course. What gentleman would not? But she can be flighty, very flighty, I fear. You might perhaps put it to him that... she has something of a reputation for changing her mind. I would put it no stronger than that, for she is very young... very innocent, naturally. And her mother being so... well, not able to supervise her as a mother should, perhaps. She has had a little too much freedom. Nothing that marriage to the right man would not knock out of her, but still, she is a little flighty yet."

Edward was offended on Tess's behalf at so cavalier a disregard of her concerns. "I think she knows precisely what she wants," he said with some heat, "but she is not yet certain of the best way to achieve it."

"She wants marriage, of course," the earl said dismissively. "What woman does not? All she needs to do is settle on the man — an eligible man, naturally, not Shapman. Not suitable at all. Strong, are you shooting tomorrow? How is your new gamekeeper settling in?"

Edward was too restless to enter into a discussion of game birds and the prospects for good sport, so he quietly slipped away to the great hall, where Wellum, the under butler, was loitering, directing footmen into the dining room or drawing room, as required.

"Do you know where Miss Nicholson is?" Edward said. "She did not come in to dinner."

He looked startled. "No, my lord. Is she in the castle? There were no instructions to the kitchen for a tray to her room, or anything of that nature. We assumed she had gone out for the evening."

"Was the carriage ordered?"

"No, my lord."

"She would hardly go out to an evening engagement on foot, would she?"

"No, my lord."

"Then find her maid and footman, and see what they have to say about it."

"Yes, my lord."

"At once!"

"Yes, my lord!"

He dispatched two footmen to the nether regions to find the two servants, while Edward paced impatiently back and forth.

Captain Edgerton emerged from the dining room and crossed the great hall to intercept Edward. "Are you concerned about Miss Nicholson, too, Lord Tarvin?"

"I am. She was distressed when she discovered that Shapman had married, and it would reassure me to know that she is not still suffering on that account. She is usually very good at shrugging off disappointments."

"Indeed. Is she still about the castle somewhere? Although it is a very large castle, and she is a small person, well able to hide herself away if she wishes it."

"I have sent for her maid and footman, and if they assure me that she is still within the confines of the building, then I shall start at the attics and work my way down until I find her."

Eventually, the maid and footman were tracked down, but both were confident that Tess was within the castle.

"She's not in her room and she's not asked for any food, but all her outdoor clothes are still here," the maid said.

"Even the old cloak she keeps by the garden door," the footman said.

"Where might she be?" Edward said, but neither had any idea. When they had been dismissed, he went on, "Well, then. The attics first. Then the bedrooms."

"If I might suggest," Edgerton said quietly, "there is a place she might be." He pointed to a small balcony overlooking the great hall. "She has been known to hide there."

"We would see her, surely."

"In a black gown? At this time of night, the light is so poor that if she sits below the rail and keeps still, she would be invisible. It would be worth a try, anyway. I shall wait here. If she is not there, wave down to me and I will help you search the rest of the castle."

Edward nodded and made his way up the stairs. The balcony was not hard to find, once one knew of its existence, hidden by an innocuous velvet curtain. Flicking that aside, Edward stepping into the dark space beyond.

Very little light penetrated, for the great hall's chandelier hung below the level of the balcony, and the glass roof above was dark at this hour.

She was there. At first, it was a muffled sob which gave her away but as Edward's eyes adjusted to the darkness, he made out her outline sitting on the floor, her knees drawn up and her face buried in the folds of her skirt. In one hand she held a tiny square of lace, with which she dabbed ineffectually at her tear-stained cheeks now and then.

"Ah, Tess," he murmured, settling on the floor beside her and reaching one arm around her shoulders. "My poor darling. He is not worth so many tears, I assure you."

Her head shot up. "Tom? That is not it."

"Then what?" What else had happened that day? "You wanted money for wedding clothes? I can give you money for clothes if—"

"I want *my* money, Edward! *Mine!* The money my father left me, and now it will all go to *him*, to my uncle, who has more money than he knows what to do with already, and I shall have nothing at all. It is so unfair!"

"Why do you think it will go to the earl?" he said cautiously.

"I heard you talking, you and Captain Edgerton and the lawyer from London. My father stole it all, filched the tenants' rent money and bought those gold bars, so it has to go back to my uncle, and I know it is the law, I understand that, but it is so hard! I hoped to get my hands on it before anyone realised anything about it. But that lawyer is too thorough. He asks too many questions."

"So you knew? That your father was embezzling from the late earl's estate?"

"I knew he was up to something, and guessed the nature of it. So much money, and it should have been mine. He intended it to be mine, and now I shall be penniless."

That brought another flood of tears. Silently, Edward handed her a handkerchief.

"I have one," she sobbed, waving the scrap of lace.

He laughed. "That little thing is useless for a real crying session. You need a man's handkerchief for so many tears."

That brought a wan smile to her face, as she accepted the offered handkerchief. "At least Ulric is safe from me now. There is no point in marrying if I have no dowry."

"Oh Tess, I am so sorry," he said. "I never wanted you to marry Ulric, but I truly wanted... I still want you to have your fortune. At the risk of being boringly repetitive, would this be an appropriate moment to remind you that you can still marry me? I would give you your fifty thousand pounds, free of all conditions, so you could do as you pleased."

"But it would still be *yours*. You could change your mind at any time, and I would have no freedom with a string of babies to tie me down."

"Well, a trust fund for the money, then, and a marriage of convenience, so no babies. Would that be acceptable?" He despised himself for the pleading tone in his voice, but surely she would marry him now? What alternative had she?

She turned her tear-streaked face to look at him. "You still want to marry me, even though I have nothing?"

"Dearest, I have never cared a straw for your fortune, except that it was of interest to you. I have a large fortune of my own, as it happens, which I should be delighted to share with you."

"Would you do that for me? Why?"

"Because I love you, Tess. Surely you know that now. I want you beside me for the rest of my life."

"But I do not love you. I could never love you."

Oh, if she only knew the pain her words gave him! "I do not ask for love," he said with what dignity he could muster. "Am I truly so unpalatable to you, Tess?"

"You are stuffy, like all men of your rank... like the earl, denying me even a thousand pounds of my own money. So patronising! He barely even listened to me."

"Is there nothing about me that you like?" he said in desperation.

She whipped round to face him, mischief written on her face. "Why, yes! I like the way you kiss me."

And to his delight and astonishment, she curled up against his chest and pulled his head towards her.

Edward melted. She was a minx, of course, and should have been reined in years ago, but he adored her waywardness with all his being. At first, he simply allowed her to have her way, her lips, salty with tears, warming him and sending hope fizzing through him. She could think him as stuffy as much as she liked if she would only kiss him like this more often. But gradually, when she made no move to break away from him, he could not help himself from responding to her with more passion. And she matched him every step of the way, until he was dizzy and shaking with the multitude of nameless emotions roiling through him.

When eventually she pushed him away, laughing, he gasped at the sudden change, like a drowning man suddenly reaching the air at the surface.

"That was fun!" she said happily.

Fun! That was not the word he would have used. Incredible, perhaps. Exhilarating. Magical. Good Lord, mere *fun* did not begin to describe it.

Breathlessly, he said, "Well, you can forget the marriage of convenience. If you are going to kiss me like that, there is no way I shall be able to keep my hands off you."

She beamed at him. "Now that is better than Tom. He tells me it is most improper when we kiss, and there can never be anything between us. Or he used to," she added sadly.

Edward almost pushed her away in disgust. "I wish you would not compare me with Tom Shapman. It is most unhandsome of you."

"Jealous, are you?"

"I am not jealous of a common labourer, Tess."

"He is *not* a common labourer, he is a skilled craftsman, an artisan, someone to be respected, as he respected me."

"Tom Shapman is a working man who respected you because you are the niece of an earl. If you had ever had the misfortune to become his wife, you would have found out just how much he respected you. As his wife, he would have owned you, body and soul, and you would have had to do whatever he wanted. Not much freedom in that, is there?"

"If I had had my money—"

"He would have owned that, too. Tess, the only man who will treat a lady with the respect due to her rank is a *gentleman*. No working man, however worthy, can truly appreciate the world you inhabit, the restrictions society places on you. Your father understood that, and it is time you did, too."

She jumped to her feet, obliging him to stand, too. "Go away, Edward! Go back to London or wherever you were, and stop meddling in my life. What *you* need to understand is that my life is my own, and I will not be pushed around by you or anyone else. You are just like my uncle — you think all I need is a suitable husband, and suddenly everything will be wonderful. Well, it will not. If I cannot have my own money, then I shall not marry at all, and certainly not you!"

With a swirl of her black skirts, she was gone, leaving Edward torn between anger and despair.

20: Captain Edgerton Investigates

Captain Michael Edgerton rode slowly down the road to Birchall village, and thence to Westwick heights, home of Mr George Atherton, younger brother to the Earl of Rennington. Mr Atherton, a genial man of around fifty, was at home and received him at once.

"John Whyte, eh?" Atherton said, handing Michael a glass of Canary. "He is an excellent groom, Edgerton. I sincerely hope this is a routine enquiry, and you are not going to haul him off to York Gaol."

"I do not anticipate that, no, but he is Arthur Nicholson's natural son, the only one we know of, and he discovered that fact shortly before the man was murdered. Added to which, his family is... well, inclined to be argumentative. There was a rowdy meeting at the White Horse with a great deal of anger expressed about Nicholson, and then mere days later the man is dead. I have to look into it, and would have done so sooner if Whyte had not been away in Lincolnshire with Mr Bertram Atherton. By the time he returned, Shapman had confessed and it seemed unnecessary to look at Whyte. But now…"

"Quite, quite. Shapman has retracted his confession and your attention naturally switches back to Whyte. I do see your point."

"The visit to Lincolnshire… Whyte did not return with Mr Bertram, I understand?"

"No, he travelled separately with Bertram's horse, Catullus, and there was an incident at a toll-gate. The horse was slightly injured, and Whyte thought it best to walk him home, all the way from Lincolnshire. Then he was so terrified of arriving with an injured horse that he stayed at his sister's farm until he was quite sure there was no permanent damage. None of which we would have minded, but he was missing for two weeks with not a word, and we were worried, I can tell you. We had visions of the boy lying dead in a ditch somewhere, and how would we have faced his mother? And naturally we wondered if he had run off because he knew you wanted to talk to him. Bertram entrusted him with a very expensive horse and a purse heavy enough to cover all possible contingencies, so if he had been guilty, he could have quietly disappeared and that would have been the end of it."

"But he came back," Michael said thoughtfully. "That alone testifies to his innocence."

"Yes, indeed. Not that we truly doubted it, since the other grooms swear he was in his bed all night, and I know them well enough to take their word for it. Besides, he is a good lad, Captain, a hard worker and willing, which not all the grooms are. When Bertram marries, he will take one of our footmen to the Dower House and I plan to train Whyte up to replace him. Just whenever we need an extra pair of hands, of course, for he is far too good with the horses to be banished from the stables entirely."

"The legacy of growing up in a smithy," Michael said easily.

"Indeed. How do you wish to talk to him — alone?"

"The boy is only sixteen. It might be helpful if someone he knows is with him, if only to reassure him that he is not in danger of losing his place here."

"Of course. Then I shall accompany you, if I may, Edgerton. Such a reassurance will be most effective coming from me, I warrant."

They had to wait a few minutes at the stables for Whyte to return from exercising one of the horses, but it gave Michael an opportunity to observe how comfortable he was in the saddle. He was riding a spirited hunter, yet controlled him without effort despite being a shade undersized for his age. His face was aglow with enthusiasm, but as soon as he saw Atherton and Michael waiting for him, his expression froze into sheer terror.

"There you are, Whyte!" Atherton called to him cheerfully, as soon as he clattered into the yard. "Here's Captain Edgerton come down from Corland to have a word with you. Let Moreton see to Bradwell, and you come into the office for a few minutes."

"Yes, sir. Of course, sir," he muttered, dismounting with youthful agility and watching sadly as the horse was led away. It was clear he would have infinitely preferred the mundane chore of rubbing down to the horror of questioning by Michael.

The stable office was the usual scatter of papers, bits of tack, a couple of saddles, and shelves laden with all manner of unidentifiable oddments. Atherton moved things off chairs for Whyte and Michael and himself took the worn leather chair where the head groom usually sat.

"Now then, Whyte, since Shapman's confession has fallen apart, Captain Edgerton is back in search of Nicholson's murderer, you see, and you can help him."

"I don't know nothing about it, sir!" Whyte said, panic in his eyes. "I didn't do it, don't know who did. I were here all night, the other lads will vouch for me."

"Indeed they will," Michael said soothingly, "and already have, in fact. So no one suspects you of committing the murder, Whyte."

"Certainly not," Atherton said hastily. "No thought of that whatsoever, and no danger of you losing your place here, none at all. But you might still know something that would be useful to the captain."

"But I don't, sir, truly I don't!"

"Ah, but you may not be aware of it," Michael said. "Just imagine, if you should have noticed something odd, perhaps a day or two before the murder, if you were to mention it to me, it might be the vital clue that leads me to the murderer. Think what a hero you would be then."

"Oh... a hero..."

"So let us start with you, shall we? When did you first know you were illegitimate?"

"I've always known it, Captain, sir. Leastways, I don't remember a time when I didn't."

"What did your mother tell you about your father?"

"Only that he were a married man, an *important* man, but he were kind to her... special, she called him. A proper gentleman. I were a gentleman's son, she said, so I were special, too."

"But she never told you his name?"

"Never. Said it were best I didn't know."

"But then, somehow, you found out."

Whyte shook his head. "Not me. I weren't there. It were around Easter, when one o' the Wishaw girls were wed, and ma took most of a bottle of old Ma Wishaw's gooseberry wine. She came right out w' it, seemingly, that it were Mr Nicholson done it. Mind you, she remembered nowt about saying it afterwards, but everyone else remembered it, right enough, and two o' me uncles came up here to tell me. But it's nowt to me, sir. I never cared who it was got me ma wi' child. I had a good family round me, and never felt no lack. And now I've a good place here, and Mr Moreton says if I keep doing well, happen I'll end up as head groom when he retires, which is more than I'd ever dreamt when I were a lad. There's no way I'd ever do anything that'd put me in a hangman's noose, not when I got prospects here."

"Of course," Michael said. "But some of your family were quite angry about it, I understand. There was a meeting at the White Horse one evening, and tempers were high. Or so I heard."

Whyte shifted uneasily. "Aye, that were me grandda and me uncles. When they've had a few, they get a bit wound up. Two of me uncles had bumped into Mr Nicholson one day, and asked him straight out if he intended to do anything for me ma, seeing as how she's nobbut a laundry-woman still, and he said he didn't know her! They were spitting fire about that, I can tell you! So they got a bit agitated and talked a lot of nonsense about going up to t'castle to force him to own up to it, but me ma told them not to be so stupid and it all died down again."

"So none of your friends or relations went off to the castle that night and took an axe to Nicholson?"

"No! Course not! They'd have marched in and thumped him on the nose, maybe, but creeping around at night? Not anyone I know."

"Can you think of anything odd that happened around that time?"

"Oh, the vital clue?" Whyte said. "I wish I could think of something, but I don't remember anything out of the way happening. And no one I've talked to has the least idea who might have done it."

Which was no more than Michael had been told by countless others. He let Whyte return to his duties, and tucked his notebook away with a sigh.

"It is a frustrating mystery," Atherton said sympathetically. "One would suppose there would be *some* evidence left behind to identify the culprit, but everyone seems to have been virtuously tucked up in bed on the night in question."

"Not necessarily virtuously," Michael said, "but tucked up in bed, certainly."

Atherton chuckled. "Yet one person at least was not, and I do not believe it was merely a passing stranger. It must surely have been someone who knew Nicholson, and bore him a grudge for some reason."

"That is the very heart of the matter. *'For some reason'*. I can find any number of ways in which the sainted Mr Nicholson was less than perfection personified, but none that would rile a person so much as to plan his murder."

"It was planned, was it?"

"Oh yes. The axe was carefully hidden away, ready for use."

"I thought it was part of the display on the stairs? One of my nephew Eustace's assemblages of weaponry, where anyone could have removed it on the spur of the moment."

"That was certainly what we thought originally, but experiment showed that it could not easily be removed from the display in the middle of the night. When I tried it, I brought the whole edifice crashing down. It would take the utmost care to remove one item from the display."

"I see." Atherton frowned. "So someone saw the opportunity, removed the axe at a convenient moment, hid it away until needed and then retrieved it on the night of the murder. I will not ask how you know all this, Captain. But what will you do now that you have talked to Whyte?"

"I must go back to Pickering," Michael said, "and pick up the threads that were dropped there when Shapman confessed. Foolish man! So much time has now been lost. And I have taken enough of your time, sir. Thank you for permitting me to see Whyte."

"Anything we can do to help," Atherton said. "It is a ghastly business, and the sooner the murderer is apprehended the better."

Out in the yard, as Michael waited for his own horse to be brought out, another horse was being saddled.

"What a fine creature!" he said, walking all round the animal.

"That is my son Bertram's mount, Catullus," Atherton said. "Ah, here he is now."

Bertram Atherton was a slender young man of scholarly inclination, who would, one day, be just such another as his father, a respectable country gentleman spending much of his time shut away in his book room, letting the world pass him by unnoticed. It was perhaps unfortunate for both of them that the Earl of Rennington's marriage had been rendered invalid and his children illegitimate, and Mr George Atherton was now heir presumptive to the earldom, and his eldest son after him.

"Captain Edgerton!" Bertram called out, as he strode into the yard, dressed for riding. "It is always a pleasure to see you, naturally, but I am very sorry that Shapman's confession has now collapsed and you must begin your endeavours again."

Michael had no wish to dwell on the dispiriting prospect of beginning again, so he made some bland response and then added, "I have not yet seen you since your betrothal to Miss Franklyn. May I offer my felicitations, sir?"

"Thank you!" Bertram said, his face lighting up. His father made a noise that might have been laughter, and Bertram chuckled too. "My family think I am insane, since I protested so vehemently against her when she threw over my cousin Walter and set her sights on me, but I am very happy with my choice, I assure you."

"Have you set a date for the wedding yet? Mrs Edgerton will want to know."

Bertram laughed. "Not yet. It all happened rather quickly, so we are not rushing things, but I hope it will be before Christmas. Ah, this must be your horse, Captain. No one else rides with a sword strapped on. Are you going back to Corland? If so, I can accompany you part of the way. I am bound to Highwood Place to ride with Miss Franklyn."

"I planned to head out onto the moors for a while," Michael said. "I need to ponder my next steps, and I can do that best if I can clear my head with a good dose of fresh air."

"Then you may ride onto the moors with us, if you wish," Bertram said easily.

"With a betrothed couple? I should be very much *de trop.*"

"Not in the least, and it would reassure Miss Franklyn to have you and your sword with us. She has become a somewhat nervous rider of late."

"Oh? She had a fall? That can be distressing, even if no injury results."

"Nothing like that," Bertram said. "On several of her rides recently, she felt she was being watched. Spied on, possibly. On the last occasion, she was certain there was someone observing her from the woods to the north of Highwood Place. She turned her horse into the trees and gave chase, and heard noises but could not see the fellow. Happily, when she returned to the track, my cousin Mr Eustace Atherton was coming along, and he escorted her home. Since then, I have always accompanied her when she rides."

"Was she riding alone? That is not a good idea, even without strangers wandering in the woods."

"She had a groom with her, but she had outridden him, and it was not sensible to leave the track alone to pursue the fellow, whoever he was."

"If Miss Franklyn does not object," Michael said thoughtfully, "I should like to see the place where this man was lurking."

"I am sure she will be happy to show you," Bertram said.

The two mounted their horses, waved farewell to Mr George Atherton and trotted out of the yard.

Miss Beatrice Franklyn was a young lady of exuberant character, who had set her heart on marrying the Earl of Rennington's son and heir in order to make herself a countess. When he had lost his inheritance, she had turned her gaze on Bertram instead, and somehow, in between her attempts to ensnare him and his to avoid this fate, they had contrived to fall in love. Even though it now seemed likely that the earl would marry again and sire a son or two to put Bertram out of the inheritance, Miss Franklyn was not troubled by the loss of the title. She had discovered the joys of Latin, and looked set fair to become just as scholarly as her betrothed.

She was delighted to see Captain Edgerton, and very excited to show him the spot where she thought the man had been hiding. Riding ahead of the two men, her abundant black curls bouncing vigorously, she stopped at a point on the track where the trees pressed close.

"In there," she said, pointing with her whip.

"What precisely did you see?" Michael said.

She thought about that. "A movement. A glint of something shiny."

"Any sounds?"

"No, not then, but when I turned the horse into the trees, I heard the fellow crashing through the undergrowth. I could not get very far, not without damage to Blackthorn's legs, so I retreated and it went quiet again. But then Eustace came along, and when my groom caught up, Eustace went off himself to see what he could find, but there was no trace of anyone. He made me think I was imagining it, but I was not, I assure you."

"Are there Romanies in the area just now?" Michael said.

"Not at this time of year," Bertram said. "We had a small group of discharged soldiers last year, but they kept to themselves and quickly moved on."

"I think, if you do not mind, I shall go and have a look for myself," Michael said. "There may be traces of a fire, or rabbit snares, if anyone was camped out here."

"You believe me, then?" Miss Franklyn said in some surprise. "Everyone else thinks I imagined the whole thing."

"But it happened more than once, I understand. And the sounds of a man running away are very distinctive. You would not have imagined *that*. You will appreciate, Miss Franklyn, that I have a strong interest in any news of a stranger wandering these parts, a stranger who might have been here in June when Mr Nicholson was murdered."

"Oh!" Her eyes widened. "Then... perhaps I saw the *murderer!*"

"It is possible. Or it might simply have been a worker taking an unscheduled rest from his labours, who knows. But I suggest you two enjoy your ride together, and I will brave the undergrowth to see what I can find."

"I think we have the best of the arrangement, Captain," Bertram said.

Michael grinned. "By no means, Mr Atherton. There is nothing I enjoy more than pottering about in woods looking for clues."

He waved them away, then led his horse a few paces away from the track. Unstrapping the sword from its carrier on the beast's side, he fastened it to his belt. He had no expectation that he would need it, but he felt vaguely undressed without it.

Within ten paces, he encountered the problem that had deterred Miss Franklyn, for the way was thick with brambles and other impenetrable growth. He pressed on, however, wielding the sword on the densest patches, hoping his boots and thick buckskin breeches were stout enough to survive more or less unscathed. Before too long, as the tree canopy closed fully overhead, the brambles died away and the going was easier.

It was less easy to be sure he was following the precise direction defined by Miss Franklyn's pointed whip, but before too long he saw a small clearing ahead and was tolerably sure that this was the right location. A small rise and a conveniently positioned fallen tree trunk marked a comfortable spot where a man might sit to rest. And from there, he could see not merely back to the track where his horse was just visible, but a long section of track that curved away from the woodland. From here, a man with a telescope, say, could easily watch Miss Franklyn galloping along the curved section. She would be hidden by trees for a moment, only to reappear at the more open section where she had stopped and noticed the glint of something shiny — the telescope, perhaps.

The clearing held no clues, however. There was no fire, nor signs that there had ever been one. There were no horse droppings... but no, the man had run away, so he had no horse. Where would he run to? On the far side of the clearing were more brambles and other undergrowth, which presumably he had crashed through as he fled. Not far beyond lay a narrow track running at right angles. That would be much easier going for a man making a hasty escape, but which way would he go? Michael was a thorough man, so he explored both. To one side the track wound away through the woods, leading ultimately to the moors. In the other direction, the track soon led to a much larger clearing, where horses had been tethered quite recently — or one horse on several occasions, perhaps. From there several tracks led off in different directions, but it was impossible to tell which had been used recently.

Michael returned to his own horse in thoughtful mood. He could not find a way to connect this to the murder, for a man would hardly linger in woods nearby more than three months after the event. Yet he could not quite set it aside, either. It was yet another oddity that could not be explained.

21: Highwaymen And Elopements

The letter from James Neate was terse and to the point. Michael read it aloud to Luce and Pettigrew.

'To Captain M Edgerton, Corland Castle, West Yorkshire. Michael, Entry has been gained to the house, but Mrs Mayberry and her four nieces are gone, fled in the night, according to the neighbours, taking the servants with them, destination unknown. We do not yet know precisely what else they may have taken with them, but the safe is still there, the contents untouched. Do you think Miss Nicholson and her maid, who have seen the interior of the house, would be willing to come to Pickering to see what might be missing? If not, the bailiffs are compiling a detailed inventory which they might look at. Yours, J Neate.'

"This is what happens when one gives due notice to people," Michael said disgustedly. "They disappear. Poof! Vanished in the night."

"At least they did not manage to break into the safe," Pettigrew said.

"Shall you try to find them?" Luce said. "If they have not stolen anything—"

"But they know so much!" Michael cried. "And Mrs Mayberry, if that is even her right name, *lied* to us! She told us that Nicholson never went to the house, but that is clearly not the case, for all his account books are in that room above the coach house. We must find out where she has gone and question her closely until she tells us the truth."

"And yet," Pettigrew said placidly, "I seem to recall his lordship expressing the wish that the lady should not be inconvenienced."

"She is no lady!" Michael said hotly. "She is a brothel keeper and a thief."

"The first I will grant you, but the second is yet to be established. If indeed items are missing, then you will have every justification for pursuing Mrs Mayberry, but otherwise, she is hardly pertinent to the murder."

"Everyone is pertinent to the murder," Michael muttered, but without heat now. "Very well, Pettigrew. Have it your own way. Unless there has been thievery, Mrs Mayberry may be left in peace. Miss Nicholson told us of a cash box containing four hundred and twenty pounds. If that is still there and the exact amount remains within, we may assume that nothing has been stolen. However, if I should happen to be in Pickering and should happen to talk to a postilion, it would do no harm to enquire as to whether he transported a group of ladies away in the middle of the night, now, would it?"

Pettigrew laughed, and shook his head but said no more.

It was Luce who added quietly, "If you should happen to be in Pickering, Michael, I hope you will not forget poor Peachy, who has been missing for more than a month now."

"I do not forget Miss Peach, but unless we have some unexpected luck, I fear it may be impossible to pick up her trail now. But she is a resourceful lady. I do not believe she has come to any harm. She is merely busy on secret business of her own, that is all."

"I hope so, Michael. I do very much hope so."

***

Tess could not remember a time when she had not had a Plan. As a child, she had fully intended to be a sailor and fight to keep the seas free from the marauding hordes of other nations. Captain Nicholson would save the day for Britain, and she had kept a particularly straight stick in her bedroom for practising her swordplay. But her first visit to Scarborough and the sight of real ships being tossed about on tempestuous waves had scotched that notion.

Her next idea was to be a highwayman, living wild and free like the Romanies, and only occasionally, when living on berries and herbs palled, would she hold up a carriage and take a few coins with which to buy meat. Rich people could afford to share their wealth, after all. But no amount of persuasion succeeded in convincing her father, uncle or cousins to teach her about guns, and since she did not see how it could be done without weapons, she was forced to rethink.

Eventually she decided that she would be a spy, and sneak into France to find out what Bonaparte was up to. The government would be extremely grateful to her, she was sure of that, and she might even be knighted for her efforts. Sir Teresa Nicholson. Naturally she would have to speak French like a native to be able to pass unnoticed, and the governess of the day was startled to find her such an enthusiastic student all of a sudden, after showing little interest in any other subject.

But the seep of reality from her mother and aunt, the various governesses and her female cousins brought home to her that the only acceptable career for a woman was to marry and breed children. As first Izzy and then Josie married, and even Olivia, her confidante in all things, turned her thoughts in that direction, Tess had realised she was alone, and trapped. The only escape was marriage, but that was just another trap, to keep a woman subservient to a man.

That was when she had met Tom Shapman, and her Plan had taken a different turn. Why should she not marry, but to a man of her own choosing, who would not keep her in subjection as men of her own class would? And when her father had died, she had, for a brief moment, believed that all she wanted would at last come to her — money, and the man with the strong arms and clever hands, and most of all, freedom. Freedom from this stultifying castle and all the people within it.

Now that was gone, and even her emergency plan to marry Ulric Frith had flown out of the window. She would be penniless and would be a prisoner all her life.

She could not summon the energy to go anywhere, to do anything. She could not go to Birchall for fear of meeting Tom or, even worse, the poultry maid. There was no point in going to stay with Lady Tarvin at Harfield, or with Josie at Throxfield, or even Aunt and Uncle Lochmaben, because the walls would press her just as close anywhere else.

Nor could she sit tamely with the other females in the parlour, so she often took her cloak and found a secluded corner of the gardens where she could sit and be miserable by herself. There was a small sunken garden with arbours built into the surrounding wall where she could shelter from whatever wind or rain the skies saw fit to inflict on her. Somehow, the days were all filled now with wind and rain, with not a ray of sunlight to be seen. Even the fountain in the centre of the little garden was still and silent, as if in sympathy with her mood. There she huddled day after day, pondering her future and finding no answers.

Here it was that Edward found her one morning.

"I have caught up with you at last," he said cheerfully, sitting down beside her. "What an elusive girl you are, Tess Nicholson! I began to think you had grown wings and flown away."

"If only I could," she muttered.

"Why is the fountain not working? I am sure I have seen it splashing away cheerfully."

"It is broken. Kent will mend it. He has done so before." Her legs were stretched out on the bench, but now she drew her knees up to her chest and wrapped her arms around them. "Go away, Edward. Why are you still here, anyway? You have ruined my life — is that not enough for you?"

"I want to make your life better, Tess," he said gently.

"Nothing you could possibly do could make my life better!"

"Then make your own life better. What do you want, more than anything?"

She laughed. "Are you serious? I want Tom Shapman!"

"Then take him. Go down to Birchall village and seduce him away from his wife. You have the power to do that, if you truly want to."

For a moment, for a very brief moment, she actually considered the idea. To have Tom with her for always! And who cared if he was married to someone else?

She cared, she discovered. Marrying a woodworker was one thing, but running away with him when he had a wife was just wrong. She could not do it. Even telling herself she hated the poultry maid, she could not do it. Ruby, that was her name, and no doubt she loved Tom just as Tess did, and she had won him fair and square. And what would it say about Tom if he were willing to leave his wife? She would not want a man who could so easily desert her.

"No," she said slowly. "Even I have some moral standards."

That made Edward laugh. "You astonish me. Well, then, what else do you want? Because whatever it is, if it takes money, I can make it happen."

She swung her legs to the ground in sudden excitement. "I want to be a highwayman."

That made him laugh even more. "A highway *woman*, you mean. Great heavens, Tess, I did not expect that! What would we need? Masks and cloaks, of course. A pair of—"

"We?"

"Of course. You do not imagine for one moment that I would miss out on an adventure like that, do you? If I am going to be hanged, and clearly in your company that is inevitable, it might as well be for something exciting. Pistols, then, and a good, fast horse each. We will probably need a base somewhere, because I suspect sleeping under hedges would become tiresome in the winter. A remote cottage, perhaps, where our nocturnal activities would be unobserved, but quite close to the turnpike. Oh, do you have a particular road in mind? It might be as well to give a wide berth to your home area to avoid the embarrassment of holding up your own mother."

"Or yours," she said, grinning.

"No, that would be an essential part of the enterprise, holding up my mother at regular intervals. I should enjoy that excessively."

He looked suddenly fierce, and she had a curious feeling of affinity with him. She was not the only one who disliked her own mother!

"Do you think we would be hanged?" she said. "They would have to catch us first."

"To be honest, being hanged would be the least of our worries, Tess. I cannot be the only man who travels with a loaded pistol at the ready. A far more likely end is a bullet through the heart. I am quite prepared to risk it, if it would amuse you, but I should hate to see you die young, my love. I should not particularly like to meet my own end that way, but if it were you..."

"Then we will not do it," she said at once. "I am not quite ready to die yet, although I should like to learn to shoot. Will you teach me?"

"I would love to, but I would need your mother's permission."

Tess groaned in frustration. "It always comes down to that! I cannot do this or that because Mama would not approve. How can I ever be free of her?"

He slid closer to her on the bench, taking her hand in his and gently stroking the back of it. "You know the answer to that, my darling. If we were married, we could do as we pleased, go where we want, be whatever we want to be." She pulled a face, and he went on, "It could be a secret marriage, if you wish."

She turned a little to face him, laughing. "A *secret* marriage? How would that work?"

"Well, we would have to get a special licence and be married somewhere we are not known, but we need tell no one about it. No announcement in the *Gazette.* Then when we meet in public, we can pretend not to know each other. *'Miss Nicholson, do you know Lord Tarvin? He is most anxious to dance with you.'* And you would say loftily, *'I believe we have met before — a slight acquaintance.'* Then we would dance and talk about the weather and the state of the roads and what a crush there is. We would have to leave separately, of course, but we would return to wherever we were staying and retire to bed together, laughing at those credulous people who knew nothing."

"Bed? What about the marriage of convenience?"

"I told you — I could not hold to that when you kiss me with such fire. You need not worry about that side of marriage, my darling. When you kiss like that, I know you will enjoy the rest of it."

"With Tom, I would have."

He dropped her hand abruptly, a look of such pain on his face that she was shocked. He jumped to his feet and paced across the sunken garden and back again.

"Well! You do have a way of puncturing a man's vanity, Tess," he said, his voice shaky. "And I thought we were getting on so well, too."

"I beg your pardon," she said, contrite. "I did not mean... it was a stupid thing to say."

"Perhaps I should take up woodwork," he said, sitting down with a whump on the bench again. "Would that help? I could roll up my sleeves and replace the cravat with a red spotted neckerchief and make chairs. Perhaps then I would be less *stuffy*. I cannot imagine why I ever thought I could win you over, Tess. I must have been mad. You have a heart of stone, clearly. Have you any idea how many caps have been thrown my way in town? Daughters of earls and viscounts... wealthy heiresses... all of them accomplished and educated and *suitable* for a man in my position. I could have had my pick, but no, they were all boring. Stuffy, even. I foolishly imagined that a chaplain's daughter who wants to be a highwayman would be a more interesting wife. What an idiot I have been!"

For answer, she slid along the bench towards him and put an arm around his slumped shoulders. "Hush. I am the foolish one. If you had an ounce of common sense, you would run back to London as fast as you can, and marry one of your heiresses. You are supposed to disapprove of me, you know."

He raised his head, and she saw the humour shining in his eyes. "But that would be no fun at all."

She laughed and, because she could not at that moment resist the twinkle in his eyes, she leaned forward and pressed her lips against his. He responded with such fierceness that all the breath left her lungs and her legs turned to jelly. It was as well she was already sitting down for otherwise she would have fallen down. She clung to him in fear that she would simply collapse at his feet, but he held her tight in his arms and after a while, when she realised that she was in no danger of falling, she surrendered utterly to the glory of his embrace. Such a man! Such a kiss! Such joy bubbling up in her heart... but she could not... it was impossible... what on earth *was* this that she was feeling? It was like nothing she had ever experienced before, and it was terrifying.

Pushing him away, she slid away from him, breathing heavily. And then she felt bereft.

"Oh, Tess, Tess!" he groaned. "Marry me, my love, *please!*"

She took a deep breath, then another. Deep inside, her heart was screaming, *'Yes, yes, yes!'*

But her head was still just about in charge. "I cannot possibly marry you, Edward."

"Why not? *Why not?* Give me a single reason why we should not be married at once."

"Because my mother would approve of you."

He stared at her in astonishment, and then, very slowly, he began to laugh. "We will just have to elope, then. She would certainly not approve of me then."

Tess laughed, too. Such an infuriating man, in so many ways, but he had the power to surprise her, too. And if he was truly willing to elope with her... that was not stuffy at all, was it?

***

Edward's mother wrote almost every day, in increasingly strident terms.

'My dearest son, Where are you? I do not expect you to dance attendance on me, for I am well accustomed to the loneliness of widowhood and the sorrow of having no daughter to console my declining years, and I know you have business that occupies you from time to time, but please assure an anxious mother that you are well. You know how I worry about you. I write to Corland as you directed, but having no response for some time, I now wonder if my letters are reaching you at all. Are you back in town? The Williamsons are there at present for Lady Serena to consult her physician. Or if you should happen to be in York, Lady Anne is visiting her cousins there. This would be a good time to fix your interest with her, too good an opportunity to miss by dallying at Corland. What business keeps you there? I do trust you are keeping well away from Tess Nicholson, who is nothing but trouble. Do write soon, Edward, if only for the reassurance your reply would furnish to your affectionate mother, Alvira Harfield.'

He wrote back as he thought appropriate.

'My dear mother, I am quite well. I am fixed at Corland for the present, and do not yet know my plans beyond that. I am fully aware of Miss Nichol-

son's nature. My regards to Aunt Myrtle and to you from your dutiful son, Edward.'

He smiled as he imagined his mother's reaction when she read it. Lord, how she badgered a man! But he was not a child any longer, obliged to account for every lesson with his tutors and every boy he befriended. And while it had amused him to pretend to be considering this or that eligible female during the season, he was not about to tell her that he had been climbing trees and chasing about Yorkshire in pursuit of Tess Nicholson. His mother would have an apoplexy if she knew the half of it!

It was true that Tess appeared superficially to be a demure maiden. She had returned to the dinner table each evening instead of skulking in her room, and they always sat together, ignoring Lady Alice's invitations for Edward to sit next to her. Afterwards, they played chess, and he had to concentrate hard to have any chance of defeating her. Quite often he was able to persuade her to ride with him, with a groom for propriety, and it amused him to think that even his mother could find nothing amiss in Tess's person or behaviour.

Yet their conversation, had she overheard it, would have given her palpitations. They planned in great detail how they would live as highwaymen. When that had been agreed, they discussed being pirates or running a gaming hell or simply disappearing to America, not telling a soul where they were going. And sometimes Edward raised the issue of elopement, and how they would plan that.

"We would need four horses to our post chaise," Tess had said. "Just in case Mama sends Captain Edgerton after us."

"Why a post chaise? I have a perfectly good carriage," Edward protested.

"Oh, the one with your crest on the door, I suppose? So that every toll gate keeper between here and the border will say, *'Oh yes, Lord Tarvin passed this way three hours and ten minutes ago.'* Do have some sense, Edward. It must be a post chaise, and we must run away in the middle of the night, so that our flight will not be discovered for some hours."

"And how are we to get a post chaise out here in the middle of the night with no one noticing?"

"It will wait for us on the road, of course. I am afraid we will not be able to take much luggage with us, only what we can carry."

"It is a pity I cannot take Deakin with me, for he is a strong fellow and could carry quite a bit, but one does not quite like to take one's valet on an elopement. It does not have the proper romantic sensibility to it, somehow. And you would have to leave Betty and Harold behind, too."

"With pleasure. How long will it take us to reach Scotland?" she said.

"Two or three days. Do you really think Lady Alice would send Captain Edgerton after us?"

"I do, and he is very likely to catch us up, too. He may not be very good at catching murderers but I think chasing an eloping couple would be something he would do very well."

"We shall just have to elope when he is not here — as now. Shall I order the post chaise for tomorrow night?"

She only laughed and said, "Silly boy."

But the next day, the captain returned from Pickering with James Neate and two other men, and were shut away with the earl and Mr Willerton-Forbes for some time. Edward, alerted by Deakin of the event, loitered in the library watching the door to the earl's study to see the newcomers as soon as they emerged. But when the door opened, it was only the earl to speak to the footman stationed outside. The footman nodded and then pointed across the room to Edward. The earl waved him across.

"Come inside, Tarvin, for I have news that affects you. It affects Tess most of all, but Edgerton has told me— Never mind, just come inside."

The two newcomers were a goldsmith from London, brought in to value the gold in the safe, and a bailiff who specialised in valuing houses and their contents to defray debts. The gold, it now appeared, was worth a great deal more than they had originally supposed.

"The goldsmith who valued the one bar we had removed assumed we wanted to sell, so he offered us a low price for it," Edgerton said. "When the whole collection was properly valued, by weighing every bar individually, it was worth a great deal more. And the house... the house is stuffed with precious objects. A whole room in the basement full of silver. Expensive rugs on the floor, fine furnishings, porcelain ornaments, exquisite glassware, some excellent paintings on the walls... In all, that house and its contents, plus the money in the bank, are worth some hundred thousand pounds."

"And... how much of that will go to Tess? After allowing for the late Mr Nicholson's thievery?"

"I cannot account for more than fifty thousand pounds stolen, if that," Willerton-Forbes said. "Miss Nicholson will inherit a fortune of at least fifty thousand pounds. She is a very wealthy lady."

Edward slumped into a chair. His dreams were over. Tess would marry Ulric after all, and be free.

22: An Invitation

Tess could hardly take it in.

"Fifty thousand? And it is certain?"

"It is at least fifty thousand pounds," Mr Willerton-Forbes said. "I cannot be precise about the exact sum yet, but I can assure you it is at least that much. I will know very soon. You will have a very pretty dowry when you marry, Miss Nicholson. I congratulate you."

"But how is it possible? The gold I understand, it was undervalued initially, but all these valuable items in the house — surely my father did not buy them? I never recall him taking any interest in art."

It was the earl who answered. "My father bought the house and furnished it many years ago, so most likely it was his doing."

"Did he use the house himself?" Tess said, but the men exchanged uncomfortable glances. "Why else spend so much money on it?"

Mr Willerton-Forbes said carefully, "We believe there was a lady living there, whom the late earl visited from time to time."

"His mistress, you mean?" she said.

"Tess!" the earl said. "A girl of your age should know nothing of such matters."

"Well, I do. Was it Mrs Mayberry?"

The earl sighed. "I never knew her name. She was not mentioned in his will, however, only the house, which was left to your father. No one knew at the time just how valuable a bequest that was. But what became of the lady, I know not."

Tess at once went looking for Edward. He was not in any of the principal rooms, but a visit below stairs soon ascertained that he had not gone out riding or in the carriage, nor had he asked for his outdoor clothes. He was still in the castle, therefore. She had no compunction about going straight to his room. He was not there, but there was a faint hint of him in the air, a subtle manly scent that she immediately recognised as unique to him. Idly she ran her fingers over his brushes laid out on his dressing table. They were silver-backed, with his crest on the handle, and of an old-fashioned design embossed with his crest, perhaps inherited from a previous holder of the title. Stuffy, as he was.

But he was not there, and she had run out of places to look... no, there was one place he might be. It was her own refuge, but perhaps he needed a place to hide away, too.

She made her way along the upper corridor, and ducked behind the curtain that hid the balcony overlooking the great hall. He was there, sitting on the floor with his knees drawn up, head lowered.

"Edward?" She knelt beside him on the floor. "You have heard, then. Are you not pleased for me?"

He lifted his head a little to look at her, and she was shocked to see how grey his face was, how anguished his expression. "You will marry Ulric," he said in flat tones.

"I have to. It is the only way to get my money... to be sure that I have full control of it."

"You cannot be certain of that. Ulric is unpredictable."

"His mother and I can manage him."

"I pray you are right, Tess. I thought... I hoped... that you might actually marry me. If we eloped. I thought that would make me less stuffy."

"Oh, Edward, that was only a game! I would never... although it would have been fun, if I had *wanted* to marry you. It would have put my mother in such a pelter! Not that she ever truly gets in a pelter. I might get on with her better if she did. Does your mother get in a pelter?"

He gave a wry smile. "No. She harangues me. *'Edward, you must do this. Edward, you must do that. Edward, you must marry at once.'* I go to a lot of trouble to arrange *not* to do all those things she says I must do without fail."

She smiled back at him. "You are a rebellious son."

"And you are a rebellious daughter. Is there nothing I can say to dissuade you from marrying poor Ulric?"

Tess gently stroked his face. "I mean Ulric no harm, you know that. He will be perfectly happy living at Myercroft with his mother and his half-brothers and sisters, and all his horses conveniently to hand."

"You intend to marry him, and then leave him there with his mother?"

"I do not think his life would be enhanced by having me underfoot, do you? Or mine in living with him. Nor is his mother sensible enough to leave in charge. I hope I can depend on you to look after Ulric, even when he is married."

Edward looked at her, frowning. "And how am I supposed to do that?"

"By tying up his income so that his mother cannot get hold of it. You are his trustee until he marries, so you can surely deal with the legal wrangling, and you seem to be rather good at keeping mothers in check. No, do not shake your head like that, for I know you can do it if you set your mind to it."

"No, I cannot. My hands are tied. By the terms of his father's will, the income goes directly to Ulric when he marries... but of course, if he were to *ask* me to manage it for him... yes, it could be done that way. And you will persuade him to put all your money into your hands. But this is still madness, Tess. You would do far better to marry me."

"And join the peerage? Wear fancy robes for state occasions? Everywhere I go, it would be my lady this and my lady that, and I could never slink about in the shadows again. I could not!"

He gave a wry smile. "Too stuffy for words. I can see that."

"Edward, can you not understand? I do not need a husband. I have never needed a husband, not even Tom. He was only ever a means to achieve a degree of freedom, and much as I regret him in many ways, I take your point that he would perhaps have become a domineering husband in time, and expected me to play the obedient wife. That would not have ended well! Perhaps you and I are better suited, but we are still at odds more often than not, and if I were your wife, sooner or later you would start throwing your weight around. But Ulric... he will never be a real husband. He is only necessary to allow me to gain control of my money... my *own* money, after all. I want nothing more from him than that."

"But you cannot live independently, Tess. No woman can. She must live under the protection of a father or uncle or brother, or else she marries.

That is how the world works. If we were married, then I would protect y ou."

"I do not need to be protected. What you call protection is more like a cage."

"No, no, no! I only want to be there to pick up the pieces when you get yourself into trouble."

She laughed. "What an opinion you have of me! I doubt I shall ever be in such trouble as to need rescuing."

His smile widened. "Tess, my darling, you will always be in trouble. That is one of the reasons I love you so much... why I want to be your husband so I have the *right* to protect you. Not to constrain you, any more than I would trap a butterfly in a bottle. I want to see you fly, my love, but someone needs to be there to watch out for danger and to take care of you when you singe your wings by flying too close to the flame."

She gazed at him, chastened. He truly meant it, the foolish man! She leaned forward and kissed him gently. "How sweet you are, when you are not shouting at me. I wish you were not quite so respectable, so that I might consider marrying you. It is a pity."

"A great pity, but I cannot escape the barony, unfortunately."

"No, but if you were to kill a man in a duel, say, we could flee the country together and live as wandering outcasts on the continent. That would be amusing, would it not?"

"It would. Presumably we would be penniless, so we would have to live on our wits, by thievery or cheating at cards, and there would be the constant threat of discovery and being hauled back to England to be hanged. How charming a life we should lead. Short, no doubt, but exciting while it lasted. Sadly, I fear I am too stuffy to kill a man to bring this delightful situation into being."

He wrapped an arm around her and pulled her close, as she snuggled against him with a sigh of contentment. Edward was so much fun in this mood!

"You are a good friend to me, Edward," she murmured into the smooth wool of his coat.

"I have no wish to be your *friend.*"

She lifted her head to gaze up at him. "I may not need a husband, but I shall always need a friend. Will you not be a friend to me? Help me to keep Ulric happy, at least."

"That much I can and will do."

"And climb trees for me... and kiss me when I am upset."

He laid his lips on hers for a moment, and with his free hand softly stroked her cheek. "Ah, Tess! I had my life just as I wanted it until you came along and upended everything. I do not want to be only your friend, but if that is all I can be, then I shall be the best and truest friend there ever was."

And then his lips were on hers again, burning into her with a fervour that seemed to be more desperation than desire. She surrendered happily to the moment, content in his arms. Her life might be strange and unsettled just now, and the future uncertain, but none of that mattered when Edward was there to hold her tight and kiss her worries away.

Her friend... her best and truest friend.

***

The letter was so unexpected that Tess had no idea what to make of it.

'To Miss T Nicholson, Corland Castle, North Riding. My dear Miss Nicholson, Forgive me for writing to you when we have not been introduced,

but it seems to me that your betrothal to Mr Ulric Frith permits me to make the approach. My husband, Sir Ernest Peterson, and I are very fond of Ulric, regarding him almost as a son, and wish to do everything in our power to forward his happiness. To that end, we feel it would be helpful to both of you if you and Ulric were to pay a visit to Myercroft for a few days, so that Ulric might show you around your future home. There may be changes or improvements you will wish to undertake before your marriage. The only other person we have invited is Lord Tarvin in his capacity as a trustee of Ulric's estate. It will be helpful while you are here to discuss the winding up of the trust fund, your marriage settlements and the arrangements for us to depart from Myercroft. Although our lease runs until Lady Day, for Ulric's sake we will vacate the house before that date, if that is what you wish. I shall also be writing to Lady Alice Nicholson to request her permission for you to come to Myercroft. Respectfully yours, Jane Peterson.'

The letter to her mother had clearly arrived at the same time, for Tess was summoned to her mother's sitting room.

"Are you persisting in this foolish marriage, Tess? Lord Tarvin told me the truth about Mr Frith, you know, so you cannot pretend that this is a match of affection."

"I have never pretended any such thing," Tess said with dignity. "If you dislike it, you may blame Papa, who tied up my inheritance so that I have no alternative but to marry."

"But not to a half-wit!"

"Ulric is not a half-wit, Mama. He is not a man of much brain, but so long as he has horses about him, he is perfectly content."

"Why can you not marry a proper gentleman, as your father intended? Lord Tarvin, for instance."

"Lord Tarvin, Lord Tarvin!" she cried, pacing angrily across the room. "What is so wonderful about Lord Tarvin?"

Her mother sat placidly, hands neatly folded in her lap, her sightless eyes following the swish of Tess's skirts back and forth. "I am sure it does not matter to you that he is a baron, and very wealthy, and would make you mistress of a great house, and that attitude is very proper. Such details do not weigh with me either. So long as your husband can keep you in comfort, and support a family, rank and position do not matter very much. But Lord Tarvin is a pleasant young man. I like the sound of his voice, his manners are good, as far as I can judge, and I am told he is well-favoured. And he loves you, Tess. There can be no better husband for a woman than a man who adores her."

"But I do not love him."

"No. The only person you love is yourself, Tess. I live in hope that one day you will grow up and realise that there are other people in the world who care about you, and are hurt by your selfish ways."

"No one cares about me! You and Papa have never cared about me, or whether I am happy or not. You only ever wanted me to creep away and not bother you, to be silent and behave like a little mouse and do whatever *good* girls are supposed to do. And now you want me to go away and marry Lord Tarvin so that you will not have to think about me ever again! Well, I will not creep away or be silent, nor will I marry a dull old stick like Edward, so you need not think it! Pleasant young men bore me to tears, Mama, and if you knew anything about me, you would understand that. So I am going to manage my own life, in a way that brings me the most happiness, and you may as well accept that."

Irritatingly, her mother only smiled. Did nothing dent her composure?

"I cannot blame you for that, Tess, since it was precisely what I did myself. You think me a helpless creature, I dare say, and physically I am, but just because I am blind does not mean I must... how did you put it? Creep away and be silent. No, when my father wished me to marry the late Lord Tarvin and I did not, I made arrangements to see that matters turned out just how I wished. I had a little help, but it all resolved most satisfactorily, and no one suspected a thing. Except your father, of course." Her smile softened. "No one ever pulled the wool over *his* eyes."

"No, the shoe was very much on the other foot," Tess said savagely. "Papa was a wicked, deceitful man."

"Nonsense," Lady Alice said robustly.

"How do you think he compiled this fortune that I inherited? Not legitimately, that much is certain."

"This house that the late earl left him—"

"—is but a small proportion of it!" Tess cried. "The largest portion of that money came from embezzlement of the earl's rentals from his tenants. A farmer would hand over twenty-five pounds and Papa wrote down twenty in the earl's books and pocketed the difference. And that house in Pickering... Mrs Mayberry was not a respectable woman, and nor were her nieces. They were not her nieces at all, I expect."

"No," Lady Alice said firmly. "You are mistaken, Tess. You have misheard something, or misunderstood it, I am sure. Your father was a good man."

"Such a good man that he never bothered to tell the earl that he had never been ordained, and look at the damage that has caused."

"I am sure that is a mistake... Arthur would not... he would not have intended... the last thing he would have wanted was to harm the late Lord

Rennington. They were the best of friends, always, despite the difference in their ages."

"Such good friends that the earl never complained when Papa somehow always won at piquet. Did Papa ever lose? I do not remember a time. That was another way he lined his pockets, Mama."

"No," Lady Alice whispered, hand to throat. "No, he was a good man... on the whole. All men have their weaknesses, naturally, and perhaps the lure of money was too strong for him, but he always meant well and to me that made him a good man. A *kind* man who loved us both dearly."

"Well, he had an odd way of showing it," Tess said. "But since he has amassed this fortune, and not all of it can be identified as thievery, I shall have at least fifty thousand pounds, which I have no intention of handing over to a husband. So I am going to marry Ulric Frith, Mama, because I can persuade him to give me full control of it, and he will not trouble me as a real husband would do, and then my life will be my own at last. Are you going to give me permission to stay at Myercroft? I am going to go, regardless of your opinion."

Lady Alice sighed. "I know. I have never been able to stop you from doing whatever you want. All I ask is that you take Betty and Harold with you, and since Lord Tarvin is also invited, you may as well travel with him. A baron's private carriage will be far more comfortable for the journey than travelling post."

Tess laughed. "Very well, Mama, it shall be as you wish, although I expect we will quarrel all the way there." Kneeling at her mother's feet, she took her hand and said quietly, "I know I am a great trial to you, Mama, but once I have my money and I am free to live my life as I please, you will not need to worry about me again."

Her mother squeezed her hand. "Mothers always worry about their children, Tess, and especially daughters. While I applaud your spirit, I cannot approve of the direction you are taking. I wonder sometimes if you have not got the worst of both your father and me in you — my determination to forge my own happiness, and his obsession with money. Both of us employed somewhat unorthodox methods of obtaining our own way, but I never stepped beyond what was proper, and your father had a charm that carried him through many difficulties. You are more like a hound racing after the faintest scent. It is irrational, this desire to control your own fortune at all costs. I hope you are not making decisions about your life solely to thwart your father's wishes or mine."

"Oh, no. Not *solely* for that reason, Mama," she said mischievously.

Lady Alice sighed. "That is what I feared, Tess. I shall reply to Lady Peterson that you have my permission to visit Myercroft, but I have misgivings... deep misgivings about the entire enterprise."

"Thank you, Mama. I hope one day you will understand that this is all for the best."

"For whom? Not for you."

"Yes, for me, for who else knows what will content me except myself? But also best for Ulric and his family, too, and certainly best for Lord Tarvin, who will be spared a most troublesome wife. I want my freedom too badly to marry at all, in truth, but if I must, then better by far to bind myself to Ulric than a man who will keep me in subjection forever."

Lady Alice shook her head sadly. "Oh, Tess, Tess! Marriage to the right man, a man who truly loves you, is not subjection, it is glorious. I wish above all things that you could experience that too."

23: Apstead House

Edward found that the journey to Myercroft was not to be a straightforward one. Captain Edgerton had requested that Tess and her maid might look around Apstead House, to see if they could determine whether anything had been removed from it by Mrs Mayberry, so they were all to go to Pickering first. Mrs Edgerton joined Edward and Tess in Edward's carriage, while Captain Edgerton rode alongside them, leaving his own carriage for the servants and luggage. Mr Neate had vanished, to make his way there by some other means.

The journey was made less tedious by a small travelling chess set that Tess had produced from some dusty recess of Corland, so they beguiled the time with a demonstration of Tess's superiority in the game, much to Mrs Edgerton's amusement.

"How is it that you are able to defeat Lord Tarvin so comprehensively?" she asked Tess. "He seems to me to be playing quite well, but then everything collapses and you put him into checkmate with ease."

"He forgets about his queen," she said at once. "It is the most powerful piece on the board, yet he seldom uses it. But is that not typical of a man, to overlook the capabilities of the female?"

"I might have done so once," Edward said, "but the longer I am in your company, Miss Nicholson, the greater my respect for female ability."

"A gallant answer," Mrs Edgerton said.

"Which has the added virtue of being entirely true. And I shall remember the queen next time."

"I hope you will, for you might perhaps defeat me once in a while. Next time we play, I shall explain how best to use your pawns."

"How did you learn to play so well?" Mrs Edgerton said. "Who is the chess champion at Corland?"

"Kent taught me. You would not know it, for he is always funning, but he is very clever. He understands how all sorts of machines work. Whenever the fountain in the garden breaks, Kent makes it work again, and he loves clocks... engines... mill machinery. He says he wants to be an engineer, but Uncle Charles will not let him."

"That is hardly fitting work for the son of an earl," Edward said at once.

"Even so, if he has a skill in that direction, it is a great pity he is not permitted to build a career on it," Mrs Edgerton said.

"Engines! Who needs engines?" Edward said. "Noisy, smelly things with their great chimneys belching smoke."

"They bring us cheap cottons and woollens for our gowns," Mrs Edgerton said with a smile, "and provide employment for many people."

"And thereby put thousands of cottage weavers out of work," he said seriously. "I do not like all these mills that are springing up here, there and everywhere. Yes, they employ many people, but they must live in cramped accommodation in smoke-filled towns, and watch their children play in filthy streets crowded with horses and wagons. Is it not better to live in a cottage in the country, surrounded by clean air and fresh water, with a bit of land to grow vegetables and keep chickens? The man has employment on the farms or for the local squire, and his wife sits at home with her loom and the baby on her knee."

"And they all live in poverty, town and country dwellers alike," Mrs Edgerton said. "At least the mills and their engines make goods cheaper, and so help those who have little money to make the pennies stretch a bit further."

"Would you then encourage the farm labourer to go to the nearest town and seek employment there?"

"Perhaps. A man may be better off taking employment from whichever mill owner will pay him the most money, and find his own lodgings, rather than working on a farm with a tied cottage such that a single disagreement with his employer would see him lose his livelihood and his home as well. But in all cases, it is for the employer to ensure his workers are contented. So many of them will pay as little as they can, even though they make vast profits."

"And how do you make them pay more?" Edward said. "If there is an abundance of workers, wages need not be high. Only if there is a shortage will pay increase."

"I do not have the answer to that," Mrs Edgerton said with a sigh. "I should like every family to have enough to live on and a little to spare, and nobody have to depend on the parish for the necessities of life, but I do not know how that is to be achieved."

"All we can do, those of us who own land and have tenants, is to ensure our rents are fair, and that we offer a helping hand to those who might need it. We cannot fix the world, only our own small part of it."

Tess was listening intently to the discussion, and now she said, "I think you could do more. Those with money can always do more. Why must mill-workers live in cramped accommodation? Why do their employers not build decent housing for them, with a little bit of land to each cottage for vegetable and chickens?"

"That would be expensive," Edward said frowning.

"But you have money to spare, do you not? It could be a charitable project… or *I* could do it!" she cried, an excited smile lighting her face. "I do not need fifty thousand pounds, after all, for my wants are small. I only need a cottage myself—"

"With a drawing room and dining for twenty-four," Edward said, chuckling.

"Well… a large sort of cottage, certainly, but the rest of my money could be put into something of the sort… decent housing for families."

"Who would pay rent, so it would be an investment," he said.

"Oh, yes! So it would."

She beamed at him happily, and since they were approaching Pickering, the subject was allowed to drop. To Edward's surprise, the carriages drove directly to Apstead House.

"Should we not secure accommodation first?" he said.

Mrs Edgerton smiled. "Michael has already made arrangements."

The front door opened, revealing the blond Scotsman, Mr Alexander, and James Neate, who had contrived to reach Pickering before them. Behind them stood two neatly dressed maids. Captain Edgerton dismounted swiftly enough to open the carriage door and assist first his wife and then Tess to alight.

"Since the house is presently uninhabited, I thought you might like to stay here while you are in Pickering," Edgerton said to Tess.

"Stay here? Am I allowed to?"

"It is your house, Miss Nicholson," he said gravely.

"Is it? This is not a part of my inheritance that Uncle Charles will take from me?"

"My understanding is that he will take what is owed to him in gold bars, and you may have the house and everything within it. Which you may choose to sell, if you have no need for it."

"Or I could live in it," she said, her face alight with enthusiasm. "It is the size of a large cottage, is it not?"

Edward laughed, although Edgerton looked mystified.

"Only if your trustees agree," he said quickly. "Sandy, have you acquired a cook?"

"In a manner of speaking," the Scotsman said. "Ye'll have a good dinner, Michael. Come away in. Yer attracting some attention from the neighbours."

It was true that a little crowd had gathered to watch the arrival of two carriages, laden with luggage, outside Apstead House, where such occurrences had not been commonplace. The watchful neighbours were no doubt aware that the ladies of the house had fled in the night, after which a number of men had come each day, and now it seemed there would be people staying there, perhaps living there. Naturally they were curious.

Edward crossed the road to the largest group of onlookers. "Good day to you all! I am Lord Tarvin. I shall be staying at Apstead House for a day or two."

"Is it your house now?" one of the crowd called out.

"Not mine, no. You see the young lady in black? Miss Nicholson. It is her house now."

Heads craned to see the new owner. "Better than they women," one of the men said. "This were a respectable street before they come along."

"There will be nothing like that in future," Edward said soothingly. "Miss Nicholson is the daughter of Lady Alice Nicholson, sister to the Earl of Rennington."

There were murmurs of approval at this news, and Edward felt it was safe to retreat to the house. He had never seen the main part of it, but he knew that it contained many valuable furnishings and works of art, so he was not surprised to find it well appointed. Its glory was somewhat faded, leaving it looking rather shabby and neglected, but he detected the hand of a person of excellent taste in the arrangements.

There was a great crowd of people in the hall, including some that Edward did not recognise. The Scotsman was waving his arms about excitedly, his accent suddenly impenetrable. An unknown gentleman, for some reason carrying a small child in his arms, was laughing at him, while a small, dark woman talked back in an accent just as strong. Tess was watching the three of them in bemusement, while the servants milled about shifting boxes and bags and umbrellas.

"Lord Tarvin, come and meet my cousin, Jeanie," the Scotsman called. "She's frae Edinburgh, too. And this is her husband, Rycroft of Melverley, in Leicestershire. The wee man is Archie, their son."

Rycroft inched through the mayhem to Edward's side, shifting the child onto one hip to offer his hand. "Delighted to meet you, Lord Tarvin. We have been hearing all about your exploits with tree-climbing and the like. Quite an adventure!"

"It was indeed. But what brings you north? You are a long way from Leicestershire."

"My wife brings me north," he said with a grin. "Finding that Cousin Sandy was fixed in Yorkshire for a while longer, Jeanie decided she would like to take the sea air at Scarborough. Then, when a cook was needed, she brought her skill with dumplings to Pickering."

"Mrs Rycroft is to cook for us? Surely we can eat at an inn? I do not like to think of her trapped in the kitchen."

"There is nothing she likes better," Rycroft said. "In fact, if ever she disappears at Melverley, I know precisely where to look for her. We have assigned the best room to you, Lord Tarvin. May I show you the way?"

"If young Archie will not mind being taken away from his mama."

"So long as he is carried by someone, even Papa, he is as good as gold. He only protests when he is put down. This way."

The room was surprisingly masculine. He had expected a former brothel to be strongly feminine, and some of the other bedchambers were decidedly so, from the glimpses he caught of floral wallpapers and delicate bed hangings. His room, however was almost unrelievedly sombre in tone, apart from a garish swathe of pink fabric adorning the bed.

"What do you make of it, Deakin?" he said, finding the valet busy unpacking evening clothes. "Strange place, is it not?"

"I've been in stranger," the valet said. "Kitchen seems to be running smoothly, anyway."

"My wife keeps a very orderly kitchen," Rycroft said a little smugly. "Most houses have the principal rooms at the front, but this seems to be the best room, and the most appropriate for a lord, so you have a view over the gardens."

"And the coach house," he said, glancing out of the window and recognising the apple tree he had climbed. "Quieter at the back, too. Where have you put everyone else?"

"Miss Nicholson has the middle room at the front, with the Edgertons to one side and Sandy to the other. Mrs Rycroft and I are next door to you."

"And Mr Neate?"

Rycroft laughed. "We were told he would make his own arrangements. He will eat his dinner here, but after that he may well disappear to one of the inns for a spell to listen to the locals talking. He is a very good listener, apparently."

The afternoon passed with Tess and her maid walking from room to room, looking about and declaring that they could notice nothing missing. Indeed, it seemed as though there was hardly a space anywhere on mantels or shelves or sideboards where another piece might be inserted. Even a small display cabinet of pill boxes, small, portable and valuable, was full.

Captain Edgerton walked behind the ladies with his notebook, but there was nothing to write down. They finished in the principal room, a rather handsome saloon fitted up in a style fashionable some twenty years earlier.

"It is strange," Tess said. "This house is excessively well furnished, yet I never noticed it when I was here before pretending to be a housemaid. My eyes were constantly fixed on the floor — the rugs to be swept, the wood to be mopped and the fireplaces! Oh, the time I spent on my knees before those fireplaces. Those I know intimately! But the mantel above was not my responsibility and so I never looked at it. But that is a very beautiful ormolu clock. My uncle has one rather similar, although surrounded by lions, not elephants. I have never seen an elephant. Is it a good likeness, Captain Edgerton? You must have seen plenty in India."

"Yes, it is rather a good likeness, and the monkeys, too. The ear is not quite right for the Indian species, though. The artist may have confused African with Indian elephants. It is still an exquisite clock. And still here, along with everything else, seemingly. It does not appear that Mrs Mayberry and her nieces were light-fingered. Even the cash box in the room above the coach house retains the full amount you reported. It seems we shall have no reason to pursue the widow," he added sadly.

"Ye'll have enough to do without chasing round after people who don't want to be found," Sandy said.

"Oh, they will have set up in business somewhere," Edgerton said. "They would not be hard to find. However, it is not my principal concern just now. There are Mr Nicholson's papers to be gone through, to see if we can discover any murderous enemies in his life. Apart from that, it is six weeks since Miss Peach disappeared, and I cannot now believe that she will simply turn up one day, none the worse for her adventure."

"That is a long time to take up the chase," Edward said. "What can you do that you have not already done?"

"I can begin again, with a new eye," Edgerton said. "I thought at first that she had simply gone away on her own, and was living incognito somewhere in her quiet, unobtrusive way. Whatever she was about, it would not keep her away for ever, I should have thought, and so I supposed that one day she would simply reappear, and laugh at us for worrying about her. But I cannot deny that I am now very concerned for her welfare. So I shall talk again to everyone who had dealings with her, and see if I can prod loose any useful memories." He sighed. "I am not hopeful, however. Not after all this time."

"Poor Peachy," Mrs Edgerton said sadly.

***

Tess felt very strange that evening. The house — *her* house, she had to keep reminding herself — had never been more than a means to an end, a way to recover her fortune, which was still sitting in the safe, awaiting instructions from Lord Rennington to convey it to a bank for safe keeping. But now that her gold bars had been put out of her reach, there was still the house. And it was beautiful, she discovered. A little faded, and where draperies had been replaced, overpoweringly feminine and downright vulgar, but on the whole tasteful and elegant.

As they gathered in the saloon before dinner, Edward had leaned close and whispered in her ear, "Shall you live here, do you think?"

"My uncle would never permit it."

"Why not? With a respectable companion, someone mature enough to lend you countenance, you could be independent here without the need to marry at all."

"Ah. You are still trying to dissuade me from marrying Ulric."

He smiled. "Indeed I am. I understand your reasons, but I think with an appropriate companion, even Lord Rennington might be convinced to make you an allowance from your fortune."

"Until I am thirty, at which time, if I am still unwed, the money disappears to Pembroke College, to finance some unworthy young man... or men, I suppose, given the size of it. That gives me precisely ten years of independence."

"Long enough to find a husband more to your taste, or at least postpone the evil day when you must surrender your freedom. What do you think? I had not thought it would be possible... a nondescript little villa seemed unworthy of you, somehow. But this is very elegant, and with some new paint and wallpaper, would be a very suitable setting for your charms."

That made her laugh. "Flatterer! You do not believe I have any charms at all, do you? And where am I to find this appropriate companion? I should not want some penniless widow who will chatter non-stop and eat until she bursts, at my expense, and I have no distant relations to call upon. None with whom I am on speaking terms, anyway."

"How about a close relation, then?"

"Mama cannot leave Corland."

"Not your mama. Your aunt."

"My *aunt?* Oh! Aunt *Caroline?* That aunt?"

"Why not? Now that your uncle is set on remarrying, she has no fixed home at present, and it might suit her very well to live here, with you. And your uncle, you know, could hardly object to you taking his own wife as companion and chaperon. Who more suitable?"

And he grinned at her, delighted with his own cleverness.

24: Raindrops

Tess did not know what to make of Edward's proposal. The thought of living at Apstead House had barely crossed her mind before, except as just another ineligible scheme, but he made it seem so reasonable. And if her aunt were there… Uncle Charles could not possibly object, could he?

But almost as soon as she began to consider the question seriously, any number of objections arose in her mind. Uncle Charles might not object to Aunt Caroline, but he still held the purse-strings. Would he allow them enough to live on comfortably? He had no idea of money at all, she knew that. And at the least whim he could withhold or rescind his permission, so Tess would still not be free.

Then there was Aunt Caroline. Tess did not dislike her, but she had no especial affection for her, either, for she had ignored Tess almost as much as her own parents had done. Her aunt was very close to Mama, too, and all things considered, she did not feel that Aunt Caroline would be a comfortable sort of companion.

She did not say that to Edward, however. To him, she mentioned only that Aunt Caroline liked to travel about to stay with Josie and Izzy, and that she might not like to settle in Pickering. He nodded, but said no more.

Soon after, they went into dinner, and there was a little jostling for position amongst the men. Mr Rycroft thought that he and his wife ought to have the head and foot of the table, while Sandy argued forcefully that it should be Captain and Mrs Edgerton. In the end, Edward pulled rank, and set Tess at the head and himself at the foot, with the others allowed to dispose themselves as they would. Tess found she had the Scotsman on one side and Captain Edgerton on the other, while Edward had the other two ladies, Mrs Edgerton and Mrs Rycroft. The remaining gentlemen, Mr Rycroft and Mr Neate, took the middle seats. As the table was reduced to its smallest size, conversation was general for the entire meal, with the gentlemen competing to entertain the company. It was a contest which Captain Edgerton was bound to win, with his bottomless fund of stories from India, but Tess liked his lighthearted tales, where there was danger but also great bravery. Not that she believed them all, but he told them so well that it hardly mattered.

The meal was sparse, having only one course and a couple of removes, but what it lacked in quantity, it more than compensated in quality. Mrs Rycroft was clearly an accomplished cook, her husband had raided the wine cellar to good effect, and with the two valets serving, no deficiency was felt by the diners.

When the ladies withdrew, Mrs Edgerton and Mrs Rycroft settled down with their needlework in the saloon, but Tess was restless and wandered through the connecting door to the room next door, which was at the front of the house, facing the street. The curtains had been left open, but a little light filtered into the room from the lamps hung at the front door, enabling her to look around. It was another saloon, similar to the first, the air a trifle stale, as if it had not been used for a while. There was some aroma detectable which reminded her of the study at Corland in her grandfather's day, where he had sat up until the small hours, playing piquet with her father and drinking brandy. Perhaps this room, too, had been the scene of cards and drinking. Those gentlemen she had seen walking through the garden had perhaps sat in here, playing and gambling and enjoying a convivial evening with Mrs Mayberry's nieces.

She stood by the window gazing out. It was raining, and drops chased each other down the panes. In the tiny front garden, several tall shrubs were tossed about by the wind. No one was about on the street at this hour, everyone sitting at home by the fire, warm, secure and *happy.*

Tess was not happy. All her careful plans had fallen apart. Just a few months ago, she had been happy because she had been in love with Tom, and had thought herself loved in return. She had always known, of course, that it might take years of painstaking effort to convince her parents that her future lay with such a man, but she had *hope.* A small hope, but it had kept her optimistic.

And then her father had died — had been murdered in his bed, and appalling as that was, it had given her a real chance of freedom. Her father's gold, which no one knew of but her, could set her free. She could marry Tom and be rich and happy. Now Tom was gone, the gold was gone — no, still sitting in the safe, infuriatingly, but out of her reach. Her choices had narrowed... to marry Edward and embrace the hideous prospect of life as a peeress, to live meekly with her aunt or her mother, as if she were still a child, or to marry Ulric and be free.

And yet... to be tied to Ulric forever... was that truly what she wanted? Yes, if it would give her the fortune that was hers. She could even live here, in Pickering, without her aunt or anyone to look disapprovingly at her.

Without anyone to play chess with, her mind instantly responded. Without anyone...

She was aware of him the instant he entered the room. There were voices in the saloon next door, but *he* was here. How she knew it was him she could not say, but she was quite certain of it, so when he came up behind her and put his arms around her waist, she was not alarmed. Nothing Edward did could ever alarm her.

"What are you doing?" he said quietly.

"Watching the raindrops run down the window."

"That sounds boring."

"No, not at all. Rain is never boring."

"But people are? Is that why you are in here, because the raindrops are more interesting than the company next door?"

"The raindrops are more in tune with my mood." There was the lightest touch, so light she might almost have imagined it, on one of her shoulders. "What are you doing?" she said sharply.

"Kissing your shoulder."

"You should not be doing that."

"I know, but you have the most enticing shoulders, do you know that?" His lips moved delicately along and then up her neck. How improper it was! Yet she made no move to stop him. If only he were not so tempting! Life was much simpler when he did nothing but rant at her, his face stern and unyielding. But this gently affectionate man was very, very hard to dislike.

"Have you ever wondered why it is," she said pensively, "that a lady prepares for the evening by exposing her neck, her shoulders and half her chest to the world, while covering her bare arms decorously with long gloves? A man, on the other hand, is covered from neck to toes. Only his face is uncovered."

The kissing paused. "I suppose it must be because a man chooses a woman for her beauty, so she must needs display her charms, whereas a woman chooses a man for his position in society, and he has no need to display anything."

"Yet in reality both choose according to money — her dowry and his income."

"You are cynical, my love. You forget that some people, men and woman alike, may choose for love. As I do."

"What is love?"

He shifted a little at her back, and she heard the surprise in his voice. "A profound question. Who can say? Writers from time immemorial have tried to encapsulate it, but I suppose we each of us experience it differently."

"But how can one tell one is in love?"

"One simply knows," he said, his arms tightening around her momentarily, as if for emphasis. "You knew you were in love with Shapman. I know I am in love with you."

"But if I were to fall in love with someone else, would it be the same or different?"

He chuckled, a low rumble that she felt in her back as he held her tight. "An unanswerable question. But you will know. Are these questions leading anywhere? Or are you merely tormenting me?"

"Tormenting you? How am I tormenting you?" She slithered out of his hold and spun round to face him.

"Dearest Tess, you know how I feel about you. If I thought you were talking about me—"

"You flatter yourself!" she said coldly, then winced at the pain on his face. Impulsively, she reached out and laid a hand on his chest. "Forgive me. I spoke thoughtlessly. I am only... it is just that... I cannot tell..."

She drifted into silence, quite unable to formulate a coherent sentence. How could she raise his hopes by telling him anything of her confused feelings at that moment? These intimate moments brought her very close to loving him, and she was not at all sure she wanted that. It would only complicate her life still further.

"Shall we play chess?" she said briskly. "There is a set in the other room."

His expression shifted, no longer hurt, merely resigned, she thought. But he nodded, and they joined the others in the saloon, and no one commented on their long absence.

She could not concentrate on the game, and expected to lose, but perhaps Edward was out of sorts too, for once again she defeated him, which he accepted graciously.

"My mind is elsewhere tonight," he said. "I think I shall retire."

"Of course. Are you quite well?"

"Oh... I suppose so. What ails me is not anything which can be fixed by a sleeping draught or a dose of laudanum, anyway. Goodnight, Tess."

The Edgertons and Rycrofts had got up a game of whist, but between rubbers, there was a shift as Sandy begged for a turn, so Captain Edgerton wandered across to the chess table.

"May I give you a game, Miss Nicholson? Or backgammon, if you wish for a change."

"By all means let us play backgammon. There is a board on the shelf over there."

He set up the pieces and they began to play, but he too seemed preoccupied, and after one rather muddled game, they abandoned the board, refilled their glasses and settled down to conversation.

"Do you truly believe you can find Miss Peach?" Tess said, before the captain could begin one of his anecdotes from India.

He sighed. "I am not optimistic. Nor do I feel I make much progress on finding your father's murderer. This investigation is turning out to be one of my most spectacular failures."

"I am sorry Tom Shapman threw everything off course by his foolish confession," she said quietly. "And for my part in that, I also apologise. I am too prone to speak without considering the consequences."

"There is no need for any apology, Miss Nicholson. You did not ask him to confess, after all. But even if he had not done so, I am not at all certain that I would have been any further forward. There is no trace left behind at Corland to point a finger. The axe was accessible to anyone. The room was easy to find, your father's habits known. No one appears to have benefited by his death, apart from you, but I do not see you as a murderer. No one had a grievance deep enough to suggest murder as a solution. Until I can find a reason why anyone should have wished to murder your father, I cannot begin to guess his identity."

"My father was a wicked, thieving man, Captain. Someone must have hated him."

"Actually, no. He was generally well liked. Not generous, but despite the penny-pinching, he paid his bills on time. The managers of the businesses he owned all said he treated them respectfully. No bullying or shouting, nothing untoward at all. He would call once a week to collect the takings, leaving the agreed sum for wages and expenses, sign the account books, drink a glass of sherry and chat for ten minutes, then away. He belonged to a political society here, but they all speak well of him, too. If he had any vices, he kept them well hidden."

"Any vices other than stealing from people, you mean," she said acidly.

The captain grinned. "Yes, apart from that, but none of those defrauded knew of it. There might have been suspicions, but nothing more than that. But while it is infuriating to be unable to find his killer, I find myself fascinated by the man himself. For thirty years he has been quietly lining his own pockets, amassing a fortune, and for what? He had no need of money, one might think. He was very comfortably situated at Corland, happily married, wanting for nothing, and yet all the time he was squirrelling away his gold bars. Have you any idea why?"

She sipped her wine, considering the point. "He said to me once that money is the real power in the world, that money means not being beholden to anyone. It is freedom... oh, and the ability to recover from a disaster. I wonder if he feared a disaster?"

"Ah... if someone were to find out he was not ordained, perhaps? That would be a crime too great to ignore, but if his secret were uncovered, with a fortune in his hands, he could make a run for it and start a new life somewhere else."

"Do you think someone found out?" she said. "That would be something that might drive a man to murder, perhaps."

"It might," he said thoughtfully. "But if he wished to hide that secret, murder is not going to help, and if he wished to expose it, there are better, safer ways, without risking the gallows. It is a puzzle, is it not, Miss Nicholson? An insoluble one, perhaps, yet I cannot quite let it go. Then there are all those strange little disconnected matters that niggle at my mind.

Hiding the axe in the urn, for instance. Mr Eustace collecting a lady from a Pickering house of ill-repute. Miss Peach's disappearance, muttering about laudanum and mule droppings. Miss Franklyn seeing a man in the woods, watching her. And that clock..."

He turned his gaze on the mantelpiece, where the ormolu clock ticked away.

"I have seen a clock very like it somewhere else, but I cannot for the life of me remember where."

***

It took Michael just two days to find the clock again, although it was pure happenstance. He had begun again on his round of all those who had known Mr Nicholson, and after the distinguished members of the Pickering Political and Philosophical Society, he had moved down the social scale to the businesses that Nicholson had owned. The chandlery was the most important, for it was where Miss Peach had taken lodgings, and so he talked to all the other residents. The last of them was a well-dressed widow of around sixty, Mrs Clegg, who lived in two rooms on the top floor.

"I am so sorry to trouble you again, ma'am, but Miss Peach is still missing, and I should like to ask you one or two more questions, if it would not be too much of an imposition."

"Not at all, Captain Edgerton. Do come in. May I offer you some tea? Or a glass of wine?"

"Thank you, but Mr Cartwright downstairs filled me full of port and macaroons. If I take another mouthful I shall burst."

She laughed, and ushered him into the room. And there it was on a shelf, for it was too large for the mantelpiece, an ornately exotic ormolu clock in a room filled with unpretentious furniture and virtually no other decorative piece. When she had repeated all that she knew of Miss Peach, none of which was new to him, Michael asked the question buzzing in his head.

"What a lovely clock! Elephants — so unusual."

"A parting gift from my employer," she said, but he thought her smile seemed a little strained.

"Do you know Apstead House?" he said.

"I do, yes."

"Have you ever been inside it?"

"Why do you ask, Captain?"

"Because there is a clock there which is almost identical to this one. Perhaps it *is* identical, for I can detect no difference. That is a curious coincidence, is it not? One might almost suppose that two such similar clocks might have been intended for the same house, one for each saloon, perhaps. One wonders just how such a handsome timepiece comes to grace the lodgings of a widow of modest means."

"You think I stole it?"

"Did you?"

"No! You are right that it came from Apstead House, but that was my home for many years — over twenty-five years. Those clocks were bought for me, Captain Edgerton, a gift from Lord Rennington. Such a generous man! When he died, Mr Nicholson came and asked me to leave. No, he didn't ask. He *ordered* me to leave, standing over me while I packed my personal effects, but he wouldn't let me take anything from the house, not a thing, even though so much of the art and porcelain had been bought for my pleasure. I don't doubt his right to do it, and he was perfectly civil over it — sympathetic, even — but it was hard, very hard, to leave my home after so long. That clock had been undergoing repairs at the clockmaker's, so when it was ready, I quietly paid the bill and brought it here. It's almost the only thing I have left of Henry now. That and the jewels he gave me over the years, which pay for my rent and keep me in tea."

"You mean there was no annuity? No settlement? After twenty-five years as his mistress?"

"Nothing. Not a penny piece. He left the house to Mr Nicholson, and perhaps he assumed that he would look after me, but he threw me out and installed those girls there. A mistress would have cost him money, you see, whereas a brothel would make a profit and he could still take his pleasure whenever he wanted."

"So you were Nicholson's mistress, too?"

She bridled a little. "I was Henry's mistress. The late Lord Rennington. He owned Apstead House and paid the bills. However, I used to oblige Arthur from time to time. No one else, but he was a great friend of Henry's and more my age. Henry came to me more for companionship by that time, so he thought I'd be pleased to have a younger man, and he always assumed that Arthur would look after me when Henry was gone. They used to drive over together at first, go to their political meeting, then come here for a good dinner and cards or music or whatever Henry wanted. Latterly it was just Arthur, but I still thought of myself as Henry's mistress. He used to write to me, you know, when he couldn't see me for a long spell. He had others before me, but no one else after he met me. Just like an old married couple we were." She smiled, lost in memories. "He was a lovely man. Not like Arthur. He had a certain... well, a superficial charm, but the way he treated me... that was not charming."

"You must be angry at the way he has treated you."

"Angry? No. I never expected to be kept in luxury for the rest of my life, Captain Edgerton. A mistress rarely has a prosperous old age. Henry was very generous, so I'm quite comfortable here, with enough jewels still in the bank to feed and clothe me for a good few years yet. An annuity would hardly have made much difference. I would have liked a little cottage, perhaps, furnished with a few bits and pieces from Apstead House. There was a lovely little davenport… and the spinet, although it would be too fine for these rooms. And perhaps the lacquered vases in the hall. They were a birthday gift from Henry. I'd have liked to leave my home in some dignity, instead of all in a rush. But I bear Arthur no grudge."

"So you did not kill him, then?" Michael said in innocent tones, and waited to see how she would react.

She burst out laughing. "And how would I have done that, Captain? He was murdered in the middle of the night, wasn't he? In his bed at Corland Castle, a place I have never been to in my life. I might have poisoned him, if I'd had a mind to do away with him, but slashing him with an axe? Not likely."

"I should be happier if you had someone who could vouch for you being here on the night in question."

"What was the exact date?" she said, rising, and opening a drawer.

He told her, and she pulled out a small book and flicked through the pages. "Ah, here we are. I was at a musical evening at a friend's house. A respectable friend," she added with a wry smile. "The widow of a corn merchant. She will remember it, for her daughter spilt wine on my gown. Shall I give you her name and direction? She will tell you who else was there — about a dozen of us, altogether. Dinner beforehand, music till eleven, then I walked home with the milliner from across the street."

25: An Unpleasant Journey

Tess was fascinated to hear of Mrs Clegg.

"But she must be Miss Carlisle!" she said delightedly. "It is her good taste in all the furnishings. Things were much better in Miss Carlisle's day, according to Mrs Harris, the cook. Best cuts of meat, and plenty of it. Then, when my father took over, penny-pinching was the order of the day. I should so like to meet Mrs Clegg. Might we invite her here? She could show us the davenport she would like, because there are at least two. The spinet she may have, and the vases, for I do not care for them."

"Lord Rennington would not like you to give away such objects, however worthy the cause," Edward said. "He and the other trustees have a duty to look after your inheritance."

"Well, perhaps I shall invite her to live here, then. The house should not be left empty."

"Again, it is for your trustees to determine what happens to the house. They may decide to sell it."

"But I do not want it sold. Perhaps I shall live here myself, with Mrs Clegg as my companion."

Edward huffed in annoyance. "Tess, you are incorrigible! Your uncle will never approve of such a woman as your companion. If you want to live here as a single woman, and personally I do not see why you should not, you must at all costs have a companion who can also act as chaperon, and who will give you consequence. You could not choose anyone less suitable than Mrs Clegg."

"Then I shall just have to marry Ulric. Then I could live here with whomever I choose, and my uncle would have nothing to say about it."

Edward's face darkened, but he did not deign to respond to this provocation. He had reverted to his stuffy self, and there had been no more kisses, but he followed her everywhere she went, looking thoroughly disapproving. She had found a few outstanding bills in a drawer, so she had filled her purse from the cash box in the room above the coach house, and walked around town discharging the debts. Edward walked beside her in silence for the whole time.

He was with her when she called upon Mrs Clegg.

"You have a look of your father," that lady said when she saw Tess. "The chin in particular, and around the mouth, I think, although your hair is much darker than his."

She had tea brought, with a plum cake, and the three of them sat, the two ladies chattering away as if they had known each other forever, and Edward sitting stiff and silent on the edge of his chair. He sipped his tea, but refused the cake. Tess had three cups of tea and four slices of plum cake, and felt pleasantly full.

"You see?" she said, as they walked back to Apstead House afterwards, Harold following at a respectful distance. "What a charming lady! She would suit me perfectly as a companion. I shall write to Uncle Charles and see what he says. Naturally, I shall describe Mrs Clegg as a respectable widow, which she was, once, before she met my grandfather. And if he agrees to it, I need not marry Ulric at all. There! That should please you."

He raised his brows disdainfully. "Do you care whether I am pleased?"

"Not a great deal, no, although you are vastly better company when you are in a good mood."

"Do you want to cry off this visit to Myercroft?" he said.

She frowned while she thought about it. "No, for Uncle Charles may say no, and then we should need to arrange the visit for another time. It is not as if I can marry Ulric before the spring anyway. Let us go to Myercroft as planned. Besides, it might be disruptive to Ulric to have everything changed at the last minute."

"Do you know, that is the first sign I have seen of you considering Ulric's feelings. Well done."

"I am not quite the unfeeling monster you imagine me to be, Edward. I have no wish to upset Ulric... or anyone. It is only that sometimes what I wish to do is in conflict with other people's ideas of what is proper."

"It is not merely about propriety, Tess, for that would affect only you. What you choose to do affects a great many people. This proposed marriage to Ulric affects all of his family, and the Petersons, too. It affects me, and through me, my mother and aunt. It affects your own mother, and her family."

"Yes, yes, I take your point! I do understand, I promise you, and if there were another way—"

"There are plenty of other ways," he said, his voice icy. "You just will not see them. We leave for Myercroft tomorrow. If you wish to write to Lord Rennington, I suggest you do so today. He can direct his reply to you at Myercroft."

He strode ahead of her, his long legs soon leaving her behind.

Now why did she feel so bereft?

***

The journey north was not a pleasant one. Two days on the road with Edward glowering and silent on the opposite seat was enough to put even the calmest person out of frame, and Tess was far from calm. She was unaccountably nervous about meeting Ulric again, for one thing. It was six weeks since she had seen him, and it was entirely possible that he had forgotten that he was betrothed to her. That would make life difficult! Then there were the Petersons to face, and while Lady Peterson's letter was polite enough, they must resent her coming, for it heralded the loss of their home for many years.

Most of all, however, there would be nowhere to hide herself away at Myercroft. Even if she knew the house intimately, as the guest of honour she would be expected to be visible at all times. She was not sure she could cope with that. Her greatest comfort in difficult times was to keep to the shadows and the safe places where she would be, not precisely invisible, but overlooked.

And beneath all these surface worries was a deeper one — was this truly the best way to proceed? She no longer knew. Marrying Ulric was a risk. There were risks whoever she married, for marriage was itself a chancy business, but Ulric was even more of an unknown quantity than most husbands would be. If he decided not to cede control of her fortune to her, as he certainly could, then she would have tied herself to him for no purpose. Perhaps it would be more sensible to withdraw, and wait for a better choice to come her way. It would be humiliating to be forced to admit that she had made a mistake, especially as Edward would be triumphant, but it would be foolish to marry Ulric just to spite Edward.

Ah, yes. Edward. She knew perfectly well that her feelings for him were utterly confused. When he was lighthearted and teasing, as he could be when he talked about eloping or being a highwayman, he was the greatest fun to be with, and she had no quarrel with him. When he climbed trees for her, she could admire him. When he pressed her to marry him with flattering urgency, and was wreathed in gloom when she refused, she could even pity him. And when he kissed her… oh, yes, when he kissed her, she could almost surrender to him entirely.

But then he would revert to his unyielding expression, as if he disapproved of everything around him, and she remembered why she disliked him so much.

"Are you angry with me?" she asked him as they waited for a change of horses. Betty had gone to find food, so they were alone in the carriage.

He looked startled. "Angry? No, of course not."

"Then why do you glare at me so?"

"I was not aware that I was doing any such thing," he said stiffly. "I shall try to avert my gaze in future if it offends you."

"You may look where you please, I am sure, but will you not at least talk to me now and then?"

"I am not minded for conversation at present."

"A game of chess, perhaps?"

"No, thank you."

Tess gave it up. As soon as they left the posting house, he closed his eyes and leaned his head against the squabs, but he was not asleep, Tess was sure of that. Still, it was an effective way of avoiding her and it left her free to look at him as much as she chose.

He was certainly worth looking at. She had always thought Tom the handsomest man she had ever met, but Edward was even more well-favoured, when he was not looking down his supercilious nose at her. And he always looked so well turned out, as if he had just that moment stepped out from his dressing room. He never had a wayward curl in his hair or wilting shirt points or a waistcoat of an odd, mismatched colour. He was effortlessly elegant, as most men of his rank were, and she could not help despising him for it. All it proved was that he was rich and had neither the need nor desire to do anything useful with his life. Men of his class frittered away their lives in idleness or pointless pursuits that served only to fill the endless hours between breakfast and dinner, and between dinner and whenever the brandy ran out.

Edward was just another effete aristocrat, drifting effortlessly through life on charmed wings.

And yet he loved her! That was an astonishing thing, and if she had been any other girl, the daughter of a gentleman and niece of an earl, she would have grabbed him with both hands. A baron with twelve thousand a year! Such a triumph to attach such a man — how could she possibly turn him down?

It was a difficult question to answer rationally. She had told him that she could not do it because her mother would approve the match, but that was a foolish reason. If she married Edward, all the uncertainty that plagued her regarding Ulric would vanish. She would have her fifty thousand pounds without conditions — he had promised it. At a pinch, she could pretend she was not Lady Tarvin, but was merely Mrs Edward Harfield.

But then there would be babies and houses to run and servants to manage and tenants to be visited, and all the trappings of the aristocratic life that she so fervently wished to avoid. And there was no knowing which manifestation of Lord Tarvin would step out of bed each morning — the amusing and agreeable one, or the sternly disapproving one. Did she want to live her entire life wondering what sort of husband she was going to meet over the breakfast table each day?

For the whole journey, these thoughts cantered around in Tess's head in a most disagreeable manner, and at the end of two days, she was no nearer to finding a resolution.

They were to spend one night at Harfield Priory, so that Edward's mother could dote on her only child for a few hours. Tess had no objection to that, for Edward would be the great attraction and she could hide herself in corners.

Mrs Harfield fell on her son as if he had travelled to India and back, instead of trotting round a small portion of Yorkshire. Wreathed in smiles, she led him into the house and it was only with an effort that he disentangled himself and escaped to his room. Within minutes, she was banging on his bedroom door to urge him to hurry downstairs, for she had received a letter from Lady something-or-other with great news which she could not wait to impart.

Edward, naturally, took his time, and Tess had been seated in the Blue Saloon making desultory conversation for some time before he put in an appearance.

"There you are, dear Edward!" his mother cried. "Do come and listen to this for it is such an opportunity for you."

"In one moment, Mother," he said, and proceeded to make his bow to Lady Tarvin, seating himself beside her to make the usual enquiries as to health, while his mother squirmed with impatience.

Eventually, she could bear it no longer. "Edward, what do you think! Lady Henrietta is in Durham — there! Is that not fortuitous? She arrived just two days ago and is fixed for at least a sennight, perhaps longer, so if you make haste—"

"I am bound for Myercroft, Mother."

"Oh yes, but the Petersons will not object if you delay for a few days in such a cause."

"I have no intention of doing so, however."

"But Edward, such a splendid opportunity may never again arise. The daughter of a marquess, you know. What could be better?"

He rose and walked across to the fireplace, where a low fire burned unenthusiastically. "Mother, let us be clear on one point. I have not the least interest in Lady Henrietta."

She raised her eyebrows in delicate disbelief. "No interest? After you pursued her so relentlessly in the spring? Oh — have you quarrelled with her? But that can be remedied if—"

"No!" he said forcefully. Then, more gently, he went on, "No, Mother. Say no more of Lady Henrietta."

"Oh. Very well, dear. But Lady Anne—"

"Enough! I have no wish to discuss my marriage prospects."

"But, Edward, you must take thought for the future. You must—"

"I must? I must, Mother? Do not tell me what I *must* do! Neither you nor anyone else has the right to order me so."

"Not an order, Edward. Heavens, what do you take me for? My only aim is to be of service to you. Since you do need to marry, and sooner rather than later, my only object is to assist you along that path."

"If you had any care for my feelings," he said, his anger barely suppressed, "you would not mention the subject. I believe now that I shall never marry. I intend to take an interest in my cousin Tostig, to see that he is properly educated and trained to take my place after my death, so you may forget about Lady Henrietta and Lady Anne and all these other dull, uninteresting women. There is not one of them who has a spark of life about her, and I would rather die a bachelor than marry any of them. Pray do not mention this subject in my presence again. I have letters to write, so I shall see you at dinner, Mother. Lady Tarvin. Miss Nicholson."

With a sweeping bow, he left the room in haste, shutting the door behind him with some force.

"Oh, dear," Lady Tarvin murmured.

Mrs Harfield burst into tears. "I suppose he fell in love with one of them and she rejected him," she sobbed. "My poor Edward! How he must be suffering!"

"He will make a recover, I am sure," Lady Tarvin said. "Young men are resilient. He will find another young lady before too long. Who do you think it was? I cannot recall that he spoke more of one lady above another."

This was a happy thought, for it diverted Mrs Harfield out of her tears and into lengthy speculation as to which of the high-born young ladies from town had broken his heart. Neither of them looked across the room to where Tess was quietly leafing through a journal, or suspected that the wayward daughter of a murdered chaplain might hold the answer to the question.

Dinner was a somewhat strained affair, with Edward studiedly polite, his mother silent and Lady Tarvin, not much of a chatterer, struggling to eke out what little conversation there was. Tess would have contributed, but there appeared to be a prohibition on every topic. Apart from asking after her mother — or *'poor bereaved Lady Alice'*, as Lady Tarvin put it — and the rest of the earl's family, there seemed to be nothing left to say. The murder was too dreadful for the delicate female sensibilities of the Priory ladies, and Tess had no wish to discuss her inheritance, for fear of veering off into difficult areas like pretend housemaids, tree climbing barons and embezzling chaplains.

So she and Lady Tarvin talked with great perseverance of the journey north, the state of the roads and, when all else failed, of the unsettled autumn weather. Edward contributed the odd word, but it was so obviously such a strain for him that Tess took far more than her usual share of the conversation to spare him.

When the ladies withdrew, leaving Edward to his solitary port, Mrs Harfield at once burst into voice. "My poor boy! I see it now, his pain and sorrow. How he must feel it! She rejected him, no doubt, but in what manner? I hope she was kind to him. Perhaps if he tries again... it must be Lady Anne, I think. Considering all that he said over the last few months, I feel it will be the lady he spoke about the least who has captured his heart, and he seldom mentioned her, you know, after the first time or two. One never talks about matters closest to the heart. That will be it — Lady Anne is the one. My poor, poor Edward!"

Tess said nothing, although the words *'I hope she was kind to him'* echoed guiltily in her head. She had not been kind to him at all, and now he was suffering because of her. Was that why he had been so silent on the journey? He had looked so severe that she had assumed he was angry with her, but was he simply hiding a broken heart? Poor Edward indeed. And it was her fault, she admitted uncomfortably. She had never quite taken his proposals seriously, for why would a man like that even look at a contrary girl like her? And then he had protested that she was tormenting him.

She determined that she would mend her ways and be kinder to Edward.

When Edward joined the ladies in the Blue Saloon, he said, "Mother, Jeffries tells me that this Ramsbottom fellow called here again."

"Oh, I had almost forgotten that in all the excitement of your arrival. I wish you would get rid of him."

"I would do so if I had the slightest idea who he might be, but I am not acquainted with anyone of that name."

"Acquainted! I do not believe he is a person one would be *acquainted* with. He has the air of a tradesman about him."

Edward raised delicately arched eyebrows. "And what is a tradesman doing bouncing all over the north of England looking for me? He has been here twice, and to Corland once, and at one point he was sent to York."

"Well, Jeffries sent him back to Corland," Lady Tarvin said. "I must say, it is most intriguing, Edward. What on earth can the man want? Whatever it is, he is most determined to see you, and he will not write any message for you. Jeffries even suggested he might care to talk to an attorney, and make his approach that way, but he would have none of it."

"Whoever he is and whatever he wants, we do not want him here," Mrs Harfield said firmly. "Edward, dear, ring for the tea, will you, and perhaps then we might have a rubber or two of whist before bed, if that would amuse you."

He did not look as if it would amuse him at all, but perhaps he had no more energy for fighting, for he tamely agreed to it at once, and for the rest of the evening not a syllable of consequence was uttered.

26: Myercroft

The next morning, Edward took rather a stiff leave of his mother, and once again handed Tess into the carriage. Tess had to admit that her mother was right — Edward's luxurious travelling carriage was a great deal more comfortable than travelling post. Betty always settled into her seat with a sigh of pure satisfaction, and the baronial arms painted on the door not only afforded them priority on the road, but ensured that they received instant attention from the ostlers at every posting house.

There was no change of horses needed on this journey, for Myercroft was but a few miles from the Priory. They stopped first, however, at Holly Cottage for Edward to talk to his aunt about Tostig, and explain his proposals for the boy.

"I hope you will consider the girls, too," Tess said as the carriage rolled smoothly along. "They could benefit from a proper governess."

Edward frowned. "I do not believe there is room in that house for another female."

"There are rooms in the attic, and a school room, of a sort."

"I shall discuss it with Aunt Joan, another item to add to the long list of items to be discussed."

"Shall we arrive at Myercroft this month, do you suppose?" Tess murmured as they turned into the drive of Holly Cottage.

She was rewarded with the glimmer of a smile from Edward. "I shall be as quick as I can," he said. "Will you come inside? There will be a fire to warm you."

"I am not cold," she said, for although the morning had begun with a sharp frost, the sun was now shining enticingly. "I shall walk about the gardens, I think, to stretch my legs. I will not go far, not beyond hailing distance."

He nodded, the smile widening a fraction. "I wish I could go with you. Enjoy the sunshine."

It was a welcome sign that his mood was improving.

There was nothing in bloom in the wilderness of a garden. The flower beds were choked with weeds, and the crunch of the path under Tess's boots owed more to fallen leaves than to the gravel beneath. Tess recalled the neatness of the grounds at Apstead House, and Mrs Mayberry's enthusiastic work with a trowel, but there was no sign of interest in the gardens here. A strip of lawn was more mud than grass, and in the distance was something that might once have been a pond, but was now so overgrown that it was hard to make out at all. As she turned a corner, she saw a lone gardener tending the vegetables.

Still, it was pleasant to walk in the crisp autumn air, the sun adding enough warmth that even Betty, following dutifully behind, had nothing to grumble about.

Of course, her thoughts turned instantly to Edward, who seemed to have accepted her rejection finally, and was now turning to his heir.

How sensible of him to— Sensible! What was happening to her? Here she was, a person who had always revelled in her own idiosyncrasies, admiring Edward for taking the sensible option! She, who tried never to be sensible if it interfered with her comfort. If she were sensible, she would never even have thought of marrying Tom or Ulric. The sensible course would have been to marry Edward. But then, if she had been sensible, she would never have set her sights on Ulric, Edward would not have come tearing up from London to protect his cousin, and they would never have been thrown together. What a strange, dull life it would be, if she were sensible.

She had seen enough of the unkempt garden and made her way back to the carriage. Edward arrived shortly afterwards with Mrs Jack clinging to his arm, crying piteously. He shook her off, not unkindly but firmly, made his farewell and the carriage set off for Myercroft.

"Is she upset at the prospect of Tostig being sent away to school?" Tess said.

Edward's face softened into a tiny smile. "Oh no. She is quite happy for me to spend money on her sons. She is cross because she has not been invited to Myercroft."

"Why has she not been invited?"

The smile broadened. "Because she steals things."

That made Tess laugh. "Oh dear. Although it was her home for many years, so I suppose she regards the contents as hers."

"That is a generous interpretation. She is a grasping avaricious woman who will destroy Ulric's inheritance if left unchecked."

"I depend upon you to check her," Tess said.

He only grunted.

As they turned into the drive of Myercroft, he said, "Ulric has been here for three days, and there is no knowing quite how he will take your arrival. Will you allow me to take the lead in dealing with him?"

She agreed to it, and leant forward to catch the first glimpse of the house. Having only visited the stables before, she had not yet seen the front façade in its full glory from the carriage drive. It was a fine house, it was true, not as large as the Priory but with greater symmetry and well maintained. The hedge surrounding the turning circle was neatly trimmed, the drive free of weeds and the windows sparkled in the autumn sunshine.

Servants emerged at once to attend to them, followed by three people whom Tess had no difficulty in identifying as Sir Ernest and Lady Peterson, and Miss Peterson. Lady Peterson was as plump as her daughter, whereas Sir Ernest was thin to the point of emaciation. The ladies were dressed in the latest modes, but his coat was of the full-skirted style fashionable twenty years earlier and he wore the sort of wig that made him look like an attorney.

They smiled and were perfectly amiable to Tess, however, displaying no resentment at the disruption her coming heralded. Lady Peterson and her daughter both accompanied Tess to her room, a charmingly appointed chamber overlooking the terrace and pleasure grounds full of pleasantly winding paths.

"Your garden is enticing me out of doors," Tess said. "So many charming walks! Would it be very rude of me to wish to explore at once?"

"You couldn't have paid me a greater compliment," Lady Peterson said, her face lighting up. "The garden is my passion, I confess, and I spend many happy hours out there, winter and summer alike. I'll fetch my cloak and bonnet, and we may take a turn together. Fanny, will you join us? Your father will be entertaining Lord Tarvin in the library if you prefer to stay close to a fire."

"I'll come with you," she said. "We could walk past the stables if you wish to see Ulric, Miss Nicholson."

Mindful of Edward's words, Tess said, "I shall see him later. The garden first, if you please."

Miss Peterson looked disapproving at this casual disregard for Tess's betrothed, but she and her mother were soon equipped with warm outdoor clothing, and leading the way to the garden.

Lady Peterson had not exaggerated in saying that the garden was her passion. She could name every plant, and recite its history, what it offered of flower or fruit and the best season for each. Even the pests to which each was prone, and the remedy thereof, she knew and was happy to describe, until Tess's head was spinning. They walked about here and there, and eventually came to the furthermost point of the flower garden, which ended in a low wall with a gate set in it, providing access to the meadow beyond.

A horseman could be seen cantering across it, heading at first directly towards the stables, but seeing their party, he diverted and rode directly towards them. Tess knew with a sinking feeling that she was about to meet her betrothed again, and without Edward's reassuring company.

"Fanny!" Ulric shouted across when he was still some distance away. Then, as he drew near, he wheeled the horse and leapt from the saddle. "Lady Peterson! Fine day!" He glanced at Tess, looked slightly puzzled, and then turned back to Fanny. "Fine day, Fanny. Good riding day."

"Every day is a good riding day to you, Ulric. Here is Miss Nicholson come to see you. She is to stay at Myercroft for a while, too, remember?"

Again, he turned bemused eyes on Tess.

"Good day, Cousin Ulric." She curtsied. "I am come to talk about our wedding, as I am sure your mama explained."

"Wedding..."

"Your wedding to Miss Nicholson, Ulric," Fanny said. "Once you're married, you'll be able to live at Myercroft all the time and think how pleasant that will be."

His frown lifted. "Like to live at Myercroft."

"Of course you would," Fanny said.

"Like to live at Myercroft," he said again. "Always good dinners here. Like to play Beat the Knave with you, Fanny. I like that game."

"And so do I, Ulric, but I shan't be here once you are married to Miss Nicholson."

The frown returned. "You going away, Fanny? Don't want you to go away."

Fanny threw Tess a sideways glance, as if to say, *'You see what disruption you are causing?'* But she only said quietly, "Not for a while yet. We can still play Beat the Knave."

"You will have to teach me how to play the game," Tess said brightly. "Perhaps you can show me after dinner tonight."

His frown deepened. "You staying for dinner? Why?"

"I am staying at Myercroft for a few days just like you, Ulric," Tess said evenly. "We can talk about our wedding, and you can show me around the house."

He smiled. "Show you around the house, cousin. Fine house, Myercroft."

"I can see that it is," Tess said. "Enjoy your ride, Ulric. I shall see you at dinner, if not before."

He nodded, remounted and rode off. Tess heaved a sigh of relief to have brushed through the first meeting without disaster.

"He has forgotten all about me," she said, with a quick laugh. "What a set-down for me!"

"No, he hasn't forgotten," Fanny said seriously, as they turned towards the house once more. "He knows he's betrothed to you, and he remembers you well enough, for we've been talking to him about you ever since he arrived. But seeing you out here, and unexpectedly — that's something which throws him. If he'd met you in the drawing room, having been warned in advance that you would be there, he would have had no difficulty."

"Lord Tarvin said something of the sort, too. He wanted to be present when Ulric and I first met, so that he could smooth things over, but you managed it beautifully, Miss Peterson."

"Fanny gets on very well with Ulric, don't you, dear?" Lady Peterson said. "She's the ideal person to advise you on the best way to manage him."

"He doesn't need to be managed, Mama," Miss Peterson said, flushing slightly. "He's perfectly sensible if he's not taken by surprise."

Sensible… that word again. Ulric was sensible, but Tess was not.

Oh, this was madness! What was she thinking of, marrying a man like Ulric Frith?

The answer was instantaneous. Her fortune. She was thinking of her fortune. The thought of it stiffened her resolve.

Lady Peterson wished to speak to the gardeners on some matter regarding some danger to her precious plants — thrips, it might be — so Fanny and Tess walked back to the house alone. Tess thought it politic to address head on the matter that most pricked her conscience.

"Miss Peterson, I am deeply grateful to you and your parents for the welcome you have accorded me today, and your forbearance in what must be a very difficult situation for you. I would not have you removed from your home if there were any other way of proceeding, but I understand how distressing it must be for you all."

"For Mama, perhaps," she said. "She'll miss this garden so much. There's scarcely a shrub or flowering plant that she hasn't planted and nurtured with her own hands, and the prospect of starting again in a new garden is one she dreads. As for my father, he has good friends amongst our neighbours here that he will be loath to leave behind. He loves his card parties, and he's a beloved figure to all the tenants. But for myself — a house is just a house, Miss Nicholson. It's not the loss of Myercroft that upsets me. It's Ulric's future that gives me sleepless nights." She stopped abruptly and clutched at Tess's arm. "You will look after him, won't you? Take good care of him for me. Stay with him, play his simple card games, ride with him, because if you simply marry him and then leave him here, he'll have no friends looking after him. His trustees will be gone, and I'll be gone, too. He needs someone to take care of him, and protect him from—"

She stopped, biting her lip.

"From his mother," Tess said crisply. What was it about mothers that made them such a trial to their children? It was an excellent argument for never having children.

"I shouldn't have said that," Miss Peterson said. "I shouldn't even have thought it. That was very bad of me."

"I have asked Lord Tarvin to continue his watchful care on Ulric after his marriage," Tess said. "He will not be a trustee any longer, but I believe Ulric can be persuaded to permit him control of his affairs."

"But he won't be here!" Miss Peterson said with a flare of passion. "Ulric needs a friend always by his side. Lord Tarvin lives in London, or else at his own house. Even as trustee, he only comes here a few times a year. Papa takes care of the day-to-day management of the estate. If you were to live here... but you'll marry him to fulfil the terms of your father's will, and then abandon him."

Tess could hear the bitterness in her voice. "It is true that I do not care for Ulric in the same way that you do," she began hesitantly.

"Nobody cares for him as much as I do," Miss Peterson said, subdued suddenly. "I wish with all my heart that I could stay with him. If I'd known he wanted to marry, I'd have married him myself, and I think... I truly believe that would have been better for Ulric. Forgive me for speaking plain, but it's what I think."

***

For several days, Lady Peterson painstakingly showed Tess over the whole house, from the kitchens in the basement to the lumber rooms in the attics, and from the crimson saloon, kept only for the most formal occasions, to the balcony of the clock tower on the roof. She saw the coal, wine and silver stores, looked into the linen cupboard, was formally introduced to the butler, housekeeper and cook, had the workings of the still room explained to her and was shown the account books. She even saw the nursery, empty but immaculately clean and ready for occupation. For a strange moment, Tess had a vision of it filled with children, but not with Ulric's golden hair. Instead, it was Edward's stern visage that rode the rocking horse and played spillikins. How odd.

Outside, she toured the stables, and won the respect of the head gardener by admiring the still fruitful kitchen garden. In the evenings, she played cards with Ulric. He still frowned at her if he met her somewhere unexpected, and once he yelled, "What are you doing here?" at her, but luckily Miss Peterson was with her, and able to smooth things over. Otherwise, in the dining and drawing rooms, at least, he called her *'Cousin Tess'* and seemed to understand that he was shortly to be married.

Yet Tess herself was less and less sure of it. Miss Peterson's words echoed in her head — *'I'd have married him myself, and that would have been better for Ulric'.* Tess could not find any point of disagreement. Yet this was the only way to have both her fortune and her freedom.

One afternoon, Edward had gone out riding with Ulric, and the Peterson ladies were out in the garden, accompanied by a pair of gardeners. Tess found a sheltered spot on the terrace and, wrapped in her warmest shawl, watched the little group crawl from one flower bed to the next. Footsteps behind her caused her to turn her head, but it was only Sir Ernest, emerging from his library in daylight hours for once.

"May I join you?" he said. When Tess assented, he sat on the other end of the bench she occupied, but he said nothing, seeming content to watch the party in the garden, just as Tess was.

"What are they doing, do you know?" she said. "They seem to spend an age over one plant, then they move along a little way, and begin again."

"Lady Peterson is selecting plants which she wishes to take with her when we leave Myercroft," he said. "Not the whole plant, necessarily, but seeds or cuttings. Favourite blooms that she would miss greatly."

"How you must hate me," Tess said sadly.

"Not in the least, I assure you. Myercroft is Ulric's house, and if he wants it back, he must have it. We cannot stay here once he has a wife."

Unless the wife is Fanny Peterson.

The instant the thought entered Tess's head, she knew it was the right thing to do. If Ulric were to marry Fanny, the Petersons would stay on to manage the house and estate, Sir Ernest could oversee financial matters and Ulric's mother would not need to move to Myercroft at all.

It was the obvious solution... the *sensible* solution. The only question was whether Tess was unselfish enough to relinquish Ulric. It was the primary question that kept her awake at night.

The secondary question was even more troubling. It had gradually dawned on her that she ought to marry Edward, despite it being the sensible option. He was not quite irredeemably stuffy, given his willingness to climb trees for her and at least talk about being a highwayman, but he was still an effete aristocrat. How she lamented the loss of Tom's manly proportions, but that could not be helped. Edward's great advantage was that he loved her . *He loved her!* The very thought of it sent thrills through her entire body. A man who loved her, truly and steadfastly, as Tom never had. At least, she hoped his love was steadfast, and he would not change overnight into severe disapproval if they married.

And so she stumbled through the days, growing more uncertain by the hour, and at night lay awake long after she should have been asleep.

She was awake one night when she heard noises in the corridor outside her door. She could not tell what the time was, for it was too dark to make out the hands of the clock on the mantel, but the house had been silent for some time.

Slipping out of bed, she crept to the door and listened. Yes, there was no doubt — someone was creeping along, making no noise, but bearing a candle, for the flickering light filtered under the door. There was no time to do more than pick up a heavy candlestick as a makeshift weapon, then open the door.

It was Ulric. The light from the candle lit up his golden head so that he was recognisable even from behind. He was still fully dressed, except for his shoes, which he carried in one hand. He turned round, gazing at Tess with a puzzled expression.

"What are you doing?" he said in his flat voice.

"I was just about to ask you the same question, cousin," Tess said.

"That's a silver candlestick."

"Is it? I had not noticed."

"Why are you stealing the silver? You are a thief." He dropped his shoes, set down his candlestick on a table and walked steadily towards her.

And only then did Tess see the danger she was in. Fear roiled through her as she backed away from him. "Ulric, it is I, Cousin Tess — your betrothed. We are to be married, remember?" Her voice rose in terror as he continued to approach, his face suffused with anger.

"You are a *thief!"* he cried, and seized her by the throat.

She screamed once before her cry was cut off. Then there was only pain, and panic, and the terrible, overwhelming fear that she was about to die.

27: A Change Of Plan

Somewhere in the darkness of her pain, Tess was aware of a voice yelling, the movement of someone rushing past her... no, not past her, stopping beside her and then the terrible pain eased as Ulric's hands were prised from her throat.

Released, she slipped to the floor, curled up on her side. Breathe, breathe... it hurt to breathe. What had happened? As her breathing slowly eased, she opened her eyes to see.

It was Edward! Edward had come to her rescue, wearing only his nightshirt, open at the throat and the sleeves rolled up. He held Ulric by the wrists, and as Tess watched, he pushed Ulric away from him and hit him with such force that Ulric was carried a little way down the corridor and fell, silent and unmoving.

Edward rushed across and knelt beside her. "Tess! Oh my God, my darling! Are you all right?"

She nodded, quite unable to speak. Her throat still hurt abominably, but she could breathe. At least, she would be able to breathe if only there were not a half-naked Edward before her. His throat and half his chest was exposed to her mesmerised gaze, and his arms! Such strong, well-muscled arms! Arms which picked her up as if she weighed nothing at all.

He sat on the floor and laid her across his lap, those astonishing arms holding her tight, and murmured into her hair. She had no idea what he said, and in truth it hardly mattered. In those few moments, her life had changed. Tom was forgotten. She need no longer regret his masculinity when she had her own perfectly formed specimen. Every difficulty was resolved in the sight of Edward's unclothed chest and arms.

Wonderingly, she lifted one hand to touch the nearest arm. So powerful! Mrs Edgerton, it seemed, was right after all when she suggested a gentleman might very well appear to manly advantage if the outer trappings of his rank were removed. Why had she never suspected that this athletic Edward lurked beneath the artfully arranged cravat?

"Does it still hurt?" he said.

"A little. I shall be bruised but nothing worse, since you arrived so quickly."

"I was still awake when I heard your scream."

"Thank you," she said shyly, smiling up at him.

"Happy to be of service."

"And thank you for not gloating. You warned me of this, after all. You told me Ulric was not a suitable husband, and you were quite right."

More voices arrived, and wavering candles. Exclamations of dismay, as they discovered Ulric. Fanny Peterson's anxious voice, then her father's calmer one. Edward's, explaining what had happened. "He attacked Tess, so I hit him," he said succinctly. Groans as Ulric began to come round. Fanny's quiet tones again. Ulric's roar of displeasure, then a great deal of angry nonsense about thieves. But Fanny talked to him steadily, her voice reassuring, and gradually he calmed down and was persuaded to return to his room. He remembered his shoes, but Sir Ernest collected them, and gradually Fanny's placid voice disappeared into the distance.

Lady Peterson's face appeared, bending over Tess. "Miss Nicholson, I am so dreadfully sorry this has happened. A terrible misunderstanding... he is not normally aggressive... are you much injured? Shall I send for the physician?"

"No, no! I am... I shall be perfectly well. There is no need for a physician."

"Well... if you are quite sure..."

With a smile of reassurance, Tess nodded and she drifted away. Silence fell.

Tess was disinclined to move. In Edward's arms, seeing him in this new and wonderful light, she was utterly content. Happiness seeped through her, filling her with warmth. She would marry him and put up with the baroness business for the sake of those splendid muscles. Edward seemed no less reluctant to move. One arm was still clasped securely around her waist, and with his free hand he played with her hair, twisting one curl round his finger and then releasing it.

"I suppose I ought to return you to your bed," he said eventually. "Shall I send Betty to you? You will not want to be alone after this."

It was true that she had no desire to be alone, but it was not Betty she wanted. Edward's bare chest and muscular arms were sending a powerful message to her. "Not Betty," she said firmly. "She will only fuss."

With a little laugh, she reached up to draw his head nearer to hers.

To her surprise, he hissed and pulled sharply away from her. "Stop it, Tess!"

"What is the matter? Kiss me, Edward."

He scrambled upright and dumped her unceremoniously on her feet. "Every time I think you are acquiring some sense, you revert to stupidity," he spat. "Will you never, ever learn to consider the *consequences* of your actions? Get back to bed, Tess, and leave me alone. Which is your room?"

"That one."

He threw open the door. "In!"

She went, turning to gaze at his furious countenance.

"Lock the door," he said curtly, then slammed it shut. She could not hear him walk away, for his bare feet made no sound on the deep carpet, but the thin line of light under the door from Ulric's candle wavered and then vanished. She heard a door close some distance away, and then there was silence.

The room was utterly black, the fire having long gone out. Tess rested her head against the unyielding door and wept as if her heart would break. And perhaps that was only the truth.

***

Tess was woken by a rattling outside the door, then a knocking. It was still dark, but the girl had come to see to the fire, and the door was locked. Letting her in, she opened the shutters and curtains, and, swathed in her thickest shawl, sat by the window watching the sky slowly lighten.

Despair. That was the emotion that held her in its icy grip. All the warmth of her joy in the night had been swept away by Edward's peremptory words. *Leave me alone.* He had loved her once, and she had never properly appreciated that before. He had *loved* her, as no one else had ever done, and now that was gone. She had driven him away once too often, and just at the point when she could happily accept him as her husband, he no longer wanted her.

But she could not marry Ulric. She had already decided that Fanny was a much better match for him, and she must do what she could to make that happen. No, she should not interfere. She would release Ulric from his betrothal, and then she could leave it to Fanny to persuade him to marry her. If that was what he wanted to do.

Lady Peterson and Fanny came to see her while she was sipping her morning chocolate, to report that Ulric was fully recovered, and to assure themselves that she had not expired in the night.

"There's some bruising," Lady Peterson said. "I've brought some arnica—"

"I have some with me," Tess said. "My maid has already applied it."

"Excellent. Miss Nicholson..." She twisted her hands nervously. "Miss Nicholson, I shouldn't like you to imagine that Ulric often becomes... *enraged* in this way. He likes to watch the full moon from the clock tower when he's here, but he'd never before met anyone on the way there. When he grows more accustomed to you—"

"No," Tess said quietly. "I was wrong to use Ulric in this way, for my own selfish purposes. I intend to release him from this foolish betrothal, and perhaps he will find a wife better suited to him, who knows?" She smiled at Fanny Peterson. "I shall leave Myercroft as soon as Lord Tarvin can arrange it, and then you may all return to your usual occupations and be easy."

Fanny flushed and then laughed. "I believe this is the right decision, Miss Nicholson, but it's a pity you had to be almost throttled before reaching it."

Tess could not help smiling. "No, I had already realised what needed to be done, as anyone... any *sensible* person would have understood long since. I am very sorry to have caused you all so much trouble."

"It's of no consequence," Lady Peterson said. "All's well that ends well. Oh, I had almost forgotten. The letters came in late yesterday, and there's one for you, franked by the Earl of Rennington."

Tess waited until the Petersons had left before opening the letter, but it did nothing to improve her mood. Her uncle had considered all that she had said most carefully, but he did not consider it proper for an unmarried lady of only twenty to set up her own establishment, no matter how respectable her companion. She would be married in a few months and have a perfectly good home of her own, so what was the need? He would not sell Apstead House for the moment if she wished to keep it, but her husband would decide what should become of it in the end.

She had expected nothing else, so she was not disappointed. It did nothing to lift her spirits, however, nor did the morning bring any relief. She had to see Ulric first, which necessitated finding him, but she had no more than an hour to loiter in the stables before he returned from his morning ride. She took the precaution of asking Fanny to accompany her, in case of misunderstandings, but Ulric was a very different character this morning. He gave no hint of remembering their encounter the night before, accepted his dismissal with a nod and said only, "Pity. Should have liked to live at Myercroft with Fanny."

The opportunity was too good to miss. "Then perhaps you should ask Fanny to marry you," Tess said sweetly.

"Marry me, Fanny," he said at once, turning vivid blue eyes on her.

"Thank you, Ulric, I should like that very much," she said calmly. "Are you riding out again, or should we go and tell my parents that we are betrothed?"

"Not riding out yet. Time for breakfast."

"Very well. Shall we go inside?"

Ulric set off at once, leaving the two ladies watching his retreating back. Fanny laughed. "That was easier than I expected!"

"And since you are already of age, you can be married as soon as the banns can be called," Tess said.

"Oh, it might take a little time to coach him through the marriage service," she said. "Still, time is one thing we have in abundance. But what of you? What will you do now? Marry Lord Tarvin?"

That cut Tess to the quick! Oh, if only she could answer as she wished! Instead she said only, "Unlikely, I think."

"Really? You two are so well suited."

It was true enough, but oh, how it hurt to hear it spoken so casually!

***

Tess was obliged to seek out Edward in order to put forward her plan to leave Myercroft that day. He was not at breakfast, so she had to send servants back and forth with messages. She had no idea which Edward she would encounter when she found him, the stern, implacable one or — No, there were no other possibilities, not after last night. He would be his disapproving self.

But he was not. If anything, he looked flustered, countered her stumbling apology for one of his own, and asked her three times if she had slept well. Each time she replied, "No, not at all," but only on the third repetition did it register.

"I am so sorry," he said, for at least the tenth time. "Of course you could not sleep. I should never have left you alone. You must have been terrified."

"No... my door was locked... I was not afraid. I was just..."

What could she say? That she was desperately unhappy, and it was all his fault? That she would humbly marry him now on any terms? That she understood now that she loved him, just as he had once loved her?

Impossible. So she forced a smile. "I spent a great deal of time thinking. You will be relieved to hear that I have released Ulric from this betrothal, although I am afraid he has wasted no time in betrothing himself to someone else."

His lips softened into something approaching a smile. "Miss Peterson? An excellent choice. But I must discuss this with Sir Ernest."

"Will it take long? I should like to leave today, if possible. It would be less confusing for Ulric if I disappear completely."

That brought back the frown. "True, and some details may be put in a letter, but there is much that must be said now. Very well, give me... oh, two hours, say. That should be enough, although we will have to overnight at Harfield."

In the end, it was nearer three, but they were eventually on the road, Betty grimly pleased. She had already voiced her disapproval of households where a guest could be throttled in the night, so it suited her notions of respectability to beat a retreat.

Edward's discussions with Sir Ernest had brought a degree of calm to Edward's demeanour. He had handed her into the carriage with studied courtesy and now appeared to be making an effort to entertain her. When several attempts at conversation ran into the ground, he said, "We could play chess, if it would amuse you."

Just a few days ago, she would have replied that no, it would not amuse her, but the new, chastened Tess said mildly, "Thank you, but I am not sure my mind has sufficient powers of concentration just now, but if you would like to—"

"No, no. I thought it might pass the time, but it is not far to Harfield."

It might as well have been at the furthest end of the country, however, for they were not destined to reach it. Just a few moments later, they heard shouts, the whinnying of horses and thundering hooves, followed almost at once by an almighty bang. Betty screamed, the carriage lurched, and there was an ominous splintering sound, followed by more shouts, more whinnying and a gradual settling of the carriage to one side, as Betty slid slowly sideways onto Tess's lap.

"Oh, wonderful," Edward murmured. "Anyone hurt? Tess?"

"I am quite uninjured. Betty?"

Some muffled noises were all that could be heard at first, but once she had extricated herself from the rug over Tess's knees, she agreed that she too was unhurt. The carriage was not so overset that they could not escape from it, but it was firmly fixed in the ditch.

"Carriage goin' the other way, milord," the coachman said. "Took the corner too fast. No way to avoid it."

"It was not your fault, Purbeck, but we must get help," Edward said. "There is a village ahead of us, and is that an inn I see? That is convenient. Do you and Harold stay with the horses, while I take Miss Nicholson and Betty to shelter. I will send someone back to help you directly."

It was not much of an inn, more of a tavern for the locals, having only a taproom, but the occupants had heard the crash and a party was already setting off to render what aid they could. It was not much, they soon discovered. The horses, alarmed but not hurt, were speedily accommodated in the stables behind the inn, but the carriage could not even be shifted from the ditch, let alone mended, and there was no other conveyance available. There was not even a horse, whereby a message could be sent to Harfield.

"It is under ten miles from here, but we will not reach it tonight," Edward said, ushering her into a hastily prepared private parlour. "The innkeeper has a room for you and Betty. I dare say the food is appalling, but it is only for one night."

"Is there not a room for you?" Tess said, surprised.

"There is, but I cannot stay here. There is a church at the other end of the village, so I shall beg the parson for a bed for the night."

"If you are thinking of my reputation—"

"Someone has to!"

"—that is all nonsense. Who is to know that we slept under the same roof? Besides, I have Betty to protect my virtue, should I wish to protect it."

"Should you wish—! Good God, Tess, even now you still have the power to shock me. This is not a time for your wilfulness. I want to be able to look your mother in the eye when I return you to her care."

"Do not abandon me here!" she cried, suddenly terrified.

His face softened instantly. "Oh, Tess! Of course I will not. I can sleep above the stables — it is a separate building."

"No! Edward, I need to know that you are nearby... please... *please!* Stay with me." Tears trickled down her face. She knew she was pathetic, to plead with him, beg him like a child, but she could not help it.

He took her face in his hands. "Hush, my darling," he whispered. "I will not leave you, but you must understand that if this is ever discovered, we will be expected to marry. Nothing would please me more, but I know—"

"What?" she said, startled. "Then what was last night all about? You would not even kiss me!"

He groaned. "I dared not! My sweet innocent girl, you do not know your own power over men. There we were, both in our nightgowns and your hair all tumbled about your shoulders... have you any idea what the consequence of a kiss would be, in those circumstances? It would have ended in your bed, and then we would have had no choice at all but to marry. The last thing I want is to force you into something you find so distasteful."

"But I do not."

He stared at her, speechless, breathing heavily.

"Edward, I fell in love with Tom Shapman because I could see that he was a real man, capable of more than dancing the cotillion or shooting fat birds. Last night I realised that you are a real man, too."

"Because I hit Ulric?"

"That, and because I could see your arms." She giggled suddenly. "That sounds ridiculous, does it not?"

"So you saw me in my nightshirt and you instantly fell in love with me, is that it?" he said, his voice soft.

"I think I have been falling in love with you for a long time," she said, serious again, resting her hands on his chest. "I thought you were dreadfully stuffy at first, but that is just a mask you wear to fool the world. When you rushed about climbing trees for me, or talked so amusingly about being a highwayman or a pirate, or... oh, Edward, those times when you were so gentle with me... No one had ever treated me that way before, but it was still fixed in my stupid head that you were just another effete nobleman underneath. So I loved you as a friend... a wonderful friend... a kissing friend. But then last night I finally saw you as a *man*. Do you understand?"

He nodded and drew her into his arms. "I always knew those boxing sessions would come in handy one day. I just never guessed it was the key to winning the heart of the woman I love. Will you marry me, Tess? Please?"

"I will, if you will forgive me for all my insults over these past weeks. Sometimes the words just come out of my mouth with no conscious thought, but I will try very hard not to hurt you with my thoughtless words in the future."

"Darling girl, there is nothing to forgive. We have traded insults equally, it seems to me, but now that we understand each other, I trust we will both do better."

"We will." She smiled at him happily. "And now will you stay with me tonight?"

He kissed her forehead. "We shall eat dinner together, and then we shall retire to our separate rooms and you will have Betty and a locked door to protect your virtue. Now that we are betrothed, I am not to be trusted, my dear one."

"But you could kiss me, could you not? There is no harm in that, is there?"

His answer was made without a word being spoken.

28: Apricot Tartlets And Tea

It was late the following day before the carriage was mended and they were able to continue the journey to Harfield, but Tess did not mind. She existed in a glow of such happiness that nothing could puncture it, although the bed at the inn was intolerably lumpy, the food was no better than average and the locals thronged the inn to ogle at the stranded baron and his entourage.

She spent the day in the tiny parlour with Edward, pretending to play chess but in reality talking unstoppably about everything and anything, and stealing kisses whenever the opportunity arose. By the middle of the afternoon, however, the coachman was satisfied that they could safely proceed, so into the carriage they went, Betty eyeing them with a knowing smile and even the innkeeper and his daughter, their pockets unusually full of coins, were aware that something had changed since their arrival.

A sleety shower came and went, but the wind was still icily chill as they arrived at Harfield, to find a post chaise and pair drawn up outside, its window down as the butler spoke to the occupants, a man and a woman.

"Wait here a moment while I see what is going on," Edward said to Tess. Walking across to the post chaise, he called out, "What is it, Jeffries?"

Tess could not hear what Jeffries said, but she saw Edward peer into the chaise and then recoil abruptly, his face black with rage. Moments later, he opened the door and a man of around forty descended, and was hustled into the house by Edward, the butler scurrying after them.

This was so intriguing that Tess called for Harold to open the door for her and strolled across to the post chaise. The woman inside had drawn up the window again, but Tess opened the door.

"Good day, madam. Will you not step inside to warm yourself? The wind is bitterly cold out here, and if your friend is to be engaged for some time with his lordship—"

"No, no! Thank you kindly, but it's best if I stay out here." She was young, not much above twenty, very pretty, and rather showily dressed, making a little money go a long way. Her accent was not a northern one. Not a lady, Tess deduced, but she could not quite work out where she fitted into society.

"I must disagree with you. Come inside and let me find you a fire."

She hesitated. "I should not. If I should meet one of the ladies..."

"It is a large house. There is little danger of it. Do come inside."

Another gust of icy wind settled the matter, and she stepped down from the carriage and followed Tess into the house, Betty hurrying in their wake. A rather harassed footman admitted them, showed them to a small antechamber and lit the fire.

"Where is Lord Tarvin?"

"In the small study, madam."

"Tell him where I am, will you? And send in some tea for Miss—?"

"Goodlake."

"Very good, madam." He bowed himself out.

"Tea... I really shouldn't."

"Why ever not? Since your gentleman friend has business with Lord Tarvin, you are just as entitled as he is to the hospitality of the house."

She gave a throaty laugh. "I don't think so, dear. The ladies wouldn't like it if they knew."

"Lucky they do not know, then, is it not? Do take off your coat, Miss Goodlake. There is no knowing how long your friend may be. Is he a friend... or a brother, perhaps? He is too young to be your father."

Another laugh. "Let's just call him my friend, for now. You know my name, but I don't know yours. I know you don't live here, because it's only two older ladies."

"At present that is true, but before too long this will be my house. I am Miss Nicholson, and I am betrothed to Lord Tarvin."

Miss Goodlake squealed. She had already untied her bonnet, but now she hastily began to fasten the ribbons again. "There, you see, that's just what I was afraid of. You shouldn't have anything to do with me, miss, you being a lady an' all, and bein' his *wife* before too long."

"Are you an opera dancer?" Tess said interestedly. "Or... oh, you are not Edward's *mistress?* Oh, you are! How delicious! How absolutely delicious! And to think I thought he was stuffy!"

Miss Goodlake stared at her, but Betty harrumphed in dismay. "You really shouldn't be in the same room with the likes of her," she said to Tess. "It's not right, bringing her under the same roof as good Christian folk."

"That's just what I say," Miss Goodlake said. "I shouldn't be here, by rights. Edward would be so cross with me."

The door opened, and a small train of footmen entered, bearing trays of tea and an array of cakes and pastries. Miss Goodlake eyed them hungrily.

"There, now! Sit down and let me pour you some tea," Tess said calmly. "Oh, these apricot tartlets are very good. Mrs Johnson's speciality. Or would you prefer the cherry cake?"

Miss Goodlake would have needed an extraordinary level of willpower to resist these offers. She removed her bonnet and pelisse, and by the third apricot tartlet and second cup of tea, all restraint had been swept away. Only Betty, glowering in the corner and refusing to be appeased by a macaroon, was still disapproving.

It was at this point that the door opened and Edward stormed in, with the man from the post chaise behind him. Before Edward could say a word, Tess jumped up and laid a hand on his arm.

"Is this not delightful? I do not suppose you expected to see Nellie here, did you?"

"I most certainly did not!"

"Nellie, will you not introduce me to your friend?"

"This is Mr Ramsbottom, milady... Miss Nicholson."

"Oh, Mr Ramsbottom!" Tess could not help laughing. "You have been following us all over the north of England. Have you concluded your business with Lord Tarvin satisfactorily?"

"I have, yes. It's all right, Nellie, he said yes."

"Oh, thank goodness!" Nellie turned to Tess. "He wants to marry me, you see."

Tess burst out laughing. "And you had to get Edward's permission, of course, to release his mistress."

"Tess!" Edward said with an enormous sigh. "What an incorrigible girl you are! You should know nothing about mistresses, especially mine. You are supposed to believe me as pure as the snow."

She only laughed harder. "Edward, you are twenty-seven years old and a single man. Why should you not keep a mistress if you want to? Once we are married, of course, it will be a different matter."

"That's the spirit!" Nellie said. "You keep him in line, dear."

He shook his head. "Yes, this is very timely, Nellie, and I am sure Ramsbottom will look after you very well. It is a better arrangement for you to be a respectable baker's wife rather than a mistress, but really, you should not be in this house."

"Why should she not be here?" Tess said. "This is your house, Edward, so it is for you to say who comes into it and who does not."

"My mother would not like it," he said.

"Are you going to be driven by your mother forever? All those games you played, pretending to be courting and having no intention of marrying any of those insipid society ladies. Is it not time to put all the secrecy behind you and run your life however seems good to you? And if your mother dislikes it, she has a perfectly good house of her own to live in."

With impeccable timing, the door opened again, and Mrs Edward Harfield came in, her eyes scanning the room, lingering on Tess, and then settling on Edward.

"Here you are, Edward. We were expecting you to join us in the Blue Saloon as soon as you arrived."

"I had business to attend to."

"Was it so urgent that you must keep your poor mother waiting? No news from you for a week, apart from a brief note to say that you had arrived at Myercroft. I was in terror that some dreadful mishap had occurred. Then you appear without warning, and I find you entertaining guests in my house."

Edward hesitated, and Tess could see the precise moment when his face settled into a harder expression.

"This is my house, Mother, and I will entertain whomever I please within it."

Two spots of colour appeared on her cheeks. "And whom does it please you to entertain?"

"Oh, do you want an introduction? Certainly. This is Nellie Goodlake, my mistress — no, I beg your pardon, my *former* mistress, and this is Ramsbottom, who is her intended. He is a baker from Clerkenwell."

Mrs Harfield's mouth opened and closed soundlessly. Tess was enjoying the scene enormously, but she did wonder if Edward had perhaps pushed her too far, and she might actually swoon away. She was made of sterner stuff, however.

"We shall discuss this later, Edward. For now, will you get these persons out of my house?"

Nellie and her middle-aged swain were all too ready to escape from a family fight, and within moments were gone, Edward accompanying them to the door. Betty took the opportunity to disappear, too.

"Would you like a cup of tea, Mrs Harfield?" Tess said in her most affable tones. "An apricot tartlet, perhaps?"

She did not deign to reply, but as soon as Edward returned, she said icily, "Edward, I have never been so outraged in my life! Bringing disreputable females here, ignoring your own mother and now that girl is usurping my position as mistress of this house."

"First, you have never been mistress here," Edward said calmly. "Lady Tarvin is mistress of Harfield Priory until I marry. Second, Tess is merely practising for when she becomes my wife."

"You would marry that disgraceful chit? If she has led you astray—"

"Not another word! Tess is my future wife, and I will not stand by and hear her abused. She is the woman I choose to share my life, the woman I love with all my heart, and you had better learn to like it."

"If you think I will stay under the same roof as that girl, then—"

"Excellent. That saves me the bother of asking you to go. You have a fine house of your own at Hunsworth Hall, and it has never seemed wise to me to leave it empty. You may leave as soon as you have packed."

She had one more throw of the dice to attempt. "If I must go, then Myrtle must go, too. If you are going to install a wife here, however unsuitable, she cannot stay either."

Edward actually laughed. "Good try, Mother, but Aunt Myrtle has a right to be here. She has been mistress of the Priory for thirty years, and it will be helpful to Tess to have her advice while she settles into her new duties. If, later, she wishes to leave us, the west lodge is a suitable size."

"So *she* is to be always on hand, is she, while I — your own mother — am banished!"

Edward sighed. "Enough, Mother." He held the door open for her. "I shall see you at dinner. In the meantime, you have some packing to organise."

Head high, she marched out. When she had gone, he closed the door gently and turned to Tess with an expression that she could only interpret as guilty triumph.

"Too much?" he said.

"That was magnificent," she breathed. "What a man you are!"

He caught her in his arms and kissed her with a passion that left them both breathless.

***

Tess was pleased to discover that they were only to spend one night at the Priory. The evening was one of the most uncomfortable she had ever spent, as Mrs Harfield tried anger, icy contempt and even tears to change Edward's mind, but he was implacable. He was never less than polite with her, and an outsider would have thought him rather affable, but Tess could detect the steel beneath the gentle words.

Only Lady Tarvin was there to see them off the next morning, and since the rain was sheeting down, there was no lingering over the farewells.

"With such an early start, we will be at Corland well before dinner," Tess said as the carriage splashed down the drive. "What time do you think we shall arrive?"

"At Corland? Not for several days."

"Oh. Are we going somewhere else first?"

"We are indeed."

"Are you going to tell me where?"

"I am not sure I should. I fear you might be disappointed."

"Why would I be disappointed?"

"Because you wanted to do this in the middle of the night in a hired post chaise, but I hope you will agree with me that this way is more comfortable. And we are taking Betty, Harold and Deakin with us, too."

"Do you mean... are you seriously telling me that we are eloping?"

"We are. At least, if you agree, we are. If not, it will be an abduction instead. We are only sixty miles or so from the Scottish border, so if all goes to plan, we can be married over the anvil today."

"Ohhh! My mother will hate it!" She laughed out loud. "How clever you are!"

"My mother will hate me marrying you, however it happens. My darling, I am afraid we will still have to have the banns called in the regular way. There must be no shred of doubt over the validity of our marriage."

"But if you plan to call the banns anyway..."

"Tess, if you think I am going to wait weeks and weeks for you, then you are very much mistaken. If we go to Corland unwed, there will be a great deal of fuss about wedding clothes and a ball and doing things properly and any amount of nonsense. And the longer it takes, the greater the risk that you will think better of it, and that I could not bear. So, elopement it must be. We can call the banns later, or we could bolt for town and get a special licence, if that would amuse you more, but it must be done properly under English law. I am sorry to be so stuffy, but there it is."

"An elopement followed by a special licence... that would be very amusing. And a honeymoon as far from Corland as you can contrive."

"Oh, a challenge! Let me see... Cornwall, perhaps? Ireland? Or—"

"No ships, if you please. The very thought of bobbing about on water makes me feel ill."

"Then it will have to be Cornwall, or else back to Scotland. Although I suspect the weather is better in Cornwall. I am not fond of relentless cold rain."

Tess laughed and rested her head on his shoulder. "Dear Edward! It is going to be so much fun being married to you."

"I hope so," he murmured, placing a soft kiss on her brow. "I do very much hope so."

THE END

The next book in the series is *Loyalty*, in which Mr Kent Atherton is torn between his duty to his family and his growing affection for shy Miss Katherine Parish, there is news of Miss Peach at last and the murder investigation takes a shocking new turn. You can read a sneak preview after the acknowledgements. For more information, go to my website at https://marykingswood.co.uk.

Thanks for reading!

If you have enjoyed reading this book, please consider writing a short review on Amazon. You can find out the latest news and sign up for the mailing list at my website at https://marykingswood.co.uk.

A note on historical accuracy: I have endeavoured to stay true to the spirit of Regency times, and have avoided taking too many liberties or imposing modern sensibilities on my characters. The book is not one of historical record, but I've tried to make it reasonably accurate. However, I'm not perfect! If you spot a historical error, I'd very much appreciate knowing about it so that I can correct it and learn from it. Thank you!

Isn't that what's-his-name? Occasionally characters from an earlier series pop up, or are mentioned. Jeffrey Rycroft and his wife Jeanie were previously in *Stranger at the Hall*, when Jeanie's brother Cameron became Lord Saxby.

About the series:

Book 0: The Chaplain: a man adrift, dreaming of a home (a novella, free to mailing list subscribers).

Book 1: Disinheritance: a man freed, looking for a new purpose in life

Book 2: Determination: a man pursued, forced to outwit his adversary

Book 3: Anger: a woman alone, trying to choose a different path in life

Book 4: Secrecy: a woman neglected, scheming to secure her own happiness

Book 5: Loyalty: a man of dreams, torn between the past and the future

Book 6: Ambition: a woman thwarted, unswervingly set on making a brilliant debut in society

Any questions about the series? Email me at mary@marykingswood.co.uk - I'd love to hear from you!

About the author

I write traditional Regency romances under the pen name Mary Kingswood, and epic fantasy as Pauline M Ross. I live in the beautiful Highlands of Scotland with my husband. I like chocolate, whisky, my Kindle, massed pipe bands, long leisurely lunches, chocolate, going places in my campervan, eating pizza in Italy, summer nights that never get dark, wood fires in winter, chocolate, the view from the study window looking out over the Moray Firth and the Black Isle to the mountains beyond. And chocolate. I dislike driving on motorways, cooking, shopping, hospitals.

Acknowledgements

Thanks go to:

Allison Lane, whose course on English Architecture inspired me.

Shayne Rutherford of Darkmoon Graphics for the cover design.

My beta readers: Charles Crouter, Julie Desbrus, Sharon Flaherty, Melissa Forsythe, Donna Sue Holly, Corinne

Lehmann, Tina Miles, Pat Oen, Kristen Pinto-Coelho, Rosemary Paton, Wendy Stubbs, Carol Sturtz, Jeanne Thomas, Andrea Usami

Last, but definitely not least, my first reader: Amy Ross.

Sneak preview: Book 5 of The Chaplain's Legacy: Loyalty

BRANTON, LANCASHIRE: MARCH

Miss Katherine Parish waited in the hall, bonnet and pelisse on, her gloves and reticule beside her. At her feet were the two boxes of personal effects she was permitted to keep. She sat on the elderly wooden settle since it was fixed to the wall, and might therefore escape the attentions of the bailiffs. Nothing else escaped their notice. The silver was the first to go, and the paintings from the drawing room and dining room. Then the good furniture — the escritoire, Papa's desk, the pretty lacquered console table. She had closed her eyes when her pianoforte had been carried past. In the last hour or so, it had been boxes of books, the contents of the linen closet and the big copper pans from the kitchen. Soon their attention would be drawn to the smaller items, like the battered chairs from the kitchen and the rows of preserves in the larder.

The afternoon wore on, and even the bailiffs began to slow down. But then, on the road outside, were the sounds of a carriage arriving, slowing, then stopping. Her uncle, at last.

He strode into the hall, the skirts of his greatcoat flying, another younger man behind him. Katherine jumped to her feet.

"Katherine! My dear girl, what are you doing here, watching all this? And alone — is there no one who could have sat with you? Where is your maid?"

"She had another position arranged, so I let her go first thing this morning."

"But have you no friends who could have borne you company?"

"Some offered, but I did not wish it," she said quietly. "No one else should witness our disgrace."

"My dear girl!" he said again, wrapping her in an embrace so tight that her nose was pressed against the damp wool of his greatcoat, her bonnet sent askew. "My poor niece! How dreadful for you! Oh... you remember James, of course. He has grown a little since you last saw him."

"I should hope I have, Father! I could not have been more than four or five when last Cousin Kate saw me."

Katherine straightened her bonnet and dipped a curtsy. "Cousin James."

She had a vague memory of a scruffy and nondescript little boy, bigger than her despite their similar age, who had pushed her about unmercifully. He had grown into a nondescript man, only a little taller than she was, and not at all scruffy. Like his father, he looked like a country gentleman, a well-dressed one with a good tailor and an efficient valet.

A footman in livery came in, and he and James manhandled the boxes out through the front door. Katherine donned her gloves and picked up her reticule.

"Are you ready to leave?" Uncle Cathcart said gently. "Is there anything you need to do? Any farewells to make?"

"I have made all my farewells. I am ready, uncle."

"Then let us go. I shall be glad to leave this smoky town behind. So many great, tall chimneys! You will be astonished how much cleaner you will find the air at your new home, my dear."

He offered her his arm and she rested one hand on it. There were times when the support of a man's arm was no more than a courtesy, but today her knees trembled so much that she was glad of it. Head lowered, she walked slowly beside her uncle, out through the door of the home she had lived in all her life.

A great crowd had gathered on the street. Some, no doubt, were drawn to the spectacle of the bailiffs' wagons filling up, but many of the women held handkerchiefs to their eyes, and the men were grim faced. Many she recognised from the mill, men who had lost their livelihoods now, but bore no resentment. They knew her father had been doing his best for them, and it was not his fault he had died when he had just borrowed a great deal of money to install the huge beam engine.

"God bless you, Miss Katherine!" someone called out, and many others took up the refrain. Several women rushed out from the crowd, sobbing, to hug her fiercely. Clusters of children looked on, wide-eyed and silent, taking it all in. Her Sunday school children, she realised. Who would teach them their letters now?

A little way down the street, beyond the bailiffs' wagons, sat the Cathcarts' carriage, a fine equipage drawn by two pairs of post horses, the postilions waiting patiently. The door was held open by the footman, and her uncle handed Katherine in, then went to supervise the arrangements for her luggage to be strapped on. Outside, the crowd on the street moved to surround the carriage, waving handkerchiefs at her. Hesitantly, she waved back, and someone shouted out, "Three cheers for Miss Katherine!" and the whole crowd set to whooping and cheering. Katherine blushed and blushed again, hanging her head low in embarrassment, but they seemed disinclined to stop.

Her uncle appeared at the door. "Other seat, my dear. Ladies always ride forwards. James, do you sit opposite. There now, I think we are ready."

He climbed in to sit beside Katherine, the footman closed the door and set the carriage swaying as he climbed up behind. Then the postilions called to the horses, the crowd cheered again and the carriage lurched into motion, moving slowly away down the street. Katherine did not look back. What was the point? She would never forget the house as long as she lived, and she did not want to have a single memory of it as it was today, with everything dear and familiar loaded onto the bailiffs' wagons. Better to remember it as it had been... when Papa was alive, or better still, when Mama was alive, too, and her brother Harold, and they had been just another mill owner's family, slowly rising to prosperity.

Debt and disgrace were best forgotten.

***

They travelled only two stages that day, as far as Skipton, where rooms were already reserved for them at the Black Horse, and Mr Cathcart's very grand valet waited. Katherine had never stayed at an inn before, but her uncle made everything easy for her, and paid for a maid to help her dress and undress, and to sleep in her room at night.

"Just in case," he said.

"In case of what?" she said.

"Well... should anything occur during the night," he said vaguely.

Nothing did occur, except that coaches came and went at all hours, seemingly, with great noise and bustle and confusion in the yard below. In the quiet spells, the walls and roof and even under the floorboards were alive with scratchings and patterings and odd little muffled squeaks.

The second day was longer, four stages, and a lengthy delay at Boroughbridge, where there were not horses enough. At first, they waited for some to arrive, but after some discussion with the ostlers, they went on with only a pair. At Thirsk, they were able to get two pairs again, and got on a little better.

Having not slept the night before, Katherine dozed on this early part of the journey, although every lurch of the carriage or the rumble of a passing farmer's wagon or remark by her uncle or cousin brought her jerking awake again. After Thirsk, the scenery became more interesting as they came into the hills of the North Riding. She had never been so far afield before, so she peered out of the window with great interest, but neither the hills nor the small villages they passed through were wildly different from Lancashire.

At Helmsley they made their last stop, collecting Uncle Cathcart's own horses and coachman for the final climb to her new home. Cathcart House. Katherine had no idea what she would find there. Uncle Cathcart was a gentleman, so it would be a gentleman's house, but what would that mean? The largest houses she had seen were on the hill at Branton, and the largest of those was the Ridwells' fine house, but Mr Ridwell was only a mill owner like Papa. He was not a gentleman. There were proper gentlemen's houses outside Branton, but they were all hidden behind high walls or hedges, and she had never seen them, let alone been inside one.

The horses strained up a long hill, turning this way and that, before the road levelled off somewhat. There was not much to see. They passed gateposts or smaller roads, but with no sign of any habitation. Trees closed in beside the road, then became fields, then more trees. Once or twice a vista opened up to one side, as if they were overlooking a deep valley, but the trees pressed close again before Katherine could examine the view. She supposed she would have many opportunities to travel this road in future, for the family went often to Helmsley for the shops, James told her.

"Here we are," Uncle Cathcart said, as they turned in through two neat brick gateposts.

The horses put on a little burst of speed, aware that they were almost home. The drive was short, and in a moment they were turning, the carriage slowing and then stopping. The footman on the back of the carriage hopped down and opened the door, and they all descended.

Katherine looked up at the house — her new home. It was rather plain, apart from a small portico at the front door and a tiny amount of decoration above the windows. But no statuary anywhere, nothing ornate or overwhelmingly grand, and it was not even as large as the Ridwells' house, a little longer than it was tall, with three stories only in the middle section.

But there was no time to take it all in, for the front door opened and people poured out. So many! An older couple, her great-aunt and great-uncle, smiling and waving from the top step. Her aunt, sister to Mama and just a little like her, beaming and rushing down the steps, arms wide to embrace her. Two young men, Alex and Neil, at eighteen well grown and handsome, not quite identical but very alike. And the three daughters, Aveline, nineteen, Susan and Lucinda still in the schoolroom. Aveline she recalled only slightly as a rather stout child. Now she was an elegant young lady, eyeing Katherine up expressionlessly. At only a year younger than Katherine, they would be expected to be friends, no doubt. A friend! Something like a sister, perhaps. How odd that would be.

Wrapped in her aunt's soft embrace, with many kind voices expressing their welcome, Katherine felt the strangeness of it all. Having been herself an only daughter, and for many years now an only child, she was unaccustomed to being part of a large family. Three generations in one house, six children not yet fully grown, and so many servants to look after them! Footmen and maids poured out to help with luggage, and a butler and housekeeper stood on the steps overseeing activity.

Now the younger girls took an arm each and towed Katherine up the steps and into the house, while their mother remonstrated ineffectually with them.

"Girls! Girls! Do give Katherine a little room to breathe. Think how tired she must be after her long journey! Susan, Lucinda, do not tug her arms quite out of their sockets. There now, my dear, let me look at you. Ah, you look so pale, but that is your mourning clothes, of course. Such a *draining* colour, black, I always say. But it is some time since your dear papa passed away, so perhaps we shall persuade you into half mourning soon."

"It is only three months, aunt."

"Well, true, but that is long enough for so young a girl, and you will be going into very different society now, my dear."

Katherine felt the now familiar spasm of terror at these words. When her aunt had written to her, just after Papa's death, and offered her a home, she had mentioned society and balls and finding a husband. Katherine had existed quite happily without such things for all of her twenty years. She had plenty to do at home, or at the mill, or amongst their workers' families, and then there was church to keep her busy. There were occasional evening engagements with their friends, but a ball! What would she find to do at a ball? She had never participated in a formal dance in her life.

Susan and Lucinda towed her on, up the stairs and then up again, into a pleasant bedroom, plainly but expensively furnished, everything solid wood and polished to a high shine. There were windows on two sides, with a view over tidy flowerbeds from one, and trees and shrubs from the other. She was relieved to discover that she was not to share a room with Aveline. Her aunt chased her daughters out of the room, and helped Katherine removed her bonnet and pelisse.

"Well, these are very suitable for travelling," she said, holding them up to examine them more closely. "Excellent stitchwork! You must have had a very good seamstress in Branton."

"I make all my clothes myself, aunt."

Her aunt stared at her. "Goodness me! Well, you will not need to do so any more. Ah, here are your boxes. Just the two? And here is Jenny, who will be looking after you."

"Looking after me?"

"Acting as your lady's maid... taking care of your clothes and so forth. She looks after Susan and Lucinda, but she can easily accommodate you as well. Now, which box holds your evening gowns? This one? Unpack this first, Jenny. I need to see if you have anything suitable for Tuesday."

"Tuesday, aunt?"

"We are to dine at the Castle. Corland Castle, with the Earl of Rennington and his family, so you will need something... well, not so plain as your travelling gown."

The Earl of Rennington! Katherine's horror must have shown on her face, for her aunt laughed, and said, "Now, now, child, you have nothing to fear from the Athertons. They are very grand, of course, and live in a style we can only dream of, but you will find them not at all high in the instep. We dine with them half a dozen times a year, and sometimes they condescend to dine with us, and we always enjoy a very pleasant evening."

"Must I go? I do not know them, so—"

"Naturally you must go. You are included in the invitation. Lady Rennington is always most particular about such things. She wrote that if you had arrived by Tuesday, then she would be delighted to welcome you to Corland Castle. So you have nothing to worry about. Well, you have not many dresses, have you? We shall have to increase your wardrobe quite substantially. Ah, lay the blue one on the bed, Jenny. Now, let me see... Hmm, it is excessively plain for an evening gown."

"Aunt, I cannot wear colours! I have a black evening gown if I must go, but I should much sooner not. Indeed, I never expected to be treated like my cousins. It would be inappropriate for me to set myself up as a lady of fashion, like them. Plain gowns are very suitable for my station, and I shall be very happy to make myself useful to you, in the kitchen or still room, perhaps, running errands, helping the governess... That is my place, surely. It is what I am used to."

Aunt Cathcart sat down on the bed, drew Katherine down beside her and took her in her arms for a long hug. "My dear Katherine, you are my niece, and my sister's only surviving child. The very idea that we would treat you as some kind of unpaid servant! Whatever you may have been obliged to do at Branton no longer applies. Your father may have left you in poverty, but your uncle is to settle a little money on you— No, no, do not protest, for he is quite resolved upon it, and we are agreed that we will treat you exactly the same as our own daughters. You will have your own pin money, and naturally you must wear suitable clothes. You would not wish to shame us by appearing less well dressed than your cousins, surely? What would our friends say if we appear to neglect you in that way? You need not be a lady of fashion if you dislike the idea, but you must be a lady o f *quality*, Katherine. Above all else, you must be a lady, and there is no need to mention your father's mill. No need at all."

"There is no mill to mention, not any more," Katherine said sadly. "But what shall I do with myself all day if I may not help with the domestic duties? What does Cousin Aveline do?"

"Why, I hardly know, but she manages to fill her days. We make and receive calls, of course. She rides, sometimes, and... well, she finds plenty to do. If you like, you may sit with Susan and Lucinda and listen to Miss Harkness. She teaches French and Italian, as well as music, drawing and the usual things. That will help to fill in any gaps in your education, you know, for if you have been busy making clothes and mixing pastry, I am sure you have not been keeping up with your lessons."

"You have a pianoforte? May I practise?"

"Certainly, my dear. That is a very ladylike accomplishment. Most suitable. Yes, you may practise on the pianoforte as much as you like."

Well, that was something to be grateful for. There had never been enough time for music at Branton, but now she could play as much as she wished.

***

The next morning, Katherine rose at her usual time. She had been warned that the family would not emerge from their bedrooms until breakfast at ten o'clock, so she recited the morning prayers, as she continued to do even without Papa, and then wrote letters to several friends in Branton who would be anxiously awaiting news of her safe arrival. She filled the rest of the time by reading soothing passages from the Bible.

Breakfast was like dinner the previous evening, the table groaning with food, of which only a small amount was eaten. The waste shocked Katherine, but she supposed that a gentleman had to live in a higher style than a mill owner. No one at Branton would think to offer such an excess of food. She was even more shocked that no one said grace, either before or after the meal. What sort of Christian family would not give thanks for their meal, especially with such abundance placed before them? It was not her place to criticise, however, so she made a small prayer in her head before she began to eat.

"Mama, may we take Katherine to Birchall this morning?" Susan asked. "She will want to see all the shops."

Katherine had no great desire for shopping, and would much rather have spent the morning at the instrument, but she did not like to be unsociable. Shortly after eleven, therefore, she awaited Aveline, Susan and Lucinda at the foot of the stairs. The first person to appear was a thin-faced woman of around thirty, as plainly dressed as Katherine was. The governess, no doubt.

"Good morning, madam," she said, dipping a curtsy. "I am Miss Harkness. The governess."

"Yes," Katherine whispered. Never having had a governess, she was not at all sure how to address one. "How do you do? I am Katherine Parish."

The governess gave a little smile. "I know who you are, Miss Parish. I hope you will be very happy at Cathcart House, despite the sad reasons for your move here. Ah, here are the girls now. Come, ladies, let us be off before the day is half gone."

Birchall village was only a mile away, by way of the gardens and some pretty woodland, the bluebells just showing through but not yet in flower. The village was just like a thousand other villages, being no more than one main street with a few short side roads, lined with cottages and a scattering of more substantial houses. A few people walking about stared openly at them, making Katherine feel very uncomfortable.

The Cathcart girls instantly ran off to a haberdashery, which seemed to be a focus for a number of other young ladies, but Katherine looked longingly at the church.

"Would you mind if I were to sit in the church for a while?" she said to Miss Harkness.

"By all means, Miss Parish. There are some fine memorials in St Timothy's, and the rood screen is much admired."

The chilly air inside the church made Katherine shiver, but it was still preferable to being stared at, or jostled in the busy haberdashery. Above all, she wanted quietude, and the church brought her a welcome sense of peace, with its familiar smells of damp wool, dust and candle smoke, and the echo from its high roof as her booted feet tap-tapped up the aisle. She found the Cathcart pew, one of the better ones, and sat there letting her thoughts wander. She was grateful to her uncle and aunt, naturally, and they were very kind, but oh, how she missed Branton and the familiarity of home. Everything here was strange. She would make friends in time, she knew that, but just at that moment she felt quite alone.

Behind her, the door creaked open, and someone entered quietly, staying near the door. A few moments later, someone else came in and she heard low voices murmuring. Little of it was audible, but she caught *'thirty barrels'* and *'is that all?'* and something about storms at sea. Then, a sudden exclamation, and she heard footsteps approaching.

A man peered over the pew wall at her, a man not much older than she was herself, slender and with a smiling face.

"Good morning to you, madam, and an excellent morning it is, too."

His eyes twinkled with such good humour that she could not be afraid of him. "Is it?"

"Why, indeed it is, for it is not raining, which is sufficient in itself to qualify as an excellent morning. Also, my brother has been shooting and I am promised duck for dinner. I am excessively fond of duck."

That made her smile.

"Ah. And I have brought a smile to your face, which makes the morning even better. How do you do, madam? Kent Atherton at your service."

Kent Atherton! One of the Earl of Rennington's family. She need not fear the evening at Corland Castle so much if this cheerful and friendly man were there.

"Katherine Parish."

"I am delighted to meet you, Miss Parish, quite delighted! I hope we shall meet again very often, so that I may have more opportunities to make you smile. You looked so sad when I first saw you, and since you wear black, you have reason to be sad, but is there not still so much in this world to be enjoyed? Every day brings us some new delight to beguile the eye or the ear, or even the tongue. You see, I am thinking of my duck again. May you find some small ray of hope every day to enchant you and relieve your sadness for a while. And one day, I very much hope that you will not be sad at all."

"Thank you, sir."

"And now, I must not disturb your contemplation any longer. Good day to you, Miss Parish."

"Good day, sir. Enjoy your duck."

He grinned. "I shall! I most certainly shall."

And then he was gone, leaving her smiling and cheerful. What a charming man! She felt a delightful warmth inside which stayed with her until she heard Aveline's voice behind her.

"There you are, cousin! What are you doing hiding away in here? Come on, there are new bonnets at Miss Prinkley's."

Katherine rose obediently and followed her from the church.

END OF SAMPLE CHAPTER *of Loyalty; for more information or to buy, go to my website at https://marykingswood.co.uk.*

Printed in Dunstable, United Kingdom

71686849R00221